ALSO BY BEN COES

INDEPENDENCE DAY

INDEPENDENCE DAY

BEN COES

ST. MARTIN'S PRESS ♨ NEW YORK

INDEPENDENCE DAY. Copyright © 2015 by Ben Coes. All rights reserved. Printed in the United States of America. For information, address St. Martin's Press, 175 Fifth Avenue, New York, NY 10010.

www.stmartins.com

"The Witnesses" copyright © 1945 by W. H. Auden and renewed 1973 by The Estate of W. H. Auden; from *W. H. Auden Collected Poems* by W. H. Auden. Used by permission of Random House, an imprint and division of Penguin Random House LLC. All rights reserved.

The Library of Congress Cataloging-in-Publication Data is available upon request.

ISBN 978-1-250-04316-0 (hardcover)
ISBN 978-1-4668-4126-0 (e-book)

St. Martin's Press books may be purchased for educational, business, or promotional use. For information on bulk purchases, please contact the Macmillan Corporate and Premium Sales Department at 1-800-221-7945, extension 5442, or write to specialmarkets@macmillan.com.

First Edition: June 2015

10 9 8 7 6 5 4 3 2 1

This book is dedicated, with the deepest love a father can feel, to my dear daughter, Esmé.

When the green field comes off like a lid,
Revealing what was much better hid—
  Unpleasant:
And look, behind you without a sound
The woods have come up and are standing round
  In deadly crescent.

The bolt is sliding in its groove;
Outside the window is the black remov-
  er's van:
And now with sudden swift emergence
Come the hooded women, the hump-backed surgeons,
  And the Scissor Man.

— W. H. AUDEN, *THE WITNESSES*

INDEPENDENCE
DAY

PROLOGUE

DNEPROPETROVSK, UKRAINE
CRIMEAN PENINSULA
SOVIET UNION
JULY 4, 1986

Pyotr Vargarin, age five, removed a wrinkled piece of paper from his raincoat, then unfolded it.

My dear son, Pyotr,

While you are perhaps too young to understand what I am about to say, I feel I must nevertheless do my best to explain to you why your mama and I have decided to do what we are, as a family, about to do. And while no five-year-old should be given the power to determine a family's fate, I above all else respect you and always will seek your understanding, sympathy, and approval whenever possible.

Why, you ask, must we move to the United States of America? Is not the Soviet Union our country? Isn't it I who always says Moscow is the most beautiful place on earth? Who points out the way the icicles hang down like great sabers from the roof of the palace? Or the chrysanthemums, along the Moskva, how they wave to us in the springtime, like old friends?

Do I not remember, you ask, lying in the field at the dacha, staring up at the summer sky, then watching as the clouds moved in from the horizon, remaining there as the warm rain poured down upon you and me, and how we giggled at it all and how mad Mama was when we returned, covered in mud? Of course I remember! We will always have that memory to cherish! And now we will create new memories!

The gift of adventure, this is what I shall give to you, my one and only love, my brilliant prize, Pyotr, my little cloud . . .

The man in the front seat of the limousine turned and smiled at Pyotr.

"What are you reading, Pyotr?" he asked.

He had a kind demeanor, a gentleness, despite the scar beneath his eye, which made his eye blink in a funny way, as if something was stuck in it.

Pyotr looked up at him. He quickly folded the letter and tucked it back inside the pocket of his mackinaw.

"Nothing."

"Nothing?" he asked, laughing heartily. "I wish I could get as much happiness from reading nothing as you do."

Mr. Roberts was his name. He was the American man Papa talked about. He would take them to the boat that would take them to Istanbul, then to the airplane that would fly them to the United States.

"A letter."

Pyotr looked up at his mother. She stared out the window of the limousine at the passing countryside.

"Do you like fireworks, Pyotr?" asked Roberts, keeping his head turned. "You might get to see some when you land in New York tonight. It's Independence Day in your new country."

Pyotr said nothing.

"Are you as intelligent as your father?" Roberts asked.

Pyotr glanced up at his mother. She met his look, then nodded imperceptibly; it was okay to talk with him.

"Yes," said Pyotr. "I am the smartest one in all of the Soviet Union."

"The smartest?" asked the American, laughing. "Most humble too."

"It's true," said Pyotr calmly. He looked up at his mother.

"Don't brag," she said.

She looked at Roberts for the first time.

"It is true," she said, placing her hand on Pyotr's leg. "He scored the highest score of all five- and six-year-olds on the standardized tests."

Roberts's eyes seemed to bulge a little.

"In all of Moscow?" he asked. "That's incredible. There must be—"

"In all of the Soviet Union," she replied tartly, before turning back to the window.

Roberts looked at him.

"Well, that is most impressive, Pyotr," he said, nodding his head up and down enthusiastically. "Perhaps you will be famous like your father, Dr. Vargarin? Would you like to be a scientist too?"

When Pyotr awoke a few hours later, his head was in his mother's lap. She was rubbing his cheek, trying to wake him.

"We're here, little dumpling," she whispered.

Outside the limousine, two men were standing. Like Roberts, they wore dark suits. One of the men clutched a submachine gun.

They followed Roberts along a dirt path through the woods. They hiked for more than a mile. In the distance, through the trees, came the sound of water slapping against a rocky shore. When at last they came to a clearing, the Black Sea spread out before them. A red motorboat was tied to a small wooden pier. Pyotr's father was standing in the clearing, surrounded by more men with weapons. His arms were behind his back. His right eye was swollen shut. His nose had blood beneath it.

"Pyotr!" he yelled when he saw his son.

Pyotr started to run toward his father, but one of the men grabbed his collar.

"Let him go," said Roberts.

Pyotr scrambled toward his father. He was crying now. He slipped and fell, then got back up. His father's clothing was covered in dirt and blood, torn in places. He had on one shoe.

"I don't want to go to America," Pyotr sobbed as he reached for his father's arm.

"We're not going to America," whispered his father, looking sadly at his son. "Your instincts were correct, Pyotr. The wisdom of a child; I should have listened. I'm sorry. Please, someday, please forgive me for what I am about to do to you. For the terrible, terrible wounds today will create inside you, wounds I will not be there to help heal."

Roberts stepped toward them. For the first time, Pyotr saw the American's smile disappear into a haunting look of anger. The scar, instead of looking out of place, seemed to make him complete.

"We've been patient, Doctor, but our patience is running out. *Where is it?*"

"'Patience'? Is that what you call this? Bringing a man's family to watch him die?"

Roberts stared at Vargarin. He reached into his jacket and removed a gun. Without removing his eyes from Vargarin, he aimed the muzzle of the weapon in the opposite direction, then fired. The gunshot made Pyotr jump. He turned to see his mother collapsing to the ground, a large bullet hole in her forehead.

Pyotr started to run to his mother, but Roberts grabbed his hair, then thrust the muzzle of the gun into his mouth. It was warm and tasted of smoke and oil.

"Where is it?"

Pyotr looked up. It was the first time he'd ever seen his father cry.

"At the institute," he said, sobbing. "Beneath the card catalog drawer. The letter 'O.'"

Roberts yanked the gun from Pyotr's mouth. He trained it on Vargarin and fired. The slug struck his chest, kicking Vargarin back, killing him instantly. He tumbled awkwardly to the dirt.

Pyotr's mouth went agape. He screamed, but no noise came out. Then he fell to the ground, next to his father. He stared at his father's face. Pyotr's eyes were like blank pools, transfixed by the sight of his dead father, there on the ground.

"Put them in the boat," said Roberts to one of the men. "Remove the cuffs, leave a gun, set it adrift a mile offshore. I'll go to Moscow and get the disk."

"What about the kid?"

Roberts aimed the gun at the back of Pyotr's head. He kept it there for several moments. After almost half a minute, he lifted the gun and put it back in his shoulder holster.

"Bring him to the local orphanage."

I

An orange-and-white Ducati Superleggera 1199 roared through the neighborhood called Presnensky—empty, dark, and deceptively quiet at a little before dawn on a balmy Moscow morning.

The superbike's black-helmeted driver had the machine gashing down Rilsok at more than a hundred miles an hour, barely under control, as if he was testing the outer limits of his skills. He was an experienced rider, but know-how went only so far when crouched atop a machine that boasted the highest power-to-weight ratio of any motorcycle.

Presnensky was a clean, incongruous neighborhood of stunning mansions and luxury apartment buildings alongside industrial warehouses. The thunderous decibel of the bike's Superquadro liquid-cooled engine was neither unusual nor even noticed. Here, more than in any other borough in Russia's sprawling capital city, Presnensky's inhabitants had long ago learned to keep their mouths shut, their eyes lowered, and their curiosity at bay.

At a street called Velka, the biker abruptly leaned to his right, leading the Ducati with him, nearly toppling over as he glided in a smooth arc around the ninety-degree turn at 86 mph. His knee scraped the ground but he didn't slow down. In fact, he feathered the throttle, surging into the corner. Then, as his gloved fingers brushed the tar, he flicked his wrist yet again, juicing the engine on with a last-second splurge of speed that seemed to defy logic and gravity. A moment later, the rider pulled a powerful, dazzling switch-back, banking abruptly in the opposite direction—hard left—then ripping the throttle to the max as the front tire burned a cloud of rubbery smoke and the back tire caught a squall of air.

He tore down the last half mile of empty, unlit street, then skidded to a stop in front of a three-story white brick building, its only window tinted crimson. He turned off the bike and put the kick-stand down. He climbed off, then removed the all-black helmet. He left it on the seat. The Superleggera made a taunting statement, and the helmet, there atop the seat, was like the proverbial cherry on top.

Steal me, it seemed to say, *and see what happens.*

Presnensky was the neighborhood where Moscow's mafia lived and breathed, a city, a government, unto itself. Everyone, including the police, knew it. Moscow was, for a certain precious few, lawless. Presnensky was the epicenter of that lawlessness.

The man walked toward the building's entrance. A low beat echoed from inside.

He pulled the door open. Like a bomb going off, music exploded out into the dark street. It was a chaotic electronica of synthesizers, infused with a dull, seismic drumbeat.

Inside was a cocaine-fueled pandemonium of bodies, music, lights, and smoke, with a dark, dystopian edge. At least a thousand men and women danced frenetically beneath flashing blue, orange, and yellow lights as a bizarre, thunderous strain of arbitrary-sounding synthesizers and drums caused the floor to undulate. The air was fetid with sweat, cologne, perfume, and marijuana smoke.

He moved into the crowd. The drugged-out eyes of young Muscovites registered him as he pushed his way through, almost

8

knocking people over as he cut straight across the jam-packed dance floor. He was charismatic; his blond Afro was flamboyant, with clumps of unmitigated curls bobbing about. The eyes of every female within ten feet were drawn to him. His face was thin and gaunt, youthful and, above all, captivating.

At the back of the massive dance floor was a red velvet curtain. The man pushed through, immediately encountering the muzzle of a silver MP-448 Skyph 9×18 pistol, clutched by a lone security guard. The gunman, hulkish and mean-looking, wore a tight black silk shirt unbuttoned to the navel. He eyed the stranger as he pushed through the curtain and moved toward him. He trained the gun on the stranger's forehead.

"*Sem'desyat dva*," muttered the man.

"*Da.*"

The guard holstered the Skyph beneath his left armpit. He patted him down, then nodded, without looking into his eyes, indicating he could pass.

The man descended a set of stairs into the basement, then moved along a dimly lit corridor. At the end of the hallway, a pair of gunmen stood like pillars outside a steel door. Both men clutched submachine guns. Reflexively, they trained the muzzles on him as he approached.

If being held in the sight lines of a pair of submachine guns bothered him, he didn't show it.

The guard on the left repeated the pat-down, more invasive this time, looking for anything that the visitor might have been concealing. Finding nothing, he nodded to the other guard, who reached for the door handle.

The man stepped inside the room as the security guard shut the door behind him.

It was a large, windowless room, meticulously neat. On one side was a glass desk, empty except for a small laptop computer, a thin stack of papers, and a handgun. On the other side of the room was a seating area. A huge plasma screen hung on the wall. A video game was being played. In the specific frame was an image of a battlefield in remarkably clear relief, almost like documentary news footage. The vantage point was that of a soldier moving across the battlefield, shooting people.

On a black leather couch, directly in front of the screen, sat a man with slicked-back brown hair, parted in the middle, a tank top, and, around his neck, a mess of gold chains. He continued to stare at the screen and fire off rounds.

"Hello, Cloud," said Malnikov, the thirty-four-year-old head of the Moscow mafia.

"Alexei," said Cloud curtly.

Malnikov fired a few more rounds, then abruptly stopped the game. He turned and looked at his visitor. He smiled and stood up from the sofa.

"Can I get you something?"

"Vodka."

"Sure."

Malnikov walked to a bar in the corner. He poured two glasses, then returned.

"Please," said Malnikov, handing Cloud the vodka and pointing to a different sofa, near the desk. "Have a seat, my friend."

The sofa was long, curving slightly in a quarter-moon, and covered in light yellow leather. Malnikov and Cloud sat down at either end of the sofa, leaving a wide space between them. Each man took sips from his glass, glancing at the other in silence.

"Let's make this quick," Cloud said. He took a gulp from his glass as his eyes darted about the room. "I don't like being here. How much?"

Malnikov laughed.

"What's wrong?" he asked, looking around the office, a hint of offense taken in his voice. "You don't like my office?"

Cloud shot Malnikov a look of contempt, unafraid even of the head of the Moscow mob.

"I grow tired of your games, Alexei," snapped Cloud. "If you wanted to kill me, you would've had one of your men put a bullet in my head. You have a nuclear weapon. There is precisely *one* individual on the face of the planet who can take it off your hands without raising the eyebrows of the Central Intelligence Agency. How much, you greedy fuck?"

"How dare you—" Malnikov started, his face flushing.

"*How much?*" Cloud screamed, interrupting Malnikov before he could finish his sentence. Cloud raised his index finger and pointed it at Malnikov's reddening face.

Malnikov sat back. His nostrils flared. His teeth flashed. He had a murderous look in his eyes, as if he was debating in his head whether to kill Cloud right then and there.

The door burst open. One of the gunmen stepped inside and trained the submachine gun on Cloud.

Malnikov held up his hand and shot his guard a look. "*Get the fuck out!*" he barked.

After the door shut, he turned back to Cloud. For a few moments, Malnikov was silent. He tried to cool off and regain his composure. He knew he needed to be rational, especially now.

Malnikov's life, thanks to his father, was already one of privilege. It was his father who spent two decades fighting for control of organized crime in Russia. Alexei Malnikov was the recipient of a generation's worth of blackmail, bribery, extortion, and murder. When Yuri Malnikov was arrested, Alexei became the boss of the Russian underworld. That was when he moved to acquire his nuclear leverage.

Three weeks before, after more than two years of bribes, threats, and more bribes, Malnikov had finally succeeded in pressuring a corrupt Ukrainian general named Bokolov into selling him a stolen 1953 Soviet-made thirty-kiloton nuclear bomb. Malnikov had bought it in order to create leverage for himself. It was an insurance policy, which he intended to use only if he was ever incarcerated by FSB or a foreign law enforcement agency, as his father had been the

11

year before. Yuri Malnikov had been arrested on his yacht off the coast of Florida by the FBI and was now confined within the Colorado prison called ADX Florence, aka Supermax, where he would likely spend the rest of his life.

But Alexei Malnikov was wrong. Very wrong. It took less than one day for him to regret the move. He hated the nuke and wished he'd never bought it. The leverage he thought he would garner by owning it was soon replaced by paranoia.

Malnikov, who moved more heroin than any other mobster on the face of the earth, had let hubris take over. Not content with the money, the unfettered access to women, luxury homes, art, rare wines, and whatever else a black AmEx could buy, he somehow came to think possession of the bomb would insulate him from the one thing every mobster feared: the lawman. But he miscalculated. When you tried to buy or—God forbid—own a nuclear weapon, you were no longer fucking with the lawman. You were fucking with nations.

Malnikov had made a grave error and wanted desperately to get rid of it.

There were the jihadists. Already a representative from ISIS had made entreaties through an affiliate in Chechnya. Hezbollah would not be far behind. How ISIS knew about the nuclear device he didn't know, but it scared him to his core. Eventually, if he was unwilling to sell, the day would come when the towel heads would send a suicide bomber to the nightclub or his home.

But the jihadists were not what worried Malnikov most. It was America, specifically the CIA.

His drugs and other vices were not a top priority of the CIA. They had bigger fish to fry. The nuclear bomb made him one of those bigger fish, and being a target of the CIA was the last thing he needed. If Langley suspected he possessed the bomb, his Russian ass could end up in a Guantánamo Bay sweatbox for the next decade. Unless the Americans decided to simply kill him and be done with it.

It was time to move the fucking nuke. And it was Cloud who held the key.

He took a deep breath and looked at Cloud.

"Let's calm down a little," suggested Malnikov. "We're on the same page."

Malnikov felt Cloud's eyes on him. The genius computer hacker was either oblivious of the risk of owning the bomb, or he simply didn't give a fuck.

Malnikov, like everyone who came into contact with Cloud, feared him. He was flamboyant, ruthless, and creepy. It was rumored that he'd helped manipulate U.S. air traffic control systems in the days leading up to 9/11, participating in the greatest terror attack in American history.

If he crossed Cloud, Cloud could do a great deal of damage, and very, very quickly. In Cloud's hands, computers were weapons.

Malnikov took another sip of vodka, then glanced in Cloud's direction.

"One hundred million dollars," said Malnikov.

Cloud was silent. His eyes looked like a calculator as they blinked and darted about, his brain conducting calculations in his head. After more than half a minute, his eyes shot to Malnikov.

"One hundred million?" Cloud asked. "That sounds reasonable."

Cloud leaned toward Malnikov, his hand outstretched.

"Good," said Malnikov, smiling, relieved.

"When will you be wiring me the money?" asked Cloud.

Malnikov did a double take.

"What did you say?"

"When will you wire me the money?" Cloud repeated, an innocent smile on his face.

Malnikov stood up from the sofa. He took two steps, raised his arm, and started to swing at Cloud.

Cloud held up his hand, interrupting Malnikov.

"I assume it will come from your account in the Guernsey Islands?" continued Cloud, just before Malnikov struck him.

Malnikov caught himself, stopping his swing just inches from Cloud's cheek.

"In fact, I took the liberty of taking the first fifty million before coming over," said Cloud. "You know, these encryption keys are very difficult to penetrate these days. It took me nearly ten minutes to get inside the bank. They really are becoming much more sophisticated with these firewalls and other accoutrements."

Malnikov stared at Cloud, his mouth agape, then staggered to his desk. He typed into his laptop, frantically signing into his bank account. After nearly a minute, he looked up at Cloud.

"What have you done?" he whispered, hatred in his voice.

Malnikov reached to the gun on top of his desk. He lifted it, chambered a round, then pointed it at Cloud.

Cloud stood up, clutching his crystal highball glass, staring back at Malnikov, then at the muzzle of the pistol. Cloud's smile abruptly vanished. He shook his head.

"What am I going to do with you, Alexei?" asked Cloud empathetically. "You don't seem to understand, do you?"

Cloud swigged the last of the vodka, paused a half second, then dropped the glass to the concrete floor, where it shattered into a thousand pieces.

Malnikov moved around the desk and stepped in front of Cloud. He was half a foot taller than Cloud and dramatically wider. He could've broken Cloud in half with his bare hands. Any other man, and he would have. Malnikov moved the muzzle of the gun to within an inch of Cloud's right eye.

"I want every cent of my money back, you little *fuck*!" Malnikov seethed. "As for the nuclear bomb, you can fuck yourself in the ass. Look into that muzzle, you little nerd, because it's the last thing you'll ever see."

Cloud's demeanor remained placid, even dismissive.

"Who do you think had your father thrown in jail?" asked Cloud. "The most powerful mobster in Russia, perhaps the world, and I had him set up, then chopped down like a weed. It was so easy

I found myself laughing afterward. He will never leave the U.S. prison, not for the rest of his life."

Malnikov's mouth opened in shock and disbelief. He reached for his chest.

"*Why . . . ?*"

"Why? Because I knew your father would never be stupid enough to acquire a nuclear bomb, and you would."

Malnikov tried to speak, but couldn't.

"If you want me to take the bomb, you will pay me, Alexei. If you complain, I'll drain the rest of the account. Delivery of the nuclear device will be to a dock in Sevastopol tonight, at midnight."

"I don't even understand what you're threatening," whispered Malnikov, his hand shaking. "I don't have the time to get it to Sevastopol by tonight."

Cloud took a deep breath.

"I should also mention that if I'm not back to my dacha in"— Cloud checked his watch—"seventeen minutes, you will be destroyed. Forget your money for a moment. Your entire organization will be rolled up, then locked up. *Everything!* United States, Hong Kong, Europe, Russia, Brazil, Australia. Do you realize how much heroin you've sold to those poor little American schoolchildren? Not to mention the electronic signature of the entire transaction with General Bokolov? Actually, now that I think about it, you'll simply be sent to Guantánamo Bay. If I'm not back in . . . sixteen minutes, my guess is you'll be in shackles by dawn. And you'll wear those shackles the rest of your days on earth."

Malnikov stared at Cloud. He was beyond anger or hatred. He was speechless, numb, and confused. He lowered the gun.

"You can kill me right now, we both know it," said Cloud reassuringly. "This is not about being a man and who is tougher, Alexei. *You* are tougher. But where I am going, it requires something different. It requires hatred."

Malnikov took a small step backward. "You're insane—"

"Yes, I suppose that's true," said Cloud, nodding. "So kill me. You have the gun. Just shoot me. The thing is, I wouldn't care. I could take dying just as easy as getting up in the morning. You, on the other hand, do care. And that is why you will pay me one hundred million dollars to take this nuclear bomb off your hands, an amount that, I'm guessing, is about one hundred million less than I actually could pressure you into paying. But, you see, I'm a generous man."

Cloud turned from the muzzle of the gun and walked to the door. He placed his hand on the doorknob.

"One more thing," he said. "They will come to you. As soon as the bomb is moved, they will find out and they will somehow track it to you. This is unavoidable. My guess is, it will be the United States. You can attempt to lie, but it will be pointless. They will wire you up and, if you are lying, they will use various methodologies to elicit the truth and ultimately they will succeed. So do yourself a favor, Alexei, tell them everything you know. As much as you hate me right now, the truth is, I am grateful to you. I mean you no harm. And I wish you a long and prosperous life. You made a mistake, we both know it, the day you shook hands with Bokolov and acquired the bomb. *Do what they say.* It is the only way you will be able to put it behind you."

"They'll ask for my help to find you," said Malnikov.

"Give it to them. I will not be found, at least not until it's too late."

"What will you—" Malnikov began to ask a question, then stopped, as if fearing what the answer might be.

"What will I do with it? Is that your question?"

"Yes."

Cloud glanced back as he turned the doorknob and opened the door.

"Something I should have done a long time ago," he said quietly. He paused and looked once again at Malnikov. "Sevastopol. Midnight. Don't be late."

2

THE CASTINE INN
MAIN STREET
CASTINE, MAINE

On the first Saturday of summer, at a little before eight in the
morning, a crowd was gathered in front of the elegant, slightly dilapidated buttercup-colored Castine Inn. There were approximately
two hundred men, women, and children, from infants in Baby Bjorns
to grandparents clutching wooden canes, talking, laughing, catching up after the long winter, sipping coffee, hot chocolate, and cider,
waiting. All were from Castine but one, the boyfriend of a Castine
girl, a nice-looking fellow from San Francisco who'd come up with
her for the weekend from Andover, in all likelihood unaware of the
fact that his first visit to the pretty, remote, slightly ornery seaside
town would feature a grueling six-and-a-half-mile race, and that
he'd be expected to participate.

Thirty-three runners—thirteen men, twenty women—stood in
the road behind a strip of yellow police tape, stretching, jogging in
place, and getting ready for the race. They had on a motley assort-
ment of shorts and T-shirts in a variety of colors and styles. The one
unusual aspect to the group of runners was that no one wore running shoes. Everyone had on work boots.

At the back of the cluster of runners stood a big man off by himself. At six-four, he was the tallest in the group, and stocky. He had on beat-up Timberland boots, madras shorts, and a green T-shirt. His brown hair was long and looked like it hadn't been brushed in weeks. His face was covered in a month's worth of stubble. He leaned casually against the front bumper of a rusted light green Ford pickup truck.

At precisely eight o'clock, Doris Russell, Castine's seventy-two-year-old mayor, stepped off the curb and into the road. Doris looked gentle, even matronly, but, as everyone knew, she possessed the wit, and the mouth, of a sailor. Doris waved her arms in the air, trying to get everyone's attention. Gradually, silence settled over the crowd.

"Good morning, everyone," said Doris in a high-pitched, slightly squeaky voice. She had a large smile on her face. "I hope you all had a wonderful winter."

"It sucked," someone shouted from the back of the crowd.

Laughter burst out from the throng of people.

"Who's that?" Doris asked, peering into the crowd. "Is that Tom? Yeah, well, mine was a stinker too, Tom, if you want to know the truth. I broke my hip falling down the stairs and my granddaughter was expelled from Miss Porter's. But thanks for asking."

"He didn't ask," yelled someone else.

Another ripple of laughter spread through the crowd.

Doris shook her head, trying not to laugh.

"If you don't let me get this thing started, we'll be here all day. Which means, odds are, I'll be dead."

"We'll miss you, Doris."

Doris laughed, shaking her head, along with the rest of the crowd. Finally, she raised her hand.

"Well, anyway, as you all know, today is the first Saturday of our beloved Castine summer, and thank God for that. I'm so goddam sick of winter I could kill someone."

"My wife would like to volunteer for that," yelled someone.

Laughter once again erupted from the crowd.

"I'd want to be dead too if I was married to you, Burt," said Doris. "Now, as I was saying, it being the first Saturday following the beginning of summer, it's time once again for the annual Wadsworth Cove Marathon."

Loud clapping and a chorus of enthusiastic cheers swept over the crowd.

Like many towns along the beautiful winding, rocky coast of Maine, Castine tolerated its summer visitors, the wealthy people from away, who came in June and left at Labor Day. But the long, hard, bitter-cold winter months were the province of the people who lived there year-round: the fishermen, teachers, nurses, construction workers, bus drivers, farmers, electricians, plumbers, police officers, doctors, a lawyer, and even a few artists.

Most towns in Maine had their own peculiar tradition to mark the end of winter, the season they'd all just suffered mightily through, mostly pent up inside their homes. In Castine, it was the Wadsworth Cove Marathon. The course was a punishing six and a half miles to the cove, then up a dirt path along Bog Brook to a large, well-known birch tree, then back to town. Running shoes were not allowed, only work boots, symbolic of the fact that the race was meant for working people, not city slickers, though technically anyone could run if they wanted to.

This year, an unusually large crowd was gathered to watch the race. A celebrity was in town. Not a celebrity in the traditional sense, just a kid from town whom everyone knew—the thirty-nine-year-old kid with the mess of brown hair.

"Now, as many of you know, this is the twenty-fifth running of the Wadsworth Cove Marathon," said Doris. "I can remember the very first race. It was that New York city slicker Jed Sewall's idea. Jed's son was the captain of the Harvard University cross-country team at the time."

"Yale," someone yelled.

"What?" asked Doris.

"Yale. He went to Yale."

"Oh, for chrissakes, Harvard, Yale, it doesn't make a goddam bit of difference as far as I'm concerned," said Doris, shaking her head. "They're both asshole factories. Give me a Maine Maritime Academy man and a glass of gin and I'll be perfectly happy. Anyway, the point of the story is, Jed concocted this cockamamie race so Jed Junior could beat everyone in town."

A low wave of hoots and hollers echoed from the back of the crowd.

Doris paused, smiling as she worked the crowd into a lather.

"Of course, Jed hadn't considered the fact that a certain fourteen-year-old Castine kid might decide to enter the race!" Doris yelled.

A chorus of cheers erupted from the crowd. A few people even shouted out his name: *"Dewey! Dewey!"*

"A kid who, I'm happy to say, is back here twenty-five years later, and, from what I've heard, is prepared to defend his title."

Doris raised her hand and pointed at the man leaning against the pickup truck. He didn't move, in fact, he didn't seem to be listening.

Dewey Andreas was Castine's son, as much a part of the town's fabric as the hard, wind-swept place was part of him.

He was born in the three-room Castine hospital, delivered by Doris Russell's late husband, Bob. He was raised on a pretty rambling farm called Margaret Hill, up a winding dirt road behind the golf course. He was a boy like any other boy in town until that one day everyone saw Dewey wasn't like every other boy in town. He was eight years old at the time. The occasion was the annual Independence Day picnic at the Castine Golf Club, attended by everyone in town along with all of the summer folks.

Dewey was playing tennis, barefoot, with his older brother, Hobey. At some point, one of the summer kids, a prep schooler named Hampton, told the Andreas brothers to get off the court.

They weren't supposed to be playing in bare feet. When Hobey told the older boy to wait his turn, he'd called Hobey a "townie."

What happened next on the green-grassed #2 tennis court lives on in Castine infamy. Dewey charged over and slammed the fifteen-year-old in the chest, knocking the taller boy over. When Hampton stood up, he lurched at Dewey, taking a big swing at his head. But Dewey ducked. Then he punched Hampton in the nose. Hampton dropped to the court, screaming in agony, as blood gushed from his nostrils. But Dewey wasn't done with him. As horrified onlookers watched from the terrace, Dewey jumped on him, straddling him, then punched him over and over, beating the living crap out of him, stopping only when a combination of Hobey and their father, John Andreas, was able to pull him away from the bloody, bawling St. Paul's freshman.

From then on, it wasn't considered a wise move to fuck with the younger Andreas brother, the one with the mop of uncut, unmanageable brown hair, the kid who liked to ride his horse to school, the handsome, quiet one with the blue eyes as cold as stone. It wasn't that people were embarrassed that day Dewey beat up Hampton. It was the opposite. Dewey had stood up for his brother and, by extension, his town.

They watched him grow up. By the time he was in sixth grade, he was six feet tall and had the gaunt, sinewy physique of an athlete. He had few friends, choosing mainly to hang out with his brother. Those friends he did have had been selected largely based on their interest in shooting things and by a shared dislike of talking, girls, and summer people.

By high school, he was six-four, two hundred pounds, and had the posture and gait of a prizefighter. After breaking every high school football scoring record in the state, Dewey ventured south to Boston College to carry the ball for the BC Eagles.

To say the town of Castine was proud of Dewey would've been an understatement. Every fall, twice a season, a bus was rented to ferry a crowd down to Chestnut Hill to watch BC's hard-nosed 225-pound tailback tear through every defensive line in the Big East.

After college, Dewey returned to Castine long enough to steal away the prettiest girl in town, Holly Bourne, daughter of a professor at Maine Maritime Academy. Everyone in town went to the wedding. By then, Dewey was getting ready to try out for the U.S. Army Rangers. His hair was short. That was when some people started to recognize that Dewey's aloofness, his standoffish demeanor, his confidence, the meanness in his eyes, the hint of savageness in his stride, that all of it had been given to him for a reason. No one was surprised when Dewey graduated first in his Ranger class out of 188 recruits.

There were tough people in Castine. There were tough people in Maine. And then there was Dewey.

When he left Rangers for Delta, people stopped gossiping altogether. It was no longer about pride. Dewey, they all knew, was being groomed to be one of America's most elite soldiers. Not only was he serving his country, he was being trained to be part of America's jagged front edge, the place where secrets were killed for, in cities no one had ever heard of, where nations clashed in the fog-shrouded dark of night. Dewey was in the middle of it all. He was in the maelstrom. A palpable sense of intrigue was always there, even when he wasn't anywhere near the town.

The few times he came home with Holly and their toddler, Robbie, what had been a quiet, laconic nature became distant. Dewey's silence told of a world the people in Castine would never know, a world Dewey didn't want them to know, not because he didn't like the people in town—because he loved them.

Where I'm going, you cannot come. I'm going there so you don't have to.

Castine's pride turned into something deeper then. Something quieter. When Dewey would return, on those rare occasions, back from an operation, his arrival was noted but not discussed. He was, they all knew, engaged in activities on behalf of the U.S. government that could never be talked of. Dewey, *their* Dewey, was at the bloodstained front edge of America's covert war on terror. He *was* the razor's edge, the tip of the spear, the hunter. It all made sense then, the toughness, the fierceness, the inability to be stopped, to feel pain.

And then, like a lightning bolt thrown from a cruel sky, it was all destroyed. Leukemia stole Robbie at age six. The town gathered at the cemetery, speechless and numb, to help Dewey and Holly bury their boy. A month later, Holly was found dead in an apartment near Fort Bragg, North Carolina, and Dewey was accused of murdering her. The town's grief turned bitter. Its character was shaken to its core. Yet instead of destroying the town, the tragedy brought everyone together. There was never a moment of doubt. Dewey could never do such a thing. Every family in town donated money so that Dewey could hire a good lawyer, a gesture he appreciated but refused to accept. In fact, he didn't hire a lawyer, despite the fact that he faced the death penalty. He represented himself, standing alone against a well-heeled prosecution, and told the truth. He stood tall, just as he'd done so many years before, back on the tennis court.

When he was acquitted after only thirty-one minutes of deliberations, it was the coda to a terrible chain of events that had physically and emotionally exhausted the entire town. No one talked about Dewey after that. They all knew he fled the United States, but no one asked where he was going or what he was doing. They let him be. His parents, John and Margaret, aged. They left Margaret Hill only on rare occasions. Hobey moved to Blue Hill. A decade passed, with vague rumors about Dewey working on offshore oil platforms in faraway countries, and that was all.

And then he returned. It was a week after the greatest terror attack on American soil since 9/11, crafted by the Lebanese terrorist Alexander Fortuna. Maine's largest employer, Bath Iron Works, had been destroyed in the attack. But someone had stopped the terrorist, though no one knew who. Several news reports mentioned a roughneck—an oil worker—with a military background, though the government refused to comment. Yes, that was when Dewey came back, and no one dared ask him if he was the one. They didn't have to.

Now he was back again. Everyone knew why. It had been in the news for weeks. Dewey's fiancée, Jessica Tanzer, the national security advisor to the president of the United States, had been killed in Argentina. Dewey had returned that fall, shell-shocked and broken. Most people assumed he'd leave after a few days, but days turned into weeks, then months, and it was then when people in Castine started to comprehend the fact that perhaps Dewey wasn't ever leaving again. Perhaps this time, something had finally gotten to him. He'd survived the death of Robbie, then Holly, but Jessica's killing had struck a blow that he didn't seem to be able to recover from. The proverbial straw that breaks the camel's back.

As Doris pointed to Dewey, a cacophony of clapping and cheers came from the crowd.

"Hey, Dewey, you gonna win it this year?" yelled someone.

From the front of the pickup, Dewey turned but didn't answer.

"Talkative as ever, eh, Dewey?" someone else yelled.

A few laughs rippled out from the crowd. Dewey glanced in the direction of the remark, remaining silent.

"Hey, Dewey, how's that new talk show of yours coming along?" someone shouted from the back.

At this, Dewey's lips spread into a smile. He glanced in the direction of the remark.

"I got him to smile!"

Dewey started laughing.

"I wasn't smiling at you, Uncle Bill," said Dewey.

"What were you smiling at, then?"

"I was thinking about the time we went duck hunting and you shot yourself in the foot."

More laughter erupted.

"That was an accident, goddammit."

"Sure it was," said Dewey.

"No hurtin' anyone if you don't win, Dewey!" came another voice. More laughter this time.

"Now, leave the boy alone," said Doris, holding up her hand. "Was that Dickie? I don't see your fat ass out there, Dickie."

"That ain't fat, that's one hundred percent muscle, and stop staring at it."

"Richard Pye, the only muscle you got left is the one you use to keep your money hidden at the bottom of those Grand Canyon pockets of yours."

"I got five dollars right here for whoever wins this here race, Mayor," said Pye, holding up a five-dollar bill for the crowd to see.

"Look at that," said Doris. "Abe Lincoln is squinting because he hasn't seen the sun in so long."

As Dewey listened to the banter, he leaned forward, off the bumper of the truck, then walked to his niece, Reagan, who was standing next to her boyfriend.

"Can you beat her, Will?"

Will smiled and shook his head.

"No way," he said. "She's the fastest runner at Andover, boy or girl."

"Prettiest too, right?" added Dewey, smiling and patting Reagan's shoulder.

"That goes without saying," said Will.

Reagan scowled and looked at Dewey, then her boyfriend.

"I know what you two jerks are trying to do, and it's not going to work," she said. "I'm not going to be distracted. Will, I will *definitely* destroy you. You're the one I'm worried about, Uncle Dewey."

"What's your best mile?" asked Dewey.

"Four fifty-five."

"You'll beat me," said Dewey. "I won't even get to State Street by four fifty-five."

"It's not going to work. You can't hustle me. I see through you."

"Then again, running in boots is a little different," said Dewey, ignoring her. "Starts to hurt a little. It's the skin on the back of your foot that goes first. Scrapes right off. Then comes blood. Gets a little muddy in there."

"Ewww," said Reagan.

"Yeah, it's nasty," continued Dewey. "Like pea soup. Only it ain't pea soup, know what I mean?"

Reagan glanced down unconsciously at her feet.

"I bandaged them."

"Oh, then you should be fine," said Dewey. "Bandages never fall off."

"You should also point out the extra weight, Dewey," said Will, smiling as he pitched in. "These boots are heavy."

"Excellent point, William," said Dewey, nodding. "That extra weight'll make your legs get all muscly and big, like an Amazon lady. Will, what do you think, are guys into girls with big, thick tree trunk legs these days?"

Dewey and Will were now doubled over in laughter. Reagan seethed with a mixture of anger and annoyance, though a small grin did manage to sneak through.

"Look, I usually don't talk like this, so please forgive me in advance," said Reagan, "but fuck off, both of you. I hope the dust I kick up will settle down by the time your lame asses come crawling along behind me."

She stormed off, shaking her head.

Just then, Doris Russell let out a loud whistle.

"Let's get this shindig going," Doris said loudly. "It's time for this race to start. I got eleven people coming for dinner and I don't even know what the hell I'm going to make."

"Trust me, Doris, no one comes to your house for the food," yelled someone from the back.

"Good luck getting that lobster license, Lincoln," said Doris, grabbing the police tape and preparing to yank it out of the way. "Now, on your mark . . ."

The runners crowded up toward the tape, except for Dewey, who remained a few feet behind everyone else.

"Get set . . ." she continued.

"*Wait!*" came a voice from up the road. "Wait for me!"

Doris waved her arms, stopping the countdown.

Over the crest of the hill, a boy came sprinting down Main Street. He was shirtless. His face was painted black and green in some sort of hellish-looking camouflage. He wore Nantucket red cutoff shorts and was barefoot. He was holding a boot in each hand, though one was long and orange, the other short and brown.

A smile spread across Dewey's face. He looked in Reagan's direction. She was shaking her head.

"Oh, for fuck's sake," she muttered.

The sight of thirteen-year-old Sam Andreas, charging down Main Street, elicited laughter, a few cheers, and some clapping, though most people just watched the kid in silent amusement.

He barreled down the last few yards to the starting line.

"Sorry, Aunt Doris," said Sam, panting as he came close. He shot his older sister a demonic stare as he sat down on the curb to put on his boots. "Reagan hid my boots."

"I did not," said Reagan.

"Yeah, right," he said. "Which is why I gotta wear these stupid things."

Sam pulled a bright orange knee-high rubber boot onto his left foot. Then he pulled a worn-out L.L. Bean hunting boot onto his right foot.

"I don't even know who these belong to, for chrissakes."

"Watch your language, Sam," came a voice from the crowd.

"Sorry, Grandma," said Sam. "I didn't know you was back there."

"*Were* back there," corrected Margaret Andreas. "And even if I wasn't, young man, you do not have license to use the Lord's name in vain."

"I know," he said, eyeing Reagan with a huge grin on his face. "I apologize."

Sam finished tying his boot and stood up. He ducked under the tape and walked up to Reagan. He stood in front of her. He was at least half a foot shorter than her. His blue eyes stared out from the dark camouflage.

"Good luck out there, sis," he whispered derisively. "You're about to learn what it feels like to lose to a thirteen-year-old wearing his grandma's boots."

"Actually, the Bean boot's mine," said Dewey.

Sam looked up. A smile creased his lips.

"Hey, Uncle Dewey," he said, still eyeing his sister. "Thank God you're here. I thought I wouldn't have any competition."

"Glad to be of service," said Dewey as Reagan gave Sam the finger. "What's with the makeup?"

Sam suddenly looked crestfallen.

"It's camo," said Sam. "I got it at the Army-Navy store in Brewer. What, you think . . . it doesn't look good?"

"No, you'll blend right in. If there are any Viet Cong in the woods, you'll be fine."

Doris clapped her hands, then whistled again.

"Okay, everyone, now that we seem to have the entire field of runners here, let's get going. On your mark, get set, go!"

Doris ripped the tape down from in front of the runners and the tightly packed throng moved out, Reagan Andreas at the lead. The crowd was cheering as the runners moved up Main Street.

Dewey started in last place, at the back of the pack. He smiled at Doris as he ran by her.

"I'm rooting for you," she said as he passed by.

As he crossed the starting line, Dewey's eyes were drawn to the right, down a side street. Parked halfway down the block, tucked in behind a line of Subarus and pickup trucks, was a black sedan, its engine idling. A spike of warmth jabbed at the base of his spine, then shot through his body, a warmth he hadn't felt in a long time. He scanned the sedan one extra moment, then turned back to the race.

The sedan was a heavily customized Cadillac CTS with tinted bullet-proof windows, steel side paneling, an undermounted bomb plate, and low-profile steel-meshed escape tires. In the backseat sat a large, dark-haired man in a navy blue suit. On his lap were two sheets of paper. He studied the documents as he sipped from a coffee cup adorned with a red-and-yellow Tim Hortons logo.

Both documents were printed on the letterhead of the Senate Select Committee on Intelligence. SSCI was responsible for providing congressional oversight of the U.S. intelligence community, including the CIA, NSA, and an alphabet's worth of other agencies. In this capacity, SSCI had the right to conduct whatever investigations it deemed appropriate in order to ensure the CIA was doing its job properly. The man was reading one such file: a top secret analysis of a CIA operative who some believed had gone "off the rails." The two documents were actually different versions of the same document. One was heavily redacted; the other was the clean, unredacted version, obtained surreptitiously by the man through a contact on the staff of the committee.

Most CIA agents, when on assignment in foreign land, assumed a position at an embassy or other benign department of government, giving them official diplomatic immunity, or *cover*, thus protecting them from the harsh punishments typically handed down to captured spies. An official agent, if captured, was usually escorted to the border and kicked out of the country.

There also were those agents who ventured into enemy lands without diplomatic immunity, unprotected. It was called *non-official cover*. If captured, these agents faced severe criminal punishment, up to and including execution. They operated alone, across enemy lines, without a safety net. Inside Langley, they were nicknamed *illegals*. Officially, they were known as NOCs (pronounced "knocks").

If infiltrated correctly, a NOC had more freedom to roam because he or she would not necessarily be on any government's watch list, as embassy workers were. But the value in being unsuspected by enemy governments was only part of it. NOCs were the most lethal combatants America's intelligence and military were capable of producing. NOCs were culled exclusively from CIA paramilitary, Delta, and Navy SEALs. The NOC was Langley's most effective and most dangerous human weapon. Some had been trained to be NOCs. Others migrated there because there was nowhere else to go.

Unfortunately, NOCs were also the most likely agents to develop severe psychological problems, and when this did occur, the results were unpredictable, and sometimes catastrophic. NOCs had the highest suicide rate of any federal employees, by a wide margin. They had the second-highest divorce rate, trailing only members of Congress. Alcoholism, domestic abuse, and a variety of other lesser travails plagued NOCs. The problems tended to occur when they were nonoperational.

Much more worrisome was the threat of a NOC being recruited into an enemy intelligence service. In the past decade, it had occurred six times. In each case, Langley was faced with a hard dilemma: kill the NOC, or let him sell whatever secrets he could—usually tactical operation design parameters—to America's enemies. In each case, the decision had been made to terminate.

The subject of the SSCI investigation was a NOC.

The man scanned the two documents for the umpteenth time, beginning with the redacted version:

U.S. SENATE SELECT COMMITTEE ON INTELLIGENCE
Washington, D.C. 20510

FOCUS: ▬▬▬▬▬▬
▬▬▬▬

SANCTION: SSCI RK667P
AS PER ASSIGNEE: US SEN. FURR

NOVEMBER 19

FIELD VISIT: JANUARY 24–25
FEBRUARY 7–10

ASSIGN: COVER BLACK WIDOW
████████████████████

SITUATION: ██████ IS A ████████ MALE SUSPECTED OF
EXHIBITING TRAITS ASSOCIATED WITH POST-
TRAUMATIC STRESS DISORDER (PTSD). TRIGGERING
EVENTS INCLUDE ████████████████ U.S.
INTELLIGENCE OPERATION. ████████████
████████████████████████████
████████████████████████
████████████████████████
████████████████████
█████████████

CONCLUSION: ANALYSIS INCOMPLETE
HUMINT INSUFFICIENT

REC: WITHOUT PROPER THERAPIST/SUBJECT
COMMUNICATION, SANCTION MUST BE DEEMED
INCONCLUSIVE. ████████████████
████████████████████████████
████████████████████████
████████████████████████
████████████████████████
████████████████████████
██████████████████████
█████████████

CITATION: DR. EDWARD HALLOWELL
TS #9773921A

SUBMISSION: SUDBURY, MA

                 MARCH 1

Next, he looked at the unredacted analysis:

U.S. SENATE SELECT COMMITTEE ON INTELLIGENCE
Washington, D.C. 20510

FOCUS: ANDREAS, DEWEY

                 NOC 295-R

SANCTION: SSCI RK667P

                 AS PER ASSIGNEE: US SEN. FURR

                 PER DDCIA GANT

                 NOVEMBER 19

FIELD VISIT: JANUARY 24–25

                 FEBRUARY 7–10

ASSIGN: COVER BLACK WIDOW

                 DO NOT SHARE (PER DEP DIR GANT)

SITUATION: ANDREAS IS A 39-YEAR-OLD MALE SUSPECTED

                 OF EXHIBITING TRAITS ASSOCIATED WITH POST-

                 TRAUMATIC STRESS DISORDER (PTSD). TRIGGERING

                 EVENTS INCLUDE DEATH OF FIANCÉE DUE TO U.S.

                 INTELLIGENCE OPERATION. GIVEN POSSIBLE PAST

                 SOCIOPATHIC TRAITS EXHIBITED BY SUBJECT, THIS

                 OFFICE WAS ASKED TO DETERMINE IF ANDREAS

                 REPRESENTS A SECURITY THREAT TO THE UNITED

                 STATES OF AMERICA.

CONCLUSION: ANALYSIS INCOMPLETE

                 HUMINT INSUFFICIENT

REC: WITHOUT PROPER THERAPIST/SUBJECT COMMUNICA-
              TION, SANCTION MUST BE DEEMED INCONCLUSIVE.
              HOWEVER, ANALYSIS OF ANDREAS PERSONAL,
              MILITARY, AND INTELLIGENCE HISTORY SUGGESTS A
              UNIQUELY CAPABLE ASSET WHOSE REHABILITATION
              SHOULD BE A TOP AGENCY PRIORITY. ALTERNATIVELY,
              THE SAME SKILLS THAT MAKE HIM A PRIORITY
              AGENCY ASSET ALSO MAKE HIM, UNREHABILITATED,
              A UNIQUELY DANGEROUS POTENTIAL ADVERSARY.

CITATION: DR. EDWARD HALLOWELL
               TS #9773921A

SUBMISSION: SUDBURY, MA
                MARCH 1

The man's focus was interrupted by his driver.

"You think Andreas will win?" the man in the front seat asked, nodding toward the runners as they ran up Main Street.

The man in the backseat glanced up, meeting his eyes in the rearview mirror.

"No."

By the time the pack of runners reached Bog Brook, marking the halfway point in the race, there were two people out in front, and the rest of the field was scattered about, far behind. Reagan was leading, and Dewey was just a few steps behind her. The two were both panting hard and drenched in perspiration.

Every time Reagan looked back at Dewey, he gave her a confident, relaxed smile, toying with her. He pounded the ground behind her as they ran down from the brook toward the road which, in a little over a mile, would conclude at the finish line.

At the outskirts of town, as the dirt path popped them out onto

Battle Avenue, Dewey made his move, cutting to Reagan's left. He knew that in order to beat her, he would have to pass her suddenly, and forcefully, at a pace that was dramatically quicker. To move on her in a gradual way would only spur her on.

By the time Dewey reached the small wooden sign marking the entrance to the Castine Golf Club, he was at least a hundred yards in front of Reagan.

His lungs burned. His legs ached as he pushed himself harder and harder. Dewey didn't look back. The truth is, he didn't want to see the look in Reagan's eyes. Part of him felt guilty about beating her. As he turned onto Main Street for the final stretch, he could hear the crowd cheering in the distance. A smile came to his face as he pushed himself toward the finish line.

Dewey's eyes suddenly shot left. It was a runner. Dewey hadn't heard the approach, but it was why everyone was cheering, he now realized. He watched, helplessly, as the wiry, shirtless figure of his nephew Sam went whizzing past him, orange boot on his left foot, Bean boot on his right, his skinny arms pumping up and down as he almost seemed to take flight.

"Oh, shit," muttered Dewey.

Dewey broke into a sprint, looking for the extra gear he realized he would need in order to catch up to his nephew. But it was futile. He could only watch as Sam coasted away from him. Sam seemed to pick up speed the closer he got to the finish line, as if he himself wasn't fully aware of his own God-given swiftness.

The crowd was going nuts as Sam approached the yellow police tape marking the finish line. Dewey was at least twenty feet behind him. No one else was even in sight yet.

Just before the finish line, Sam stopped. He leaned over, in pain, catching his breath, as Dewey approached. Sam stood just in front of the line, waiting for Dewey.

"What are you doing?" Dewey panted.

Sam shook his head as he tried to catch his breath.

"I want you to win," he said. "Next year'll be my time."

Dewey pushed him across the police tape. The crowd let out a wild chorus of cheers.

Dewey waited for Reagan to arrive at the finish line. He watched with a big smile on his face as she ran the last few feet and crossed. Finally, he stepped over the police tape, taking third.

Sam lumbered over to him.

"Why'd you do that?" he asked, panting. "I wouldn'ta run if I knew you was going to do that."

"*Were* going to do that," corrected Dewey. "You won, Sam. Deal with it."

He put his hand on his nephew's shoulder. As he did so, he again registered the foreboding sight of the black sedan, parked along Court Street, vapor rising from the tailpipe into the air.

"Wanna go get some pancakes?" asked Sam.

Dewey smiled.

"Sure. Give me a few minutes."

Dewey walked slowly to Court Street. As he approached the sedan, the back door suddenly opened. A man in a suit climbed out. He was tall, a bit heavy, with thick black hair. The man, Hector Calibrisi, director of the Central Intelligence Agency, stared at Dewey for several seconds without saying anything. Finally, he spoke.

"Hi, Dewey."

"Hector."

"How you been?" asked Calibrisi.

"Good."

"You win the race?"

"No."

There was a brief pause in the conversation, then Calibrisi cleared his throat.

"I need to speak with you," he said.

"I told you on the phone, I'm not interested in coming back."

"Jessica died six months ago, Dewey."

"Did you fly up here just to remind me of that?" Dewey glared at Calibrisi.

"I'm sorry. That came out wrong."

"Who were those people up here skulking around? Did you send them?"

Calibrisi shook his head.

"No, I didn't."

"Who did?"

Calibrisi crossed his arms and leaned back against the car. He shot the driver a look, telling him to turn the car off.

"Some people are worried about you."

"Who were they?" Dewey asked again.

"Shrinks hired by the Senate Intelligence Committee," said Calibrisi. "Senator Furr."

"If anyone tries to fuck with me, Hector—"

Calibrisi held up his hand.

"Stop," he said, as he cast his eyes about, instinctively aware of the danger of their conversation being listened to through electronic surveillance.

"Stop what?"

"Just don't say it."

Dewey bent over, putting his hands on his knees, and stared at the ground. He was still breathing heavily from the race.

Calibrisi crouched so that he was close to Dewey.

"Why were they here?" whispered Dewey.

Calibrisi was quiet. He looked away, avoiding the question.

"What are you not telling me?"

"Someone is attempting to have you classified as a *breach risk*," said Calibrisi.

"*What the fuck does that mean?*" Dewey said, his temper rising.

"You have knowledge," said Calibrisi. "All NOCs do. If that knowledge fell into the wrong hands, it could be devastating."

"That's insane."

"We lost two NOCs last year. One to China, one to Russia. That's just a fact."

Dewey stood.

"I never wanted the designation and you know it."

"You agreed to it."

"I'm not a security threat," said Dewey. "Go tell them to fuck off."

"That's the last thing we want to do," Calibrisi said. "We need to be calm here."

Dewey nodded.

"What do they do with breach risks?"

Calibrisi took a deep breath.

"It could mean a few sessions with a white coat," said Calibrisi. "A CIA psychologist. Lying on a couch. I told you you needed it."

Dewey read Calibrisi's face.

"Is that it? Doesn't seem so bad. I could take a nap."

"It could also mean a few weeks at a clinic somewhere," added Calibrisi.

Dewey remained silent.

"Or it could be worse," Calibrisi continued, "a lot worse. It's called 'institutional clinical management.' It means incarceration at a CIA hospital somewhere where you'd be managed with pharmaceuticals and not allowed to leave for a few years. Depends on your probability level for failure."

Dewey's eyes were blank and emotionless. He stared at the ground.

"*Probability level for failure?*" he whispered. "What am I, a toaster oven? Aren't you the boss?"

"Why do you think I'm here?" asked Calibrisi. "The way to protect you is to bring you back in."

Dewey shook his head.

"I'm not ready," he said.

"We'll get you ready."

Dewey shook his head.

"I don't want to run ops anymore, Hector. I want to be left alone."

"That's not an option."

"I'll call Dellenbaugh," said Dewey.

"No, you won't."

Dewey stared at Calibrisi. His look wasn't one of anger or even resentment. Rather, it was a look of sadness.

"Who is it?"

"His name is Gant. He's a career Agency man. I don't know what his agenda is. He's clever. Machiavellian."

Dewey looked away. He understood that Hector was there to help him, that he'd flown up to try to warn him, that he wanted to bring him back in because he cared for him. But what Hector couldn't know was something only Dewey understood. He really *wasn't* ready. He wasn't just saying it.

"It's a straightforward project," said Calibrisi.

"A project?" asked Dewey. "You already have me assigned?"

"A cocaine refinery down in Mexico. You're on a two-man team, the other guy is good. He's already in-theater. It'll be like riding a bike."

Dewey stared calmly into the distance.

"It's happening tonight," continued Calibrisi.

Dewey turned and looked at the crowd of townspeople. He saw Doris handing Sam the winner's trophy.

"I don't blame you for wanting all this," said Calibrisi, waving his arm toward the crowd gathered at the finish line. "It's a wonderful place. But it'll be here when you're done. Right now, I need you back inside the fold."

"How much time do I have?"

Calibrisi glanced at his driver. Suddenly, the car started.

"We're leaving right now."

3

Josh Gant stood at the island in the middle of his kitchen, holding a cup of tea and reading the morning newspaper.

Across the room, his wife, Mary, was contorted on top of a purple yoga mat, deep into her daily routine.

Gant had on a blue button-down with white collars, a yellow tie, suspenders, tortoiseshell glasses, and olive pants. He looked meticulously neat and well put together. His hair was slicked back and parted down the middle. He scanned *The Wall Street Journal.*

"Honey, don't forget, we have therapy at two," said his wife in a lockjawed Connecticut accent, her eyes closed.

Gant's eyes shot up for a moment, a hateful look in them. Then, as if flipping a switch, a smile creased his lips.

"I have it right on my schedule, sweetie," he said.

One of Gant's two cell phones started ringing.

"Hello?"

"Mr. Gant, it's John McCauley at the country club. You wanted to speak?"

"Hi, John," said Gant. "Thanks for calling. It's somewhat of a delicate matter."

"You have my promise of utmost discretion, Mr. Gant."

"Good, John. You see, it's just that one of the men I play tennis with seems to have a problem obeying the club rules."

"The rules, Mr. Gant? Is he . . . cheating?"

"No, nothing like that," said Gant. "But he doesn't wear whites, as club rules dictate. I mean, yes, sure, sometimes he does, but he's just as likely to wear a pair of colored shorts or a striped shirt."

McCauley, the Bethesda Country Club general manager, was temporarily silent.

"I see, sir. Did you have an opportunity to discuss your concerns with the member, Mr. Gant? Often I find that many issues can be 'cut off at the pass,' so to speak, with a few simple words."

"No," said Gant, "and I don't necessarily want to. I play tennis with him."

"Of course, I see. Would you like me to say something to the member?"

"Per club rules, I believe it is the responsibility of the rackets committee to address the issue," said Gant, his lips flaring for a brief second as he contemplated the anonymous reputational strike he was making at the member, a player who had now beaten Gant for four consecutive years in the club singles championship.

McCauley was silent.

"Anonymity is of the essence."

Gant's other cell started to vibrate. He looked at the screen:

::   US SEN FURR   ::

Gant hung up one phone as he answered the other.

"Hello, Senator," he said.

"We have a problem," said Furr, the junior senator from Illinois, barely above a whisper.

"Where are you?" asked Gant. "You sound like you're in an elevator."

"Who the fuck cares where I am," said Furr. "We have a problem. Someone leaked the Andreas file to Calibrisi."

"I expected it, Senator," said Gant. "There's nothing wrong with
what we did."

"He's going to rip your head off."

"Calibrisi? I'll be ready for him. In the meantime, you need to
continue demand access to any other aspects of Andreas's life that
are even remotely questionable. The death of his first wife. His time
on the oil rig. Jessica Tanzer's death. *Push it.*"

"Look, Josh, I don't like the guy either," said Furr. "I was willing to run the psych eval, but I'm not about to start ruining his life.
We're talking about a bona fide American hero. For fuck's sake, he
was awarded the Presidential Medal of Freedom. Dellenbaugh loves
the guy."

Gant took a sip of his tea.

"You don't get it, Senator," said Gant. "This isn't about Dewey
Andreas. He's a means to an end. He's a pawn, a poker chip."

"Yeah, I know," said Furr. "But if he's innocent—"

"The question is not whether Andreas is innocent," interrupted
Gant. "It's about image. This is a political campaign. We're going
to expose a security risk at the highest levels of the Central Intelligence Agency. We'll be notorious, Senator."

"I'm not sure I want to be notorious."

"Notorious is the rung on the ladder just before ubiquity," said
Gant.

There was a short silence.

"It would be a front-page story," agreed Furr, calming down.
"The American public likes their heroes until they're exposed as
something else, then they tear them down and kick them to the curb.
The press would have a field day, Josh."

"We need to be patient," said Gant. "Calibrisi might say something, but I can handle it. We need to be patient and bide our time."

4

A rusty light blue CMK 12.5-ton crane spewed diesel smoke out into the Sevastopol sky. The smoke blended into the thick fog shrouding the port city as dawn approached. The sun would burn off the fog by 6:00, but now, at 4:30 A.M., it hid the port well enough to obscure any possible observation from satellites overhead or Ukrainian patrol boats.

The operator of the crane sat in the cab and smoked a cigarette as he maneuvered the boom. He swept it above a flatbed semitruck. The truck was parked on a concrete pier sticking out into the ocean. He stopped the boom when the hook and ball were above a brown-skinned man named Al-Medi.

He was tall, with a thin, sinister-looking mustache, a beaklike nose, and long black hair. He was shirtless. His chest, shoulders, and torso were thick with muscles.

He was standing near the back of the flatbed, next to a wooden crate. The crate was four feet tall, eight feet long, and wrapped in thick steel cables, drawn around to a thick steel padlock on top.

"*Lower!*" yelled Al-Medi to the crane operator. "One foot. *Hurry!*"

Moored alongside the pier was a fishing boat, a 211-foot vessel built for use in deep ocean all over the world. The ship had been in dry dock for several years before its current owner purchased it, in cash, just a week ago.

Cyrillic letters spread across the bow. Roughly translated, they meant *Lonely Fisherman.*

The ship was black, old, and ugly, with long streaks of rust and slash marks along the hull, earned over decades. A half dozen men stood on the deck. They were young, all in their early twenties. There was not a smile to be seen among them. Their eyes scanned the dirt road behind the pier, the small area of visible waterfront, and the foggy sky, looking for any unexpected visitors.

The hook and ball were lowered down next to Al-Medi. He grabbed the hook and moved it to the top of the crate. He latched it to a steel ring at the center of the large container.

Slowly, the crate was lifted into the air. The crane boom creaked as the object stressed rusted bolts and pulleys. The crane operator swung the crate gingerly through the air toward the deck of the ship. Once the boom was above the center of the deck, he lowered the crate until it came to rest. One of the men unhooked it.

A distant noise interrupted the low din of the crane. Every man turned. A brown cloud of dust and dirt accompanied the sound of a car engine. It was a dull blue Porsche 911 4S. Two of the men on the deck of the ship lifted submachine guns reflexively into the air, training them at the approaching vehicle.

"*Put the guns down!*" yelled Al-Medi angrily.

The Porsche stopped at the end of the pier. The driver's door opened and a man stepped out. He was joined by an older man, in his seventies, with gray hair and glasses, who carried a steel briefcase.

Al-Medi jumped down from the flatbed to greet the visitors. As he walked, he looked at the six men aboard the ship.

"Get ready to cast off!" Al-Medi barked. "Tarp the crate. *Now!* Faqir, come with me."

One of the men jumped off the boat and walked with Al-Medi toward the visitors.

"Cloud," Al-Medi said as he stepped toward the parking area to greet him.

Cloud was wearing black jeans and a leather jacket. He had on white-framed sunglasses. His Afro of blond curls stuck up in an unruly pattern. In his right hand was a small duffel bag.

Al-Medi put his hand out as Cloud approached, but Cloud made no effort to return the gesture.

"Is it ready?" asked Cloud, with urgency in his voice.

"Yes," said Al-Medi. "They will push off within the hour. This is the captain, Faqir."

Cloud scanned the other man.

"How old are you?" asked Cloud.

"Twenty-seven," said Faqir.

"And you are capable?"

"I have made six transatlantic crossings in my life," said Faqir. "Yes, I believe I am ready, sir."

"Have you ever been at the helm when making those crossings?"

Cloud stared into the Arab's eyes. He already knew the answer to his question, but he wanted to hear what Faqir would say.

"No, sir, I have not."

Cloud nodded impassively. But Faqir's answer pleased him. He was not a liar.

Cloud handed him the duffel bag.

"This is a VHF radio," said Cloud. "It was bought in Nova Scotia and is registered to a Canadian citizen. Its AIS beacon will indicate that it is a Halifax cod dragger. When you get to Georges Bank, initiate contact with whatever vessel you can find. Do not send a distress signal. You simply are having engine problems. Inform whoever you can raise that you're in need of engine filters. When they come close, do what you need to do to take over the boat. No witnesses. Move the bomb, then sink the dragger."

"I understand," said Faqir.

"Dr. Poldark has potassium iodide pills for the crew. You'll want to start taking them today. They won't stop the radiation sickness, but they'll delay it. After that, you know what to do. The specific maps and time lines have already been sent to you."

"Yes, I have studied them."

Cloud nodded to the older man with him.

"This is Dr. Poldark," said Cloud. "He'll inspect the device and connect the detonator. Give him whatever assistance he needs."

Faqir nodded at the older man.

"It's an honor to meet you, sir," he said.

"Is my equipment here?" asked Poldark. "Lathe? Soldering devices? Explosives?"

"It arrived last night. It's been placed aboard."

"Very good," said Poldark. "What about hazmat suits?"

"Yes, they're on board."

"And did you cover it in the tarp I sent?"

"Yes, sir. What is it for?"

"The Americans measure radiation from satellites in the sky," said Poldark. "Uranium depletion emits a signature that enables them to pinpoint and track the bomb from stationary locations in outer space based solely on molecular level air characteristics. Soon, the United States will know the bomb is moving. They will scan the coast. If their Milstar satellites attempt to find the radioactive signature that matches the bomb, the covering will obscure the readings and cause them to lose track of the bomb for several hours. By then, we will be out of their imprint lines. Hopefully, they won't know where it's gone."

"If the Americans somehow find us—" said Faqir respectfully.

"There are too many boats and the ocean is too busy and too wide for you to be caught," said Cloud, interrupting. "However, if the Americans catch you, tell them whatever you know. There's no glory in trying to protect me. They will torture you to get at the truth. I am deeply grateful for your service and your sacrifice. I wouldn't want you to suffer torture. Now get going. I'll be in touch after you're through the Strait of Gibraltar and are free and clear."

He turned to leave, then reached into his pocket and removed a small remote.

"Faqir," he said, tossing it in the air. "The detonator."

Faqir caught the device, a panicked look on his face.

"It's not connected yet," said Poldark, shaking his head.

Cloud moved up the driveway. Al-Medi followed him. He stepped close, so that Poldark and Faqir couldn't hear him speak.

"I must tell you something," he said in a low voice. "At dinner last night, there was talk. Chatter. Everyone is talking about the next nine/eleven. They know something."

"This is because of your jihadists," said Cloud, nodding toward Faqir. "We need them, but they have big mouths."

"What if the Americans—"

"You seem worried," interrupted Cloud. "Do you remember nine/eleven? Do you remember coming to me after school and asking for my help? You didn't have any fear back then, did you?"

Cloud stepped forward so that he was only inches from Al-Medi's face. He glared into Al-Medi's eyes.

"Let me worry about the CIA," continued Cloud. "You have one job to do. Get that boat moving, then get back to Moscow."

He handed Al-Medi a cell phone.

"Keep this on you," said Cloud. "I want to be able to reach you."

"What about my payment?"

Cloud moved up the hill. He climbed into the Porsche and started it, then revved the engine as he looked at Al-Medi, standing in front of the car. He stared at the cell phone as Al-Medi stuck it into the pocket of his jeans.

He lowered the window.

"You get paid when the boat is through the strait," said Cloud. "That should be Friday or Saturday. Saturday I'm having a dinner party at the dacha. Come by. It will be fun. I'll pay you then."

Cloud cranked the wheel hard clockwise, then slammed the gas, burning a fiery, dust-choked cloud into the air behind him.

5

A white Chevy Suburban, windows tinted sunglass silver, ripped along a decrepit, pothole-rutted road at a hundred miles an hour. It was just past midnight.

The vehicle sent a simple, ominous message to the locals as it cruised by: *Stay the fuck out of the way.*

Everyone assumed the shiny white Suburban was from the Sinaloa cartel, or someone having to do with Sinaloa. The locals feared the psychos who ran the cartel. Gunning down a local was not only possible, it happened all the time, often without provocation or explanation. No one dared even look at the vehicle as it moved along Iguala's winding roads.

Sinaloa was Mexico's largest criminal enterprise. It was a drug-trafficking, money-laundering, and organized crime behemoth believed to rival the Moscow mafia in its size and scope. Both groups had tentacles deep inside the United States, Europe, and Asia.

But the Suburban wasn't from any cartel.

Inside the vehicle, two men sat quietly, one driving, the other in the backseat. They hadn't spoken since departing Mexico City two hours before.

"We're five klicks out," said Pete Bond, glancing in the rearview mirror at Dewey.

Dewey didn't look up. His eyes were focused on the window and the passing countryside.

"Hey, Dewey?"

Dewey gradually moved his eyes away from the window and toward Bond. He remained silent.

"I need you briefed up," continued Bond.

"Sure," said Dewey. "Take me through it."

Bond was Central Intelligence Agency; a senior officer inside the National Clandestine Service's Political Activities Division. He was dressed in clothing that could only be described as ostentatious: black Lanvin slacks, white Givenchy button-down, gold chains, Prada shoes. His hair was long, black, and slicked back. He had a mustache. Bond's get-up was highly planned, in case they were stopped along the way. He looked like a high-level capo inside, or affiliated with, Sinaloa, come to pay a visit to the refinery.

Dewey had on jeans, a black synthetic shirt that clung to his chest, arms, shoulders, and torso, a flak jacket, and a Lycra ski cap. His face was camouflage black.

Across his lap was an unusual-looking assault rifle: HK MR762A1-SD. Dewey had selected the gun based on his experience as a Delta fighting cartel gunmen. It was a stealthy, very powerful piece of killing hardware, a gun that could silently take out a guard from two hundred yards without being seen or heard, then, a minute later, could be used to mow down a dozen of that guard's colleagues after they discovered the corpse on the ground and went to guns.

The refinery was located in remote territory several hours south of Mexico City, technically part of the sprawling city of Iguala but twenty miles from the city's decaying urban edge. The roads leading to the refinery were bordered by squalor. Shacks were scattered every hundred feet or so. Old steel oil barrels tossed flames into the sky from gasoline fires. Front yards were overrun by chickens and mongrel dogs.

The refinery was situated at the end of a weed-covered, mile-long dirt road. A hundred years ago, the road led to a sugarcane mill, but the buildings had long since been boarded up, abandoned, then burned to the ground by vandals. Now the site was occupied by a neat-looking corrugated steel warehouse. Inside, a small state-of-the-art cocaine and heroin refinery turned out street-ready narcotics that left in semitrucks bound for the United States.

For the Sinaloa cartel, the refinery was neither important nor valuable. It was one of more than one hundred such coke fabs that dotted the Mexican countryside. Portable, tremendously profitable, totally expendable.

Bond was a highly trained operator, but his true métier was in-theater intelligence acquisition, synthesis, analysis, and strategy. The operation was his design.

Dewey was there to execute that design.

"Beneath the seat," said Bond, "grab the scans."

Dewey reached down and found a manila folder, placing it on his lap. He took his SOG combat blade from his vest and triggered a small light built into the hilt. He put it in his mouth and aimed it at the photographs inside the folder.

"Those are fresh off NGA SAT an hour ago," said Bond.

NGA, the National Geospatial-Intelligence Agency, was a key CIA operations support agency, providing real-time imagery of areas of operation, looking primarily for signs of unexpected enemy manpower.

Several of the photos were taken during daytime. They showed a rectangular warehouse, along with a few semitrucks backed up to a loading dock. There were also night shots, from the sky, using advanced holographic-imaging technology. They looked like X-rays. One of the photos displayed a close-up of the side of the building; a red circle had been stenciled around a door.

Dewey finished looking at the photos and tossed them on the seat.

"You'll approach on foot in a northeast pattern, coming at the building through a side door. The location is on the scan. Eliminate anyone you see, then hit me up on commo. I'll get down there, we'll set munitions, then split. We'll detonate it remotely. We should be able to fly Air America out of Acapulco. SEAL Team 4 is prepared to exfiltrate if things get nasty."

Dewey stared out the Suburban's back window. As hard as he tried to listen, Bond's words sounded like they were coming from a thousand miles away. As hard as he tried to concentrate, he couldn't.

"Cartels your first desk?" asked Dewey, willing himself back to the present.

"Second," said Bond. "I spent five years in Russia."

"Doing what?"

"I was part of a team that was trying to destabilize Putin before he got elected. Obviously it didn't work too well."

Dewey closed his eyes and pictured Jessica. It was the afternoon she was killed. She was on a horse, riding in Argentina. He was riding behind her. For some reason, this was the image that popped into his head as he stared out at the moonlit Iguala countryside.

It had been almost precisely six months to the day since she was killed. He and Jessica would've been married. The first bump of a child might've appeared on her stomach by now.

He shut his eyes for several moments, then opened them, steeling himself against the sadness he knew would soon come on like a fever.

"I heard you spent some time chasing down the North Valley cartel," said Bond, referring to one of South America's most notorious cartels, a group that was now largely gone.

"Yeah," said Dewey, meeting Bond's eyes, forcing himself back to the present, to the Suburban, to Bond's words, to Iguala.

"What was the biggest coke fab you hit?"

Dewey stared at Bond in the mirror. He remained silent.

Stop thinking about her.

"I don't remember," said Dewey. "They all sorta blend in."

"I studied how North Valley was taken down. You were right in the middle of it."

"If I was, I didn't realize it," said Dewey.

Dewey looked at Bond in the rearview mirror.

"Can I ask you something?" said Dewey.

"Sure."

"And not have it leave here?"

"It stays between us."

"You know someone at the Agency named Gant?" asked Dewey.

Bond's eyes flashed in the rearview.

"The new deputy director," he said. "Yeah. Why?"

"Just wondering."

Bond paused.

"Steer clear of him," he said. "I don't trust him. Politicians are bad enough, but the guys who get them elected? They're assholes."

Bond slowed the Suburban.

"We're here," he said as he pulled on a set of thermal night optics, killed the lights, and banked left into the driveway, accelerating down an empty dirt road. After a minute, he came to a stop.

Dewey reached to the seat next to him. He lifted a half-moon-shaped mag and slammed it into the gun. He opened the door and climbed out. He reached to his ear.

"Commo check."

"Roger," said Bond. "See you in a few."

Dewey started a quick-paced run off the driveway, into a low field of brush and dry scrub grass.

He had night optics, but he kept them strapped to his weapons belt, preferring to let the moon guide him. After several minutes of running, he came to a crest of a hill and for the first time saw the lights of the refinery, just a few hundred feet down a steep slope.

Dewey paused, catching his breath. He checked his weapon one last time. He skulked down the hill toward the near side entrance, raising the rifle as he moved.

At the bottom of the hill, he moved to the side door that had been circled on the scans. He felt his heart racing. He could barely breathe. His hand reached out to grab the door handle. He felt paralyzed, watching as his hand reached for the door. In the dim light, he could see what he already knew was happening, the trembling of his hand as it reached out for the handle. Dewey stared for more than a minute at the warehouse. The minute became two, then three. Yet still he didn't move.

Suddenly, he heard a faint whisper in his ear.

"How we doing?"

It was Bond.

Dewey reached for his earbud. His arm remain paralyzed, extended toward the door, shaking like a leaf.

"Dewey, you okay?" whispered Bond.

"No."

"I'll be right down. Stay where you are."

Dewey took a step backward, then another, moving slowly away from the warehouse. He heard the engine. His eyes turned to the driveway. The Suburban barreled toward him, skidding to a stop. Bond climbed out, submachine gun raised, and charged toward the front door of the warehouse, around the corner from Dewey.

Bond glanced at Dewey just as he was about to open the front door. He flashed Dewey a smile. Then he raised the SMG and pulled the door open.

The staccato of automatic weapon fire thundered from inside the warehouse. Dewey stood still, not moving, for what seemed like an eternity. Finally, Bond emerged. He walked to Dewey. When he came to within a foot, Bond reached out for Dewey's rifle, pulling it from him.

"You think you can help me carry the bomb?" asked Bond.

Dewey nodded.

"Yeah," he said.

Bond stared for one last moment at Dewey.

"You're not the first," said Bond reassuringly. "You won't be the last. Now let's torch this place and get the fuck out of here."

6

SOVETSKYA AVENUE
ELEKTROSTAL, RUSSIA

Cloud parked the Porsche on a side street, behind the Elektrostal train station. He had on dark black sunglasses. Behind the
lenses, his eyes were bloodshot and red rimmed from a lack of sleep.
He wore black leather pants, boots, and a green T-shirt. He was
gaunt, so thin he appeared unhealthy. He walked quickly, stopping
at a building several blocks from the station. Glancing in both directions, he made sure he hadn't been followed, then inserted a key
into a large steel door.

The building was four stories high, constructed in mustard-
colored brick. Like most buildings in Elektrostal, it long ago took
on a look of dilapidated resignation, its exterior stained in rust and
mildew. It had once contained the administrative offices of a steel
pipe manufacturer who'd gone bankrupt in the 1970s. It was the
fourth location over the course of a ten-year period for Cloud.

The locations shared certain characteristics. Each was inside a
city large enough to provide a level of anonymity and infrastructure,
yet small enough to be off the radar screens of intelligence agencies. Each was within a few hours of Moscow and accessible by train.

All the cities were economically depressed, guaranteeing plenty of vacant office buildings.

Elektrostal was a small industrial city located an hour's drive east of downtown Moscow. A handful of heavy equipment manufacturers, metallurgical plants, and chemical processors were located in the grayish city. The streets of Elektrostal were laid out in a mathematical grid, with straight, sweeping blocks of concrete apartment buildings and half-empty strip malls that ran in precise lines for miles. Other than an underground nuclear waste storage facility at the northern outskirts of the city limits, Elektrostal was unimportant, a minor place that produced little of great consequence. At least a quarter of the city's low-rise concrete office buildings were dark and empty. There wasn't a single warehouse that wasn't partially covered in rust.

Cloud didn't like or dislike Elektrostal. For him, the dirty city, its shabby, woebegone people, its lousy restaurants, its crappy weather, and its foul mood were all irrelevant. Elektrostal was the entry into the world he actually lived in. The way a scientist might live deep within the infrastructure of a cell, Cloud lived within the digital pathways of the Internet.

Inside, Cloud climbed the stairs. The first two floors sat dark, empty, and unused. The third floor was dimly lit. Glancing through the fire door, Cloud could see that fully half the floor was taken up by high-powered computer servers, fifty-eight in total, enterprise-class, Chinese-made Huawei servers, all in steel cases that could be wheeled and repositioned. They'd been stripped and sanitized of all digital identifiers that might enable remote tracing or real-time location discovery. A half dozen large industrial air conditioners were kept on around the clock, no matter the time, weather, or season, to moderate the heat generated by the servers. Even in the dead of winter, the temperature in the room never fell below eighty degrees.

Cloud arrived at the fourth floor. The space was cavernous, open, brightly lit, and immaculate. All interior walls had been removed.

At the center of the room, a series of tables were set up in a large U shape. On top of the tables sat computer screens, long lines of them, and before the screens were chairs. There were thirty-six separate computer screens in all.

Every square inch of the floor, walls, windows, and ceiling was covered in a thin layer of copper mesh, epoxied like wallpaper and designed to prevent eavesdropping or other forms of electronic signals capture from outside the building.

Sascha looked up at him as he came inside, barely registering his entrance.

"Hello, Cloud."

"What about Malnikov?" asked Cloud. "Has he been contacted by the Central Intelligence Agency?"

"Not that we're aware of."

"'Not that we're aware of'?" snapped Cloud rhetorically, annoyance in his voice. "What does that mean? I thought we are intercepting every phone call and electronic communications Alexei Malnikov makes."

"My only point, Cloud," said Sascha sheepishly, holding up his hands, "is that we technically wouldn't be aware if someone walked up to him and started talking."

"We just acquired a nuclear bomb," said Cloud. "Don't be so fucking literal. You scared the shit out of me."

"I'm sorry."

Cloud nodded.

"It's okay," he said. "You always were the boy who cried wolf, weren't you? I should've left you at Saint Anselm."

Cloud walked to Sascha at the far end of the room and stood next to his chair. He glanced at one of the screens in front of him. It showed an online chess game.

Cloud did a double take.

"You took one of my rooks," he whispered, shaking his head in disbelief.

"You're distracted," said Sascha. "Otherwise I know you would not allow me to get within a hundred miles of your rook, Pyotr."

Cloud stared at the screen.

Sascha was one of the few people in the world who had known him back before Cloud existed, when he was Pyotr Vargarin, little Pyotr, son of the famous scientist Anuslav Vargarin, who'd killed himself and his wife in a motorboat for reasons no one knew, leaving Pyotr an orphan.

They met at the only home he could remember, a dank, dreadful place in Sevastopol called Saint Anselm by the Sea, the city's only orphanage, a cruel and horrible place, run by an alcoholic priest named Father Klimsov.

"Pyotr," said Cloud. "I haven't been called that in a long time."

A memory flashed.

"Pyotr, please come in," Father Klimsov said one day.

It was raining. Whenever it rained at Saint Anselm, there would be small puddles everywhere from the holes in the roof. On Father Klimsov's desk, a tin bucket was half filled with water.

"Pyotr, this is Dr. Tretiak," said Father Klimsov as he stepped into his office.

After more than six years at Saint Anselm, it was his first time in Father Klimsov's office.

Pyotr didn't like Father Klimsov. He was an obese, cruel old man.

"Dr. Tretiak is the president of Moscow Technological Institute. It is the most prestigious educational institution in all of the Soviet—I mean, in all of Russia."

Tretiak had a kind smile on his face. He extended his hand to shake Pyotr's, but Pyotr did not return the gesture.

"I heard you were shy," said Tretiak, laughing. "It's all right. I don't bite."

"Dr. Tretiak brings good news," said Klimsov.

"Yes, Father," said Pyotr.

"You have been granted entrance to Moscow Technological Institute," said Klimsov. "Next fall, you shall move to Moscow."

"You're a very smart young man," said Tretiak. "But then, you know that already, don't you?"

Pyotr didn't move, but not because he was scared, or rude, or indifferent. Instead, it was because he was transfixed by the sight of an object on Klimsov's desk.

"Yes, I know," said Pyotr, staring at the object.

"What do we say when someone compliments us, Pyotr?" asked Father Klimsov.

Pyotr didn't look at Klimsov or Dr. Tretiak; instead, his eyes remained fixed on the thing on Klimsov's desk.

"It's not a compliment if it's the truth," said Pyotr.

That night, after curfew, Pyotr snuck into Father Klimsov's office, where he turned on the computer, only to be thwarted by its demand for a password. It took almost a month's worth of nights for Pyotr to guess it. But once he did, it was like stepping out of a cave and suddenly seeing the world for what it was. He read and read and read for what seemed like forever, newspapers and magazines from all over the world. He stared mesmerized at photos of places he had never heard of. And then, at some point, at the sight of an error screen, he went behind the Web site into its code base. He studied it for hours, then returned a night later and studied it more, going back and forth between the code and the Web site. He could never explain what happened then, but one night, at the sight of the white screen filled with meaningless symbols, words, and spaces, he suddenly felt it all coalesce. He could see vague outlines in the code of what was being created visually. Soon, he could pore over a wall of computer code and know exactly what would be created by its code.

Within a few months, Pyotr taught himself enough programming to hack into the Union Bank of Sevastopol, where he established a bank account and then stole $25,000 from an account inside the bank. He used the money to buy a laptop computer and a wireless router, which he arranged to have delivered to the post office down the street from the orphanage. After splicing the Internet cable that came into the building, he added the router to the orphanage's dusty utilities closet. It was his escape hatch. Every night, he climbed through it, venturing out into a world beyond Saint Anselm by the Sea, beyond Sevastopol, beyond the shores of a country that had bequeathed to him a destroyed and hateful heart.

Sascha was the only person in the world who knew him from the orphanage. Sascha was the only one who knew the truth about Cloud's father. That he hadn't killed himself. That an American had done it, a man with a scar.

He trusted him because when you are orphans together, something happens between you that is stronger even than the ties of siblings. It is what you have when you combine self-hatred and anger, when violence and deceit are inflicted upon you at the youngest of ages; it is the feeling of trying to scratch an itch that will never go away, the itch that is the answer to the question: Why did they leave me?

Why did this happen to me? What did I do to deserve this?

The unsung chorus of the orphan.

Within the hell that is the sole real thing that an orphan possesses, misery pools like molten lava and eventually hardens into rock, then steel. It bonds orphan to orphan, and it can never be broken.

"Do you remember Klimsov?" asked Cloud, returning from his memory, looking at the chess game on the computer screen before Sascha.

"Yes. What about him?"

"He was such a crappy chess player," said Cloud, studying the chessboard. It was his move.

"I never played him," said Sascha.

"I did. He sucked."

"Why did you think of that old bastard?"

"Because I was wondering if he taught you how to play," said Cloud.

He leaned forward and typed into the keyboard.

"Checkmate, Sascha. Now go fuck yourself."

7

ANDREWS AIR FORCE BASE
CAMP SPRINGS, MARYLAND

A white, unmarked Gulfstream V touched down at precisely two o'clock on a cloud-covered, brutally humid afternoon. Dewey followed Bond down the jet's stairs as, in the distance, a black Chevy Suburban sped across the tarmac.

"Speak of the devil," muttered Bond.

"Who is it?"

"Gant."

The Suburban made a beeline for Dewey and Bond, stopping directly in front of them. Dewey and Bond stood still. Both men were still dressed in tactical gear.

The back window opened. Sitting in the backseat was Gant. He had a stern look on his face.

"How did Iguala go?" he asked, looking at Bond.

"Fine."

"What happened?" asked Gant, his eyes scanning Dewey from head to toe as he waited for Bond to answer.

"We achieved the objective of the mission," said Bond. "Now, if you'll excuse us, we're both sort of tired."

"Take me through the minute-by-minute," said Gant.

"Sir, it'll be in the brief."

"Right now."

Bond took a deep breath, trying to control his temper. He nodded at Dewey and they started to walk away.

The back door of the SUV suddenly opened. Gant stepped out and caught up to Dewey and Bond, stopping directly in their path.

Gant crossed his arms, fuming. His attention shot to Dewey, again looking him up and down. Dewey didn't react. In fact, he didn't look back, choosing instead to simply stare off into the distance, ignoring Gant.

"I want the first debrief," said Gant, pointing at Bond.

Bond looked at Gant's finger, pointing at him.

"No disrespect, but I report to Bill Polk," said Bond, barely above a whisper. "He gets the brief, not you."

8

Dewey sat at the bottom of a winding, carpeted stairway, on the first floor of an old, beautiful, impeccably designed town house, drinking a beer. It was his fourth beer. On second thought, it might have been his fifth. He was leaning against the wall, legs crossed in front of him, still dressed in tactical gear.

Dewey owned the town house now. Jessica had left it to him. It was the first time he'd stepped inside it since her death.

Next to him was a case of beer, five bottles missing. Two six-packs were Bud Light, two were Yuengling, a slightly heavier concoction. Dewey drank a Bud in between Yuenglings. He looked at Bud Light as being the equivalent to drinking water, a way to make sure he didn't get too drunk. Of course, the bottle of Jack Daniel's still inside the paper bag would soon make that whole thought process pointless.

His eyes were glued to the wall, at a large oil painting of a green iris. It was Jessica's favorite painting. Dewey wasn't thinking about the painting, however. He wasn't thinking about Jessica either. He wasn't even thinking about Gant, though he knew he'd likely come to Andrews for the sole purpose of eyeballing Dewey.

Dewey was thinking about Mexico.

He could count on one hand the number of operational failures he'd experienced. Invariably, they had been failures due to circumstances beyond his control. All of them occurred on complicated, difficult operations. Mexico should've been easy. It wasn't particularly dangerous, complicated, or logistically challenging. It was a brilliantly planned operation, which is why it was so relatively safe and simple. Yet he froze like a deer in the headlights.

Dewey was searching for the meaning of it all. Why had he not grabbed the door handle? Where had that paralysis come from? But the harder he searched for an answer, the more elusive it became. Yet he knew he needed to find the answer. He didn't have a choice. Calibrisi hadn't come to Castine to recruit him. He'd come to rescue him.

Dewey pulled out his cell phone and hit a speed-dial number.

"Yeah?" came the voice.

"Hey, Rob."

Tacoma, an ex–Navy SEAL, was Dewey's closest friend, that is, if he actually had friends. Dewey hadn't spoken to Tacoma since a few days before Jessica's funeral.

"Dewey."

"I'm good, thanks for asking," said Dewey.

"Like I'm the one who went off grid, asshole. What are you doing? Are you still up in Maine? What are you gonna become, a fucking lobsterman?"

"Maybe," said Dewey. "I like lobsters. Sorry for not calling. I've been . . . well, I've been getting my head straight."

"Uh-oh. Are you doing yoga or some shit like that? Acupuncture? No, wait, you're a fucking vegan, aren't you? I knew it. Just tell me you're not driving a Prius. I swear, I'll never talk to you again."

Dewey laughed.

"No, I still have my balls. I'm in D.C. I'm at Jess's."

"Really? Awesome."

Tacoma did his best to act positive, despite the mention of Jessica and the fact that Dewey was in what was to have been their future home, obviously alone.

"I'll be back in a few days," continued Tacoma. "You want to get together?"

"Yeah, that sounds good."

"Listen, they're telling us to shut off our phones," said Tacoma. "I'll call you when—"

"I have a quick question."

"Uh-oh. Let me guess. You're in jail. Call fuckin' Hector, man." Dewey laughed again.

"You still fight?" asked Dewey.

"What do you mean, 'fight'?"

"Mixed martial arts. That UFC shit you're always talking about." Tacoma paused.

"Yeah," he involuntarily offered. "Why?"

"You like it?"

"It's not as much fun as it used to be. There are some punks out there. Last time I was at a gym, I almost got my neck broken. All these guys think they're gonna be famous. Scouts from UFC are always there, so they're showing off. That being said, it's the only way to keep sharp, other than running ops, of course."

Dewey reached for the brown bag. He unscrewed the cap and took a large swig.

"There's a decent gym in Adams Morgan. Some good fighters."

"Is that where you almost got your neck broke?"

"No," said Tacoma. He paused for several moments. "Dewey, look, I know you."

"What the fuck does that mean?"

"I know you've been drinking."

Dewey looked at the case of beer. He picked up the Jack Daniel's and took another gulp.

"Tell me the name of the gym," said Dewey. "I promise I won't kill anyone."

Tacoma laughed.

"I'm not worried about them."

"Rob."

Tacoma let out a sigh.

"Okay, fine. It's in southeast, out near Redskins stadium. It's called Whitewater. Don't say I didn't warn you."

The neighborhood was one, possibly two steps up the economic ladder from ghetto. A few stores had hand-scrawled signs advertising their wares. Others sat vacant, shuttered in graffiti-covered corrugated steel. People were gathered on the stoops of boarded-up, burned-out town houses, drinking and smoking.

At eight o'clock, the night was still young. But darkness had long ago descended on this forgotten part of the nation's capital.

The taxi driver dropped Dewey at the back edge of Lincoln Park, unwilling to go any farther into the neighborhood. Dewey climbed out, without tipping, and walked the last dozen blocks to Whitewater MMA.

Dewey had on jeans and a green T-shirt, along with running shoes. He walked down the sidewalk, a hard look on his face, staring a thousand miles away as he moved toward the gym. He stepped through the steel door of the gymnasium as, a few blocks away, a siren started to wail.

The inside of Whitewater was humid, with a sharp, acrid smell that stung the nostrils. Years' worth of body odor hovered in the cavernous gym. To most, the smell sent a wave of disgust, even nausea. But Dewey breathed it in. It was an odor he knew well, a smell he'd hated, then come to love, first at BC, the stench of the varsity football team locker room. In Rangers, it was the CQB room, where Dewey learned the basics of hand-to-hand combat, alongside the rest of his Ranger class. It's not that the memories were fond ones, but they were part of him.

There was a large crowd, fifty or sixty people, mostly young men, black or Hispanic, in their late teens or early twenties. The few who were older had on street clothing. These were, Dewey guessed, coaches and scouts.

A few heads turned as Dewey stepped through the door. He was greeted with cold stares.

There were three rings. Two were smaller sparring rings, used for practice. Both were occupied. In one, a small tattoo-covered Hispanic kid was working with a coach. He had on red Lycra shorts and no shirt. He was barefoot. The coach was working on his kicking attack. Every few seconds, he would launch a vicious series of kicks, his feet sometimes slashing above his coach's head.

The other ring had a bout going on. A few people were watching as the two barefoot, muscled fighters circled each other. One of them suddenly charged the other, leaping, kicking his right foot toward his opponent's head, striking it, sending the man tumbling down to the mat as blood surged from his mouth. But the man on the ground was up in seconds, side-crawling away from a second strike, standing quickly, then slamming a fist into his opponent's torso, followed by another, then tackling him to the mat.

"Hey, it ain't free."

Dewey's head turned. A man in a wheelchair was looking at him.

"You wanna watch, fine, but it ain't free."

"How much?"

"Ten bucks."

"How much for one of the rings?"

The man in the wheelchair looked Dewey up and down.

"What do you want it for?" he asked. "You gonna do some Pilates?"

Dewey looked at him, ignoring his taunt.

"How much to fight?"

"Spar?"

"Fight."

The man grinned.

"What'd you watch some UFC on TV? This ain't the place for amateur white guys from Alexandria to learn how to fight."

Dewey scanned him with his eyes.

"How much for a fight?"

The man reached for Dewey's right arm, grabbing him by the wrist, tugging it down toward him. He lifted Dewey's T-shirt, revealing a long, nasty-looking purple-and-pink scar, which ran from his shoulder blade down the front of his biceps.

"What the fuck is that from?"

Dewey ignored the question.

"Tough guy. Okay, you want a fight, I'll get you a fight."

The man took a whistle from around his neck. He blew it. A moment later, a tall black man approached.

"Daryl," he said, nodding at Dewey, "get Chico or one of the other young guys. Put 'em in the big ring. Pretty boy here wants to relive his youth."

The man in the wheelchair turned back to Dewey.

"Fifty bucks, up front."

In a small locker room off the main gym, Dewey removed his shoes, jeans, and T-shirt. Beneath, he had on cutoff khaki shorts, covered in paint stains. They were the only shorts he could find at the town house.

He walked back inside the gymnasium. The smaller rings were empty now. The crowd had gathered around the center ring. Dewey pushed his way through.

Daryl was standing in the middle of the ring, there to officiate. Behind him was a short, stocky Hispanic kid who wore a bright yellow Lycra body suit. His arms, neck, and legs were covered in colorful tattoos. He had short-cropped black hair. A tattoo of a large tear was painted below his left eye. He was stacked with muscle, punching the air in place and bouncing on his bare feet as Dewey climbed into the ring.

Daryl looked at Dewey's shorts, then at his scar, then at him. He walked to Dewey, leaning toward him.

"Hey, man, no shame if you wanna bail now," he whispered, "know what I mean?"

Dewey didn't respond.

The truth is, he barely heard the words.

Maybe it was the smell of the gym. Or the eyes, filled with doubt, now upon him. Maybe it was the sight of the fight before, in the sparring ring, the kick, the blood spilling onto the mat. Whatever it was, he started to feel the warmth that for too long had gone missing. The warmth that should've found him in Mexico. Adrenaline. It was only the faintest hint of it, and yet it was unmistakable. He glanced down at his right arm. He saw the small black tattoo of a lightning bolt. And then whatever warmth was there flamed into fire.

Daryl motioned for the two to come to the center of the ring.

"Three-minute rounds. Only rule is, when I say stop, you stop. Other than that, feel free to kick the shit out of each other."

The Hispanic looked at Dewey from head to toe.

"Voy a matar a ti, viejo."

I'm going to kill you, old man.

Dewey didn't even look at his opponent. He said nothing.

Each fighter returned to his corner.

The crowd was getting hyped. A few catcalls to the other fighter got him to smile as he bounced on his bare feet.

"Chico! Kill the fucker!"

Daryl nodded to someone seated next to the ring. He slammed a hammer into the bell.

Dewey stepped slowly into the center of the ring as Chico danced left. Dewey glanced left; the man in the wheelchair was positioned next to the ring, watching. They made eye contact. Then Chico started his charge. He sprinted toward Dewey, swinging wildly, left right, almost too fast to see, his fists swinging for Dewey's head as he lurched across the ring.

Dewey waited, guard down, calmly poised, his knees bent slightly. As the swings came closer, he heard the roar of the crowd anticipating the fight, wanting a rapid, brutal ending to the spectacle.

Chico charged into Dewey's range. Dewey sensed a left hook slashing the air, and ducked. Chico lurched past him, whiffing completely, his momentum thrusting him forward. In one fluid motion, like a cocked spring, Dewey crouched, spun clockwise, and coiled his right foot skyward in a brutal roundhouse strike. His foot smashed into Chico's face, hitting his jaw like a hammer, crushing it, breaking it in several places. Chico went flying sideways, tumbling awkwardly to the mat, unconscious. Blood gushed from his mouth and nose.

The kick silenced the crowd.

Dewey stepped to the center of the ring. His chest, torso, arms, and legs were red from adrenaline and the momentary exertion. He was ripped, his muscles hard and toned. He circled the ring, looking at the crowd. A few started clapping politely, then stopped.

Dewey stepped in front of the man in the wheelchair as a pair of gym workers carried the unconscious fighter out of the ring.

"You ready to stop fucking around?" asked Dewey.

9

Will Parizeau sat in front of a pair of brightly lit plasma screens arrayed in a slight concave atop a long steel desk. Parizeau's bespectacled eyes darted back and forth between the two screens. A look of concern adorned his youthful, ruddy face as his eyes raced between the screens. Then came a look of fear. His mouth opened slightly. His eyes bulged.

"*Sweet Jesus,*" he said aloud.

On the left screen was a grid displaying four satellite images. On the right was a wall of numbers plotted against a spreadsheet.

Parizeau was a senior-level analyst within the Defense Intelligence Agency's Directorate for Science and Technology. Employing radar intelligence, acoustic intelligence, nuclear intelligence, and chemical and biological intelligence, the DIA detected and tracked fixed or dynamic target sources, such as nuclear weapons. If the National Security Agency was about scouring e-mails, phone calls, Internet traffic, and other signals intelligence, looking for bad people who might do harm to the United States, DIA was about scouring the earth for the objects those bad people might use in those efforts.

Parizeau's desk sat in a cavernous, windowless, dimly lit room two floors belowground, in a respectable if unspectacular-looking brick building. It was one of several old, well-maintained buildings, built in the 1920s, on a 905-acre military base in southwest Washington, D.C., called Fort Bolling. Parizeau was one of more than a hundred analysts, all surrounded by visual media, and all of it related to nuclear weapons deemed vulnerable to theft or purchase by terrorists.

Parizeau's job was to keep track of all suspected nuclear weapons inside the former Soviet republic and now sovereign nation Ukraine. DIA believed that four nuclear devices still were hidden in Ukraine, their existence denied by both the Ukrainian and Russian governments, and yet their telltale chemical signatures were like beacons to the highly purposed satellites that hovered in geostationary orbit looking down.

When the Soviet Union collapsed in 1991, tens of thousands of nuclear weapons were at risk all over the newly independent breakaway republics. Due to geography, these small countries now owned nuclear weapons. Impoverished regional governments, often run by peasants and farmers, suddenly possessed a variety of valuable objects; nuclear weapons were at the top of the list. Indeed, they *were* the list.

Several years of negotiations between Russia and the West ensured that all Soviet nuclear weapons were accounted for and in safe storage. So concerned with the chaotic approach of the Russian government to its nuclear arsenal, America decided that it would be prudent to "invest" more than $300 billion in an effort to help Russia secure its own nukes. But even with the massive bribe, a few weapons went missing.

Behind the complex negotiations between the United States and Russia to safeguard the rogue bombs, there lurked a more alarming set of negotiations between Russia and its former republics. On the one hand, Russia wanted the United States to think they had the power to bring all of the weapons back into the fold. On the other hand, Russia had a smorgasbord of newly created republics, independent of Russia, that wanted a cut of the U.S. bribe. In the end, America bought—for Russia—its own weapons back from the republics. It was inevitable that some bad characters, in places like the Ukraine, would keep a few for themselves.

Ukraine had officially handed over all nineteen hundred of its nuclear weapons in 1994, giving them to the Russian Federation in exchange for its sovereignty and a variety of economic concessions, forgiveness of debts, and cash. A discrepancy of four out of the nineteen hundred had never been fully explained by either the Ukrainian government or Russia. It had taken technology and nearly two years to pinpoint the telltale tritium emissions and locate the four rogue weapons. Ever since then, it was Parizeau's full-time job to monitor the supposedly nonexistent Ukrainian-domiciled nukes.

Parizeau relied on an advanced communications satellite operated by the U.S. Air Force, one of five that hovered in geostationary orbit above the earth. Parizeau spent his time tracking a variety of telltale chemical and biological symptoms, including plutonium depletion, keeping an eye on the nuclear devices.

It was a scan fewer than twenty-four hours old that Parizeau now stared at, transfixed. What the numbers showed was that one of the nuclear bombs in the Ukraine had been moved. In fact, it had disappeared.

Parizeau picked up his phone.

"Get me Mark Raditz over at the Pentagon."

Mark Raditz, the deputy secretary of defense, sat behind his desk on the second floor of the Pentagon. His phone buzzed.

"Mark," said Raditz's assistant, Beth. "Will Parizeau is on one."

"Who?"

"Will Parizeau. Ukraine desk at DIA."

"Put him through."

Raditz flipped on a tan plastic device that looked like a large radio. It was an air filtration machine. He opened the top drawer of his desk and removed a pack of Camel Lights. He stuffed a cigarette between his lips, then lit it. He sat down on his large red leather desk chair, leaned back, and put his cowboy boots up on the desk.

"What is it, Will?" asked Raditz, crossing his legs, yawning slightly. "How's the Ukraine these days?"

"We have a rover," said Parizeau.

Raditz was still for a brief instant, then lurched up and leaned over the phone console on his desk.

"Come again?" Raditz said.

"There's a nuclear bomb missing. This is one of four devices we believe Ukraine still possesses."

"Where and when were the last hard readings made?"

"As of four days ago, the two bombs we believe to be housed at a warehouse south of Kiev were both present and accounted for. Plutonium depletion levels have dropped by fifty percent as of two this morning. One of the bombs is gone, sir."

Raditz took a last puff on his cigarette. He lifted his left foot and stubbed the cigarette out on the bottom of his boot.

"Will, I'm about to walk into Harry Black's office across the hall from mine," said Raditz, referring to the secretary of defense. "In turn, Secretary Black will call the president of the United States. Are you one hundred percent goddam motherfucking absolutely sure your math is correct?"

"Yes, I am."

Raditz took a deep breath.

"Stay on the line," he said. "I want to patch in interagency."

Raditz hit another button on the phone.

"Get me Josh Brubaker over at the White House," Raditz told his assistant. "Then get Torey Krug at EUCOM. I also need Hector Calibrisi, Piper Redgrave, and Arden Mason. Better get Sarah Greene at 4th Space Operations Squadron too. *Hurry.*"

"Is everything okay, Mark?" Beth asked, fear in her voice.

Raditz paused and stared at the phone.

"No. Everything is not okay."

Within eight minutes, a dedicated, highly secure communications link had been established among the Pentagon, the Defense Intelligence Agency, Langley, the National Security Agency, Joint Special Operations Command Eurasia Directorate, 4th Space Operations Squadron, the Department of Homeland Security, and the White House.

Raditz and Parizeau were joined by Lieutenant Colonel Sarah Greene at Schriever Air Force Base. Greene was in charge of all Milstar satellites, commanding the hardware group from a highly secure facility located inside a mountain a few miles outside Colorado Springs. They were joined by General Torey Krug, commander of the United States European Command, one of nine Unified Combatant Commands of the U.S. military. Piper Redgrave, the director of the National Security Agency, hopped on a moment later. The head of the Department of Homeland Security, Arden Mason, called in from the border of Mexico. Last on was Calibrisi, who was joined by Bill Polk, who ran National Clandestine Services for the CIA.

A variety of other senior-level staffers from the different agencies were on as well. Finally, Josh Brubaker, White House national security advisor, came on the line from the West Wing.

"Hi, everyone," said Brubaker. "What do we got, Mark?"

"Ukraine," answered Raditz. "We have a nuclear device that's on the move. Will, give everyone the details."

"Milstar night scans picked up material geographic displacement," said Parizeau, "signifying the movement of a nuclear device. This is an RDS-4, one of the so-called Tatyana bombs, made in 1953, approximately thirty kilotons. It's an old bomb, relatively small and light, originally designed to drop from a plane and take out a submarine. It would, if detonated, destroy a big area. Most of Manhattan. All of Boston. This is not a tactical weapon; we're talking about the real deal here."

"How long ago did the scans degrade?" asked Brubaker.

"The last hard reading from Milstar was three days ago," said Parizeau. "It could've been moved at any point during that time."

"Is this one of the devices controlled by former Ukrainian military?" asked Calibrisi.

"That's right. General Vladimir Bokolov."

"Piper, get Bruckheimer on that immediately," said Calibrisi, referring to Jim Bruckheimer, who ran the NSA's Signals Intelligence Directorate. "We need to find Bokolov."

"I'm on it," said Redgrave.

"Will, how long to break down the bomb and harvest the physics package?" asked Polk.

"Why is that relevant?" asked Brubaker.

"It'll determine how they're moving it," said Polk. "If they can pit it in a few hours, the bomb will be light enough to stick in a pickup truck. If that's the case, then trying to find it is a waste of time."

"It would take at least forty-eight hours to execute a clean removal of the physics package," said Parizeau.

"So what does that mean?" asked Brubaker.

"It means they're going to get it to water as quickly as possible," said Polk. "The alternative is going inland in a semitruck that will be Geigered at the border. They're not going to risk doing that."

Raditz moved to the wall, where a large plasma screen lay dark.

"Will, can you live-wire what you're looking at? Put it on IAB thirty-three. Put it on everyone's screen."

A moment later, a strikingly colorful three-dimensional horizontal map of Ukraine splashed onto Raditz's plasma screen, along with the screens of everyone on the call.

"That's Kiev," said Parizeau, narrating, focusing in on a line of lights.

Near the top of the screen, just above a red digital line representing the atmosphere, was a flashing red, white, and blue object, which represented the U.S. Milstar satellite.

"Are we watching this in real time?" asked Polk.

"Yes," said Parizeau.

"Spotlight the routes on every road to the Black Sea and the Sea of Azov," said Polk.

Suddenly, a spiderweb of yellow lines branched southeast from Kiev. These were the roads leading to the coast. There were at least a dozen different roads heading to the water.

"Will, correct me if I'm wrong, but you're able to focus in on these devices because of radioactive emissions, right?" asked Raditz.

"Plutonium, uranium, or tritium."

"Can you look at a moving truck and get an accurate enough reading to detect it?" asked Raditz.

"It would take a decent amount of luck, to be honest," said Parizeau.

"What's a decent amount?"

"One in a thousand. The movement of the truck dissipates the strength of the radioactive emissions. We readjust to try and compensate by looking for a lower reading, but we don't know how fast or slow the driver is going. So we're probably going to be wrong."

"Not to mention any sort of cloaking measures they might employ to hide the imprint," added Calibrisi.

"If their only option is getting it out of the country by water, let's send everything to the coast," said Raditz. "I want every satellite we have close to the theater focused on finding that nuke. Repurpose any assets we have in the sky over Belarus, Poland, Slovakia, Hungary, Romania, and Moldova. Immediately. Blanket the ports, especially Sevastopol and Odessa."

"Should we inform Russia?" asked Brubaker.

Silence took over the call. It was a tricky question.

On the one hand, the Russian Federation might be able to help stop the people who had the bomb. Russia would have a deeper knowledge of the players in the area to draw on.

On the other hand, a deep mistrust inhabited the upper echelons of America's military and intelligence infrastructure. After all, Russia had spent decades denying the existence of the four nuclear devices inside Ukraine. In addition, Russia's president, Vladimir Putin, was a former top-level assassin within the KGB. Deep down, beyond all the diplomatic words, all the summits and state dinners, the United States and Russia hated each other. For many in Russia, the loss of the Cold War stung every bit as much today as it did then, perhaps more so.

Calibrisi spoke first.

"No way do we tell Moscow," the CIA chief said. "That's a recipe for wasting a lot of time and energy that could be used to find this bomb. We ask for help, they deny the existence of it, we're forced to try and prove our case that there are still nukes inside Ukraine, and all of a sudden we will have burned three days trying to win a debate instead of hunting this thing down."

"I disagree," said Mason, secretary of homeland security. "We should tap into their knowledge base immediately. This is not just America's problem. It's everyone's problem."

"General Krug," said Brubaker, "any thoughts?"

"We're way behind here," said Krug. "If this bomb went missing four days ago, it's through the Bosphorus Strait by now and probably most of the way across the Mediterranean. I wouldn't bother with Russia, Ukraine, or anything other than the nine-mile stretch of ocean between Gibraltar and Tangier. If they make it past Gibraltar, they will enjoy open ocean all the way to the U.S. East Coast. There are simply too many boats and too much ocean."

"What do you look for?" asked Raditz.

"We should assume they're sophisticated enough to know they're being watched and spectragraphed," said Krug. "They'll need a vessel that blends in and also is able to make a transatlantic crossing.

My guess is they're on some sort of deep-sea fishing trawler, a few hundred feet long. There are literally hundreds of thousands of them floating around. I think we need to get UAVs over the Strait of Gibraltar immediately, along with whatever warships we have at Naval Station Rota in Spain. SEAL Team 6 has some men at Rota as well, and I'd position them in fastboats."

"How long to get everything in range?" asked Raditz.

"A few hours."

"Get them moving."

"I suggest we run this out of Langley," added Krug.

"Why Langley?" asked Brubaker.

Krug cleared his throat.

"Because the truth is, if they make it past Spain, it becomes an intelligence operation," he said. "Bill, you might as well start involving yourselves now."

"I hear you," said Polk, "and we're ready to fill that role. I'll have Control set up a secure uplink."

"I'll get the ships, SEALs, and drones moving," said Krug. "Josh, you got anything else?"

"No, not at the moment. Let's reconvene in an hour."

Piper Redgrave, head of the National Security Agency, spoke up.

"I need to interrupt here," she said. "I have to bring something to everyone's attention that could be related."

"Piper," said Brubaker, "tell me it's something good."

Redgrave was silent for a few pregnant moments. She cleared her throat.

"We broke into a server we know to be run by an Al Qaeda tertiary in Damascus," she said. "There is high-frequency chatter across the terror complex focused on a second major attack on the United States. They're calling it 'nine/twelve.'"

The conference call went silent.

"Jesus H. Christ," said Brubaker. "When were you going to elevate this?"

"We decrypted it half an hour ago," said Redgrave.

Again, the call went silent.

"Mike," said Brubaker, breaking the quiet, "we need to get the president up to speed. Bring Secretary Black with you. Brief him on the way to the White House. Hector, Bill: NCS has tactical command control. I want live protocols run in through Langley, then distributed across interagency in real time. The Milstar data is critical at this point. But it's not as critical as the chatter. Piper: NSA has to dig deeper, and it needs to happen *immediately*. Open up PRISM, MYSTIC, ThinThread, and any other signals archives NSA has access to. We need to get to the bottom of this nine/twelve chatter and determine if it's related to the nuclear device. God help us if it is."

10

Calibrisi, Polk, and several other NCS staffers, analysts, and case officers were in Calibrisi's glass-walled seventh-floor corner office when Calibrisi's phone buzzed. It was Jim Bruckheimer from the NSA.

"Tell me you found Bokolov," said Calibrisi.

"Yeah, we got 'em," said Bruckheimer. "But we have something even better."

"Let's hear it."

"We tracked Bokolov to southern France," said Bruckheimer. "Fifteen minutes ago, he bought a forty-four-thousand-dollar Rolex Daytona at a jewelry store in Cannes. They must pay those Ukrainian generals well, huh?"

"Someone did."

"That's what we assumed, so we did a little more research. A month ago, Alexei Malnikov wired him eight million dollars from a Zurich bank account."

Calibrisi looked at Polk. Both men knew Malnikov, along with his father, Yuri. Alexei Malnikov ran the largest criminal enterprise in the world. Langley had helped the FBI track down Malnikov's father off the coast of Florida the year before, providing informal "off-log" support for the highly publicized arrest of the head of the Russian mob, a man now confined to a prison cell in Colorado.

"We scanned Malnikov's bank accounts," added Bruckheimer. "No significant payments were made to him. However, four days ago, *he paid* someone a hundred million dollars."

"Who?"

"We don't know. The account he wired it to isn't there anymore. It's almost as if it was created a half second before the wire, then disappeared."

Calibrisi picked up his cell phone. He stepped to the corner of his office, out of earshot of the others.

"Control," came the female voice.

"Get me John Barrows."

A tall, gray-haired man was standing on the fringe of the seventeenth green of Augusta National Golf Club, watching one of his clients prepare to putt.

He felt a small vibration in his pocket. He wasn't supposed to have his cell phone with him. It was strictly forbidden at Augusta. Yet certain phone calls were more important than being a member of the most exclusive golf club in the world.

Barrows watched his client, a businessman from Omaha, tap the ball. He glanced down at his cell as the ball rolled in a poetic curve across the ice-hard green.

:: CALIBRISI H.C. ::

This was one of those phone calls.

Barrows lifted the phone to his ear.

"Hi, Hector."

"I need to speak with one of your clients."

"I have a lot of clients."

"He's Russian."

Barrows cut away from the green and walked toward a line of dog-wood trees, looking about for anyone who might be watching him.

"I really don't think my client is in any mood to do the head of the Central Intelligence Agency any favors," said Barrows. "Being locked up in a windowless six-by-six cell has made him a little grumpy."

"I'm not talking about Yuri," said Calibrisi, his tone polite but unmistakable. "I need to speak with Alexei Malnikov, John. It needs to happen immediately."

Barrows glanced at his client, who was walking toward the eigh-teenth tee.

"Are you prepared to work with me on a transfer of Yuri Malnikov to a more suitable facility?" asked Barrows.

"If I'm not on the phone with Alexei Malnikov in the next five minutes," said Calibrisi testily, "he'll be going to a place that makes Yuri's cell look like a suite at the Four Seasons. Got it?"

"Stay by your phone."

Alexei Malnikov stood on a terrace outside his suite at the Bulgari Hotel Milan, looking down at La Scala. He wore Derek Rose black silk pajama pants. In the darkness of the Milan evening, he was prac-tically invisible, except perhaps to the woman inside the suite.

He'd flown from Moscow to Paris, then to Milan. Somehow, he thought that getting away from Moscow would ease his mind about the entire interaction with Cloud, but it hadn't. He realized how quickly and precipitously his world could, and probably would, come crashing down around him.

His cell phone made a low beeping noise.

"Hello?"

"Alexei, it's John Barrows. Are you alone?"

"Yes."

"In exactly three minutes, your cell phone is going to ring. Answer it."

"What are you talking about?"

"I don't know what you did, and I don't want to know. But you need to answer the phone."

"Who is it?"

"Hector Calibrisi," said Barrows.

Malnikov shut his eyes.

"Why is he calling me?"

"Don't bullshit me," said Barrows. "And don't attempt to bullshit Calibrisi. If you lie, no one can protect you. For what it's worth, I don't think he's after you."

"How do you know?"

"If he was, he wouldn't have called me."

"What is your advice, John?" asked Malnikov, a hint of anxiety in his voice.

"My advice? Be honest with him. There's something going on here, and you're involved. I have a feeling you know perfectly well what it is. The last guy you want to piss off is Calibrisi. You'll disappear quicker than you can say *ciao* to that high-priced hooker in your bed."

"How did you know—"

The phone clicked.

Malnikov took a deep drag on his Gitano. He walked into the hotel suite and picked up a red silk negligee.

"Get out," he said, throwing the negligee at the woman in the bed. "Now."

In the bathroom, he splashed cold water on his face. Then his cell buzzed. Malnikov lit another cigarette and stepped onto the terrace.

:: CALIBRISI H.C. ::

"Hello."

"Alexei, this is Hector Calibrisi."

"What do you want?" asked Malnikov.

"I'm going to be very direct with you. You need to understand something. It's not a threat, it's just fact. The moment you acquired that nuclear bomb, you became a terrorist in the eyes of the United States government."

There was a long silence on the phone. Malnikov stared down at the sidewalk.

"I'm not a terrorist," he whispered.

"That remains to be seen. Do you want to help us?"

"Do I want to? Of course not. Will I? Yes."

"Who has the bomb?"

"His name is Cloud. He's a computer hacker. I don't know his real name. He's Russian."

"Was the bomb delivered to one of the ports?"

"Sevastopol."

"Is that why you paid him a hundred million dollars?" asked Calibrisi. "To take it off your hands?"

"Yes."

"Why did you buy it in the first place?" asked Calibrisi.

Malnikov tossed the remainder of his cigarette into the air, watching as it floated down toward the busy street a dozen floors below.

"Protection. A poker chip to play if I was ever in danger of being arrested."

"Where is he?"

"I don't know."

"Do you know where he's taking it?"

Malnikov paused.

"No. I asked what he was going to do with it."

"What did he say?"

"He said, 'something that should have been done a long time ago.'"

There was a pause on the phone.

"Interesting," said Calibrisi. "That might be helpful. What about the boat? Did your people see the boat?"

"No. They delivered it to a parking area outside Sevastopol. His men had on ski masks."

"How do you communicate with him?" asked Calibrisi.

"It's always different. Phone, e-mail, or else he just shows up. It's always initiated by him. Somehow, he knew about the deal with Bokolov."

"What did he say?"

"He said he wanted the bomb. I thought he was offering to buy it."

"But you paid him?" asked Calibrisi. "A hundred million, right?"

"Yes," said Malnikov. "Actually, he took the first fifty before we came to an agreement."

"Brazen."

Malnikov laughed mirthlessly.

"He's a scrawny little fuck," he said. "There's evil behind his eyes. They say he helped disrupt American air traffic control systems on nine/eleven."

Calibrisi was silent.

"He said you would come to me and seek my help. He said to tell you everything I know."

Calibrisi paused.

"He told you to help us?"

"He was quite emphatic."

"My God," said Calibrisi. "What else did he say?"

"He said he was the one who supplied the information that enabled the U.S. to arrest my father."

Calibrisi was silent on the other end of the phone.

"Are you kidding?"

"No."

"Do you have a photo of him?"

"No, I don't."

"But you've met him, right?"

"Twice."

"Stay on the line, Alexei. I'm going to bring in a sketch artist."

* * *

Five minutes later, the CIA's top sketch artist was seated in Calibrisi's office, listening to Malnikov and drawing a portrait of Cloud as the Russian mobster described him over speakerphone.

Calibrisi glanced at his watch; he was supposed to be at the White House.

He stepped outside and looked at Lindsay, his admin.

"Is Pete back?" he asked.

"He's waiting for you in two."

"Is Dewey with him?"

Lindsay shook her head.

Calibrisi walked down the hallway to the conference room. Seated, Prada wingtips up on the table, was Pete Bond. He stepped inside and shut the door.

"How did Mexico go?" asked Calibrisi.

Bond had a blank look on his face.

"We accomplished the mission."

"That's not what I'm asking."

"I know."

"So?"

"He froze up," said Bond, "just like you said he would."

Calibrisi nodded.

"Where is he?"

"I dropped him off in Georgetown."

"Thanks, Pete."

Calibrisi turned to leave.

"Chief, you need to know something."

"What?"

"Gant met us at Andrews. He was waiting for the plane to land."

Calibrisi's head turned sharply back to Bond.

"*What?*"

"He was waiting on the tarmac," said Bond. "He asked for a first look on the debrief. Gave me a rash of shit."

"What did you tell him?"

"Well, I probably shouldn't have done this, but I told him I report to Bill and he could get my brief from him."

"That's exactly what you should've done. Thanks for the heads-up."

Calibrisi reached for the door, then turned.

"Bring him in," said Calibrisi. "Whatever condition he's in."

Bond nodded at Calibrisi.

"Will do, J.P."

Calibrisi walked to the fire stairs, then descended, two steps at a time, to the fourth floor. He moved down a curving glass-walled hallway to the offices of Josh Gant, deputy director of the CIA.

Unlike Calibrisi, Gant had a fancy set of offices, complete with a large entry foyer adorned with framed photographs of Gant posing with President J. P. Dellenbaugh.

Gant's assistant stood up as Calibrisi marched into the outer office and brushed past her. He stepped into Gant's office and shut the door.

Gant held his hand over the phone. Gant had on a bow tie and horn-rimmed glasses. He was tan. His hair was brown and neatly coiffed. He had on a seersucker suit, a yellow button-down, and cordovan loafers.

"I'm on a call," said Gant.

"Get off it."

Gant stared at Calibrisi. He put the phone back to his ear.

"I'll call you back."

"What the hell do you think you're doing?" asked Calibrisi.

"I was trying to convince my daughter not to change her major from economics to French literature, if you want to know the truth."

"I'm talking about Dewey Andreas."

"Sinaloa is in my matrix, Chief. You're the one who assigned it to me, remember?"

"I'm talking about that psych eval you got Furr to order up," said Calibrisi.

"He's got a screw loose, Hector, and I don't like it when NOCs have loose screws. You shouldn't either."

"I'm not going to dignify what you just said," said Calibrisi, barely controlling his temper. "You *stay the fuck away* from Dewey. Do you understand me? What you did—using the Senate Intelligence Committee to try and build an incarceration order on Dewey, on U.S. soil—is against the law."

Calibrisi noted a slightly surprised look on Gant's face.

"You're not trying to incarcerate him, are you?" said Calibrisi, studying Gant. "You want a hit order on the man who stopped Alexander Fortuna?"

"That's absurd," said Gant. "I don't want him dead. I just want the right thing to be done. If that means sending Dewey back out in the field, great, I have no issue with that. It's not personal. If it means removing him to a clinic for a few months, or years, until his value as a breach target is diminished, then that's what I'm for. We've had two NOCs punctured in the last year. It has to stop."

Calibrisi walked over to Gant's desk.

"Either you stay away from Dewey, or I'll call Dellenbaugh and tell him what his little political hack has been doing. You'll go straight back to whatever hole you crawled out of."

Gant stared at Calibrisi.

"The president is aware of my concerns and my actions," said Gant calmly.

Gant held up a small electronic recording device.

"In addition, you need to understand that if Dewey ends up going sideways, I'm documenting every single thing you're doing to prevent me from stopping it."

"You've been recording this—" said Calibrisi, momentarily stunned.

"EPPA 7664, section H91, paragraph 2," said Gant. "*'All employees of the Central Intelligence Agency agree to certain waivers of constitutional rights, including the right not to be electronically recorded without prior knowledge and consent.'*"

Gant paused, letting his words sink in.

"National Security Act of 1947," Calibrisi shot back. "*'The Director of the Central Intelligence Agency may, in the discretion of the Director, terminate the employment of any officer or employee of the Central Intelligence Agency whenever the Director deems the termination of employment of such officer or employee necessary or advisable.'*"

"*'In the interests of the United States,'*" added Gant, finishing the citation. "An operator like Andreas could do a lot of damage to the United States of America."

Calibrisi turned toward the door.

"One last thing, Hector," said Gant.

Calibrisi paused at the door.

"Where is he?" asked Gant.

"Fuck you."

II

The man in the wheelchair stared at Dewey, then turned to Daryl. "Where's Tino?"

Daryl leaned forward, between the ropes.

"You think that's a good idea?" Daryl asked quietly.

"Get him," he snarled.

Daryl stood up and searched the crowd. His eyes settled on the window at the rear of the room. A dark-skinned man was seated on the windowsill. He had earbuds in, seemingly oblivious. Daryl motioned for him, but he wasn't paying attention. Someone reached up and tapped him on the arm. The kid looked up, found Daryl, then stood.

People started to shout and clap as Tino made his way to the ring, unbuttoning a sleeveless flannel shirt as he came close and dropping it to the floor. Reflexively, people stepped aside to let him through.

Tino wasn't overloaded with muscles, but what he did have looked sculpted, as if he managed his muscle tone around fitness, speed and, above all, violence. He walked bowlegged, bending his head side to side as he walked, stretching his neck. His chest was bare. As he climbed into the ring, and the cheering picked up, Dewey saw his one and only tattoo, a foot-wide picture of Jesus across his back.

He wore long nylon shorts that came below his knees. He climbed into the ring and walked to the corner, ignoring Dewey.

The crowd was amped. They called out Tino's name in a prideful chorus.

"*Tee-no! Tee-no!*"

Dewey glanced at Daryl.

"I'll make the same offer as before, man," he said to Dewey, "but I know what you're gonna say."

Dewey didn't respond. The truth is, though he heard what Daryl said this time, the meaning of the words seemed to sail over his head, as if they were in a different language.

All Dewey could hear now was the warmth. It had gotten there, to that level he'd grown to know and trust, when it guided him, when it spoke to him.

He'll try to kill you. He wants to kill you. The question is, are you going to let him?

Daryl stepped to the center of the ring, motioning for Dewey and Tino to meet him there.

Tino continued to ignore Dewey as the two approached Daryl. Then he looked up and their eyes met. They were dark eyes, almost black. He smiled. He had no upper front teeth, just a big gaping hole. He stared at Dewey, studying him.

"What branch?" Tino asked, barely above a whisper.

Dewey didn't answer. He was in a different place. He couldn't even hear the din of the gym. The shouting was loud now. There was a sense of riot and chaos. He heard only his own thoughts.

It's time to return. Now is that time.

"Three-minute rounds," said Daryl, yelling so that Dewey and Tino could hear him above the clamor of the crowd, now five deep around the ring.

Daryl leaned toward Tino.

"When I say stop, you stop, and I'm fuckin' serious, Tino."

Tino smiled and began to bounce on his feet, back and forth, left right, staring at Dewey.

"Other than that, well, have at it, motherfuckers," said Daryl, stepping back, motioning to the corners.

Daryl nodded to someone seated ringside. Suddenly the bell sounded, and the fight began.

Dewey stepped toward the center of the ring. Tino remained in his corner, adjusting his mouth guard. He seemed nonchalant as he did so, not even looking at Dewey. Dewey moved closer, and yet Tino seemed oblivious; he made eye contact with someone in the audience, smiled, then removed his mouth guard. He yelled something to him. His head was turned sideways to Dewey. Dewey came closer now, his fists raised, clenched, waiting for Tino to turn back to him, and in that momentary pause, Tino burst left—like a lion hurling itself through the bush at unsuspecting prey.

Dewey caught the move, but too late. He tried to block the attack, swinging at Tino's head, but by the time his fist slashed right to left, Tino's head was gone, dropped down beneath Dewey's arm as he charged at Dewey's legs—lurching viciously headfirst at Dewey's thighs. The moment of anticipation, caused by his own error, was painful. Tino's skull slammed his left thigh, as hard as a sledgehammer. The shock of the attack was unexpected, the pain brutal and immediate. Dewey felt lightness as Tino drove him hard, backward, then, for an awful second, into clear air. Before he hit the mat, Tino's arms were around his legs, his sharp fingers ripping at the back of his legs, trying to break the skin. Then Dewey landed, Tino atop him. His back struck the mat, followed by the back of his head. In the fiery moment, he heard Tino's grunt, a terrible sound, intermingled with pain in the front of his thigh and the dull, deep migraine that shot out from the back of his skull.

The gym erupted in screaming and cheers.

It took all of ten seconds, and Dewey knew he was in deep trouble.

The crowd moved closer, bunching up the sides of the ring, yelling at Tino, egging him on.

"Break it!"

"Bury 'em, Tino!"

Dewey lay on his back, locked at the thighs in a viselike grip. He slammed his fists into the back of Tino's skull, his neck, and the upper part of his back, eliciting not even a grunt. Then Tino's knee shot up from beneath him and hit Dewey squarely in the balls. A half second later, Tino's right arm sprang loose from around Dewey, swinging wildly for Dewey's face.

Dewey anticipated the move, raising his left arm, blocking Tino's swing. Then, with his right hand, Dewey grabbed whatever he could of Tino's moving fist, finding Tino's middle and index fingers, then snapping back, breaking both fingers at the knuckle just as Tino's other fist slammed hard into Dewey's right biceps.

Tino grunted in pain as he swung again with his left, striking Dewey in the shoulder. Dewey's right arm shot out, then under Tino's elbow, locking Tino in an awkward position. Dewey yanked upward with his right arm, trying to snap Tino's arm at the elbow. But Tino moved to escape. From atop Dewey, he pushed with his head, his right hand, and his legs, then jumped up into the air in a controlled pirouette, a 270-degree sideways leap that freed him from Dewey's grip. He landed on his feet.

Dewey rolled left, but not in time to avoid Tino's bare left foot, which kicked him viciously in the mouth. Blood shot out. Tino followed the first kick with another, his right. Dewey blocked it, then swept his legs across the mat, beneath Tino, kicking Tino hard at the ankle, dropping him.

Nauseous, dizzy, badly bleeding, Dewey climbed to his feet.

Daryl, the referee, stood in the corner, arms crossed, watching with a blank expression on his face.

It felt like they'd been at it for hours, but for the first time Daryl made a motion: two fingers. Two minutes left in round one. Only a minute had passed.

"Motherfucker," Dewey panted, blood coursing down his chin and onto his chest as he regained his knowledge of what it felt like to stand on his own two feet.

Bond parked his Audi S6 on a quiet residential street off Wisconsin Avenue in Georgetown. He found the alley that ran behind the line of town houses that included Dewey's. He scaled a brick wall that bordered the small backyard, slipping quietly over the top without making a noise.

Once inside the darkened property, he climbed a tree until he came to a branch that hung over a third-floor eave, then jumped to the terrace. He took a thin, hard titanium card from his wallet and slid it into the seam between upper and lower windowpanes. Bond jimmied the latch open, climbed in, and took the stairs to the first floor. There he found the case of beer along with a small collection of empties. Next to it was a bottle of Jack Daniel's, a third of it depleted. On the side of the bag, he saw a word scrawled in chicken-scratch handwriting: WHITEWATER.

Bond sighed. He took out his cell and started to dial Calibrisi. Before he hit Send, however, he stopped. He put the phone back in his pocket and stepped to the front door. He didn't want to pass it off to Calibrisi. He wanted to help.

Back on Wisconsin, he hailed a taxi instead of driving. He knew if he drove his Audi to Whitewater he'd likely never see it again.

After the first big scrum, Dewey and Tino were squared off along the edge of the ring, Dewey catching his breath, Tino studying an opponent he should've already beaten. They didn't bother circling each other. Dewey had his left hand on the rope, clutching it for stability. Blood poured from his mouth. Splatters of fresh crimson dotted the mat.

Tino's face was bright red and drenched in sweat. His left fist was shut. His right fist was open. A pair of broken fingers jutted unnaturally into the air.

The crowd was in a frenzy. In unison, they chanted Tino's name, urging him on.

Dewey glanced to his left, ringside, through the opening in the ropes. The man in the wheelchair was staring at him.

As much as Dewey wanted the rest that would come with the end of the round, he knew that if he didn't end the fight now, he would likely die in the second round or, worse, have to forfeit.

Don't be afraid to die.

Dewey stepped into Tino's range, slowly and deliberately. As he did, his eye was drawn to the wall near the door at the back of what was now a standing-room-only crowd. There, he saw Bond, his arms crossed, watching. Bond noticed Dewey's glance. He nodded at him but remained in back.

Dewey moved closer to Tino. He jabbed the air in front of him, punching left right, as if he was softening up an invisible layer of protection in front of Tino.

It's time to return, Dewey.

Tino charged. Like before, it came out of the blue. His bare feet battered the mat as screaming and cheers erupted from the crowd.

This time Dewey was ready.

Tino lurched at Dewey's midsection, diving, hands out, a low, guttural scream emanating from his throat as he again sought to take Dewey to the mat. Dewey waited one moment, then another, timing it, watching as Tino came within a few feet, then a foot, then inches, tuning out Tino's grunt, which was supposed to distract him, to instill fear in him. Dewey felt it then, not small traces or even just a burst of it. He felt the fire of the adrenaline hitting his entire body. He lashed his right foot high into the air as Tino's fingertips made their initial brush against his torso. His kick was brutal and deadly accurate, greeting the right side of Tino's skull with a punishing thud. Whatever momentum Tino had was immediately interrupted. His head snapped awkwardly sideways. He tumbled to the right and down to the mat, dropping onto his back near the rope, helpless, stunned.

The crowd was silent. Mesmerized. Dewey remained focused on his prey, wiping his bloody mouth with the back of his hand. He bounced ever so slightly on the balls of his bare feet as he stood over Tino, waiting for him to get up.

Tino gathered himself to his knees, then looked up, expecting Dewey to kick him, but Dewey remained squared off, fists clenched, blood dribbling from his mouth.

"Get up," he mumbled.

Tino got to his feet, shaking his head, trying to knock the proverbial cobwebs out. Dewey moved in. They punched at each other, back and forth, their fists flying so quickly that most could barely register the number of contacts. Every time Dewey started to create a series of successful punches, Tino's leg would come out of nowhere, either his foot or knee, catching him anywhere he could, but Dewey was winning the fistfight. Tino's left eye was cut, swollen shut, and bleeding. His left cheek was covered in a sheen of blood, as were his shoulder and arm.

Dewey punched Tino back into the corner, ignoring his kicks, absorbing them, beating on Tino's head. Tino moved his fists up to protect his head. Dewey lowered the focus of his punches to Tino's torso.

Beneath Dewey's withering pounding, Tino seemed to duck down, behind his hands.

"Stop," Tino muttered, barely above a whisper, loud enough for Dewey to hear, but no one else.

Dewey stopped punching long enough for Tino to lurch up at him, headfirst, the front of his skull striking Dewey above the left eye, sending him flying back to the mat, where Tino pounced on him and began to punch and knee him furiously.

All Dewey could feel was the numbness that precedes the sharpest of pains, and at the front of his head, the fog of a concussion.

Somewhere in the distance, Dewey heard the bell, ending the

round. Tino kept punching until, a few seconds later, he heard Daryl yelling at him to get off.

Dewey struggled to get up. He put a hand down and started to push up but spilled over onto his side. He was dizzy and nauseous. He climbed to his knees, weaving, then grabbed the rope. He vomited over the side of the rope as he clung to it. Dewey crabbed along the rope to his corner. There was no stool, but an arm handed up a bottle of water. Through his open right eye, Dewey saw a young black kid staring up at him.

Daryl came over.

"I can DQ him for the head butt," he said.

Dewey took a sip of water, spat it out, then focused his eyes across the ring. Tino was sitting on a stool.

"No," Dewey said, shaking his head.

"I thought I heard him call 'stop,'" said Daryl.

Dewey's eyes remained transfixed on Tino. His dizziness was quickly abating.

"No," groaned Dewey. "He didn't call 'stop.'"

A half minute later, the bell clanged for round two.

Dewey stepped to the center of the ring, weaving slightly, his fists down at his sides. He watched Tino as he circled him. The crowd was quieter now. There were still chants of "Tino, Tino," but they were fewer and farther between.

Dewey didn't move his feet. He stood still, moving only his head, tracking Tino out of the corner of his eyes as he circled him.

It's time to return. Your job is not done.

Dewey waited for the moment when he could no longer see Tino. The blind spot, behind him, shielded by his swollen left eye, out of reach of his right. His training came back to him: Delta, advanced hand-to-hand combat tactics, taught over a grueling summer in the Utah desert, almost always at night.

You will learn to fight during the day, but you will come to know the night. Darkness is the adversary of most, but not Delta. We will teach you the night.

Dewey shut his eyes. He listened for Tino's guttural panting. With his feet, he waited for the infinitesimal movement on the mat as Tino came closer.

He felt it behind him, then heard it, the movement, the patter, as Tino suddenly charged.

When you are the night, there is no man alive who can stop you. There is no man who you cannot kill.

Dewey waited, focusing on Tino's low grunts as he charged, feeling the mat concave slightly, hearing the footsteps, then, at the final moment, sensing the presence of another animal as it descended.

He guessed Tino would dive for his knees.

Dewey pivoted, opened his eyes, then jumped into the air.

Tino dived across the air beneath Dewey as the crowd let out a cacophonous, spontaneous cheer. Tino braced himself for the coming fall, landing on his hands, then leapt up. He turned.

Dewey raised his fists and stepped toward Tino. Tino raised his fists. They came closer, slowly hovering in front of one another, just out of reach.

Dewey moved closer, slowly, weaving slightly, and entered Tino's range. Tino swung, hitting Dewey in the chest. Dewey let the fist strike him, then another, this time across the chin, before swinging a brutal roundhouse at Tino's head. But Tino ducked. In a single fluid motion, Tino kicked his left leg out sideways, a fierce boot to Dewey's ribs, pushing Dewey backward, making him grunt in agony. Tino followed the kick with a 270-degree roundhouse recoil, left foot pivoting on the mat, right swinging clockwise toward Dewey's head.

Dewey met Tino's outstretched foot with a braced left forearm, which he slammed up just as the foot made contact, thrusting at Tino, sending him flying over backward. Tino's eyes went wide, knowing what was about to happen. The crown of his skull hit the mat before his hands had the chance to stop the fall. As Tino landed, then rolled, Dewey stepped toward him. At that moment, he could've kicked him. He could've easily crushed Tino's nose and snapped his head back hard enough to do permanent damage, the kind of damage Tino had been trying to do to him. But he didn't. Instead, Dewey stood above him. With blood still dripping from his mouth, Dewey waited, fists clenched, in case Tino decided that he wanted more.

Daryl moved to Tino, kneeling. He grabbed his ear, lifting his head slightly so that he could see him. Tino looked up, his eyes meandering around inside the sockets. He shook his head, resigning from the fight.

The crowd was silent for a few moments. Someone started clapping. Dewey looked down to see the black kid, smiling widely, looking up at him. Soon the gym grew louder as others joined in.

Dewey moved to the rope. He lifted it and climbed down. He started to walk toward the door, but turned. Then he saw the man in the wheelchair. He nodded at Dewey. Dewey returned the gesture with a blank stare.

Near the entrance, Dewey found Bond, leaning against the wall, arms crossed.

"You almost just got killed," said Bond.

"Yeah, no shit," said Dewey, touching his eye.

"You realize you just took down the top-ranked UFC prospect in the United States?" asked Bond.

"I wish someone had told me that before I got in the ring," said Dewey, rubbing his eye. "How the hell'd you find me?"

"I broke into your town house."

"That's breaking and entering. You can get a ticket for that in D.C."

"Sue me."

"Hector send you?"

Bond nodded.

"I can't imagine why he'd be worried about you," said Bond, shaking his head. "Let's go."

12

ABOARD THE *LONELY FISHERMAN*
MEDITERRANEAN SEA

Faqir stood in the wheelhouse, chain-smoking cigarettes, his eyes flashing between the rudimentary navigation equipment and the four-foot waters of a wind-driven ocean, illuminated now by halogen lights at the trawler's foredeck. It was almost midnight.

The wooden deck of the trawler was soaked in seawater. The steel along the balustrade was rusted. Near the bow of the ship, a watch tower stood thirty feet high, put there in order to spot schools of tuna. A cable was draped between the tower and the wheelhouse. Christmas lights were wrapped around the cable, though most of the bulbs were burned out. The few that remained created a dim, murky glow on the deck.

The wheelhouse had a strong stench of fish, body odor, oil, and cigarettes.

The boat was chugging along at twenty-four knots, thick smoke spewing from a pair of stacks behind the wheelhouse. The engine was loud and made an unhealthy grinding noise. It didn't, however, concern Faqir. Not only had he crossed the Atlantic in far less seaworthy vessels, he also had the preternatural calm of a jihadist.

He didn't care if he died, believing in his heart that whatever was next was paradise.

It had been twelve hours since they'd refueled in Bizerte, on the coast of Tunisia. By Faqir's estimates, the trip through the Strait of Gibraltar would take another day. Until then, Faqir did not intend to leave the wheelhouse.

He heard rapid footsteps on the deck and turned as the door to the wheelhouse burst open. One of the crew stood at the door, panting.

"*Vrach dolzhen vam srazu.*"

The doctor needs you immediately.

"*Sledit' za ognyami,*" said Faqir. "*Krichat', yesli vy vidite kakoy-libo. Vy ponimayete?*"

Watch for lights. Scream if you see any. Do you understand?

The young crew member nodded and walked to the wheel.

Belowdecks, Faqir passed the engine room, then came to a large cargo hold near the middle of the ship. Outside the room hung several pink hazmat suits, designed to protect against chemical, biological, radiological, and nuclear exposure. Each had a self-contained breathing apparatus. Faqir put one on, then opened the door.

The bomb lay on its side on a steel frame. A section had been removed, exposing a steel cylinder near the center of the device.

Dr. Poldark, also dressed in a hazmat suit, was standing over the bomb, looking at the cylinder.

"What is it, Doctor?"

"We have a problem," said Poldark. "The explosives in the gun assembly are shot. They will not work."

Faqir shook his head.

"I'm not a nuclear scientist, Dr. Poldark."

Poldark took a deep breath, then smiled patiently. He pointed at the steel cylinder that stuck out from the bomb.

"This is a fission bomb," he said. "That is the gun assembly. The way it works is simple. At the very end is a conventional high explosive. When that is detonated, it causes a bullet—made of highly enriched uranium—to fire down the barrel into a larger piece of highly enriched uranium at the other end. When it strikes the other piece of uranium, a chain reaction occurs. Critical mass. *Boom.*"

Poldark patted the steel cylinder.

"The problem is, this bomb is old. It was assembled in 1952 or '53. I was a teenager then. Your parents, Faqir, were probably not even born yet. That's how old it is. The uranium is, of course, pristine. It will last forever, or at least long enough for our purposes. But the conventional explosive that begins the chain reaction is, I'm afraid, useless."

"I brought explosives, Doctor," said Faqir.

He turned to one of the men standing against the wall.

"*Guzny, gde zhe detonatorov?*" he barked at the young Chechen.

Guzny, where are the blasting caps?

The Chechen's eyes darted about nervously. Finally, he spoke, barely above a whisper.

"*Ya iskal vezde. Ya, dolzhno byt', zabyli ikh.*"

I looked everywhere. I must have forgotten them.

Faqir's face turned red as his expression flared in anger. He pulled a handgun from a holster at his waist, raised it, and fired. The slug struck the young Chechen in the center of his forehead, spattering blood across the wall of the hold. He fell to the floor.

Faqir looked at the two other men.

"Throw him in the ocean," he ordered.

He looked at Poldark.

"I apologize for the incompetence of my man," he said.

"Without some form of propellant, the bomb is useless," said Poldark.

Faqir glared at the scientist.

"I will find you explosives, Dr. Poldark."

"How?" asked Poldark, shaking his head in disgust and resignation. "We can't go back. There is no way."

Faqir ignored Poldark.

He turned to one of the Chechens and spoke to him in Akkhiy, an Arabic-influenced dialect of Chechen: "Get the weapons ready. Night optics too."

13

Amy Dellenbaugh, along with the Dellenbaughs' two daughters, Summer and Sally, were waiting in the living room of the White House private residence. The two sisters, ages nine and twelve, both had lacrosse sticks in their hands and were throwing a ball to one another. The president walked toward them, a big grin on his face. The Dellenbaughs were headed to Montana for their annual July Fourth vacation.

"Who's psyched for Montana?" asked Dellenbaugh.

Sally tossed the hard rubber lacrosse ball to her sister. It went wide of Summer's stick, then bounced on the marble floor, ricocheted up, and struck the wooden archway over the door. The ball shot left. It sailed toward a large oil painting of a man rowing a boat in an angry ocean by Winslow Homer. As it was about to hit the canvas, Dellenbaugh's right arm shot out and caught the ball.

Sally stared at her father, whose smile had vanished.

"I'm psyched for Montana," she said enthusiastically.

He shook his head, smiled, then underhanded the ball back to his daughter.

"Sorry, Dad," she said, squinting her eyes.

"It's okay, sweetheart," said Dellenbaugh, walking to her and putting his hand on her head. He leaned over and kissed her forehead. "You're lucky you're so cute."

Dellenbaugh glanced at his wife, who was rolling her eyes and shaking her head.

"Honestly, J.P., you're the biggest softie. That girl has you wrapped around her finger. How is she ever going to learn?"

"She's supposed to have me wrapped around her little finger," said Dellenbaugh, picking Sally up and walking toward the elevator.

The Dellenbaughs entered the elevator. Summer pressed a button for the first floor, and they descended. Outside the elevator, Calibrisi was standing, arms crossed, waiting. His face was ashen.

"Morning, Mr. President," said Calibrisi. "Amy, Summer, Sally, how are you?"

"Hi, Mr. Calibrisi," said Summer.

Calibrisi smiled, then shot Dellenbaugh a look.

"I'll be right there," Dellenbaugh said to his wife.

"No, I don't think you will, sir," said Calibrisi.

Amy saw the expression on Calibrisi's face. She walked toward her husband and wrapped her arms around him.

"It's okay, honey. I'll save a hot dog for you."

"I'm sorry."

"Don't be," she whispered in his ear. "You're president of the United States. Montana will be there when you're done."

Dellenbaugh walked his family through the Map Room and outside to the South Lawn, where Marine One, the presidential helicopter, was already waiting to take the first family to Andrews Air Force Base. Behind Marine One were two more helicopters. One looked exactly like Marine One; this craft served as a combination decoy and attack chopper, lest anyone attempt an action against the president while on board Marine One. The other helicopter was the one used by the CIA director.

Dellenbaugh cut back through the Rose Garden, then through a terrace door that led into the Oval Office. Calibrisi was already

seated on one of the tan Chesterfield sofas, along with Josh Brubaker, the president's national security advisor. Dellenbaugh sat down
on the other sofa, across from Calibrisi.

"How bad is it?"

"Bad."

"Let's hear it."

"This is not going to be a straightforward deal, Mr. President,"
said Calibrisi.

"I'm not sure what you mean by that, Hector."

"What I mean is, this is developing into an attack pattern that
falls squarely into the Vulnerability Matrix, sir."

Prepared for the president's eyes only, the Vulnerability Matrix
was a top secret analysis coauthored by the CIA, the Pentagon, and
the RAND Corporation. Every quarter, the brief, highly classified
analysis laid out America's critical security vulnerabilities for the
president. It was a chilling document.

Calibrisi pulled out a sheet of paper and handed it to Dellenbaugh.

"I took the relevant page," said Calibrisi as Dellenbaugh grabbed
it from him and quickly scanned it.

POTUS EYES ONLY
VULNERABILITY MATRIX 997-A-554

KEY:

1 MANAGEABLE: THREAT IS ABLE TO BE EFFECTIVELY MANAGED
BY U.S. GOVERNMENT/LAW ENFORCEMENT

2 CRITICAL: THREAT HAS VERIFIABLE ODDS OF SUCCESS AND
WOULD BE DIFFICULT TO STOP

3 QUANTUM: RISK POSED BY THREAT HAS NO RELIABLE OR
PREDICTIBLE WAY TO BE MANAGED AND MUST THEREFORE BE
PREVENTED THROUGH FORWARD AND/OR PREEMPTIVE ACTIONS

SCENARIO A5-788

SHIPBORNE NUCLEAR DEVICE: EAST COAST

RISK FACTOR: 3

Commentary:

America's single greatest security risk remains the same as in the last 74 consecutive months: terror attack involving an improvised or stolen nuclear device, delivered by boat to a city on the U.S. East Coast. The reason for this is simple: the volume of commercial fishing vessels (est. 6–7 million) × the length of U.S. East Coast shoreline = extreme improbability of discovery. This is referred to as "quantum vulnerability," meaning that if such a plot were ever actualized, the odds of stopping it would be minimal.

President Dellenbaugh stared at the sheet of paper. He had a haunted look on his face.

"What do we know about the bomb?" he asked.

"It's a thirty-kiloton 1950s era Soviet bomb."

"Is it bigger than Hiroshima?"

"Much. There's more highly enriched uranium, and the science behind it is better. Depending on the integrity of the trigger, the yield from this device could be ten times bigger."

Dellenbaugh put the paper down. His hand was visibly shaking.

"How many people are we talking about?"

"Assuming the target's a city, at least a million."

"How much time do we have?" asked Dellenbaugh.

Calibrisi didn't answer. Instead, he looked at Dellenbaugh's cowboy hat, which was on the sofa next to the president. Dellenbaugh always wore it in Montana. He looked back at the president.

"July Fourth," said Calibrisi.

"Independence Day. That's four days, Chief. Let's get to work."

14

NATIONAL SECURITY AGENCY (NSA)
TAILORED ACCESS OPERATIONS (TAO)
FORT MEADE, MARYLAND

Serena Pacheco and Jesus June were seated next to each other inside a brightly lit office at NSA headquarters. It was three o'clock in the morning.

Pacheco and June were two of the NSA's top electronic signals intelligence analysts. They employed a wide gamut of custom-built, extremely powerful software programs that pored through Internet, phone, and satellite traffic, most of which was obtained secretly.

They'd heard of Cloud, but only in the context of other well-known Russian hackers, a group considered criminal in nature but never before rising to the level of a national security threat. When they listened to the recording of Calibrisi's conversation with Malnikov, it was the first time anyone had confirmed what had been considered an urban myth: that problems with air traffic control systems on 9/11 had been intentionally caused by computer hackers.

Now they were dividing duties. Pacheco was focused on Cloud's likeness. After receiving a high-resolution sketch from the CIA based on Malnikov's description of Cloud, Pacheco had quickly pushed the sketch out to Interpol and other intelligence agencies.

That effort was intended to find Cloud by tapping into any personal or professional knowledge or experience with him. In addition, Pacheco had digitized the sketch and run it against a number of NSA surveillance programs. One such program, PRISM, was running the photo against visual media channels across the globe. This included security cameras at both public and private institutions, like airports and train stations, as well as license scanners, and, in cities where they existed, such as London, police cameras on street corners. PRISM could scan social media networks, like Facebook and Instagram. It also included certain Web-based photo storage repositories, such as iCloud, Dropbox, Flickr, Google Drive, and dozens of others, large and small.

If an image appeared that resembled Cloud, either in real time or at some point in the past, the software would trigger an alert. By 1 A.M., four separate alerts had popped. Three were errors, but one was Cloud, an Instagram photo taken by a girl at Alexei Malnikov's nightclub. In the photo, Cloud is in the background, in a tank top, gaunt and pale. His hair is what stood out, an alarming Afro of blond curls.

In turn, PRISM shared the photo, its origin, and any other data tied to it with the other NSA surveillance platforms, expanding their arc of detection.

June was focused exclusively on the one concrete piece of data they had: digital records of the hacker's phone calls with Malnikov. There had been three in all. Because Malnikov was already on an NSA watch list, those phone calls had all been recorded. June did not even bother listening to the conversations. He wanted the phone numbers, which he quickly found and then matched to the companies that had provided cellular coverage for the specific calls.

Two of the numbers were attached to a company called Beeline. The third number belonged to a company called MegaFon.

Legally, June wasn't supposed to be looking into the proprietary data of phone companies without permission from those compa-nies. Certain companies allowed it for national security reasons, but neither Beeline or MegaFon was on that list. June, however, didn't give a damn. When a nuclear bomb is headed toward American shores, the legalities were irrelevant.

Beeline was owned by a company based in Amsterdam and incorporated in Bermuda. June was able to quickly penetrate the company's Bermuda offices, hacking into a server from which all corporate documents, submitted to taxation authorities, had been sent. Inside this server, June focused on billing records. It was a voluminous cache of data showing minute-by-minute transactions of all 220 million customers worldwide, going back several years.

When June ran the two prepaid numbers against the database, each came back with only one record: Alexei Malnikov. Cloud had called him, then presumably thrown the cards away. Both cards had been shut off the day of the calls.

June waged a similar intrusion into MegaFon's records, this time going in through a "trapdoor" he'd built several years before. A hack that should've taken days, even weeks, now took less than an hour.

As with the prepaid phones, only one number had ever been dialed with the MegaFon Samsung cell: Alexei Malnikov. June expected as much. What he did not expect was for the Samsung phone to be live. He expected the phone to have been shut down. When he entered the number into MegaFon's billing platform, he suddenly sat up and leaned in toward his computer screen.

"Call Jim," said June, typing quickly.

"What is it?"

"His cell phone is still on," said June.

When Bruckheimer entered the office, he moved behind June as, from beside him, Pacheco watched.

A map of Moscow appeared on the screen. A few keystrokes later, brightly lit gridlines appeared crisscrossed on top of the map. The feed sharpened and closed in, stopping on a street corner.

Bruckheimer leaned over next to June and hit the speakerphone.

"Get me Polk."

15

Two floors belowground, past multiple security checkpoints, in a dimly lit, windowless room walled in by high-def plasma screens, Calibrisi, Polk, and a half dozen others were gathered.

There were four mission theaters at CIA headquarters: Bravo, Echelon, Firehouse, and Targa. These were the epicenters of CIA covert operations around the world.

During a CIA operation, the mission theater served as tactical command control authority. Unless the senior case officer declared "in-theater command control," someone at Langley was calling the shots. Using real-time visual and audio media, the theaters served to connect the many disparate, shifting elements of an operation in real time through the use of technology, data, and human intelligence. By managing an operation from a central hub, the Agency could direct the operators who were out there, at the front edge, risking their lives, with information such as the arrival of hostile forces or the detection of an operator's movement.

The four CIA mission theaters occupied an entire floor two stories below ground level. Echelon was the largest, but Polk liked the intimacy of Targa. He wanted to be able to glance into the eyes of the dozen or so case officers, field experts, tactical support specialists, and analysts on his team.

A double chime sounded on the speaker, then Jim Bruckheimer came on.

"We have something and it's live."

"What is it?" said Polk.

"The phone he called Malnikov with is still on. I'm sending you the coordinates. He's in Moscow."

Polk moved behind one of his analysts, seated at the computer in front of a large black screen.

"Give me Moscow grid with all Langley assets," said Polk.

The large plasma screen lit up. A live satellite image of Moscow came into sharp relief. A few seconds later, green lights began appearing on the screen, showing all CIA personnel available for deployment in or around Moscow. There were two CIA assets in the city.

"Put the coordinates of the target up," said Polk.

In the lower left-hand side of the screen, a bright orange light, then the words "15 Prospekt Vernadskogo."

"He's near Moscow Polytechnic," said the analyst.

Polk pointed to one of the green lights—a CIA agent who was close by.

"Highlight it," said Polk.

The analyst hovered a cursor above the light and double-clicked it. A photo appeared of a young male with black hair and a mustache. Beneath the photo, an empty box appeared, asking for a password. The analyst turned to Polk.

"Sir?"

Polk glanced around the room, making sure every person present had requisite security clearance.

"553 dash TS dash 7," he said.

When the analyst typed it in and hit Enter, the man's biography spread in block letters beneath:

NOC:	344K-6T ALPHA
LTK:	4 OCT 2011
PDS:	MAYBANK, JOHN BRAEBURN, Lt.
DOB:	04/14/88, Charleston, SC
REW:	U.S. Navy SEAL Team 10 (S01)
RANK:	4 V.E.X.

Polk pulled a small device from his chest pocket. It was an ear-bud, approximately the size of a gumdrop. He stuck it in his ear.

"We are now live," said Polk. "I have *control*."

"Roger, control," came a voice of a woman on speaker.

"Protocol."

"Roger, protocol is on-screen 'IVY,' over."

"Alpha 344K dash 6T," said Polk.

"Roger Alpha 344K dash 6T. Hold for shadow."

Johnny Maybank heard the buzzing noise, then felt it at his wrist. The wrist phone had five distinctive beeping patterns. This one, a dull monotone, was a call out from one of Langley's mission theaters. It meant a live operation was under way and Maybank was being pulled in.

Maybank lay in the darkness of his Moscow apartment, giving himself one extra second, then he practically jumped from the bed. As he charged across the room to the bathroom, he typed a code into his wrist phone.

"Maybank," he said.

"Control 344K. Go commo."

Next to the sink, Maybank found a small pill bottle, flipped it open, and removed a transparent object the size of a Tic Tac—his earbud. He peeled a strip of covering from the adhesive on the side of the object, then stuck it in his ear.

"Commo, affirmative," he said.

"You have Mission Theater Targa, control leader Polk," said the woman.

"Roger."

"Morning, Johnny, it's Bill."

"Yes, sir," he said, reaching for a pair of cutoff shorts that were clumped up on the floor.

"The photograph you're about to see is a Russian computer hacker known as Cloud," said Polk. "He's also a terrorist, running a live, high-target operation inside the U.S."

Looking at his wrist, he saw a photograph of a Caucasian with blond, curly hair.

"The target is less than one mile from you," said Polk. "His coordinates will be punched into the GPS on your wrist. He is moving, could be guarded, and should be considered very danger-ous. You are to take whatever actions necessary to capture him and prepare for in-theater real-time interrogation. Do *not* kill him; we need him alive."

"Roger, Bill."

"We're gonna try and get some backup, Johnny, but don't count on it. Now get moving. Out."

Maybank stepped out the front door of the building and broke into a hard run. He had on orange Puma running shoes, no socks, cut-off khaki shorts, a T-shirt, and a blue windbreaker. He sprinted down a side street until he reached Prospekt Vernadskogo, then went right. He charged along the sidewalk for more than a mile, check-ing his wrist, whose small map guided his movements. Maybank, who'd played football at the University of Texas, was running at a 4:30 pace.

When Maybank's wrist PDA told him he was within ten feet of the cell phone, he stopped. There was only one store within ten feet, a small coffee shop. He caught his breath for a minute, then opened the door and stepped inside.

A dozen tables were filled with students, looking at their computers, talking on phones, reading, and sipping drinks. He scanned for the man with the blond Afro. He wasn't there. He checked the restroom, then went behind the counter. Nothing. Maybank could have imagined almost any one of the customers in the restaurant being a terrorist. Half were Middle Eastern, the others a mix of long-haired Russians.

He got in line, studying the GPS signal. According to his wrist device, Cloud was within four feet of him. He reached his hand to his ear.

"Target isn't here."

"Are you sure?" asked Polk.

"Yeah."

"Control," said Polk, "I need you to dial that tracker cell."

"Roger, NCS."

"You ready, John?"

Maybank stepped toward the counter, reaching his right hand into the windbreaker. He found the butt of his SIG Sauer P226. He felt the suppressor sticking into the side of his torso.

"Yeah, I'm good."

"Go, control," said Polk.

"Roger, NCS. In five, four, three, two, one . . ."

"May I help you?" asked a girl behind the counter, in Russian, as Maybank heard the low ring of a cell phone behind him.

"Espresso, please," he said, glancing over his shoulder.

A tall, thin, young-looking man was holding the phone, his eyes darting about. He was Middle Eastern, his face covered in a beard and mustache, his skin olive.

Maybank watched as the man lifted the ringing phone to his ear.

"Someone answered it," said Maybank. "Arab."

"We need a photo."

Maybank removed his hand from his windbreaker, then nonchalantly hit a button on his wrist, taking a photo of the man answering the phone.

* * *

Inside Targa, the photograph shot up on one of the screens.

A crosshatch of red grid lines spread across the man's features as CIA facial recognition software quickly synthesized his face into a precise block of metadata, or code, then pushed it across a whole library of CIA, FBI, NSA, Interpol, and other databases. In less than one minute, the screen burst into a profile sheet, with a series of photos of the same individual along with a biography:

Interpol Flash: Terror Stk: Wanted Dead or Alive

ALERT: AL QAEDA [LEVEL 2 COMBATANT]

WANTED: AL-MEDI, Zhia

CIT: Chechnya, RUSSIA

DOB: 26/02/85

HOME: Grozny, Chechnya

LKS: LAST KNOWN SIGHTING: 11/01/12—Damascus, Syria
                I case L87-34-00K

ACTIONS: Madrid, Spain +[CTU FILE WAW45] 11/3/2004+
                Madrid train bombings
                191 casualties: Al-Medi believed tertiary
                to Atocha Station attack
                Riyadh, Saudi Arabia +[CTU FILE S09U]
                12/5/2003+U.S. embassy compound bombing
                36 casualties: Al-Medi driver of pre-fuel truck from
                Lebanon (later converted by Al-Houri into bomb)
                Khobar Towers (U.S. DOD—67T el-forte)

Polk tapped his ear.

"Johnny, his name is Al-Medi," said Polk. "He's AQ with a laundry list of hostiles. Be *very* careful. He could be wearing some sort of suicide vest. Also, do not let him reach for his mouth; we don't want him munching a cyanide pill before we can grill him. We need him alive."

"Roger that, Bill."

Polk pointed at a separate green light on the screen.

"Highlight it," he said.

The analyst moved the cursor above the second green light, then double-clicked. The face of a female agent appeared. She was black, with closely cropped hair.

SAD:	55007 ZEBRA
PDS:	BRAGA, CHRISTINA CATHCART
DOB:	09/03/88, Los Angeles, CA
REW:	Recruit: RUS language desk
	Juilliard (2002–4) *Ballet/modern dance*
	Yale University, Russian Studies
	(D.Phil 2009) *summa cum laude*

"She's your best option?" asked Calibrisi.

Polk paused an extra half second, studying the Moscow grid on the wall.

"She's our only option."

He tapped his earbud.

"Control."

"Roger, NCS."

"55007 Zebra," he said.

"Hold, NCS."

Christy Braga was typing into her laptop in her third-story office at the U.S. embassy when her wrist phone made two small beeps.

She stood up, shut the door, then hit a button on the side of the watch.

"Go commo," came the voice of Polk. "We're live."

"Roger, NCS," she said, reaching for a silver locket around her neck, popping it open, and removing an earbud and affixing it inside her ear. "I'm commo, Bill."

"We're downrange in an operation near you, Christy," said Polk. "I need you to move to a set of coordinates with tactical weapons and escape options. Coordinates will be on you in a few seconds. Move by car."

Braga shut her laptop and moved to her office closet. She pulled out a steel weapons case and unbuckled it. Inside, held in place with Velcro straps, were several combat blades, a few suppressed handguns, and a pair of HK MP7A1 submachine guns. She removed a suppressed Colt M1991, a SOG SEAL Pup knife, and one of the MP7A1s, slamming a mag into it and then threading in a suppressor. She left her office and ran down the service stairs three at a time. In less than a minute, she was at the wheel of a red BMW M5, moving toward a steel gate at the back of the embassy compound.

"Can I get some intel, Bill?"

"This is an Emergency Priority recon," said Polk. "Agent Maybank is in active pursuit of a known Al Qaeda operative and will likely need support."

"What do we do when we get him?"

"Vernacular House," said Polk, referring to a CIA safe house in Moscow. "This is a *do not kill*. He's a tertiary to a planned terror attack we believe is now live. We need to talk to him."

Maybank paid for the espresso, keeping Al-Medi in his range of vision. He stepped to the end of the counter and waited for his drink. He watched Al-Medi without looking.

Maybank took the espresso from the counter and left the coffee shop. He glanced in through the window. Al-Medi held the phone to his ear, then hung up. He scanned the coffee shop suspiciously.

Maybank crossed the street. He stood behind a parked car and waited. A little while later, Al-Medi stepped through the coffee shop door.

"He's moving," said Maybank. "He suspects something."

"We have him on grid," said Polk, "as long as he doesn't throw the phone away."

The street was crowded. The neighborhood was filled with students from Moscow Polytechnic University, a few blocks away.

Al-Medi went left. From a distance, Maybank watched him, gulping the espresso, then tossed the cup into a garbage can. He walked ten feet behind him, keeping pace, but on the opposite side of the street.

As Al-Medi walked down the sidewalk, his head swiveled slowly back and forth, searching calmly around him. His laid-back demeanor was an act. The chase was on and he knew it.

The call changed everything. Had it been Cloud, he would've called back. But he didn't, and right now Al-Medi knew he was being hunted. He'd been thumbprinted the moment he answered the phone.

Al-Medi came to an abrupt stop. He peered into a storefront window, pretending to look at something. Instead, he studied the reflection for signs of a tracker. He studied each and every person as they moved past him. Nobody looked even remotely suspicious. Then, across the street, he saw a tall black-haired man staring at him from behind a Citroën.

Al-Medi started to walk casually down the sidewalk. He stopped at a mailbox, opened it, tossed the cell inside. He saw the man, moving now, running directly at him. Shielded by the mailbox, Al-Medi pulled out a gun—Helwan 9mm semiautomatic, made in Egypt.

"He tossed the cell," said Maybank. "He's moving."

"Stay on him," said Polk. "It's imperative you stay with him, Johnny. He is our only connection at this point."

Maybank charged back into the traffic-filled street, barely dodging a van whose driver didn't see him. But as he came around the van, he was trapped in the crosshairs of Al-Medi's gun.

"Oh, shit!" he groaned, lurching left just as the unmuted crack of gunfire ripped the streetscape. Al-Medi's slug missed him, and Maybank pulled his right arm up, grabbing the butt of his P226, just as a second gunshot tore the air, hitting him in the thigh.

"*Fuck!*" yelled Maybank as he continued to sprint after Al-Medi, who had gone down a side street called Baku.

"Johnny?" asked Polk, urgency in his voice.

"I need support," barked Maybank, still running, despite the slug lodged in his thigh. He glanced down. The bottom half of his left leg was drenched in blood.

"Almost there," came a female voice.

Braga had the M5 weaving in and out of traffic as she drove through the narrow, clogged streets that surrounded Moscow Polytechnic University. She glanced between her wrist piece, which showed her position relative to Maybank on a small map, and the road, trying to navigate.

"Control," she said, "I need third-party navigation."

"Control, over," came a voice. "Hold."

She shot a quick glance at the speedometer: 77 mph.

"Take a sharp right in approximately one hundred feet. *Get over.*"

Braga ripped the BMW hard right, hit the brakes, then moved the car onto Baku.

"He's coming right at you," said CIA control in her earpiece.

* * *

At the corner of Baku, Al-Medi ripped off his jacket. He sprinted down the small side street. In two blocks, there was a metro station.

He looked back. The man now had a gun, which was swinging up and down in his left hand as he tried to catch up with him. But the shot to the man's leg slowed him.

Al-Medi kept glancing back, at first fearful he might get shot but soon realizing that his tracker, whoever he was, wanted him alive.

Maybank was falling behind as the blood now sopped his running shoe and the pain became intense.

He saw Braga's red sedan far in the distance, at the end of the street. Al-Medi was now between the two of them, running toward her.

"You need to stop him," Maybank yelled.

Al-Medi moved as he'd been trained, in a zigzag, dragging in behind pedestrians, making it hard for his pursuer to catch him.

In less than a block was the metro station. He would lose the man there.

Braga stopped the car at the end of the street, watching in the distance as Al-Medi raced toward her. She could also see Maybank, well behind him, limping as he ran, his leg covered in blood.

Braga slouched down in the seat. Her head was just high enough to peer through the opening in the steering wheel.

Al-Medi came closer, sprinting along the line of parked cars. She put the car in reverse and cranked the steering wheel counterclockwise. Then she waited.

He was a dozen cars ahead, then ten, then just a few. A savage, angry look was in his eyes. When he reached the car in front of her, she glanced up, watching as he ran by her door, oblivious of her presence. He was drenched in sweat. She waited one last moment, then took her foot off the brake and floored the gas. The M5 burst left, its back end lurching into Al-Medi's legs, slamming him violently, pummeling him to the tar. He landed, both legs broken, and started to scream.

Braga climbed out and opened the back door just as Maybank arrived. Maybank wrapped flex-cuffs around Al-Medi's wrists as Braga handled his ankles. Maybank finished with a wrap about his head, muffling his screaming. They lifted him into the back of the car, then climbed in, Maybank in back, Braga driving.

Maybank unsheathed his combat blade and jammed it into Al-Medi's mouth as Braga turned around, then floored it. Propping his mouth open, Maybank searched Al-Medi's mouth. He found a fake molar and ripped it out. Inside was a small white pill: *cyanide*. He opened the window and tossed it to the street.

Maybank grabbed Al-Medi's T-shirt and ripped it down the front, tearing it in half. He took the cloth and wrapped it around his thigh and tied it tight over the wound, creating a tourniquet.

Braga had the M5 scorching along Baumanskaya at 80 mph, weaving skillfully between cars and pedestrians as she sped toward the CIA safe house.

Maybank hit his earbud.

"We have him," said Maybank, breathing hard. "I need direction."

"Get him back to Vernacular House and prepare for immediate interrogation," said Polk.

"What's the protocol?"

"Dayton protocol," said Polk. "We have a *Level-One* terror threat. Use whatever means necessary to find out the whereabouts of Cloud. *Out*."

16

NSA

Serena Pacheco was in line at the NSA cafeteria, buying a sandwich and a cup of coffee. Her cell phone started ringing. The ID indicated "June, J."

"Pacheco," she said, answering the phone.

"PRISM is going nuts up here," June said.

"Be right there."

Pacheco left her tray on the counter.

Back at her workstation inside the TAO suite of offices, Pacheco found two separate hits, or matches, based on the CIA sketch of Cloud. Both were photos of a woman with dark skin and long black hair. In one photo, the woman is seen walking out of a Moscow restaurant. Standing next to her is a man with straight blond hair, dressed in a tuxedo. The other photo showed the same woman, this time climbing into a limousine. The same man is behind her, holding the door. Pacheco zoomed in on the two photos, then placed them between the CIA sketch of Cloud and the photo from the nightclub. The first photo did not look at all like the Cloud depicted in the sketch or in the photo from the nightclub; he was handsome and clean-cut, his hair neatly combed and straight. But the second photograph gave her pause. It was his eyes. They were dark and suspicious. They were the same eyes. It was unmistakable.

Pacheco quickly ran the woman's photo through PRISM. In less than a minute, dozens, then hundreds of photographs dominoed across her screen.

Basaeyev, Katya

CITIZENSHIP: Russia

DOB: c. 09/10/1990
    Yakutsk, Sakha Republic, SIBERIA

HIST: Convent of Good Shepherd, Yakutsk
    Yakutsk, SIB 1990—2002
    Bolshoi Academy for Performing Arts
    Moscow, RUS 2002-07
    Bolshoi Ballet, *troupe ballerina,* 2007–08
    Bolshoi Ballet, *prima ballerina,* 2008–

Katya's biography went on for twenty-seven pages. In all, PRISM was able to source more than a hundred thousand photographs of the famous Russian ballerina. Of these, only two popped Cloud's photo.

One of the photos on Pacheco's screen had been taken just an hour before, then posted by someone on Pinterest. Pacheco clicked on the photo. It showed Katya's beautiful face on a large poster above the entrance to a theater. Katya's blue eyes were like jewels. An enigmatic smile was on her face, her pure white teeth visible and contrasted against rose red lips:

The Kirov Ballet is proud to present Tchaikovsky's
Swan Lake
with Special Guest Star

Katya Basaeyev
"The Siberian Diamond"
July 4–July 28
Mariinsky Theatre, Saint Petersburg

"I found his girlfriend," said Pacheco.

17

Faqir had the trawler running on only one engine, putting along the dark North African coast, a half mile or so offshore. Most boats in the area were moored for the night, anchors down, awaiting first light.

The *Lonely Fisherman*'s running lights were extinguished. Faqir navigated by a portable state-of-the-art sonar system, which was set on the wood shelf next to the wheel.

They were still in safe waters, but in a few hours, they would come to the Strait of Gibraltar. If they were going to get stopped, that's where it would happen. That one of the crew left behind the explosives only added to the anxiety Faqir felt. This side trip was unnecessary. It would add several hours onto the voyage, hours that were precious.

The front window of the wheelhouse was open. In the crow's nest at the bow of the ship, thirty feet up in the air, two of the Chechens were standing, each holding thermal night-vision binoculars, scanning the water in front and to each side of the trawler.

Their instructions were twofold. Warn him if they were approaching too close to a vessel. More important, look for a particular flag: Indonesia, Vietnam, Manila, Thailand, any African country.

Faqir tried not to think about the sheer stupidity of Guzny, but he couldn't help it. It was unbelievable. Everything they had worked for could now be gone, simply because one man had forgotten a duffel bag.

Suddenly, one of the men in the crow's nest started waving his arms and pointing to the right.

Faqir stepped from the wheelhouse and crossed the deck.

"What is it?" he yelled.

"Flag," he answered. "Vietnam."

"Get ready," he ordered. "Every man."

Faqir walked back to the wheelhouse and turned the ship toward the distant lights of a boat. It took twenty minutes to reach it. Faqir navigated to the smaller ship's starboard side. It was a beat-up old thing, a double-ended fishing scow that sat low in the water. A few lights were on, but there was no movement. Atop an aft stanchion, a flag dangled. It was a rectangle of red with a yellow star in the middle.

Faqir had spent three years aboard a similar fishing scow. Most of the fish were caught legally, but when times were slow, his captain was not above dropping explosives into the water and seeing what came up. It was highly illegal, and Faqir quickly learned the countries that engaged in the practice. Of all of them, Vietnam was the worst.

As the *Lonely Fisherman* chugged closer, a swarm of Chechens stood on the port deck, weapons raised. Faqir cut the engine just as a crew member aboard the other boat appeared on the deck, carrying a flashlight. When he saw the approaching ship, his eyes bulged, then he screamed and turned to run. One of the Chechens fired. The staccato of automatic weapons fire interrupted the relative quiet. A burst of slugs hit the man as he ran, knocking him down, the flashlight tumbling onto the wooden deck.

The *Lonely Fisherman* drifted closer and closer until, finally, it slammed into the Vietnamese boat's side. As two Chechens lashed the vessels together, the others leapt aboard the quiet scow.

127

"*No witnesses!*" yelled Faqir as his men sprinted across the deck toward the stairs that led below, to where the screw was sleeping.

Faqir stepped to the wheelhouse. As he entered the empty room, he heard screams, then the peal of submachine gun fire coming from directly below.

He ransacked the wheelhouse, ripping open cabinets, searching for explosives. Finding nothing, his eyes moved to the door. Above it was a steel box. He pulled the box down and opened it. Inside were several dozen sticks of gelatin dynamite along with a pile of blasting caps. He grabbed six of the sticks and all of the caps, then walked quickly to the door. As he climbed back onto the *Lonely Fisherman*, the first of the crew who'd gone below appeared back on deck, trailed by the others.

Faqir waved them over.

"*Hurry!*" he snapped.

The gunmen ran in a loose line back to the trawler, climbing aboard as Faqir started the engine.

One of the men stepped into the wheelhouse.

"It's done. There were fourteen men in all."

"You searched for anyone who might be hiding?"

"There's no one. They're all dead. Should we sink it?"

"With what, idiot? Explosives?"

"What about setting it on fire?"

"No," said Faqir. "That will only draw attention. Cut the boat's anchor line. Perhaps it will drift into the rocks and sink on its own."

Faqir revved the trawler's engine and put the boat into gear.

"Untie the boat," he yelled through the window. "Two men, back in the crow's nest. We need to hurry."

18

VERNACULAR HOUSE
MOSCOW

Al-Medi looked up at Maybank as he struggled to catch his breath. He was drenched, pale, and barely alive.

"Where is he?" asked Maybank.

Maybank had been at it for an hour now. He was in a soundproof, windowless basement room, with Braga watching from the door, as he tried to get Al-Medi to break.

"I told you, I don't know who you're talking about," said Al-Medi, his Chechen accent thick. "I stole the phone."

"We ran your prints. We know who you are. Stop fucking with me."

Maybank slammed Al-Medi's head down into the water. He looked calmly at his watch as he held him under. After a full minute, he lifted him back out.

Al-Medi was soaking wet. He stared lifelessly up at Maybank. Suddenly, his eyes rolled back in his head. He leaned left as he began to fall from the steel chair.

"Oh, no you don't, motherfucker," said Maybank.

Maybank lurched out and grabbed his arm, then lifted the

now unconscious terrorist from the chair. Water and sweat from Al-Medi rained down on Maybank as he hoisted him up and hurled him as far as he could. Al-Medi slammed into the concrete wall, then dropped to the floor, grunting in pain. Maybank stepped toward him and kicked him in the knee. He let out a horrendous scream.

"Where is he?" Maybank asked calmly.

"Fuck you," whispered Al-Medi. He coughed, and water poured from his mouth to the floor.

Maybank booted him in the other knee, harder this time. Al-Medi screamed and moaned, then coughed out more water.

Braga stepped to Maybank, who was growing increasingly frustrated.

"Can I try?" she asked.

Maybank towered above the diminutive Braga. He nodded.

"Sure."

Braga walked to Al-Medi and stood above him.

"When did he give you the phone?" she asked matter-of-factly. "I mean, it *is* rather odd he would arrange for the purchase of a nuclear bomb with it, then pass it on to someone else versus, for example, disposing of it. Don't you think that's odd?"

Al-Medi said nothing. He panted, then vomited more water.

"Have you been asking yourself that question?" Braga continued. "I thought he was a famous computer hacker. Surely he'd know that anyone possessing that phone could be discovered?"

Braga paused, looked down at Al-Medi, then knelt to the ground next to his head. The terrorist looked dazed; it was difficult to tell if he was even listening.

"Alexei Malnikov paid Cloud one hundred million dollars to take the bomb off his hands," said Braga. "Did you know that?"

She saw Al-Medi clench his fingers, the first sign of anger or emotion he'd displayed.

"We were trying to guess how much he shared with you," continued Braga. "Johnny thought ten million. I guessed higher. I thought at least thirty million. Which one of us was right?"

Al-Medi shut his eyes.

"Oh, my God," she said. "He didn't share it with you, did he? He hands you a phone that he knows will get you either killed or locked up for the rest of your life, and he doesn't give you a nickel."

Al-Medi stared lifelessly at the ground.

Braga tapped her ear, triggering commo with Polk back inside Targa.

"Can I negotiate?" she whispered.

"Offer him whatever you have to."

Braga took a can of Coca-Cola from the table and opened it. She leaned down in front of Al-Medi, put her hand beneath his head, then propped him up. She tipped the can of soda toward his mouth, pouring it slowly in. Al-Medi chugged it like a dog gulping water on a hot summer afternoon.

"You help us find him," said Braga, "and we'll set you free. No strings attached. We'll also give you some money."

"How much?"

"A few million."

Al-Medi slugged down the rest of the soda until it was gone.

"I don't believe you," he whispered.

"But it needs to happen right now," continued Braga, ignoring him. "You know it and I know it. Don't be an idiot. Freedom and money or a concrete cell in a prison most people don't even know exists. And if you're one of these martyr types who think death comes quickly at the black sites, you're wrong. We don't let you die. You'll live to be a hundred, chained to a wall, inside a dark room, alone. From what I hear, it's not much fun."

"How do I know you're not lying?"

"You don't."

Braga tapped her ear, getting ready to relay the information she knew Al-Medi was about to give up.

"What do you want to know?"

"What kind of boat is it?"

"A fishing trawler. Two hundred feet long."

"What about Cloud?" she asked. "Where is he?"

"I don't know. But I know where he'll be."

19

Bond stepped into a small glass-walled office within the suite of offices reserved for the National Clandestine Service. Polk was standing inside, arms crossed, reading a sheet of paper. He looked up at Bond.

"You're going to Saint Petersburg," said Polk. "I know you haven't been to Russia in a while, but I need you running second phase line."

In NCS lingo, phase lines referred to stages of an operation. Often, one stage was predicated on the one before it either succeeding or failing. Second phase line meant Bond's part of the operation would kick in only if the first stage—Phase Line One—failed or was aborted.

"I'm ready," said Bond. "Why the phase lines?"

"We have a real problem," said Polk. "A Russian terrorist is downrange with an operation to detonate a nuclear device on U.S. soil. We're going to try and capture him in Moscow. If that part of the mission fails, you go live. This guy's girlfriend is in Saint Petersburg. Phase Line Two is a hostile extract. It's a two-man team, you're running the in-theater."

"Why are you being so cryptic?"

"The bomb is on its way to the United States."

"Can't we blockade?"

Polk shook his head.

"The coast is too big. Navy could maybe shut down two or three cities, but they'll know that. We have one shot here. We have to catch him."

"Who is he?"

Polk looked at Bond, then through the glass.

"Cloud? Who is he? That's the scariest part of all. We don't know."

Bond was silent. He glanced around the office, looking out through the glass. Across the hallway, he saw Dewey talking with someone, holding a bag of ice to his eye.

"I need to know who you want with you."

Bond looked at Polk, pausing for a few moments.

"Dewey," said Bond.

Polk was motionless. He waited, thinking about his response.

"Dewey can be very charismatic, Pete," said Polk. "A lot of guys have asked to be teamed with him. But in Iguala he froze up on a relatively minor project. He shouldn't be running ops right now."

"He froze in Mexico, but six hours later he almost killed the top-ranked amateur MMA fighter in the U.S. He's ready. Trust me."

"You cannot afford a second of doubt if Moscow somehow goes south and Saint Pete goes live," said Polk. "At that point, the extraction of his girlfriend is all we have left before this nuclear bomb hits our shores. They're calling this thing nine/twelve if we don't stop it. Books will be written about the decisions we make this day. Do you understand that?"

"You asked me who I want," said Bond. "I'll work with whoever you put me with, but I want Dewey. Either put him with me or don't. But don't lecture me about what's going to happen if things get fucked up. I've been there, and if it's my choice, I want him next to me. You're the one who taught me 'trust your gut.'"

Polk smiled.

"Sorry," he said. "I didn't mean to imply that I am as close to the ground as you. But I've seen an operation or two. Your loyalty is admirable, but I think it's going to be Joe I send over with you."

"Why the fuck did you even ask me?" asked Bond.

Polk was silent.

"All right, fine," said Polk, glancing at his watch. "You're an argumentative son of a bitch, you know that? I'll think about it."

20

The lobby of the apartment building was minimalist, elegant, and quiet. Its walls were paneled in walnut, with large, abstract geometric works of art. There was a pair of chandeliers in leaded crystal and a floor of rare white marble streaked with turquoise.

Two big men dressed in dark suits stood behind a security desk. They were both active-duty GRU, highly trained agents adept at close-quarters combat, face-to-face self-defense, and human intelligence. Russia protected its important citizens, especially the famous ones.

A soft chime told the guards that someone was at the steel-gated front entrance. On a video monitor behind the desk, one of the guards studied the man's face.

"It is Mr. Vargarin," he said.

The other guard pressed a button, unlatching the gate and allowing the visitor to come inside the building.

Cloud stepped through the front door. In one hand he held a bouquet of red chrysanthemums wrapped in silver foil and tied with a white ribbon. In the other was a small wooden box. Cloud smiled politely as he approached the security desk.

"Hello, Jonas, Mikhail," he said. "How are you?"

"Very well, Mr. Vargarin," said one of the men, grinning. "Are those flowers for us?"

"I'm afraid not," said Cloud, laughing.

The transformation in his appearance was shocking. Other than the sharpness of his eyes, he was an entirely different person from the creature who strong-armed the most powerful mobster in Russia into handing him a nuclear bomb. Cloud's hair was no longer a mop of blond curls. Rather, it was straight, combed neatly down the middle, and slicked back. He had on a white button-down shirt beneath a plaid blazer, khakis, and brown wingtips. He looked stylish, immaculate, and worldly.

Cloud had learned long ago how to use his appearance to his advantage. It was the fulcrum upon which his outward identity pivoted; one day a gentle-looking, exotically handsome man of culture, the next a scrawny outcast with hints of drug addiction and dark powers.

In theory, the guards at the Margaux were trained to profile all manner of potential security threats, the most important being possible kidnappers or terrorists. But they were oblivious of Cloud's true nature.

Cloud put the wooden box on top of the desk.

"We don't need to inspect it," said one, waving his hand. "We trust you."

"It's a gift for the two of you for all you do to protect Katya."

One of the guards opened the box. Inside were two nondescript bottles.

"You like vodka, yes?" asked Cloud.

"Of course."

"This is vodka from the personal collection of Nikita Khrushchev."

The guard on the right lifted a bottle and inspected it. The glass was a bluish-green hue and looked as if it had been blown by hand.

"Mr. Vargarin," he said. "I cannot—"

"Please," said Cloud. "I personally don't like to drink anything stronger than tea. I brought one for each of you."

"Thank you," said the guard. "You're too generous."

"You're welcome."

"How did you obtain something so rare?" asked one of the men, a hint of suspicion in his voice.

At the question, Cloud's demeanor shifted. For a brief moment, a dark look crossed his eyes. Then it was gone.

"It was left to me by my father," he said.

"Your father must have been very important to receive such a treasure."

Cloud had a cold look on his face. He looked at the ground.

"He was above all else a kind man, that is all. Now, if you'll please excuse me."

In the elevator, Cloud pressed the button for the top floor. As he did so, he thought of his father. Were he alive, Cloud knew that his father would be proud of him, but only for this part of his life. For his other activities, his hacking, his thievery, his father would be deeply angry. As for the nuclear bomb and what was to come, words could not describe the shame and utter revulsion Dr. Anuslav Vargarin would feel toward him, were he alive.

Were he alive.

But he wasn't alive. He was dead, killed along with his mother by the United States. Killed in front of him. Killed like a dog. All for . . . well, all for a reason Cloud still did not understand. A computer disk, that was all. Letters and numbers that represented his father's life work. Data. Now he would turn their data back on them. The information hunters would become prey to disinformation. Their theft of his father's science would metastasize into a creation far more abominable than they ever could have imagined.

A father's debt: Cloud would repay it, even though the kindly man whose gentle touch he could never forget would not want him to.

The chime for the seventh floor awakened Cloud from his daydream. He stepped out of the iron-trellised elevator and walked to the only door on the floor. He knocked twice and waited patiently. A few seconds later, the door swung open.

"Pyotr," a woman said, staring affectionately at him. She stepped forward and wrapped her arms around his neck.

"Katya," he said, wrapping his arms around her waist.

"I miss you already and I haven't even left yet," she said.

"I love you so much, Katya," he whispered as he clutched her tightly in the frame of the open door, hugging her for more than a minute.

"I love you too," she said. "You make me so happy."

At age twenty-six, Katya Basaeyev was among the most famous women in Russia and was well on her way to being recognized as the greatest living ballerina in the world. She was from Yakutsk, the largest city in the remote Sakha Republic, a part of Siberia that bordered the Arctic Circle and was known for producing diamonds.

She had learned to dance at the convent, taught by one of the nuns who herself had been a celebrated dancer before turning to God. By twelve, Katya's skills were well enough known to draw a visit from the director of admissions at Moscow's prestigious Bolshoi Ballet Academy. After that, it took only a little while for her to sweep like a tidal wave across the ruthlessly competitive world of Russian ballet. Katya had done so effortlessly, without a great deal of strategy or deliberateness, as if it was simply meant to be, her rise predicated on a unique dancing style. Katya had an inner grace, a simplicity, really, that was almost untrained and a style that even those dancers she eclipsed admired. No one who knew Katya disliked her. Other dancers, choreographers, and conductors all loved her. The fact that she was also so pretty, and so kind, only added to her singularity.

Her nickname: "The Siberian Diamond."

They stepped into the apartment and shut the door. Cloud handed Katya the flowers.

"They're beautiful."

"Would you like to go out to dinner?" he asked.

Katya buried her face in the chrysanthemums and took a big sniff, then turned.

"Do you not have a nose?" she asked playfully.

"What do you mean?"

"I made your favorite dinner."

He suddenly became aware of the scent of chicken roasting in the oven.

"And for dessert, profiteroles," she said, stepping to him and removing his blazer, then wrapping her arms around him. "I spent all afternoon making them. Your mother must have been a saint. They are very hard to make."

Cloud looked into her eyes for several moments, expressing his gratitude, his love, silently, through his eyes.

"The day before you leave for Saint Petersburg, and you are cooking for me. I don't know what to say."

"It makes me happy to make you happy, Pyotr," Katya said, kissing him on the lips.

Katya's hair was jet-black. It dangled down to her shoulders, parted in the middle, and it shimmered in the light. Her skin was brown; her eyes were aqua, their unusual color like a flash of blue sky on a dark, cloudy day.

Her apartment was a rambling warren of odd-shaped rooms carved out of what had been the palace's attic. Yet it was the most expensive unit at the Margaux. Katya had purchased the apartment for $12 million two years before. There were four bedroom suites, a dining room, a library, a formal living room, a more casual den, a media room, a wine room, and a small gymnasium, half of which had been turned into a practice area, with a barre, mats, and mirrors.

Katya put the bouquet of flowers in a large vase, filled it with water, and then placed it on a credenza against the wall of the living room.

They had met when she was a student at the Bolshoi and he was at the Moscow Technological Institute. They met on the first day of school, seated next to each other in the large dining room the two schools shared.

Like Katya, Cloud was a prized recruit. Moscow Technological Institute, Russia's top academic institution, did not accept applicants. Like the Bolshoi, the institute scoured Russia, as well as the republics of the former Soviet Union, looking for the country's most talented individuals. It was MTI that produced the country's greatest scientific, mathematic, and computer minds.

Like Cloud, Katya no longer had parents, and they shared a similar loneliness. She had been sent to the convent at age four after her father was killed in Afghanistan and her mother died of cancer the same year. She didn't know what it was like to have a father and mother. Cloud remembered. He knew what it was like to enjoy the love of two doting parents, as an only child, a beloved child. He also knew what it was like to watch those parents be murdered in front of his eyes.

In Moscow, like two birds caught in a windstorm, Cloud and Katya became friends first, then best friends, then lovers. As Katya's renown increased, so too did Cloud's. His ability with computers grew every bit as quickly and dramatically as Katya's ballet skills.

So too did his hatred for the country that had killed his parents.

At fifteen, Katya had her first prima debut, in *The Nutcracker* at the Bolshoi's Christmas performances. That same year, using a computer in the school library, Cloud helped to manipulate air traffic control systems in the United States on the morning of 9/11. Both performances, in their own way, were prodigal.

Now, after a little more than a decade, they remained inextricably linked. But Katya's world was as transparent as Cloud's was hidden.

She'd become the most famous dancer in Russia. Her life was an open book to Cloud. Cloud, meanwhile, had become the most famous computer hacker in Russia. But to Katya, he remained Pyotr Vargarin, computer consultant, who made a great deal of money but did not like to discuss his work.

They ate dinner at one end of the large dining room table, enjoying a bottle of wine as Tchaikovsky's *Swan Lake* played softly in the background.

"Tell me about the Kirov," said Cloud, referring to the Kirov Ballet in Saint Petersburg, where Katya would be headlining the summer production of *Swan Lake*. It was a highly anticipated series of performances for which she would be paid $5 million. The shows had sold out in less than an hour.

"I thought that perhaps you would consider coming," Katya said.

"I would like that very much," said Cloud. "I have a big project at work, as you know, but I am going to do my very best."

"How long will this project take?" she asked.

"Maybe a week."

"What is this project?"

Cloud leaned forward and put his hand on Katya's.

"It's a boring project involving computers," he said.

"Computers, computers, computers," she said. "You think I would be confused if you tell me, don't you?"

"Not at all, just bored."

"Try me."

Cloud was silent for several moments. He didn't like to lie to Katya.

"I am helping to redistribute certain scientific assets," said Cloud.

"Why?"

"Well, these assets will help to bring a little heat and light to a part of the world that desperately needs it."

Katya smiled, leaned forward, and kissed him on the lips.

"I am proud of you."

"Not as proud as I am of you. I will try to see you in Saint Petersburg. Besides, I have seen you dance now about a hundred times. It seems only fair to let others have the chance to experience the wonder of your dancing."

Katya smiled and blushed.

"Flattery will get you everywhere," she said. "But I must tell you, Pyotr, that when you are in the audience, I dance differently. I run faster. I am able to jump higher. Your eyes beckon me to try harder."

Cloud looked at Katya's hand on his, running her finger over his gold signet ring. He felt a spike of anxiety, not at the terrible thing he was going to do but at the terrible deception he'd allowed into the most important relationship—the only relationship—he cared about. He'd built a lie in order to project—and protect—an image of himself in her eyes. He knew that if she ever found out his true nature, it would destroy everything he had.

"May I ask you something?" he asked.

"Yes."

Cloud looked at Katya. He reached to his pocket and removed a small red leather box. Hand trembling, he put it on the table.

"Katya," he whispered. His eyes were red with emotion. "I love you more than any man has ever loved a woman. I would do anything for you. The thought of you being gone for a month causes me great pain, because I will miss you. But I am also deeply proud of you, and I wouldn't have it any other way."

Katya smiled. A small tear came to her right eye as she reached forward to touch the red box.

"Forgive me for my meandering words, but what I am about to say is the most important thing I will ever say."

Tears of emotion now trickled down Cloud's cheeks.

"Will you marry me, dear Katya?" he whispered, looking at her with naked vulnerability.

Katya opened the box. Inside was a stunning object: a magnificently large yellow diamond the size of a person's fingertip, set upon a platinum band scrolled in an antique design.

"It . . ." Katya started to speak, then went quiet. Her mouth opened in awe as she removed it from the box, and tears of happiness began to flow down her cheeks. "It's so beautiful."

Cloud slipped the ring over her left ring finger, then held her hand up, beneath the golden-hued light of the chandelier.

"It's from Siberia," he said.

She stared at it for several moments.

For Cloud, the moment was the most beautiful of his life, as he waited, doubt choking his heart.

"Yes," she whispered.

Later, after watching Katya pack for Saint Petersburg, after making love to her, after she had long since fallen asleep, Cloud arose from the bed. He wrapped himself in a silk bathrobe and walked soundlessly out of the bedroom and through the apartment. In the front hall, he stared for several moments at the cherry credenza, almost as if he was admiring it. He got to his knees. Reaching down, he felt the bulge of a gun taped to the bottom of the credenza. Slowly, he pulled the gun out: Stechkin APS with a black silencer threaded into the muzzle.

Cloud went to the apartment door and waited, leaning against the door, listening for more than a minute but hearing nothing. He raised the Stechkin with his left hand and trained it on the door. With his right hand, Cloud turned the doorknob, slowly, until it cracked open. He spied the guard to the left, seated on the floor, oblivious. Cloud pulled the door open, then triggered the suppressed Stechkin. The slug struck the burly Russian in the temple, spraying blood and skull down the hallway.

He heard movement down the hallway, around the corner, near the elevator, out of view. He dropped his left arm to his side, concealing the gun, then walked toward the elevator.

"Miss Basaeyev?" he heard from the second guard.

Cloud stepped around the corner and found the guard, who was standing near the wall. He smiled.

"Mr. Vargarin," he said. "Is everything all right?"

"No," said Cloud. "I can't sleep."

Cloud swung his arm up and fired. The slug ripped the guard before he could even comprehend what was happening, kicking him backward.

"You, however, don't seem to have that problem," added Cloud, making eye contact as the guard slid down the wall, clutching his chest, trying to say something.

Cloud took the elevator to the lobby. As the elevator came to a stop, he raised the weapon. The doors parted. Cloud stepped forward and started firing at the front desk, before he even had time to aim. His first two bullets missed, but it didn't matter; both guards were seated, legs up. They both reacted too late, reaching for their sidearms just as Cloud pelted them with slugs, hitting one man in the left eye and the other in the forehead, decorating the walls behind them in a riot of crimson, brains, and bone.

Cloud shuffled calmly to the front desk. One of the vodka bottles was sitting there, unopened. He picked it up, yanked the wax-covered cork from the top, and took several sizable gulps. He reached beneath the desk and found the entrance buzzer, hitting it, unlatching the front door to the building. A few seconds later, a small army of men swarmed in from the outside. Two were dressed in suits, like the guards at the front desk; two were in sweaters and slacks, similar to the men upstairs; and two wore one-piece dark green work suits, their hands already covered in purple rubber gloves. Each carried a large duffel bag, inside of which were body bags, industrial cleaning equipment, plaster, wood putty, and small jars of paint for fixing the walls.

The crew went to work, packing up the two corpses. Cloud took several more slugs of vodka.

"Are they in place, Leo?" asked Cloud, looking at one of the men in the cleaning suits.

"The team is in Saint Petersburg."

"And the backup?"

"Yes, Cloud. The backup. And the backup to the backup. The two women too. They are all highly skilled. The best that money can buy."

Cloud nodded. Saying nothing, he turned and walked to the elevator.

"If anything—"

"Nothing will happen to her," said Leo. "You have my word."

21

General Torey Krug was standing with five other men on the bridge of the USS *Donald Cook*, an Arleigh Burke–class guided missile destroyer. They were all looking at the same thing: an illuminated plasma screen tied in to various naval and land-based units. The screen looked like an air traffic control screen, though instead of tracking commercial airliners, this one displayed U.S. military assets, in real time, in the geographic area south of Spain. Krug and his senior officers were tied in to a gamut of teams, including two other Aegis destroyers, two submarines, UAV command centers, and on-the-dirt commanders, including members of SEAL Team 6, now in fastboats off the coast of Spain.

At that moment, those military assets were all doing the same thing: searching for a boat.

The focus was the crowded stretch of water between Spain and Morocco known as the Strait of Gibraltar. Twenty-two UAVs had been scrambled to the area. Gray Eagles, Raptors, and several other drones were flying in low-hover lines back and forth across the narrowest section of the waterway, between Tarifa, Spain, and Eddalya, Morocco, a nine-mile stretch of water Krug believed was the best opportunity to stop the rogue nuclear bomb before it got to open water and the relative freedom of the Atlantic Ocean.

The challenge for Krug and his team was multifaceted. They had only a vague description of the boat. That description, moreover, was of a type of vessel that was extremely common. Already, they'd pinpointed ten trawlers matching the description. They had no idea how fast it was moving. In addition, it was nighttime and, despite various thermal-sensitive cameras, it was difficult to see, and what they were able to see was starting to blend into a continuum.

With the help of the Spanish and Moroccan navies, along with local police forces, a small armada of speedboats patrolled the waters, looking for anything suspicious, their officers equipped with Geiger counters. Already, several boats had been boarded, without result.

Reflexively, Krug kept looking over at the line of clocks displaying time in various countries. It was five A.M. in Spain. Dawn was coming. On the one hand, the improved visibility would help. On the other, each passing hour diminished the chances of finding the boat.

A scratchy voice came over commo.

"General Krug, I'm putting up live video. This is UAV 16-Y. We have a report of a suspicious-looking ship close to the coast, near Nador, Morocco."

"Roger, Major," said Krug, scanning the plasma for the UAV, then reaching out and tapping a small icon. Suddenly, a grainy video started running on the plasma. It showed an empty stretch of water illuminated by the UAV's powerful spotlight. A boat came into view. It was a motorboat, approximately forty feet long, with three uniformed men aboard. A hundred yards past them was a dilapidated fishing scow, running lights on, listing in the water, seemingly adrift.

"Send them in," said Krug. "Keep the bird overhead."

Krug and his men watched as the motorboat from the Moroccan Navy pulled up alongside the trawler and tied off.

A Vietnamese flag was flying from the aft of the ship. Its name was painted on the stern: *BIỂN THIÊN CHÚA.*

Sea God.

Two of the officers scaled a steel ladder and climbed aboard. They moved to the wheelhouse, the image blurry but decent enough to capture their movement.

Each officer clutched a submachine gun as he moved. A short time later, the two gunmen emerged, shaking their heads, indicating they'd found nothing.

One of the men pointed at his helmet.

"Patch him into commo," said Krug, pointing to one of his staffers.

The plasma cut into two live feeds. One was the UAV feed, the other was from a camera mounted to the officer's helmet.

The officers charged belowdecks, down a badly lit set of steel stairs. They moved along a dark hallway, opening door after door, finding nothing. Then, near the front of the ship, one of the officers opened a door, revealing a horrible scene of carnage. The ground was littered with the corpses of fishermen. The floor was a miasma of blood.

The officers moved from corpse to corpse, searching for anyone still alive.

"In the corner," barked Krug, seeing a slight movement. "Get over there!"

One of the officers stepped to a man in the corner. He was a young Vietnamese man. His chest was covered in blood. His eyes were shut. The officer shook him, softly at first, then with force, trying to wake him. The man opened his eyes.

"Put it on speaker," said Krug to the officer.

The officer set his phone near the dying man's ear.

"*Những gì họ muốn?*" asked Krug.

What did they want?

The fisherman struggled to keep his eyes open.

"*Vật liệu nổ,*" he said, coughing.

"Explosives," Krug, translated. He turned back to the image of the dying man on the screen.

"*Bạn bị tấn công cách đây bao lâu?*"

When were you attacked?

"*Dêm qua,*" the Vietnamese man whispered.

"Last night," said Krug.

Krug looked at the map. He took a ruler and did a quick calculation, estimating the time it took the trawler to travel from Sevastopol to Nador, then measuring the time between Nador and the Strait of Gibraltar.

A dejected look appeared on his face. He glanced around the table.

"Get Brubaker on the line," said Krug. "Hector too. They're through the strait. They have open water to the U.S. East Coast."

22

Calibrisi, Polk, and a half dozen other senior-level intelligence officials stepped into what looked like a small movie theater, with luxurious, reclining leather chairs arrayed in three ascending rows before a 140-inch screen.

Already seated were six members of CIA paramilitary, the six men selected to go to Russia.

Three wore tactical gear. These were the commandos who would lead Phase Line One: John Dowling, Dave Tosatti, and Benoit Fitzgerald. The other three men were dressed in casual clothing. This was the Phase Line Two team, and included Dewey, Bond, and Joe Oliveri.

"Gentlemen, beginning approximately one week ago, signals intelligence indicated a dramatic increase in chatter across the terrorist complex concerning an impending high-target strike on the United States," said Polk. "They have a name for it: they're calling it 'nine/twelve.'"

The lights dimmed as the screen abruptly lit up with the only known images of Cloud they had: the Malnikov sketch, the night-club photo, and two photos showing him with Katya Basaeyev.

"His name is Cloud," said Polk, pointing at the screen. "It's an alias. He's a computer hacker. Up to a week ago, he acquired a medium-sized Soviet-era nuclear bomb, capable of wiping out an area the size of downtown Boston. We believe he placed the device on a ship at the port of Sevastopol on the coast of Ukraine, and that the ship is now headed for the United States."

The screen flashed a photo of a modern glass-and-steel building set on a green lawn.

"Early this morning, based on intelligence from NSA, we captured a scumbag and known Cloud associate named Al-Medi. Under interrogation, he coughed up where Cloud will be tomorrow evening. This is a dacha outside Moscow where he will be attending a dinner party. That's why you're here. Your job is to infiltrate the Russian theater and capture Cloud—alive."

Calibrisi turned and glanced at the photo of Cloud.

"As of right now, Cloud is the only person who knows where that ship is going. We need to find him."

Calibrisi was silent for a few moments, scanning the six commandos with his eyes.

"I like to think all CIA missions are important, and they are. But this one is quite obviously different. This was why you joined the military. This was why, forty years ago, I joined the military. It sounds like a cliché, but it happens to be true. Your country needs you right now. You're the difference between the peace and stability, the silence, the calm, that Americans have come to know, and a catastrophe of untold horror, a catastrophe that will destroy families, neighborhoods, a catastrophe that will scar America for generations to come."

Calibrisi turned to Polk.

"Mission architecture is still being designed," said Polk. "We need to get you guys moving. Dowling, Tosatti, Fitzgerald: there's a Black Hawk on the helipad. Wheels up in five. You'll receive instructions on your way to Frankfurt."

"Yes, sir."

"Bond, Oliveri, you two are to go to CMG and get wardrobed. Then you'll fly to Saint Petersburg."

Polk glanced at Bond, then Dewey.

"Dewey, Hector and I need to see you in the director's office."

23

DIRECTOR'S OFFICE
LANGLEY

Go ahead in, Dewey," said Lindsay, Hector Calibrisi's assistant. "They're expecting you."

He pushed in the thick glass door. He stepped inside the CIA director's expansive corner office, which looked out over a neatly manicured lawn and, behind it, a dense forest of sugar maples and birch trees rustling in the morning breeze. It was a bright, sunny summer day.

Calibrisi was standing behind a rectangular glass-and-steel desk, sleeves rolled up, top button unbuttoned, leaning forward, scanning a document.

Seated in front of Calibrisi's desk was a bald man in a suit, with horn-rimmed glasses: Bill Polk.

"What do you need?" asked Dewey.

Dewey was dressed in an orange T-shirt, khaki shorts, and flip-flops.

"We want to talk to you," said Polk.

"Sit down," said Calibrisi.

Dewey remained standing just inside the door.

"It's about Saint Petersburg," said Polk.

"Bill wants to take you off Saint Petersburg," said Calibrisi. "I'm on the fence."

Dewey nodded.

"What happened in Mexico?" asked Polk, shooting Dewey a cold stare.

Dewey stared back at Polk, in silence. His eyes moved over and met Calibrisi's.

Behind Calibrisi, on the credenza, was a silver-framed photograph of Jessica.

"I froze up," said Dewey. "It won't happen again."

From behind his tortoiseshell glasses, Polk's eyes darted to Calibrisi, who remained silent.

"If something goes wrong in Moscow," said Polk, "we're relying on this man to perform at a level that right now he's just not capable of."

"I'll be fine, Bill," said Dewey.

"He's on a team with one of our best agents," added Calibrisi. "Pete asked for him."

Polk shook his head, then turned to Dewey.

"You're a talented operator. But right now, you're damaged. You need to get your head back on straight, and a mission that could get very messy, very quickly, inside a dead zone, is not the place for mental therapy."

Dewey stared back at Polk, in silence, dumbfounded.

"You know what the Russians do when they capture a NOC?" asked Polk.

Polk looked back at Calibrisi. Calibrisi remained silent.

"Fine, I'll tell him. If Russia captures you downrange, inside their country, in the middle of an operation, you'll never step foot outside Russia for the rest of your life. *Never.* We will be unable to retrieve you. They'll wrench what information they can out of you. That'll take about a month, then you'll be shipped off to a gulag in the middle of Siberia, maybe Krasnokamensk, or even worse, one of the countless prisons that doesn't have a name, a territory somewhere with a number on it."

Dewey stared down at the rug.

"It gets better," continued Polk. "They'll put you to work in a uranium mine or they'll use you for drug trials. If they determine you're a flight risk, they'll just kill you."

Dewey's eyes found Calibrisi's. He was like a father to Dewey. He could see it in his eyes. Dewey watched as, almost unconsciously, Calibrisi's eyes moved away from him to the photo of Jessica.

"I'm taking you off the operation," said Calibrisi, breathing deeply. "I think Bill is right. I think you need a little more time."

Dewey felt a sharp kick to his stomach. He tried not to show any emotion. Only his hand betrayed him; it reached back and clutched the door handle, which he gripped tightly, trying to control his anger, frustration and, most of all, self-loathing. He knew they were right. He had only himself to blame.

"I understand," said Dewey. He turned to leave.

"One more thing," said Polk. "I'm placing you on a six-month internal administrative drop. You'll be paid. We'll call it a director's project. I want you to go out to the clinic in Sedona. I'm not going to send you back into the field until you pass a psychological evaluation from Dr. Goldston."

"You're not actually serious?" Dewey asked, incredulous.

"Yeah, I'm serious," said Polk. "I want you back, but you're not ready. You need some help to deal with this."

"You call this bringing me back into the fold?" asked Dewey, looking at Calibrisi. "Protecting me? Is this what you had planned all along?"

"No," said Calibrisi.

"I don't need a fucking doctor. I need a gun and a mission."

Calibrisi bit his lip.

"Go out to Andrews and get a jet," said Polk. "I'll have Mary make sure one of the Gulfstreams is ready when you get there."

Dewey nodded and pulled the door open. He turned one more time and looked at Calibrisi and Polk.

"Good luck with the operation."

24

LANGLEY

Dewey walked down the hallway toward the elevators, scanning each office, passing various members of Calibrisi's staff. Halfway down, he found an empty office. He looked up and down, then stepped inside. Dewey moved to the desk, quickly opening drawers until he found a set of car keys. He went back out, looking both ways, seeing no one.

Dewey took the elevator to the basement, entering the cloister of rooms that housed Special Operations Group. From his locker, he picked up his backpack, which contained his mission gear for Saint Petersburg.

He saw Bond, who was getting ready for the flight to Saint Petersburg.

"You coming?" asked Bond.

"No," said Dewey.

Bond stared at him for an extra second, a surprised look on his face.

"You had to tell the truth," said Dewey. "I would've done the same thing. Good luck over there. And thanks for asking for me."

* * *

Dewey exited CIA headquarters through the south entrance, approaching the massive parking lot on the opposite side of the building where his pickup truck was parked. He stood in the shadow of the alcove, watching for several minutes, waiting. Other than a few people coming and going to their cars, he saw nothing unusual. He took out a thermal optical scope and scanned the area near his truck. There were two trackers, one seated in a car two cars away, the other in a different car several rows back and to the left of his truck.

Bill's not fucking around.

Dewey took the set of stolen keys. He hit the Unlock button, but nothing happened. He stooped and moved along the edge of the first row of cars, banging his thumb at the button. Finally, he heard a dull click. Turning, he eyed the flashing lights of a minivan. He walked to it, climbed in, then drove slowly to the exit, studying the rearview mirror for the trackers.

He didn't know what to expect as he handed his ID to a uniformed guard at the exit, but it didn't matter; he didn't have a choice.

The guard swiped it, then handed it back.

Suddenly, in the rearview mirror, Dewey eyed movement. One of the cars pulled out. It was soon followed by the other.

"Officer, can I ask you a question?" asked Dewey.

"Sure."

"If I saw a guy drinking in his car just now—"

"Drinking what?"

"It looked like a bottle of Jack Daniel's," said Dewey. "I don't mean to be a tattletale, but I'd hate to have an Agency employee get a DUI or God forbid hurt someone. That's the kind of publicity we could do without."

"I couldn't agree more," said the officer, waving Dewey through.

Dewey pulled through the gates of the CIA, watching in his mirror as the guard stepped out of the booth along with two other guards. All three held their hands up, stopping the car. Dewey registered blond hair, sunglasses, a mustache, and a frustrated punch against the steering wheel as he sped left onto Colonial Farm Road.

The trackers would expect him to take one of two busy routes out of the area, Dolley Madison Boulevard or the Georgetown Pike.

At the end of Colonial Farm Road, he went straight, passing signs that said THE POTOMAC SCHOOL, driving up through the verdant grass lawns that formed the campus. As he drove, he reached into the backpack and removed his SOG Escape Knife. He parked the minivan in a row of cars near the school, climbed out, and looked for the oldest car he could find, a red Dodge Charger. He smashed the hilt of the knife against the back window, then popped the lock and climbed in the front seat. Working quickly, he tore the plastic cover off the steering column, then found the harness connector and, inside it, a bundle of wires. He separated the battery, ignition, and starter wires from the bundle, then connected the ignition wire to the battery wire, twisting them together. Last, he touched the starter wire to the other wires. The engine rumbled to life. Dewey cranked the steering wheel hard in both directions, breaking the steering lock. Within two minutes, he was on the Beltway, heading north.

Dewey felt a sense of warmth as he escaped his CIA followers. A sense of mission, almost primal. The feeling he had was like a fever, a compulsion: he had to go to Russia. Perhaps he'd only observe the operation from afar, but he could never live with himself if he sat on the sidelines while America was attacked.

He drove north on 95, staring at the endless monotony of cars in both directions, keeping an eye out for trackers.

Polk thought he was burned out and scared. Dewey didn't blame him for thinking that. Nor did he blame Calibrisi for removing him from the operation.

Dewey hadn't been able to protect Jessica. He thought by hunting down her killers—by getting revenge—he would be able to heal his wounds. But revenge was a temporary tonic at best. What Dewey sought was redemption. It wouldn't come by running away, or lying on a couch somewhere. Redemption meant fighting for those he loved and for the country he loved. But to do it, he would need to get to Russia. And right now, there was no way he could get on a plane without being snared at the first TSA checkpoint he hit. He needed help.

At a gas station outside Philadelphia, Dewey purchased a disposable international cell phone. He dialed as he steered the car back onto 95 North.

"Yes," came a German accent. "Who is this? It's four thirty in the morning."

"Hi, Rolf," said Dewey.

25

Dewey Andreas," said Borchardt, almost spitting the words out. "The last time I saw you, you were about to hit my head with the butt of your gun."

"That's weird," said Dewey. "Last time I saw you, you were unconscious and your head was bleeding."

Rolf Borchardt was the most powerful arms dealer in the world. From his London headquarters, he was involved in arms deals all over the world, with virtually every government. He bought and sold weapons, weapons systems, ammunition, and information. He dealt with democracies and with dictators. He even dealt with terrorists. It was the sale of information that had brought Dewey and Borchardt together. Borchardt had sold a photograph of Dewey to Aswan Fortuna. Borchardt had also betrayed Dewey to Chinese Intelligence, though Dewey had anticipated it.

Yet despite his perfidy, Borchardt had also helped Dewey on numerous occasions. It was a complicated relationship. Dewey could have killed Borchardt many times but had chosen not to. Borchardt possessed a unique set of tools that could occasionally be very helpful.

"I still have a scar," said Borchardt.

"I bet it makes you look tough," said Dewey.

Borchardt laughed.

"That Dewey sense of humor," he said. "You missed your calling. You should've been a stand-up comedian."

"Thanks."

"I heard you were on some sort of . . . hiatus?" observed Borchardt. "Word on the street is you have psychological issues. PTSD. Is that true?"

"Yep," said Dewey. "I've gone batshit crazy. Which is why I need your help."

"My help? I thought you didn't trust me."

"I don't. But I don't have any other option."

"What do you need?"

"A ride."

"Where?"

"Russia."

"It's a big country."

"Saint Petersburg. It needs to be off grid, with a clean insertion and no facial recognition appliances. I also need some weapons."

"Why not hop aboard an Air America flight out of Andrews?" asked Borchardt, referring to the CIA's fleet of jets.

"Let's just say no one reserved me a seat."

"Interesting. The plot thickens. How much time do I have?"

"I get to JFK in two hours."

There was a long pause.

"Fine," said Borchardt. "The plane will be waiting at the private terminal. Look for Carlyle Aviation. It will be a red-and-black Gulfstream 100. Please don't kill anyone on board or, for that matter, throw any coffee cups. It's a brand-new plane."

"I'll be on my best behavior."

"There is a price," added Borchardt.

"I figured that. What is it?"

"I want to know why you need to get to Russia so urgently."

"You know I can't talk about it."

"Perhaps I can be of help," said Borchardt. "I have many friends in Russia."

"I'm sure you do," said Dewey. "Probably a real hip crowd. But I think I've got it covered."

"You don't seem to understand," said Borchardt. "I want to know what's happening. That's the price. Either tell me or find another way to Russia."

Dewey shook his head.

"You're a fucking asshole, Rolf," said Dewey. He hit Mute, pretending to hang up on Borchardt.

"Dewey?" asked Borchardt. "Calling me names will get you nowhere."

Dewey remained silent, listening.

"Dewey?" said Borchardt after a few moments. "Did you hang up? Dewey? Son of a bitch. If you're listening, fine, you don't have to tell me."

Dewey unmuted it.

"Hi, Rolf. Glad we worked that out."

"You really are a manipulative bastard," said Borchardt.

"Flattery will get you nowhere," said Dewey. "Oh, one more thing."

"What?"

"Promise you won't tell anyone?"

"What is it?"

"Promise?"

"Fine."

"Say it. Say 'I promise.'"

"I promise," snapped Borchardt.

"I need a ticket to the ballet."

26

REKI FONTANKI
SAINT PETERSBURG

A warm wind off the Baltic Sea rustled the leaves of the ancient white birches that lined Griboyedov Canal. It was Saturday night in the oldest, most historic, and prettiest of Russian cities. Saint Petersburg twinkled in pockets of orange and yellow as cars moved quickly along the crowded streets, and people walked, laughing, some already inebriated, toward cocktails and parties and dinners, to meet friends and family and lovers.

The temperature was in the midseventies, the air dry. It was the nicest evening of the summer. A festive glow charged the night, from golden-hued windows of crowded restaurants, from gaslit lampposts radiating honey orange flames at street corners. It all pushed out against the Russian darkness. There was a sense of giddiness about Saint Petersburg this night, a devil-may-care attitude, anything goes.

Danger.

A dark red Mercedes limousine cruised slowly down Reki Fontanki Avenue. It stopped near the corner.

Fifty feet away, a tall man in jeans and a tan leather Belstaff motorcycle jacket stood alone on Nevsky Prospekt Bridge. He leaned against a waist-high granite abutment, looking down into the black water of the canal, deep in thought.

He was tall, at least six-four, but he loomed larger. He had the beginnings of a thick beard and mustache. His brown hair was long, parted in the middle, but unruly and unkempt, hiding the big man's rugged good looks.

The man didn't seem to notice the red Mercedes limousine that had just pulled up near the corner. But he had. He knew that inside were two agents; Joe Oliveri, a commando from Special Operations Group, and Pete Bond, from Political Activities Division.

The man's demeanor was aloof, standoffish, taciturn. To anyone passing by, the message was clear: *Leave me the fuck alone.*

Had someone been able to look into his eyes, he would have found little except for a suggestion of loneliness, a hint of anger, and above all else a blank aspect. Most would mistake that for coldness, but those few with a certain type of experience would recognize it for the danger that lurked within.

He lifted a pack of Davidoff cigarettes from his coat pocket, removed one, then flicked a lighter and sent a small flame into the air. He took a long drag, exhaled, glanced at his watch, then looked across the canal at the red marble pilasters of Mariinsky Theatre.

The grand front entrance was alight as well-heeled Russians mingled outside. It was intermission of the Kirov Ballet's *Swan Lake*, starring Russia's most famous ballerina, Katya Basaeyev.

"Hi, guys, I apologize for the wait."

In the man's ear, affixed to a minuscule thread of tape, a two-way communications device the size of a Tic Tac connected him to a windowless conference room in Langley.

"We're waiting for sign-off from the White House, but I need to get you briefed right now. We don't have a lot of time."

The voice was that of Bill Polk, director of National Clandestine Services at the Central Intelligence Agency.

"We're in pursuit of a Russian," continued Polk. "He's a computer hacker known as Cloud. He's also a terrorist. A few days ago, Cloud purchased a nuclear device and that device is now on its way to the United States of America. It's big enough to do a lot of damage—a lot more than the one we dropped on Hiroshima. This may be the only shot we have at capturing this guy before it's too late. Each of you was handpicked for this mission. We need flawless execution in the kill zone."

The man on the bridge took a drag on his cigarette and stared down at the water as he registered the words in his ear.

"This is a two-phase line operation involving surgical penetration into Russia," said Polk, "so we need to be extra fucking careful. Our comrades in Red Square would not be happy if they knew we were trespassing."

The man on the bridge put a hand in his pocket, as if by reflex, making sure it was still there: weapon.

Know where your weapon is at all times.

"Phase Line One, Moscow, has the lead," Polk continued. "The team consists of three commandos, who right now are thirty-five thousand feet above Ukraine headed for the Russian border. Johnny, you guys good to go?"

"Yeah, Bill, we're good."

The voice was Dowling's, lead commando of the first phase line, Moscow, the front edge of the operation.

"Fifty miles inside Russia, you three say good-bye to your British Airways flight and perform a high-altitude high-opening parachute landing at a dacha outside Moscow. According to our intelligence, Cloud is attending a dinner party. You guys will grab him and move to a safe house about a mile away. We will interrogate him there. I repeat, this will all go down in-theater."

"Why?" asked Dowling.

"We can't risk anything going sideways during a border cross."

"Yes, sir."

"Mission video will start running when you're airborne," said

Polk. "You'll get to see the landing zone along with a few more photos NSA was able to dig up."

The man in Saint Petersburg remained quiet. He unzipped his leather coat. Beneath, he wore a red T-shirt with a faded Boston Bruins logo on it.

"Phase Line Two, Saint Petersburg, should already be active," continued Polk. "Pete, you two there?"

"All set here," said Bond from the red Mercedes.

"Saint Petersburg is our insurance policy," said Polk. "Hopefully it's unnecessary. Cloud's girlfriend is in the city. She's a ballerina named Katya Basaeyev. If everything goes smoothly in Moscow, we'll leave her alone. But if something goes sideways at the dacha, we're going to exfiltrate her. We will grab her when she leaves the theater. This is important. We don't know where she's staying or what kind of manpower she'll have around her. We need to take her off the street and get her to water. SEAL Team 6 is already in the harbor. SDV will take her to the USS *Hartford* a few miles off the coast. We'll bring her out of the country and see what she knows. But that's only if Moscow doesn't go as planned. Got it, guys?"

SDV stood for SEAL Delivery Vehicle, a small, nearly silent submarine used to ferry SEALs deep into enemy territory, just below the water's surface.

"Affirmative," said Bond.

"Can you give us any more background on Cloud?" asked Dowling from the plane.

"I told you what we know," answered Polk. "This guy's a ghost. Virtually unknown. Chief, you got anything more?"

"Yes," said Calibrisi, joining the briefing. "There's a rumor he helped disrupt air traffic control systems on nine/eleven."

"What's ROE?" Dowling asked, referring to the rules of engagement that would govern their use of deadly force during the mission.

"There are none," said Polk. "But remember, we need Cloud

alive. Try not to harm anyone else, but if you have to, your weapons and ammo are Russian and they're sanitized."

"How many are we expecting?"

"We don't know."

"What if he's not there, sir?"

"Go to your standard protocols. Everything you need—cash, ID, visa, et cetera—is at Moscow Central Station. Split up and move out of the country."

"Roger that, sir."

"By the way," Polk said, "the dacha is going to be well guarded. Expect ex-operators, Alpha Group, Vityaz, Spetsnaz. You know the type. Russians are assholes to begin with, but I'd expect these guys to be particularly ornery, especially when they comprehend you're operational."

The man on the bridge had listened to the entire CIA briefing, remaining quiet. He studied the Mariinsky Theatre, then glanced to his right, making sure no one was near him. He took a final drag on the cigarette, then flicked it into the air. He watched as the ember somersaulted through the sky and then hit the water.

Dewey wasn't supposed to be here. Not in Saint Petersburg. Not in Russia. Certainly not listening in on a live CIA OP briefing. He was supposed to be in Arizona, at the CIA's Sedona Clinic, a highly secure mountainside lair where operators with mental problems were sent to try to bring them back to reality. PTSD was the primary condition the doctors at Sedona treated. Dewey already knew he had it. It wasn't the first time either. By his reckoning, Jessica's murder, in front of him, had caused his fourth bout with the condition.

But Dewey also knew that sitting on a leather couch for six months would make him even crazier. He knew how to deal with PTSD. It wasn't the clinical way to do it, but Dewey had forged his own unique approach. Bottle it up. Put it in a box. Bury it. Then forget about it. Cut off the memory that sent you reeling. Cut it off and kill it. Like burning down a forest, the process of eradicating his memories left him a colder, harder, meaner man. But it was the only way Dewey could go on.

He felt a hard lump pressing against his torso: Colt M1911A1 .45-caliber semiauto, eight-inch Osprey suppressor threaded to the muzzle, a strip of black hockey tape wrapped around the grip.

It had been sixteen hours since Calibrisi took him off the operation. He'd flown to Russia on a private jet, courtesy of Rolf Borchardt. He wasn't sure why he'd come. He'd been kicked to the curb and he should've been pissed. And he was, but at himself. At his self-indulgence, self-pity. Most of all, his weakness.

Dewey told himself he was there for redemption. But even that wasn't true. Deep down, Dewey knew the real reason. He had nowhere else to go. He had nothing else.

He zipped up his coat and walked toward the theater. A slightly shit-eating grin crossed his lips. They'd neglected to ask for his mission gear back, including the earbud, which now allowed him to eavesdrop on the operation. If Calibrisi or Polk knew he was listening in, he'd be disavowed forever.

"Fuck 'em," said Dewey.

27

MISSION THEATER TARGA
LANGLEY

The mood inside the high-ceilinged, low-lit amphitheater was tense, even electric, despite the hush that kept the windowless CIA mission theater quiet.

Polk glanced at a large clock on the wall. He muted communications with the two phase line teams. He looked to his right at a man leaning against the wall, arms crossed, tie loosened, a mop of black hair combed haphazardly back: Hector Calibrisi, the director of the Central Intelligence Agency.

Two lines of desks were arrayed in front of the screens, staffed by technical managers who were there to feed the screens with whatever inputs the operation commander requested.

A dozen men and women stood along the back wall or else were seated. These were the various operations officers, collection management officers, staff operations officers, and targeting officers, there to answer questions that arose during the OP.

All attention, including Polk's, was trained on a pair of large, brightly lit plasma screens on the front wall that were tracking the operation.

Polk moved toward the screens and put his hand on the shoulder of one of the analysts seated below it.

"Where's the plane?" Polk asked.

The analyst, Jerry Lesesne, hit a few keystrokes. The left screen lit up. It displayed, in bright blue, a map of Ukraine extending east into Russia. An orange pictograph representing British Airways flight 319 flashed at the center of the screen.

"We cross the Russian border in four minutes, sir," answered Lesesne.

Polk looked at Calibrisi.

"We're about to penetrate Russian airspace, Chief," he said, a concerned look on his face. "We need sign-off from the president."

Calibrisi glanced at his cell. On the screen was a live CNN broadcast of President J. P. Dellenbaugh, standing on a stage, delivering a speech. He had the volume turned down. He had been following it to see when Dellenbaugh would be finished. He looked back at Polk.

"What's the call?" asked Polk.

28

President J. P. Dellenbaugh smiled and waved for the fourth time as the large crowd gathered at the Detroit Convention Center continued to applaud. Finally, he held up a hand. He waited until the crowd became quiet.

"It's great to be home," said Dellenbaugh. Cheers arose again, but he quickly quelled them by holding up his hand. "But I want to say something serious now. I want to make a wish, and I want you all to help me."

At the corner of his eye, Dellenbaugh saw his aide, Holden Weese, holding up four fingers. He'd been doing so for the past few minutes.

The CIA director is on the line, and it's urgent.

"No, it's not for world peace, or economic prosperity, or anything like that," he continued.

Dellenbaugh was dressed in jeans and a polo shirt. His thick mane of black hair was combed neatly back. The president, who was raised in a two-bedroom Cape by a father and mother who both spent their entire careers working the General Motors assembly line down the road, had a common touch that came from the simple fact that he'd been there too. That touch was like gasoline on a fire, and the blue-collar crowd—mostly Democrats—was going nuts. Dellenbaugh was American—blue-collar American—and the annual summer meeting of the Teamsters Union let him know that despite the fact that he was a Republican, to a lunch-pail-carrying man and woman they recognized J. P. Dellenbaugh was one of them.

The crowd was hushed and quiet as they awaited Dellenbaugh's final words.

"I want the Red Wings to win the damn cup next year!"

The crowd erupted into wild cheers.

"Thank you, Big D!" said Dellenbaugh. "Man, I love coming home. You all have a great Fourth, now, will ya."

Dellenbaugh waved one more time to the enormous crowd, then walked offstage.

Once on the other side of the curtain, he charged behind Weese in a hard run down the hallway. He came to a secure holding room, guarded by plainclothes Secret Service agents armed with machine guns and carbines.

Inside, a military attaché in a dark blue Navy uniform held a small black briefcase, extended from which was a portable phone. Near the attaché, two men held what looked like small antennae. These were jamming devices, which would scramble the president's conversation to anyone trying to eavesdrop, beyond the significant layers of encryption the signal would already have.

Dellenbaugh grabbed the phone.

"Go, Hector," he said.

"Sorry for the interruption, Mr. President," said Calibrisi. "We've found Cloud. I need your authority to send in some men and try to capture him. It's a tight time frame. He's supposed to be at a dinner party in less than an hour outside of Moscow, and it might be our only opportunity to capture him."

"What about the boat?" asked the president.

"It's through the Strait of Gibraltar, sir. They have open ocean to the East Coast."

"Are we working with Russia?"

"Negative."

"Why not?"

Pause.

"Enough said. What's the ask, Hector?"

"Emergency Priority," said Calibrisi, "hostile exfiltration. We have a team in the air right now. The intelligence is hours old. It's likely to be the last time we have a shot at him."

In the special language reserved for covert operations, what Calibrisi wanted was full presidential authority to infiltrate a sovereign, unfriendly nation, in this case Russia, with members of a U.S. paramilitary team. Emergency Priority was the highest classification level possible for an operation. It meant the mission was critical to the national security of the United States of America. In turn, the granting of such authority gave the front-line operators a clear message, tantamount to license to kill. In his three years running the CIA, it was the first time Calibrisi had ever made such a request.

"How many people will be with him?" asked the president.

"We don't know. It's a dinner party. We're not going to go out of our way to hurt any of them, sir."

Dellenbaugh glanced to a photo on the wall, an antique black-and-white shot of Henry Ford holding a champagne bottle as he prepared to smash it on a car.

"Do it," said Dellenbaugh. "Tell the attorney general to get me some paper. Be careful in there, Hector."

29

In a small, pitch-black compartment near the back of British Airways flight 319, three men sat pressed tightly together. Each was dressed in black tactical military gear, with special polypropylene underwear for warmth. On each man's head was an airtight helmet with tubes that led to small oxygen tanks strapped to their chests. On each man's back was a high-altitude high-opening (HAHO) parachute, designed to enable the three Special Operations Group commandos to fly a very long distance using GPS and trade winds. HAHO jumps were invented to enable special forces to penetrate deep inside enemy territory.

"Phase line in twenty, guys," said Polk.

Between each commando's legs was a ruck bag containing weapons and ammunition: each had a PP-2000 submachine gun, an ASh-12.7 urban assault rifle, and an OTs-33 Pernach machine pistol. All the guns were suppressed. Fitzgerald's ruck held a Vintorez "Thread Cutter" sniper rifle. On the right leg, each man had an extra pistol. For Dowling, a GSh-18 compact 9mm. Tosatti and Fitzgerald each carried a P-96 compact 9mm.

The three commandos had been seated for three hours in a secret hold at the back of the twice-daily British Airways Frankfurt-to-Moscow flight. Their presence was unknown to anyone on board the plane, including the pilots. The small compartment was one of England's best-kept secrets, designed by SAS, Britain's elite Special Air Service, in conjunction with British Airways, under a top secret directive in 2001.

HAHOs had an effective range of only seventy-five miles, and that was with a strong tailwind. Moscow was two hundred miles from the nearest border. This meant that urgent missions inside Moscow were effectively rendered impossible unless manpower was already in-theater, on the ground. The small compartment enabled England and, by extension, the United States to drop operators deep into the heart of Moscow on an ad hoc basis, using the cloaking anonymity of a commercial airliner.

"Roger, Langley," said Dowling.

Dowling, the senior Special Operations Group commander, clicked a ceramic switch in his glove, allowing him to talk on a closed circuit with Tosatti and Fitzgerald.

The outer glass of the commandos' helmets was dark blue, making it impossible to see inside the helmets. Dowling saw the reflection of his own helmet and that was all.

"Check your packs," said Dowling, referring to their parachutes.

"I'm good," said Fitzgerald.

Tosatti nodded, indicating he was good to go.

"I fuckin' hate HAHOs," said Tosatti.

Dowling glanced at his watch. "We're within five."

Fitzgerald reached out and hit a yellow switch on the wall. Over the next two minutes, the compartment depressurized, reaching equilibrium with the outside air. The temperature dropped to fifty degrees below zero.

"Fuck, it's cold," said Fitzgerald.

"Just got the upload," said Dowling.

Dowling clicked the ceramic. The interior upper right-hand corner of all three helmet glasses lit up. Displayed was a black-and-white photograph showing a man, young, perhaps in his twenties, and an Afro of dirty blond hair. He had a long, thin, gaunt face.

The three men studied the photo for several seconds, then Dowling clicked the ceramic again.

The photo of the target was replaced by a video, which began to play. It showed a three-dimensional topographical map, with the plane represented on the left-hand side and the word *Moscow* in bright red on the right.

A monotone prerecorded female voice accompanied the video.

"Gentlemen, you are now in Russian airspace, headed for a dacha outside of Moscow."

The video sharpened to a side view of the plane. Three small figures—representing the commandos—emerged from the back of the plane. Their parachutes opened. A red arrow appeared. It cast a line from the commandos toward Moscow, then dipped and stopped on a bright green X. This was the flight path of the HAHO team.

"From the drop point, you will travel eighty-one miles northeast," continued the woman. "Landing zone is a dacha located in a town called Rublevka, near Moscow. Target is believed on premises."

A series of photos replaced the video. They showed a modern glass-and-steel house from a variety of angles. The house was large, spreading in an L shape atop a bluff. Manicured lawns in every direction surrounded the stunning glass structure.

"There will be security as well as a hard infrared cordon. You must land on the property."

A drawing of the property plot lines appeared. The lot was long and thin.

"Property is two acres but is not wide. You will grab Target, then improvise vehicle transportation and move to safe house B."

The video showed the topo map again. A red arrow simulating the vehicle moved down the long driveway. The map scaled wider and a red X appeared, representing the safe house.

"From safe house B, you will be extracted by a team from SRR. Good luck, gentlemen."

The video froze and went off. A dull flashing red light pulsated, then went green.

"We're going airborne," said Dowling. "Follow my strobe. See you on the ground."

Suddenly, a three-by-three-foot piece of steel on the fuselage of the plane moved down. The sky was eerily dark. Dowling leaned forward and jumped out. Tosatti, then Fitzgerald followed, leaping into the bitter cold, nearly oxygenless night air above Russia.

A moment later, the steel plate on the jumbo jet slid back into place and locked as the commandos disappeared.

30

The lobby of the Mariinsky Theatre was a soaring, four-story atrium of vermillion marble, granite pilasters, and statues of Russia's greatest dancers. The building was packed. The mood was celebratory.

A massive photograph of a woman's face, more than three stories high, hung on the wall above the entrance. Her face was dark, Middle Eastern, and exceptionally beautiful. Her bright blue eyes resembled sapphires. Her hair was jet-black. A mysterious smile was on her face.

Across the bottom of the photo, in bold black cursive: *Katya.*

Dewey walked toward the entrance to the main seating area of the theater. The theater's ceilings and walls were adorned with magnificent murals, landscape scenes painted in towering gold frames. The walls were stacked with private boxes filled with Russians dressed in formal attire. The mood was festive, excited, yet hushed. There was a palpable sense of impending adventure. It was all related to Katya.

Dewey went to the bar and bought a whiskey. He'd never been to the ballet before.

A woman approached. Her long blond hair seemed to shimmer like water beneath the chandelier light, and her green eyes, as they scanned Dewey, widened, brightened, as she smiled at him with confidence. She leaned toward Dewey and said something in Russian.

"I'm sorry," Dewey responded, "I don't speak Russian."

"I asked," the woman said in English, with a pretty, soft Russian accent, "what do you think of the ballet?"

"I just got here."

"Oh, that's too bad. It was very beautiful."

The woman was in her late twenties. Perhaps a model. The eyes of at least half a dozen men were on her. Yet the only person she could look at was the tall American.

"I'm Petra," she said, extending her hand. "Are you from the United States?"

"Yes."

"Would you like to have a drink afterward?"

"Thank you," said Dewey, "but I have plans."

Backstage at the Mariinsky, the dressing room was crowded. Dozens of dancers sat before mirror after mirror, staring at themselves, some smoking. The mood would have surprised most of the audience. It was raucous, with laughter filling the room, the occasional shout.

A half dozen makeup artists moved from dancer to dancer, re-applying powder and rouge for the final act.

"Ten minutes," shouted one of the assistant directors.

A dimly lit corridor behind the cast dressing room had walls adorned with framed photographs of famous Russian dancers. Many were old, black and white, with a thin layer of dust.

The photo before the door at the end of the hallway was in color and showed Katya Basaeyev.

A hulking man with black hair and a mustache stood outside the door, guarding it.

Inside the private dressing room, a long table was cluttered with bouquets of freshly cut flowers, bottles of champagne, and unopened gifts. On the wall, dozens of articles had been cut out of newspapers and magazines, all of them showing photos of Katya and heralding her performances in Saint Petersburg over the last two weeks.

Katya was alone. She stood, naked, before an oval full-length mirror.

She shook a glass bottle filled with baby powder into the palm of her hand, then lightly dusted it into her brown skin, so that in the heat of the stage lights and the exertion of the dancing, perspiration would not make her slip in the hands of one of the male dancers there to catch her.

Katya pulled on her outfit for the final act.

A soft knock came at the door.

"A package, Katya," came the voice of the bodyguard.

She said nothing.

She sat down before another mirror.

"Katya?"

"Who is it from?"

"He didn't say."

She shut her eyes and steeled herself. She stood and walked to the door, opening it slightly, and took the package.

The box was blue and was tied with white string. She sat down at her makeup table. She put the box on her lap, then yanked up on the string. She lifted the top of the box.

Inside the box was another, this one long and thin, wrapped in light blue velvet. She opened it. Inside was a stunning diamond necklace. It was anchored by a large yellow diamond. Katya pulled the necklace out and stared at it for several moments. She fastened it around her neck and admired it in the mirror.

A small note was stuck inside the box: *I love you, my future wife.*

A light tap came at the door.

"Two minutes, Katya."

Katya let the note fall from her fingers onto the floor. She took

182

the necklace off and placed it on the dressing table, then walked to the door.

"Yes," she said, barely above a whisper.

The door opened. Katya walked past the bodyguard, saying nothing, as the lights from the theater flickered in the distance.

Bond was seated in the backseat of the red Mercedes limousine, at that moment parked one block behind the Mariinsky Theatre. He was dressed in a linen suit, his hair combed back and dyed black, a white handkerchief puffed out of his breast pocket. The get-up was perhaps overkill, but Bond had spent two years in Saint Petersburg working for the CIA, and Polk didn't want to take the risk he might be spotted in the middle of a live operation.

In the front seat, Joe Oliveri had on a chauffeur's outfit. A former member of Force Recon, the Marines' elite deep reconnaissance unit, Oliveri was considered one of Langley's top "escape men," the agent charged in a dead zone operation with getting whatever individual or materials that needed to be extracted to a drop zone.

Tonight, if necessary, it would be Bond's job to grab Katya, and Oliveri's job to get her to water, where Navy SEALs lurked eighteen feet beneath the waterline.

Bond stared out the side window, in silence, as Oliveri tapped his fingers absentmindedly on the steering wheel.

"Your kid make that baseball team he was trying out for?" asked Bond.

"Yeah," said Oliveri, keeping his eyes trained on the street ahead. "First game's tomorrow night. Hopefully, this'll all be cake and I'll be there to watch it."

An usher led Dewey to the orchestra section near the front of the theater. His seat was on the aisle.

Dewey sat next to a woman and her young daughter. Dewey smiled at the girl, who smiled back. Her mother stared at him.

His eyes scanned the left and right balcony boxes. Seated inside were elegant-looking groups of Russians dressed in evening attire. The men varied in their looks, but each woman seemed like she could have been on the cover of a magazine.

The curtain opened to the final act of *Swan Lake*.

At Katya's entrance, a wave of hushed whispers swept the theater. Even Dewey leaned forward in his seat to get a better view.

The ballerina wore a simple white dress, which looked as if it had been painted onto her body. Her black hair was braided on top of her head and shone like leather beneath the stage lights. Her skin was dark and dusted with white makeup. She stood motionless near the back of the stage. She looked sad, vulnerable, even frail. And then her head moved slightly around and her gaze ripped across the crowd.

In an instant, what had appeared weak and frightened disappeared. Her beauty shot from the back of the stage like lightning across the night sky. Audience members reflexively moved forward in their seats. The little girl two seats away from Dewey shot her arm out, pointing. The electricity in the audience was palpable, and Katya had yet to take even her first step.

And then she began her run. She moved as if galloping on the wind, toward the center of the stage, then leapt high into the air as gasps arose above the orchestra music. She seemed to hold the air for an inhuman amount of time. The lights from behind her brightened, creating a dark silhouette of her soaring figure, like a five-pointed star crossing in front of the sun. Then, just when it seemed like she would remain airborne forever, she fell like a bird in flight, a bird who's been shot, falling helplessly, listlessly, freely, with no concern for her own safety. She fell as if she had just died midflight. Inches from striking the stage, a male dancer caught Katya, swinging her up and around, landing her on one toe, upon which she proceeded to pirouette like a top, until at long last she stopped, raised her arm triumphantly above her head, then looked out across the audience. A mysterious smile creased her lips. The entire audience erupted in a cacophony of cheering as it stood up to welcome its beloved Katya.

She seemed to glow, to radiate, and yet her eyes met no one's, not the dancer who caught her, not the audience that screamed in delight. She was in a different world altogether.

Dewey had never seen anything like it. He'd never seen a woman with such beauty as the woman standing on the stage before him.

Finally, the clapping ended, and the audience sat down to watch the rest of the performance.

In Dewey's ear, the monotone Philadelphia accent of Bill Polk brought him back into focus.

"We have sign-off from the president," said Polk. "Get in and get it done."

31

Sascha nodded at Cloud. Cloud stepped around the table and walked to him.

Sascha was a gifted programmer in his own right and was the one who was able to penetrate Alexei Malnikov's father's VPN, thus enabling Cloud to anonymously set up the elder Malnikov.

"What is it?" asked Cloud.

"The trapdoor into Langley," said Sascha. "It was there an hour ago. Now I can't find it."

In hacker lingo, a trapdoor was a hole in the security of a system deliberately left in place by a designer or maintainer.

Cloud moved quickly to Sascha's workstation.

"The operation will be going live," said Cloud.

"I know."

Cloud leaned over and took Sascha's keyboard, then started typing.

"Yes, I see," said Cloud, typing away. "They found the evidence of one of the times we were inside. Like finding the ashes after a fire. But they're not anywhere near the matches or the gasoline."

Cloud gently pushed Sascha aside and took over his computer. He typed a URL into the Web browser. This was the enterprise server in Elektrostal. He went through a series of consecutive screens, entering passwords, each time pressing his right thumb to the computer's thumbprint detection security device. At the fifth screen, a large cartoonish-looking eye suddenly appeared. Cloud leaned forward, staring into the laptop's built-in camera. After a few moments, a soft musical note chimed, the eye disappeared, and the words came onto the screen.

Welcome home, Cloud

Cloud had succeeded in hacking into the CIA but not by penetrating the Agency's computer networks. The odds of being able to pull off such a "front door" intrusion were not only remote, but they would also likely lead the CIA back to him. The CIA was in large part a closed-loop user of the Internet and originator of signals intelligence. This meant there were few exposed access points into the Agency. Those that did exist were for noncore, "passive" activities, such as human resources and public relations. Those access points which allowed the general public into the CIA through e-mail or a Web browser were heavily monitored and delivered visitors to a digital world entirely separate from the important stuff, such as communications regarding live operations.

The coming attack on America was based on surprise. Although he'd stolen hundreds of millions of dollars from U.S. corporations over the years, he'd never targeted any entity that would consider it a national security violation.

Instead, Cloud had taken a more prosaic approach to worming his way into Langley. He'd written a virus, which, once downloaded, was innocuous and invisible to its users. It sat there in silence and was impossible to detect. The virus was activated by a user mistakenly clicking a link in an e-mail. Once activated, the virus targeted music files, striking the digital code of a song as it was being downloaded. Then the virus waited. For most people, it waited forever and did nothing.

The virus was designed to awaken if it was ever placed on the CIA mainframe. Then it would go live and create a single trapdoor for Cloud.

Cloud had designed the virus, then blanketed a fifty-mile radius around Langley. The goal was to have a vital employee of the Agency, with access to the closed-loop mainframe, break Agency rules and share music on a home computer with a work computer.

It took almost a year of daily e-mails, often in the millions, but eventually it happened. A young case officer had synced his iPhone with his computer at Langley. Within forty-five seconds of the insertion of the USB, Cloud, on the other side of the world, had a ladder into Langley's closed-loop mainframe.

He was soon staring at a live video, the same video being watched inside the CIA mission theater.

He typed in silence for more than five minutes, then, with a dramatic flair, hit Enter.

Sascha smiled at him.

"A lucky break," said Cloud, pretending to be modest.

In a dialogue box at the lower left of his screen, the audio communications passing between Langley and the Agency's operators in the field were transcribed in real time:

1842	phase line in twenty guys
1843	this is immediate priority
1844	its vital we capture this guy
1845	use all means necessary to bring him in alive
1846	roger langley
1847	we have sign off from the president
1848	get in and get it done

Cloud sat back, crossed his arms, and stared at the screen.

"It is beginning," he said.

32

Dowling looked down at the earth. He clicked the ceramic switch in his glove. A digital altimeter in his helmet read:

32,880.7FT
006.23M

He glanced at the mission clock, dimly illuminated in orange in the upper left corner of his glass:

1:06:32

They had a little over an hour to go. He clicked again. A digital chart appeared, displaying Dowling's position relative to where, based on trade winds and other metrics, he should have been.

The data that informed the charts was compiled and processed in real time, based on readings in their helmets, in communication with an Air Force AWACS that was flying, at that moment, above the Caspian Sea.

Dowling clicked again and looked at yet another chart, which showed the three commandos, along with data as to how much height and distance separated them.

All three commandos had spent years learning how to do high-altitude high-opening (HAHO) and high-altitude low-opening (HALO) parachute jumps as Rangers. HAHOs were exhausting. The adjustments to the steering and altitude of the canopy, based upon a constant cycling through the charts, was endless. It required intense concentration, especially for the lead navigator, who, in this case, was Dowling. A strobe on his helmet enabled the other men to follow.

The sky above Russia was clear and warm as the commando team descended. The lights of the Moscow suburbs were like a carpet beneath them—yellow, increasingly bright—as they came concentrically closer to the dacha.

They reached the outskirts of Rublevka while still a thousand feet in the air. A green light appeared in the upper corner of Dowling's helmet along with a steady beeping noise. They were directly above the dacha.

The lights of the modern glass mansion were visible below.

The three Americans circled concentrically above, funneling rapidly lower as if swirling down a drain. The lights grew brighter. Dowling triggered the ceramic in his glove several times until the plot lines of the property appeared in bright orange. He made out a line of cars in the driveway. He soared left, over the house, moving out over a dark lawn. Night-vision goggles lit up the ground in light green. Several large pine trees lay dead ahead, then a field, and he dropped rapidly now. When his feet were about to hit the ground, he adjusted his chute, letting it pull him up one last time, softening the coming landing.

A minute later, Fitzgerald landed a few feet away, then Tosatti.

The team removed their parachutes, flying packs, tanks, helmets, and anything else that was unnecessary, packing it in black nylon bags they'd carried in. All three men were sweating profusely, from the heated flight suit and from the adrenaline now coursing through them like fire.

Each commando was dressed the same: black synthetic wicking shirt and pants, light duty combat boots.

Fitzgerald pulled a thermal night scope from a pocket and scanned the property for any signs of life.

Dowling activated his commo.

"We're clear," he said.

The dacha's lights cast bright warm blue and orange light into the night sky.

Each commando unzipped his weapons ruck, removed the submachine gun and slammed in a mag. Tosatti reached for his ASh-12.7 urban combat assault rifle, equipped with night optics and an undermounted grenade launcher. Dowling and Fitzgerald followed suit, slamming in mags, then grabbed several extras and attached them to their belts.

Each man grabbed OTs-33 Pernach 9×18 machine pistols, tucking them into the holster on his belt.

They moved across the field, dead silent as they traversed toward the dacha.

Dowling reached to his wrist and triggered his commo, then whispered.

"Phase Line One, on the ground."

Fitzgerald, Tosatti, and Dowling made a wide arc across the back of the dacha, stalking along behind a canopy of birch trees, in the darkness and shadows.

The house was long and rectangular, a modern box made almost entirely of glass. It stood elevated on steel stilts. Every room in the house was alight.

On the south side of the dacha, set back from the window, was a room full of people seated around a dining table.

Tosatti snapped his fingers, pointing to the driveway.

Dowling moved his night goggles down over his eyes. Two men were standing in the driveway, between two automobiles. One was smoking. Both men clutched submachine guns, trained at the ground.

Dowling nodded to Tosatti and Fitzgerald.

"On my go," he whispered. "I got the Ivan in back; Dave, take the other guy. Fitz, backup."

"Roger that," whispered Fitzgerald.

All three men raised their carbines. Dowling aimed at the guard facing them, while Tosatti aimed at the man whose back was turned.

Fitzgerald was backup. He aimed at a spot between the two men and would fire only if Dowling or Tosatti missed.

"On three," whispered Dowling. "One, two . . ."

Tosatti and Dowling triggered their guns. Dowling struck his man above his right ear, dropping him, and in the same instant Tosatti took the top of the other guard's head clean off.

They moved quietly, at the back edge of the lawn, scanning the terrain for other guards. They didn't see any.

Dowling took out a high-powered monocular. He studied the dining room. He counted fourteen people, all seated around a large oval table, eating dinner. The low din of conversation could be heard.

He scanned each person at the table. Seated at the right corner was a tall man with an Afro of curly blond hair. Dowling couldn't see his face, but the hair was unmistakable.

"I got him," he whispered. "Front right."

Fitzgerald moved toward the driveway. He pulled a preset explosive from his weapons belt as he moved: C-4 with a remote detonator. He came to the side of the house, then stalked, pressed against the wall, toward the front. As he was about to move around the corner to the front door, headlights abruptly punctured the darkness.

The vehicle barreled through the entrance to the driveway. It was out of Fitzgerald's sight line, but he would soon be illuminated by the lights.

Dowling whistled as Tosatti raised his carbine and trained it on the approaching vehicle. Fitzgerald turned. Dowling signaled to hold his position.

A Range Rover sped up the driveway and parked just feet from the dead bodyguards. The lights on the SUV went out. A woman in a white summer dress stepped out from the driver's door. She had yet to see the dead men on the ground, but she would soon step on them.

Tosatti trained the sniper rifle on the woman, who was now walking toward the front door. The dead guards lay directly in her path. He aimed, then waited.

"Sorry, honey," he whispered.

He fired. The bullet ripped the woman's chest, exploding crimson across her white dress, pummeling her backward. She tumbled to the ground.

Dowling nodded to Fitzgerald.

Fitzgerald moved to the front entrance. The objective was simple: create a diversion at the front of the house, then enter through the back. The explosives were the diversion. He attached a small brick of C-4 to the door, just below the doorknob, then moved silently along the side of the dacha back to Dowling and Tosatti.

Dowling led the team to the back of the glass house. A swimming pool twinkled in muted subwater green light. Behind it was a stairway that led up to a deck. The three men moved rapidly now, around the side of the pool, then climbed the stairs. They stopped outside the door.

Dowling ran his hand along the perimeter of the door, studying it. He took a preset explosive from his belt, smaller than the one on the front door. He stuck it beneath the doorknob.

The men stood as silent and still as statues. Their faces were black with paint. They were as dark, as invisible as phantoms, shielded by the door.

"I have the target," Dowling whispered to Tosatti and Fitzgerald.

Tosatti and Fitzgerald nodded.

Dowling reached to his wrist, pressing commo.

"We're at the line," he whispered, telling Langley they were about to strike.

* * *

Polk stood, arms crossed, directly in front of the plasma, watching a live video feed picked up from a satellite ten miles in the sky. Calibrisi was a foot behind him, to the right. Every man and woman in the room stared at the screen.

Polk was calm. He'd stood in the exact same place many times, directing literally hundreds of operations in his storied career. He looked like a high school English teacher, with horn-rimmed glasses, a striped rep tie, a pink button-down shirt, khakis, a needlepoint belt, and penny loafers. He was considered the best in-mission commander in the history of NCS.

The thermal prints of Dowling, Tosatti, and Fitzgerald were grouped to the left of the screen, like apparitions, huddled three abreast just outside the door.

On the other side of the door, a few feet away from the waiting commandos, the thermal outlines of the dinner party attendees were similarly visible, their movements well defined if hazy: seven bodies on each side of a table, facing each other; the rapid movements of arms, heads, shoulders in the act of enjoying dinner.

One of the people stood up and started to move toward the front entrance.

Polk glanced at Calibrisi, then reached for commo.

"You have someone moving to the door," said Polk. "Get in there."

At the back door to the dacha, Dowling registered Polk's words, glanced at Fitzgerald, who clutched the detonator for the C-4 at the front door, then nodded.

Fitzgerald flipped the metal cap off the detonator and thumbed a small red button. A loud boom abruptly ripped the air on the other side of the house, shaking the ground.

The steel front door was blown like a cannonball into the dacha, down the front hallway. It slammed headlong into a woman on her way to the bathroom, hitting her at more than fifty miles per hour and killing her instantly.

Steel and concrete from above the door were kicked thirty feet in the air. Red and orange flames burst in a fiery cloud. Glass shattered throughout the front wing of the dacha as shouting, then screams, suddenly filled the air.

The wailing of the house alarm came next, a high-pitched siren that only added to the sense of chaos.

Then, at the seeming height of pandemonium, Dowling hit the button on his detonator.

A small-burst explosion ripped the back door off its hinges. It tumbled down onto the deck.

The screams from inside the dacha were louder now.

Tosatti held a small pocket mirror in the door opening, looking for security or signs of weapons. All he could see, through the smoke-clogged air, was the dining room table filled with people, all of whom had raised their hands.

Tosatti signaled the other two commandos, then moved.

They charged through the smoke into the dining room. Tosatti surged first into the room, ASh-12.7 in his grip, suppressor jutting out, then moved right. Fitzgerald was half a step behind him, also armed with an ASh-12.7, and he leapt to the left, surrounding the table.

Then Dowling ran in, moving to the man at the corner of the table as Tosatti and Fitzgerald provided cover.

The thirteen remaining guests stared at the three commandos. Several of the women were crying, hysterical with fear.

"*Comment?*" asked one of the men, his accent unmistakably French.

Dowling stepped in front of the man known to them only as Cloud. But instead of a young man, the one who now cowered before Dowling's suppressor was much older. He stared blankly at Dowling, his arms raised.

"Where is he?" asked Dowling.

"Who?" he whispered.

"Cloud."

The man was silent. His hands, raised above his head, trembled in fear.

Fitzgerald moved his wrist to his mouth and triggered commo.

"Bill, we've got a situation," he said.

But before Polk could respond, another explosion shattered the night.

It started beneath the dacha—ten pounds of Semtex, igniting in a ferocious moment that no one had time to flee. The detonation ripped the floor, scorching white-hot fire and heat through the dacha like a grenade through a sand castle. The three commandos, along with the guests, were vaporized before they could even register the white heat as it engulfed them. The glass-and-concrete house shattered in a wild, violent moment. Steel beams went flying as the force of the explosion spread sideways and up, in one horrendous sequence. The dacha burst into a mushroom cloud of flames and heat, white, red, and orange, against the desolate Russian night.

33

At CIA headquarters, Polk, Calibrisi, and the rest of the NCS mission team watched as the plasma screen abruptly lit up. A bright orange ball of flames appeared at the center of the screen, then spread out in a concentric wave, overtaking and obliterating everything in frenzied light.

Gasps came from the back of the conference room.

Calibrisi lurched toward the screen.

"*Mother of God,*" he whispered.

"*Johnny!*" barked Polk.

But there was no answer.

Polk watched the screen for a few more moments as it billowed in a silent blur of white light, then disappeared into black. A pained look crossed his normally placid demeanor. He shut his eyes for a moment, swallowed, then stepped to the left, in front of the other plasma screen. On it, the red Mercedes was visible from the sky above, the size of a toy Matchbox car.

Polk looked at Calibrisi, then triggered commo: "Saint Petersburg," said Polk calmly, "you're live."

Polk glanced at Calibrisi, who held up his left index finger, signaling Polk to tell the agents an additional piece of information.

Polk hit commo again: "This is an Emergency Priority operation. I repeat, *Emergency Priority*. Safeties off. Take whatever action is required to get the girl."

34

ELEKTROSTAL

Cloud read the words and shook his head in disbelief.

119   saint petersburg youre live

"*Idioty*," he muttered.

"What is it?" Sascha asked.

"They still don't know we're watching."

He had on black Oliver Peoples sunglasses. Behind the lenses, his eyes were rimmed with red from a lack of sleep. He wore black leather pants, Saint Laurent boots, and a sleeveless green T-shirt. His shoulders and arms were visible. His muscles were sinewy, brown, sensual, muscles that aren't made by weights or steroids but rather a gift from his lineage. He was extremely thin.

His feet were up on the table. He stared lackadaisically at the screen, reading live transcription of the CIA operation.

120   this is an emergency priority operation

121   i repeat emergency priority

122   safeties off

123   take whatever action is required to get the girl

Most people looking at a Monet in a museum see the subject of the painting: flowers, colors, water. A rare few, other masters, see beyond the visual representation. They see brushstrokes. They see layers beneath the colors that are at the surface. They see empty spaces. Motivation and passion, deceit and laziness. They see the way the painting itself is done, from the very kernel of the idea through the painting's completion. They understand it in a way only Monet himself could have intended.

Cloud was able to see the Internet in much the same way.

124	roger that bill
125	were moving into position
126	well recon as soon as she exits the theater
127	what about the seals

If the Internet was, for most, a vehicle for connection, information, and entertainment, for Cloud this surface level of interaction was a thin veneer, indeed, even a distraction. A girl might go online to read about her friends on Facebook, to buy a new shirt from J.Crew, to text her boyfriend. Each separate action involved the movement of data—numbers, letters, and symbols—over wire, or glass fiber, or through the air. These numbers, letters, and symbols, traveling at almost impossibly fast speeds, invisible to the human eye, carried, in their precise structure, very specific commands. That shirt, in this size, send to this address. In exchange for sending it to me, take money from this bank account or that credit card. They were commands. At any given moment, the world was being shaped, changed, and lived in an almost infinitely large architecture of precise data commands and responses. It was where the world was lived. The girl saw only that which had been framed and presented. She saw the results of the commands—pictures of her friends on Facebook, photos of blouses on J. Crew, letters on a screen from her boyfriend. What Cloud saw were the textual representations of the commands and their movement. Within, he saw the human beings behind such commands. He looked for the human brushstrokes, for here is where he could find the human frailties and mistakes that enabled him to penetrate.

The pathways of the data, the multilayered connections across public networks—where it moved, how it moved—were, to Cloud, like the brushstrokes upon the canvas. This was where he lived.

128	roger langley this is jacobsson over
129	are you guys ready
130	roger that
131	were in harbor awaiting your recon
132	repeat we are in harbor and good to go over
133	thank you lieutenant
134	ill hit you up when were go out

Cloud's cell phone started beeping. He looked at the number, took a deep breath, then smiled.

"How was tonight's performance?" he asked.

"Wonderful. Thank you for the necklace."

"You're welcome, Katya. Do you like it?"

"Do I like it? It's magnificent. It must have cost a fortune."

"It is only the beginning of the gifts I will give to you, my love."

"I have to go," she said. "There are fans. I must sign autographs. I will call you from the hotel."

"Please—" he began, then stopped.

Cloud stared at the computer screen. He felt his heart race.

He wanted to warn her: *Don't go near the red Mercedes.*

"Please what?" she asked.

"Please be careful," he whispered.

35

REKI FONTANKI
SAINT PETERSBURG

Bond nodded to Oliveri in the rearview mirror. Oliveri put the Mercedes in gear and started driving.

"Roger that, Bill," said Bond, tapping his earbud. "We're moving into position. We'll attempt recon as soon as she exits the theater. What about the SEALs?"

A voice came on commo for the first time; the reception was poor and he sounded like he was in a tunnel.

"Roger, Langley, this is Jacobsson, over."

"Are you guys ready?"

The Mercedes moved quickly down Reki Fontanki toward the queue of limousines waiting at the stage door entrance. Oliveri, in the passenger seat, steered it up alongside a pair of young blond women strolling down a cobblestone sidewalk in tight, nearly see-through white dresses, one of them holding an unlit cigarette, laughing as they held arms. The gorgeous, slightly inebriated girls were giggling and singing a song.

"Roger that," said Jacobsson. "We're in harbor awaiting your recon. Repeat we are in harbor and good to go. Over."

"Thank you, Lieutenant. I'll hit you up when we're go. Out."

As the Mercedes pulled into position at the rear of the line of limousines, the girl on the left caught a heel of her stiletto sandals on a cobblestone and stumbled awkwardly. She fell sideways as her companion tried to catch her, but it was too late. She toppled to the ground, her head slamming into the curb as she tumbled awkwardly into the street in front of the moving Mercedes. She let out a terrified scream as the car was about to run her over.

Oliveri slammed on the brakes, which screeched, drawing the attention of everyone within a hundred feet. The vehicle came to an abrupt halt, its right front tire stopping just as it pressed into her arm, bumping the girl, but ever so slightly.

Bond tapped his ear, shutting off commo.

"*Goddammit!*" he snapped. "Watch where the fuck you're going."

"I didn't see her."

Several pedestrians flocked to the girl.

"We need to clean this up," said Bond, frustration in his voice.

"Just get her out of the way before the woman gets here."

Bond opened the rear door and climbed out.

"*Ne dvigayutsya,*" Bond yelled, his Russian flawless. "*My dolzhny ubedit'sya, chto ona ne ranen prezhde chem my pereydem yeye.*"

Don't move. We must make sure she's not injured before we move her.

Bond jogged toward the girl, his eyes shooting right, to the stage entrance, knowing that Katya would soon be coming out.

Several pedestrians were also coming over, seeing if the girl was all right. Her friend had her arm and was trying to lift her up from the street.

Bond glanced at Oliveri, still seated behind the steering wheel. Oliveri shook his head; he didn't like the distraction.

Suddenly, a commotion ensued behind Bond. The excited yells and giggles of young girls came from the theater's side door. Bond turned. Katya had emerged and was now signing autographs and talking with her fans.

He needed to clean up the situation, and he needed to do it quickly.

Bond pushed aside a man who was helping the injured girl to her feet. Bond knelt just above her. She looked up at him and their eyes met. Her head had a gash and was bleeding badly. Bond took the handkerchief from his pocket and placed it against the wound.

"Thank you, sir," she whispered in Russian.

"Are you okay?" Bond asked.

"I feel dizzy," she whispered.

"I am so sorry," said Bond. "My driver was not paying attention adequately enough."

"It was my fault," she said, slurring her words.

"Nonsense. I will pay for everything."

"May we have a ride to the hospital?" asked her friend. "I don't know if she can walk right now."

Bond lifted the girl up by her right arm.

"Sir, may we have a ride to the hospital?" she asked again.

Bond glanced to the stage entrance. Katya was nearly to the end of the line of autograph seekers. He looked back at Oliveri. He was making a circular motion with his right index finger: *hurry the hell up.*

"No," said Bond shifting and looking again at Katya, "I'm sorry. We will pay for a taxi to take you, but I have a situation that requires my immediate attention."

For the first time, Bond saw bodyguards flanking Katya's path— one behind her, one in front. The eyes of the guard in front swept across the sidewalk, back and forth, looking for signs of danger. When he saw Bond, his eyes focused in on him.

Bond glanced to Oliveri, signaling him with his right hand.

She has two bodyguards. Get the weapons ready and prepare to engage.

Inside the Mercedes, Oliveri stared out the passenger window, beyond Bond and the two girls, watching as Katya signed a last autograph, then turned and waved with both arms at the crowd, which were still gathered.

"Come on, Pete," he whispered.

Beneath a blanket, Oliveri's right hand clutched the grip of a Desert Tactical SRS-A1, a compact, concealable sniper rifle with a thick black suppressor screwed into its muzzle and a scope mounted on top. Without looking, he flipped the safety off.

Oliveri knew full well the danger of having witnesses. But it was unavoidable now.

Emergency Priority.

A higher mission classification did not exist. It meant the achievement of the mission's objective was paramount to U.S. national security.

Leaving the blanket on top, Oliveri raised the SRS-A1 until the snub-nose of the suppressor was pressed against the passenger-side window. He leaned down and, without looking through the scope, targeted the guard in front of Katya. He placed his finger on the trigger, preparing to fire.

Suddenly, the back door to the limousine opened.

"Here's my card," said Bond, handing the girl an alias business card. "I will pay for everything. You need to go to the hospital."

Bond leaned forward, into the limousine, a desperate look in his eyes. He registered Oliveri, then the blanket raised across the front seat. He glanced right; Katya was now less than fifty feet from the line of limousines, walking quickly.

Bond ducked and leapt into the car, yanking the door shut.

But as the steel of the door was about to close tight, both of the injured girl's hands shot out and stopped it. Bond turned, a stunned look in his eyes as the girl ripped the door open.

"*No!*" he screamed, just as the second girl blew into the cigarette that had been dangling, unlit, from her lips. A small dart the size of a toothpick tore from the cigarette and stuck into the center of Bond's right eyeball. His hand shot up to his eye as he groaned in pain.

The injured girl ducked and stabbed forward into the back of the limousine, followed by the other girl, whose hand reached inside her leather purse as she too infiltrated the vehicle.

Oliveri, hearing Bond's groan, turned from the sight of Katya and the two bodyguards. Before his head could swivel all the way around, the girl tore a Glock 18C from her bag. Oliveri's eyes went wide as he registered the weapon. He ducked and tried to reach for the door, but he was too late. She pumped the trigger. A dull thud sounded as a slug tore through the back of the leather seat, then ripped into Oliveri's neck. A mist of blood splattered the steering wheel and windshield as Oliveri was kicked forward. His hand shot to his neck as he tried to scream. She fired again, this time sending the bullet into his head.

Bond, the lead CIA agent, watched helplessly as Oliveri was killed. He tried to reach for his commo to say something, but he was paralyzed by the highly lethal, fast-acting toxin in the dart. A few seconds later, unable to breathe, he suffocated to death.

The injured girl climbed over the front seat, pulling Oliveri to the passenger side, pushing his large frame to the floor.

She took up position behind the wheel, then turned.

"I can't see," she said in Russian, her view blocked by the blood on the windshield.

The girl in the backseat handed her a handkerchief to wipe what she could from the windshield. A few moments later, she hit the gas pedal and tore down Reki Fontanki.

36

*T*his is an Emergency Priority operation. I repeat, Emergency Priority. Safeties off. Take whatever action is required to get the girl."

Dewey heard Polk's frantic words just as the final act was nearing its conclusion.

Moscow had gone bad.

Stay calm.

He stood and moved quickly up the aisle, then heard Bond's voice over commo for the first time.

"Roger that, Bill. We're moving into position. We'll recon as soon as she exits the theater. What about the SEALs?"

Dewey exited through the front of the Mariinsky Theatre as, behind him, clapping and cheering echoed out from the theater.

"Roger, Langley, this is Jacobsson, over."

"Are you guys ready?"

Dewey went left, then crossed the side street. A few yards from the corner was a bench, part of it occupied by an elderly couple. Dewey walked past it and stood near the corner. From there, he could see down the street that ran alongside the theater. Halfway down the block, outside the private stage entrance, a line of limousines and dark sedans idled, their drivers waiting for VIPs and cast members to emerge. Dewey registered the red Mercedes a block behind the line of cars, but moving quickly.

"Roger that. We're in harbor awaiting your recon. Repeat we are in harbor and good to go. Over."

Dewey felt his heart racing. He reached inside his coat, feeling the butt of his gun, as he scanned the mission zone.

It was coming again. The paralysis he'd first experienced in Mexico was coming. He felt it. He tried to think of Tino and the fight at Whitewater, but all he could see now was his shaking hand, frozen in the Iguala air, unable to open the door to the cocaine refinery.

Dewey watched the Mercedes move toward the line of limousines outside the theater. He heard the old woman on the bench say something. He turned. The couple was holding hands, sitting peacefully, enjoying the warm evening. He watched them for an extra moment, trying to calm down and get his emotions under control.

Polk had been right all along. He did need help. He would've frozen up all over again.

At that moment, Dewey felt self-loathing as powerful and intense as he'd ever felt it before. Everything he'd built, all of it, was gone.

"Thank you, Lieutenant. I'll hit you up when we're go. Out."

Dewey walked away from the scene. He drifted toward the canal, lost in thought, lost in self-hatred and doubt, a knot in his stomach. He would drop his gun in the canal, along with his earbud. He'd find a hotel room, then the bar at the hotel, and drink until he couldn't walk, or think. Tomorrow, he'd fly home. He'd return to Castine. He'd stay there until he was an old man.

He turned back one last time to the theater. At the stage entrance, a commotion ensued as Katya emerged. Autograph seekers, mostly squealing teenage girls, cheered and yelled at the sight of the famous ballerina.

His eyes scanned the scene. He watched as the red Mercedes moved into position.

Then his eyes were drawn to two girls walking along the sidewalk, weaving slightly, alongside the Mercedes. Dewey looked away, thinking nothing of it.

Dewey was now at the granite abutment above the canal. He put his hand inside his jacket and found the butt of his gun. He pulled it out, clutching it by the barrel. He started to toss the gun into the dark water below . . .

The sound of screeching brakes was like a thunder clap, interrupting the quiet scene, awakening Dewey from his reverie.

He held on to the gun, then turned.

A cold chill emanated from the base of Dewey's spine. He stared in disbelief, then horror, as one of the girls pretended to slip and fall, then was struck by the limo.

"Decoy," he said.

Bond and Oliveri were in extreme danger.

Dewey moved back toward the theater. A crowd was gathering to help the fallen girl. Bond stepped out of the limo and went to her, helping her up, then led her to the back door of the limo.

Dewey crossed the street, watching as the girl reached her hands out then leapt inside the Mercedes. Just as he reached the corner, blood splashed across the inside of the windshield, like mud being thrown.

A few seconds later, the limo lurched away.

Bond and Oliveri were dead.

The Mercedes sped away from the theater. It was now coming directly toward where Dewey stood. The limo was accelerating, fleeing from the scene. As it was about to reach him, Dewey stepped into the street, directly into the path of oncoming vehicle. His hand was already inside his coat, clutching the hockey-tape-covered grip of his .45-caliber Colt M1911A1. The driver didn't slow down or attempt to avoid him.

Just before the Mercedes struck him, Dewey tore the gun out, then leaned right. He fired the gun as fast as his finger could pump the trigger. Unmuted gunfire punctuated an already chaotic scene.

Slug after slug tore into the driver's-side window, shattering glass, then the girl's head; her skull bounced sharply to the right as a bullet entered just above her ear. Blood sprayed across the front seat as the limo sped by, tires screeching, the back bumper barely missing Dewey as it swerved wildly. A moment later, it veered right and smashed violently into a parked delivery truck.

The first sirens sounded from a few blocks away.

Dewey charged, coming from behind the limo, knowing the other assassin would be targeting him. In stride, sprinting for the cover of the back bumper, Dewey popped the mag from his Colt and slammed a new one in just as bullets from the other assassin shattered the back window. Dewey lurched left, then dived to the street just as bullets pocked the tar near his feet.

He scrambled beneath the rear bumper, sheltered from the fusillade. He crawled beneath the car, feeling the heat of the engine on his back. He crawled until he reached the front passenger-side door. He came out from under the limo, then quietly opened the door as sirens grew louder. Two dead bodies, Oliveri and one of the girls, along with a sniper rifle, and a riot of blood covering the white leather seat. He climbed into the vehicle, skulking soundlessly, weapon out, trained at the back of the girl's head, loaded, safety off, and cocked to fire.

Through a crack in the seat, Dewey could see the other girl's back as she searched frantically for him behind the limo.

Dewey leapt over the seat and smashed the girl's head down. With his other hand, he grabbed her shooting arm, yanking it behind her back.

"Where's Katya going?"

"I don't know."

Dewey yanked up her arm until it snapped. She screamed.

The sirens were within a block now.

"Where is Katya going?"

Dewey grabbed the woman's neck and choked her. Her face turned bright red.

210

"Tell me where and I won't kill you."

"Four . . ." she groaned.

"Seasons?"

She nodded.

Dewey snapped the girl's neck, ripped open the door, and jumped out, running, just as police cruisers descended upon the scene.

He disappeared down Reki Fontanki, blending into the crowds that were fleeing the crash scene, making their way toward Nevsky Prospekt.

37

The mission room was eerily quiet. No one said a word. Calibrisi stood silently at the front of the room, arms crossed. Like everyone else, he looked dazed.

On the screen, a live satellite feed showed the chaos in Saint Petersburg in real time, captured by a thermal-imaging camera that was attached to a satellite several miles above the earth's surface. The images were very grainy and rendered in black, white, and gray. Heat from human beings and cars showed up as white exoskeletons. People looked like ghosts. But after observing hundreds of night operations, everyone inside the command center knew how to parse the video and, for the most part, understood what was happening.

They knew which vehicle the Mercedes was. They knew precisely where Bond and Oliveri were. They watched the collision with the girl, Bond's movement to her, then her intrusion into the Mercedes. The flash of the assassin's muzzle inside the vehicle looked like silent fireworks. They all watched as the thermal outlines of Bond and Oliveri went dim.

In less than fifteen minutes, the CIA had suffered its worst one-day casualty loss in the history of the Agency. Yet nobody was thinking about the loss of a group of operators. Rather, it was the human loss that hurt them all. Every person in the room knew the five dead agents.

It was Polk who brought everyone back. He stepped to the rear wall, where a whiteboard, unused in months or perhaps years, sat blank. He took a pen and started writing:

Cut all signals outside this room.
We are contaminated.

A case officer near the front of the room held his thumb up, indicating he understood the order. He typed furiously into his computer, then hit Enter.

"We are now a closed loop," he announced. "Targa is quarantined. All commo is off-line."

"Now play the video again," said Polk. "I want to watch from the moment the limo starts moving again."

The screen replayed the limo lurching away, fleeing the scene, the bodies of the two assassins white apparitions against the dark street. As the limo barreled down and was about to strike a pedestrian, Polk snapped his fingers.

"Freeze it there," he said. "Slow-frame it."

In painstakingly slow motion, the next few moments of the video played frame by frame. A pedestrian about to get run over. Stepping to the side to avoid the limo. Arm extending. The muzzle flash of automatic weapon fire outside the limo. The driver kicked violently to the right. The limo careening out of control and crashing. The gunman charging toward the back of the limo, disappearing underneath it, then reemerging at the passenger door, going inside, and killing the last remaining occupant of the limousine.

"What the hell just happened?" asked Calibrisi.

Polk turned to him.

"I don't know."

38

Dewey entered the lobby of the Four Seasons Lion Palace. His heart was thumping fast. It felt like it was in his throat.

Calm down.

The .45 was inside his jacket, and so was his hand, on the gun's grip, ready to swing it out at the smallest provocation.

The lobby's walls shimmered as light from the chandeliers refracted off walls and floors of polished marble. It was crowded: a couple on a sofa at the center of the lobby; three businessmen in suits to the left, talking loudly; a family of four, two adults and two girls, at the front desk checking in. Several uniformed bellmen stood nearby. Straight ahead, a tall woman was waiting behind the front desk. Dewey crossed the black-and-white-checked marble floor and approached her.

He needed time to think, to plan. Everything had backfired and was destroyed, and now he needed time to plan what would be a very ad hoc operation. *What just happened?*

"*Dobro pozhalovat'v Four Seasons—*"

"I don't speak Russian," Dewey interrupted quietly.

"My apologies," she said. "Welcome to the Four Seasons. How may I be of service to you?"

Dewey checked his watch. It was 9:45 P.M.

"I need a room," he said.

"Yes, of course," she said, typing into the computer. "A royal suite overlooking Saint Isaac's Cathedral? I'm afraid it's all we have left."

"That's fine."

He handed her an alias credit card tied to his CIA cover before he was taken off the operation. It would set off alarm bells back at Langley, but that didn't matter now. A moment later, after swiping it, she handed Dewey a small folder with keys.

"Is the restaurant still open?" he asked.

"Of course, Mr. Sullivan," she said, pointing to a door across the lobby. "The veal is excellent, by the way. Can I let the maître d' know you'll be coming?"

"Please," said Dewey. "A booth. Out of the way."

Dewey went to the lobby restroom. Looking for the first time at his coat, he saw a patch of blood streaking the sleeve. He wiped it off, washed his hands, then looked in the mirror. Other than a slight blush to his cheeks, he appeared calm, even normal. The area above his eye was healing. The remnant blackness had dissipated, though there was still enough to hint at the violence from which it had come.

Dewey stared into the mirror, trying to collect his thoughts, contemplating his next move. He pictured Dowling, one of the commandos who'd been on Phase Line One, Moscow. Dowling had saved Dewey's life in Portugal the year before. Now he was dead. Or maybe he wasn't. Maybe Cloud just wasn't at the dacha? Yet somehow Dewey felt a cold chill deep inside. It was in Polk's voice over commo. It had about it a hint of desperation.

It seemed clear to Dewey. The fact that Cloud knew about Saint Petersburg meant that he probably also knew about Moscow. He'd probably done the exact same thing: lured them in, then murdered them in cold blood.

It was obvious that Cloud had known about Saint Petersburg long before Bond and Oliveri stepped foot in-country. The girls were operatives, most likely government trained. The strike itself had been masterful. Bond and Oliveri had stepped right into a well-choreographed play.

"He ratfucked us," whispered Dewey, to no one.

How did Cloud know? That was the question. Had he been listening in? Watching? The only other explanation was that someone inside Langley had tipped him off; Dewey dismissed that possibility out of hand.

The hit on Pete and Joe had been architected. Like a play, it had its acts, its stars. If Dewey had an advantage, it was that he'd arrived in Saint Petersburg off the grid. He'd punctured the phase line midstream. The subterfuge with the stumbling girls was planned out, but their deaths were not, and now Dewey was inside, rewriting Cloud's play. Cloud thought the final curtain had been lowered, but Dewey had slipped beneath it.

Now he needed to act.

If Cloud didn't already know about the dead women, he would soon enough. When he did, he'd remove Katya from the city. Dewey needed to act quickly. He needed to find Katya and extract her before Cloud himself did it.

Suddenly, the restroom door opened and a tall man stepped in. Dewey turned. He was older, a businessman, and he nodded hello at Dewey. Dewey moved past him, heading for the restaurant.

The restaurant was softly lit, intimate, and warm, its walls a beautiful deep crimson, four crystal chandeliers hanging from a low, louvered ceiling decorated in ornately patterned green-and-white toile paper.

Dewey looked quickly about the room; most of the tables were occupied. A pretty red-haired hostess led him to a booth on the right. A minute later, a waiter approached and handed him a thick leatherbound menu across the table.

"*Chto-nibud' vypit', ser?*" he asked.

216

"I—"

"Something to drink, sir?"

"Whiskey, neat. Bourbon if you have it."

"Anything to eat?"

Dewey glanced around, trying to be calm.

"A steak, please. Rare. A bottle of wine, something red and expensive."

"Very good."

A small rectangle of high-backed red-leather booths framed half a dozen four-tops in the middle of the room. The lighting was dim.

A minute later, the waiter returned with a glass of bourbon.

Dewey took a large gulp and let it burn the back of his throat. He knew he shouldn't be drinking, but right now, his priority was calming his nerves.

He pulled out the disposable cell phone and punched in a six-digit number. It was a number that could be dialed from anywhere in the world. He hit Send. A half minute of silence followed, than it rang for several seconds, before being interrupted by a high-pitch monotone beeping noise. Dewey punched in a code. The soft, sultry voice of a woman came on the line.

"Name?"

"Andreas, Dewey."

"Flag?"

"NOC 2294-6."

"Go."

"Requesting encrypted bridge to NCS one, no commo. This needs to be routed over landline."

"Hold."

He listened to a series of clicks as his call was put through to Polk. It took almost two minutes for him to come on the line.

"Who is this?" asked Polk.

"It's Dewey."

There was a short pause.

"What the hell are you doing calling me through control?" asked Polk. "We're downrange here in the middle of an operation—"

"I'm in Saint Petersburg."

Polk was silent.

"Was that you?" he asked.

"Yes."

"Who were they?"

"I don't know," said Dewey. "It was a skill job. They're both dead. I did find out where Katya is."

"How did you get to Saint Petersburg?"

"It doesn't matter," said Dewey. "I'm here and I need direction."

There was a long silence.

"Bill?"

"What the fuck you are doing in Saint Petersburg is what I can't get over."

"Look, Bill," said Dewey, "I understand why you took me off the operation. The thing is, I'm not about to go lie on some fucking couch in Arizona while my country's under attack. This is what I was trained to do. Can you understand that?"

Polk was silent for several moments.

"Yeah, I can," he said. "Where are you?"

"I'm at the Four Seasons, where she's staying."

"What do you need?"

"An encrypted patch to whoever's running the SEAL team."

"Sure, let me take care of that."

"They had details of the operation," said Dewey.

"Langley is contaminated," said Polk. "Commo is shut down."

Dewey's eyes shot left. One of Katya's bodyguards entered the restaurant. He was big, at least six-four or -five. He had a military-style crew cut, wide-set eyes, and a thick forehead that protruded slightly. He walked bowlegged, arms out to the sides. He had on jeans with a gray sweater that hugged his chest, shoulders, and torso. He looked ex-military. An operator. He scanned the room, unsmiling.

"I gotta go," said Dewey.

"One more thing," said Polk.

The bodyguard's eyes roamed the restaurant, focusing first on the couples at the table in front of Dewey, a glance that lasted less than a second. Then he found Dewey. For several moments, the Russian stared across the dimly lit restaurant at him.

"What I warned you about before," said Polk.

"What?"

"You can't get captured, Dewey. You need to be on that SEAL Delivery Vehicle. I can't emphasize that enough."

"Don't worry," said Dewey, shifting uncomfortably under the watchful gaze of the Russian thug. "I'll be on it."

39

Roman, Katya's bodyguard, sat down at the table and took out his cell phone. He started typing:

Roman:	Possible situation
Cloud:	Explain
Roman:	CIA is here
Cloud:	Take photo

Roman stood and walked to the wall, out of the line of sight of the man. He took the cell and moved the very end of the wall, where the camera lens was, just past the ornate wooden pillar, and snapped several photos without looking. He examined the photos, finding one that caught the man as he sipped a drink. Roman texted it to Cloud.

He went back to the table, where Katya was eating.

"What were you doing?" she asked.

"Nothing," he said, placing his cell on the table as he awaited further instructions from Cloud.

40

ELEKTROSTAL

Cloud stared at the grainy photograph of the stranger in the restaurant. The restaurant was dark and the image was not good. He uploaded the photo into a facial recognition program. The computer screen scrolled rapidly through thousands of photos. After more than a minute, the words appeared:

No matches found

"Come here," he said.

Sascha walked from his computer and looked at the photo.

"Who is it?"

"I don't know. See if you can find anything at the hotel. A list of guests. We need to know more."

Sascha returned to his computer.

A news flash abruptly cut across one of Cloud's screens. It was a report from one of the Moscow television stations. At the bottom of the screen, the words:

LIVE—RUBLEVKA

Behind a news reporter, flames from the dacha lit up the distant sky. A police cordon was visible, as well as fire trucks, ambulances, and police cruisers.

Cloud stared, mesmerized, at the horrible scene he'd created. The faintest hint of sadness flashed across his eyes.

Then Sascha whistled. Cloud stood and moved quickly to him. A black-and-white photo was frozen on one of Sascha's screens. It was the man from the restaurant. The image was much crisper.

"Where did you get this?"

"I took it off the hotel security cameras," said Sascha.

He wore a light tan leather motorcycle jacket, BELSTAFF emblazoned across the chest. He had a mop of brown hair, parted down the middle, but roughly, as if by hand. The edges of his hair were dark with sweat. His hair went down past his ears, a slight, natural feather to it. He had a thick beard and mustache. He was handsome in a rugged way. He looked tough, even brutal, someone to be avoided. He was tan. His eyes revealed little; it was a blank expression, and yet there was no question. The way they looked forward into the camera, almost knowing the photo would be found and examined in the very manner it was being examined at this moment.

Cloud leaned closer, studying the photo. The jacket was unzipped. A thin strap was visible near the man's neck.

"Shoulder holster," said Cloud.

Sascha pointed at the man's arm. A large patch of dark covered the bottom inside section of the jacket, near the wrist. The hand was dark with blood.

"Who is he?"

"I don't know."

"Was there *any* intelligence involving a third man from the CIA?" asked Cloud.

"Nothing I could find," said Sascha. "After the explosion at the dacha, the feed went dark."

Cloud took over the keyboard and started typing.

"What are you doing?" asked Sascha.

"Running the photo against the GRU database," said Cloud, referring to Russia's foreign intelligence service. "There's a chance he's on their radar screen."

Cloud uploaded the photo of Dewey into the same facial recognition program. Again, the screen scrolled rapidly through thousands of photos. After half a minute, the screen froze. A photo appeared of a much younger individual, with short-cropped hair, standing on an airport tarmac. A large-caliber carbine was in his right hand, trained at the ground. He was walking point in front of a small entourage that included the former president of Afghanistan.

Cloud clicked the attached bio:

GRU CASE FILE 112-A-77
USA DIRECTORATE
SUBJECT: ANDREAS, DEWEY
INACTIVE FILE

STATISTICS:

Citizenship: USA
b. Castine, ME (c. 1973)
U.S. ARMY 1993–4
* US ARMY RANGERS 1994
    Winter School
    Rank #1 out of 188
*** 1st SFOD—DELTA FORCE

OPERATIONS (known):

  + Lisbon, POR: Jan–Mar 96 (mission unknown)

+ San Isidro de El General, COS: Oct 96–Jan 97: Anti-narcotic: NIC, COL, VEN

+ Munich, GER: April 97: Exfiltration Milos Abramovich (wanted by GUR-RUS) (mission success)

+ Buenos Aires, ARG: Sep–Dec 97: Anti-narcotic: ARG, COL, CHI, and BOL

+ Montreal, CAN: Jan 98: Assassination Milos Abramovich (mission success)

+ London, ENG: Apr 98: Assassination (attempted) Subhi al-Tufayli/Hezbollah (mission aborted)

+ Lisbon, POR: Mar 98: Assassination Frances Vibohr (Siemens VIP suspect in sale of TS info to SAU) (mission success)

+ Bali, IND: Aug 98: Assassination of Rumallah Khomeini (mission success)

NOTES:

ANDREAS is a Combat Applications Group (formerly Delta Force) officer with extensive international mission experience. GRU INTEL was asked to open a file on him following the death of LEONID PARSKY, GRU COMMANDER (1988–1997).

ANDREAS has executed at least three covert penetrations of Russia. The first (April 1997) was a fact-finding mission and field setting, in which ANDREAS spent four days in Moscow preparing various elements associated with his second penetration. ANDREAS's second visit was shorter, two days, and coincided with PARSKY's assassination (September 1997).

Though no evidence was found implicating ANDREAS in PARSKY's death, ANDREAS met with MILOS ABRAMOVICH during his first visit to Moscow. ABRAMOVICH, who was later found to be working for the CIA, was under a GRU Task Force Investigation, so ordered by PARSKY. It is GRU INTEL's assessment that the US Government had PARSKY killed in order to preserve ABRAMOVICH. ABRAMOVICH most likely provided ANDREAS with information enabling him to kill PARSKY.

ANDREAS's third infiltration took place in November 1997, in which ABRAMOVICH was successfully exfiltrated from the country in order to save his life. (In January 1998, ABRAMOVICH was subsequently killed in Montreal by ANDREAS for reasons unknown.)

ANDREAS is considered unusually dangerous, with Level 12 proficiency in all aspects of operations, including close quarters combat, face-to-face combat, firearms, explosives, cold weapons, transportation, and improvisation. He is trained in extreme condition field and wet work, and has seen multiple actions in hostile environments across the geopolitical theater.

JUL 2003: FILE DESIGNATED *INACTIVE*

Cloud and Sascha read the file in silence. Sascha furrowed his brow, then looked at Cloud with a concerned look.

Cloud picked up his cell phone and started typing a text to Roman: *Kill him.*

41

FOUR SEASONS LION PALACE
SAINT PETERSBURG

A minute later, Dewey's cell buzzed.

"Yeah," said Dewey.

"This is Commander John Drake on the USS *Hartford*. Where are you, Dewey?"

The waitress appeared carrying a plate with Dewey's steak.

"At the Four Seasons," said Dewey. "Where's the team?"

"The SDV is in harbor. I'll patch you through to Jacobsson, he's the in-water operator."

"Thanks, Commander."

A minute later, another man appeared in the restaurant. He was shorter than the first, but he was, in his own way, more worrisome. His shirt was open at the collar and unbuttoned down to his navel. Gold chains hung around his neck. He had spiky blond hair. He was wiry and pale. He wore a hard stare, his eyes sweeping the room.

A moment later, Dewey heard a voice.

"This is Jacobsson. You there, Dewey?"

"Yeah, I'm here."

"Do you have the girl?"

When the Russian's eyes arrived at Dewey, they stopped. The next moments were intense, as the thug stared for several long moments at him.

"Not yet," said Dewey. "It's going to be a little while."

"We're here," said Jacobsson, "and we're good to go."

At the man's breastplate, clearly visible, Dewey could see the telltale bulge of a gun, strapped around his neck.

"What's point of entry?" asked Dewey.

"You need to get to the canal. To the right of the hotel."

The excited voice of the hostess interrupted the din of conversations inside the restaurant. A moment later, Katya entered the restaurant.

She wore jeans and a white short-sleeved sweater. Her hair was braided back. She shook the hand of the hostess, then began speaking with her.

The four people at the table in front of Dewey all looked in unison at her, then began whispering excitedly.

The skinny guard looked again at Dewey. Dewey pretended not to notice, cutting another piece of his steak and putting it into his mouth. A moment later, the guard finally turned away, saying something to the larger man. He pointed to a booth, out of Dewey's sight line.

The hostess led Katya across the restaurant. The ballerina glanced briefly in Dewey's direction, making eye contact with him, a carefree smile on her face, then disappeared around the corner, flanked by her bodyguards.

"Got it," said Dewey. "Give me a few minutes."

42

I want all non-official covers in-theater," Calibrisi said to Polk, "with their locations."

One of the analysts typed, bringing up all NOCs in or near Russia. Three photos tiled across the screen:

1. Maybank, J	NOC 333	Moscow, RUSSIA
2. Fairweather, T	NOC 009	Poznan, POLAND
3. Brainard, T	NOC AW-22	Minsk, BELARUS

"Remember Johnny's wounded," said Polk. "He has a bullet in his leg."

"How bad is it?"

"He has a fever and hasn't left the bedroom. Christy thinks he needs a doctor."

They both knew what it meant. If Maybank's injury required surgery, he would need exfiltration. Right now, there was a higher priority.

"Get Brainard and Fairweather to Moscow," said Calibrisi, walking toward the door. "Tell Christy she needs to take the bullet out herself. Then get word to Dewey. He needs to stay in-theater. We can't afford to have him get on that sub."

43

Dewey finished his meal and paid. He was the last person inside the restaurant other than Katya and her men, who were in a booth out of his sight line. Before standing up to leave, he removed the .45 from a concealed pocket on the inside of his leather jacket. From his pants pocket, he removed a suppressor, screwing it into the muzzle of the gun beneath the table. He repocketed the gun, then stood and walked to the door. He glanced right, around the corner, to Katya's booth. Both of the men with Katya returned his look. As Dewey passed the maître d', he caught movement in his eyes, a fleeting glance over Dewey's shoulders, behind him.

Dewey crossed the lobby, looking quickly at his room key. The lobby was empty except for a woman behind the desk, who smiled and said goodnight to him.

At the elevator, Dewey heard footsteps, hard-soled shoes clicking on marble, approaching from behind him. A moment later, the bigger guard joined Dewey next to the elevator doors.

They were approximately the same size. The Russian stood close, waiting for the elevator. When it came, he stepped on first.

"Which floor, my friend?" he asked in English filtered with a sharp Russian accent.

"Four."

As the doors shut, Dewey watched the guard carefully, spreading his legs in case the bodyguard wanted to engage him in the elevator.

The bodyguard instead pressed the button for four, then a button for a floor higher than Dewey's.

When the elevator stopped at the fourth floor, Dewey stepped out. He walked down the dimly lit hall.

Dewey's back was to the bodyguard as he walked away, trying to appear nonchalant but hyperaware of the man back at the elevator. With his right hand he reached inside his jacket, removed the .45, and clutched it tight beneath his left armpit, the suppressed muzzle of the gun aimed behind him, back up the hall, inside the leather jacket, so the man couldn't see it.

Dewey heard the faint metallic click of a round being chambered.

At the end of the hall, he came to the last door. With his left hand, his free hand, he pulled a room key from his pocket.

Dewey inserted the card into the lock with his left hand while, with his right, he put his index finger on the trigger. The key slid into the lock. A red light came on. In the same moment, Dewey fired the Colt as fast as his finger could flex; several quick blasts, through the jacket, moving the .45 in a line without looking, left to right, across the hallway.

The scream from the Russian came from the second round, in the same instant a silenced slug sailed by Dewey, striking the door just above his head.

Dewey pivoted, ducking. The gunman lay on his back, a pistol at his side.

Dewey's round had struck him in the stomach. His shirt was already drenched in blood. Groaning, the Russian reached for his weapon as Dewey moved toward him. Dewey watched as the bodyguard found the butt of the gun. Dewey stepped quickly toward the

Russian, who now lay on the ground in a growing pool of crimson. Dewey had his gun out and he trained it on the killer's head, saying nothing. Then Dewey fired. A slug ripped the Russian in the right eye.

Dewey heard the door to his right abruptly open, a curious hotel guest, then the sound of a chain. As the shocked occupant of the room screamed, Dewey booted his foot at the door, ripping the chain off, then lunging into the room.

Standing in a bathrobe was a man in his seventies. Dewey pointed at the bed, training his gun on him, holding a finger to his lips, telling him to be quiet.

Dewey stepped backward, gun fixed on the man. He opened the door and grabbed the ankle of the dead bodyguard. He dragged him into the room, keeping the muzzle of the Colt trained at all times on the old man's head.

Dewey shut the door shut and left the dead thug just inside the room.

"Please don't kill me," the man stuttered.

Dewey said nothing. He came to the man, flipped him on his stomach. He removed his Gerber combat blade from his ankle sheath. He sliced apart a towel, ripping it into strips. He gagged the man tightly, then bound his arms and legs.

Dewey moved to the dead man. He had another gun—Walther PPK—and a pack of cigarettes. In a secret pocket in his left sock, Dewey found a plastic room key.

Dewey looked in the bathroom. On the sink was a plug-in razor.

Dewey took the electric razor and shaved his beard, mustache, and hair. It took him five minutes, and was rough. His hair was now short, a quarter inch of stubble. He looked in the mirror, and for a second, he didn't recognize himself.

He checked the old man to make sure he wasn't tied too tightly. He went to the door and looked out the peephole. The corridor wall had a small arc of wet blood. The beige carpet was pancaked in scarlet.

He had to move.

He exited the room and moved methodically down the hallway, soundlessly inserting the key, watching, at each door, as the light turned red. He took the fire stairs to the fifth floor, repeating the sweep. Near the far corner, a door lock suddenly flashed green and the lock clicked. Dewey removed his gun. He opened the door, then kicked with all his strength. The door swung violently in, crashing against the wall. The other bodyguard was sitting, shirt off, on one of the beds, the TV on. Next to him on the bed was a small sub-machine gun.

He looked at Dewey. His eyes shot, inexplicably, reflexively, to the closet next to the door.

Dewey turned the gun and fired into the closet as the shirtless guard reached for the SMG.

Dewey swept the Colt and fired again, ripping a slug into the man's chest.

He yanked the closet door open. On the floor was another man. His chest was oozing blood. A gun was at his feet. He looked up at Dewey, whispering something in Russian as blood drenched his chest.

Dewey shut the door. He stepped to the window. In front of the hotel, at least a dozen police cruisers had arrived, red lights flashing, along with a growing line of black sedans.

"Fuck," he whispered.

He stepped to a door connecting to the next room. He knocked.

"*Da.*" A woman's voice.

Dewey said nothing. He waited, then knocked again. The door opened. Standing in the door was Katya. She had on a white terry cloth bathrobe.

Dewey raised the weapon and aimed it at her head.

"Don't say anything. Don't scream. Don't try to run. You do that and I won't hurt you."

Katya nodded. She looked as if she was about to cry.

"Who are you?" she whispered.

"Put on some clothing," said Dewey.

He shut the connecting door and walked to the window. Flashing blue lights dotted the road surrounding the hotel. The sound of sirens came in through the window.

He kept his gun trained on Katya as he pulled out his cell. He dialed the number of the Navy SEAL, Jacobsson, who was in the harbor waiting.

"Jacobsson, go."

"I have the girl," said Dewey. "We need to move."

"Who are you?" she asked again.

Dewey ignored her question.

"Where are you?" asked Jacobsson.

"Four Seasons."

"Go out the front entrance," said Jacobsson. "Right one block to the canal. I'll be there, beneath the bridge."

"How long?"

Above the sirens, a sharp, high-pitched beeping noise suddenly roared. The hotel fire alarm. The Four Seasons was being evacuated.

"Five. By the time you get there I'll be in position."

"See you soon," said Dewey calmly.

44

FOUR SEASONS LION PALACE
SAINT PETERSBURG

Dewey pocketed Katya's cell phone. He ransacked her suitcases, purse, handbags, coat pockets, and anything else he could find. He went into the bathroom and dug into her toiletries kit, keeping the muzzle of his gun aimed out the open door at Katya.

"What are you looking for?" she asked. "Do you know who I am?"

Dewey returned to the living room of the luxurious suite, then stepped into the bedroom, the gun always aimed at Katya through the open door. He looked in the drawers of the bureaus, lifting up clothing. He went to a mahogany desk in front of the window and opened the drawers, finding nothing. He returned to the living room.

"Get dressed," said Dewey. "Get some shoes on. Now."

"Why are you doing this?" Katya asked, her voice trembling.

Dewey pulled out a sheet of paper and unfolded it. On it were photos of Cloud. He handed it to her.

Katya's hand went to her mouth, covering it.

"Is that your boyfriend?" asked Dewey.

She nodded as tears rolled down her cheeks.

"He's a terrorist," said Dewey. "He's planning an attack on the United States."

Katya wiped her cheeks, staring at the paper, then let it fall to the floor.

"He killed five Americans tonight. Lured them into a trap, then killed them. They never had a chance. Now get dressed."

Katya burst into tears.

"Pyotr," she said. "He's not a terrorist."

"What's his last name?"

"Vargarin."

Dewey took out his cell and hit Speed Dial.

"Control. Identify."

"Andreas, put me through to Bill Polk."

As Dewey waited, he nodded to Katya.

"Get dressed," he said again. "*Now.*"

Polk came on the line.

"Dewey?"

Dewey stepped to the window, out of earshot, then spoke in a low voice, all the while keeping his gun trained at Katya.

"I have her," he whispered.

"Where?"

"The hotel."

"That would explain why Metro police is going haywire."

"Yeah, I know. I need to get going, but you need to know something: His name is Pyotr Vargarin."

"She told you that?"

"She seemed genuinely shocked that he's a terrorist. She's either a very good liar or is unaware of this guy's true identity."

"Does she have a cell phone?"

"Hold on."

Dewey took out Katya's cell phone, then dictated the number to Polk.

Polk cleared his throat.

"One more thing," Polk said. "You need to stay inside Russia.

We just received word that the nuke is through the Strait of Gibraltar. Katya Basaeyev is now our only link to Cloud. Get her out, then stay in-theater and wait for further orders. You got it?"

"Yeah, I got it."

"Get going."

"Where are you taking me? Please, I ask you sincerely."

"You're the only connection we have to Cloud," said Dewey. "I'm taking you out of Russia."

"You're kidnapping me," she sobbed.

"Yes," said Dewey, "I am. Kidnapping. Abducting. Whatever you want to call it. We will do whatever we need to do to stop this attack on the United States. I don't want to hurt you, Katya. But that's up to you. Do you understand?"

She stared at him in silence. He looked back, trying not to look too long into her eyes, trying not to get to know her in any way, trying not to think about anything other than the mission. His eyes went to the window and peered down at the chaotic mess in front of the hotel.

"Please get dressed," he repeated.

In the reflection in the glass, Dewey watched as Katya removed her bathrobe and allowed it to fall to the ground. He stopped looking, even at the blurry reflection, until she had pulled on a pair of white jeans and a sweater. He saw her take a small object from the table, something that was beneath her shirt, and tuck it under a book.

"What was it?" he asked, pointing to the book.

"Nothing."

"Give it to me."

Katya picked up the object and stepped toward Dewey, staring daggers as she handed him a small leather object the size of a wallet. Dewey opened it up. It was a traveling photo album, with slots for just a few photos. There were only two. One was a color photo of a pair of teenagers, a girl and a boy. They were seated at a restaurant. In front of the girl was a piece of cake with a single candle lit on top of it. They were holding hands. The girl had pigtails and a big smile on her face. The boy had short, curly blond hair. He was smiling too.

Dewey stared at it for several moments, then looked at Katya.

"My fifteenth birthday," she said.

"Is that him?"

Katya nodded.

The other photo was black and white, its edges frayed with age. This photo showed a child. He was standing dead center in the middle of the photo. Other children were gathered to his side, all eyes looking at him. He was in front of a table, upon which was a large trophy. An adult, presumably a teacher, was presenting the trophy to the boy. Behind him, a plain-looking, slightly rotund woman was standing next to a tall, bearded man with glasses and curly brown hair. The woman had a blank, serious expression on her face. The man was smiling proudly.

Dewey studied the black-and-white photo. Cloud was very young. He wore a button-down shirt and tie. His hair sprouted up from his head in big, wavy curls.

"What is this?"

"The only photo he has of his parents," she answered. "They're both dead."

"How old is he?"

Katya shrugged her shoulders.

"I don't know," she said. "Even he doesn't know."

Dewey pulled the black-and-white photo from the leather case, folded it in half, then stuck it in his pocket.

Katya watched him do it, a look of disbelief on her face.

"It was the only photograph Pyotr—"

"Pyotr isn't going to be alive much longer," said Dewey. "I don't think he'll miss the photo."

"He would never have anything to do with terrorism," she said. "He's a kind man. I've known him since age thirteen. He's gentle. Please, you must believe me."

"It doesn't matter what I believe," said Dewey, scanning the street

237

in front of the Four Seasons, which was now a pandemonium of police cars. "Besides, there are about a hundred cops outside. They all have guns. I don't think they're very happy with me at the moment."

"Perhaps they will shoot you, like you shot my guards."

Dewey looked at her.

"At least I'm not wearing white pants."

Katya looked down at her white jeans.

"What's wrong with white pants?"

"It's an easy target for a marksman. Especially at night. They'll probably be shooting at me, but if they miss, it's going to hit you."

"Why are you trying to scare me?"

Dewey walked to Katya and stood in front of her.

"Because I need you to be scared. If you're scared, maybe you'll listen to me. There's only one way out of here. But you need to do exactly what I say."

Katya became quiet.

"Where will you take me?" she asked.

"I don't know the answer to that question."

"Please tell me your name. I have the right to know."

"It doesn't matter."

"To me it does."

Katya's English wasn't flawless. And yet the aristocratic softness of her accent made the imperfections somehow charming.

Dewey held the curtain to the side. A cordon of police were stretched across the road in front of the hotel.

"My name is Dewey Andreas."

"What did he do?"

"He acquired a nuclear bomb. He put the bomb in a boat that right now is on its way to the United States. He intends to detonate it there."

She stared at him, a look of utter shock at his words. She walked to one of the couches and sat down.

"He would never do this," she said. "It's a mistake."

"Where is he?"

"I don't know."

"You don't know much," said Dewey. "And yet you have, let's see, one, two, three bodyguards? Why would anyone need so much protection?"

"Are you implying that I'm involved?"

"I just find it strange that you have three operatives guarding you. Ex-military. Spetsnaz, if I had to guess."

She stared.

"They're provided to me. I've had guards as long as I can remember."

Dewey stared out the window.

"The first one followed me upstairs and tried to kill me," said Dewey.

He turned and their eyes met.

"Why would I kill you?" she asked softly. "There is already too much misery in this world. I would not kill you. I would never kill anybody."

She stood up. She walked to the window, next to him, and looked out.

"Let's go," said Dewey.

She pointed at the police cordon.

"Are you insane?"

"We're going to walk out the front door. I'm one of your guards."

"That will not work," Katya said, shaking her head.

"You're probably right. They'll kill me and you can go back and hang out with a terrorist and jump around in a bird costume. It doesn't mean we're not going to give it the old college try, though."

Katya smiled.

"College try? What does this mean?"

Dewey took her wrist and lightly clutched it, pushing her toward the door. At the door, he turned.

"I'm going to explain how this works," he said quietly. "I've stood where those guys we're gonna walk by are standing, and right now they're looking for a killer. You alone can convince them I'm not the one they're looking for. It's like a play, and you're the star, and your role is to be the pissed-off ballerina who doesn't like gunshots and sirens and wants to move to a different hotel. I'm the goon who's supposed to protect you. Got it? Sell that and we both live. Don't sell it and we both die."

"What if I give you up?"

"You die."

"You would kill me?" she asked quietly.

"Yes."

"I've done nothing wrong."

"If you rat on me, that qualifies as something wrong—in my book, at least."

"I'm innocent."

"If you're innocent, you won't be harmed," he said. "You're not the one we're after. You'll be asked to help us find Cloud. Then you'll be set free. It's that simple."

She closed her eyes, looked at the ground, then looked up and opened them again, staring directly into his eyes.

"I will do it. I will try to help. I still do not believe the man you say is a terrorist is the same man I know. But I will help. I have nothing but fondness for the United States of America."

He pointed at the phone on the desk.

"Call the front desk, ask them what's going on," said Dewey. "In English. I want to hear it. Ask why the police are here. Then tell them to bring the car around. You would like to move to the Grand Hotel."

Katya picked up the phone. She dialed the front desk and did precisely as Dewey instructed, then hung up.

Dewey lifted her bag.

"Dewey," she said.

"Walk in front of me, like I work for you," he said.

Dewey handed her a pair of sunglasses.

"Put these on."

"You don't trust me?"

"Don't take it personally."

Dewey followed Katya to the door. She opened it and stepped into the hallway. A pair of armed policeman in blue tactical gear were standing near the elevator.

The first officer looked at Katya, then at Dewey. Dewey maintained a cool demeanor but nodded.

"Miss Basaeyev," he said in Russian. "We ask that everyone remain in their room."

"I'm leaving the hotel," she said in English, walking toward the elevator.

The agent blocked her path.

"Get out of my way," she snapped indignantly.

The officer didn't move.

"I'm under orders, Miss Basaeyev. I'm sorry. Until the killer is apprehended, no one goes in or out of the hotel."

Dewey was behind Katya. He had the Colt .45 in his right hand, behind his back. He raised the gun, moved to Katya's side, and fired. The silenced slug hit the agent in the forehead. Before the second officer could react, Dewey fired another shot, hitting him in the mouth, kicking him backward and down.

Katya stared at the dead men, her eyes wide, momentarily repulsed by the bloody scene.

Dewey grabbed Katya's wrist and pulled her into the elevator. He pressed the button for the ground floor, then the button for the second floor. He stood in the far left corner, waiting and watching. His eyes were calm, blank, above all cold, with a hint of anger.

The elevator stopped at two. Dewey eyed Katya. Quickly, he raised his gun and trained it on the elevator doors. As they began to slide open, Dewey held Katya by the back of her jacket with his left hand.

Another agent in blue tactical gear was waiting. He had on a combat helmet and had a carbine raised and trained on the elevator as the doors opened.

The solider barked something in Russian.

"*Zapustit!*" Katya screamed, warning the agent. *Run!*

Dewey lunged toward the door, firing. The soldier ran. Dewey stepped into the hallway, firing as he moved, striking the officer beneath the lower edge of his helmet, a quarter inch above his Kevlar flak jacket, dropping him.

He turned back, looking for Katya. His eyes saw the white of her jeans, just a glimpse, as the elevator doors shut.

Dewey lurched, getting a finger between the doors just as they went tight. The elevator made a low mechanical grinding noise as the doors tried to close. Dewey fought against the elevator doors; if they closed, he would lose Katya. The mechanical grinding became louder as Dewey struggled to pull the doors apart, his face contorted. A low ringing noise came from somewhere inside the car. Inside the elevator shaft, below, on the other side of the doors, he could hear the cables tugging against the elevator housing, trying to lower the elevator. But Dewey would not let the doors shut, and finally, the low beeping noise stopped. The doors suddenly opened.

Dewey stepped inside and was greeted by a violent kick to the groin from Katya. The kick doubled him over. The elevator doors started to close again as Katya charged at him. From a pained crouch, he swung, but she ducked, spinning, then hammered her right foot counterclockwise, a vicious motion aimed at his head.

Dewey recognized Katya's martial training; his brain processed it in the split second following the kick to the groin. As her foot moved toward his head, he anticipated it, bending just as her foot cut viciously across the air above his head. In the instant that followed, Dewey slashed his left arm out, slamming Katya in the knee with a fist, then speared her in the rib cage with a brutal punch that sent her flying into the wall, then down.

Dewey stepped back, gun trained on her. He glanced at the elevator door, then back at her. Both of them knew that the first floor held a waiting army of Russian police.

Dewey put his hand in the elevator door before it closed. As it moved automatically back open, he grabbed her hand and pulled her out of the elevator, gun raised, then moved right. At the end of the hallway, he knocked several times on the door to a room. When a woman answered the door, Dewey pushed the door in, weapon raised. The woman burst into tears. He pointed to the bathroom, ordering her to go inside.

He turned off the lights in the room, then moved to the window.

Below was a courtyard, closed for the night, with tables and sun umbrellas.

Behind it was a street. Beyond that, the canal.

He dialed Jacobsson.

"I need to move right now."

"Go," said Jacobsson. "I'm here."

Dewey heard shouts from the hallway in Russian, then the loud drumbeat of footsteps. He looked at Katya just as her mouth opened and she started screaming. Dewey charged at her, catching her near the bed, and covered her mouth with his hand, silencing her. He felt her sharp teeth bite down.

Dewey pulled his hand, now bleeding, away from her mouth. He wrapped his forearm around her neck and tightened it. She struggled, kicking his legs, trying to punch him, but it was futile. In seconds, she grew weak, then went limp in his arms.

He carried her limp body to the window. He quickly surveyed the courtyard, as, behind him, a steel battering ram slammed into the door with a somber thump.

Dewey took a few steps back and aimed his gun at the window.

The battering ram slammed a second time. The door made a loud cracking noise as wood splintered.

Dewey lifted Katya's body and wrapped it around the back of his neck, clutching her legs and neck in a tight grip with his left hand as he held his gun in his right.

He charged toward the window, as, behind him, the door crashed in. He fired a slug, shattering the window, just as he leapt into the air. Yelling in Russian was interwoven with automatic gunfire. Dewey's right foot hit the windowsill as slugs erupted behind him. He hit the sill, then leapt out as far as he could, launching into the air as bullets flew just above his head. The momentum of the jump was quickly gone; Dewey and Katya dropped in a sharp line toward the ground two stories below. Dewey kicked his legs furiously through the air, trying to maintain his balance, holding Katya tightly around his neck. Their trajectory took them toward a red-and-white canvas umbrella. Dewey slammed into it, feetfirst. He ripped through the thick canvas and smashed painfully into the wooden pole holding the umbrella, snapping it in half, then crashed to the ground, his right palm, elbow, hip, and knee all absorbing the trauma yet protecting the unconscious Katya.

Dewey jumped to his feet, despite piercing pain in his leg.

The staccato of unmuted gunfire clotted the Saint Petersburg night.

He shifted Katya's body to his left shoulder, fireman style, and charged across the Four Seasons courtyard. He hurdled a wall of neatly manicured boxwoods as bullets pocked the slate on the ground around him.

They were trying to slow him, or scare him into stopping, but the gunmen did not target him directly. They would not want to kill Katya, and that fact alone offered him a slim margin of protection.

Dewey could see the iron balustrade above the canal entrance, just a block and a half away. He sprinted as fast as he could, sweat drenching him. The scene was chaos. Gunfire mixed with shouting, screams, cars honking, and, in the distance, the low thunder of a chopper moving in.

From both sides, policemen swarmed. For the first time, Dewey registered the khaki-and-red uniforms of Russian soldiers. He sprinted past a block of mansions, lungs burning, then lurched out into traffic, dodging cars as he crossed the last remaining roadway before the canal. Suddenly, to his left, he eyed a pair of soldiers running toward him.

Horns blared. Bullets struck a taxicab, shattering its windshield. Sirens mixed with hysterical screaming.

Dewey leapt to the sidewalk on the other side of the road. He had a few yards on a pair of officers who were closest, but they were gaining. He had less than a block now, a block lined with a half dozen limestone mansions. After that, he would be free and clear.

Suddenly, just past the last mansion on the block, precisely where Dewey wanted to run, a police cruiser cut across the road and bounced up onto the sidewalk, blocking him.

Dewey kept running as police officers jumped from the front and back of the sedan, weapons aimed at him. As one of the men stepped toward him, Dewey slammed his left shoulder into the officer, pummeling him backward, then kept charging toward the canal ahead.

Dewey recalled Polk's words: *The nuke is through the strait . . . get her out, then stay in-theater . . .*

Dewey was now running as fast as he could, despite the pain in his hip, just feet in front of a pack of Russian policemen. His eye shot right as a plainclothes agent lurched at him, diving toward his legs. Dewey kept running, bracing himself as the agent's arms wrapped around his thighs. He broke through the tackle, his knee striking the man's head, a loud grunt coming from him as he tumbled to the ground.

From behind, police officers swarmed, coming from what seemed like every direction, shouting at Dewey to drop Katya.

At the iron gate above the canal, Dewey threw Katya, like a rag doll, toward the water, then followed, leaping in the air, hurdling the fence. He heard a splash as Katya's body hit the water beneath him, then, suddenly, he slammed feet first into the water next to her. Dewey dived down into the dark canal as bullets hit the surface of the water just above his head.

45

GRIBOYEDOV CANAL
SAINT PETERSBURG

In the dark waters of Griboyedov Canal, a small black object floated in a stationary position next to the four-hundred-year-old stone embankment, directly across the canal from an iron railing, past which was Nevsky Prospect, the nearest entry point to the canal from the Four Seasons.

The object appeared to be nothing more than a piece of floating debris, dull matte rubber in a dark shade of gray, a sliver of glass on one side, and that was all. It could've been anything: a buoy, an old boot, an empty vodka bottle. But it wasn't just anything. The rubber was in fact the skullcap of a tactical wet suit. The glass was a specially designed full-face diving mask, equipped with night optics and a dynamic graphical user interface which, on the left side of the interior of the helmet, displayed a live video feed, taken from the sky, of the scene.

Wearing both was Navy SEAL John Jacobsson. He moved his legs slowly beneath him, inhaling and exhaling through a closed-circuit underwater breathing apparatus called a rebreather, which enabled him to recycle most of the unused oxygen from his exhale, thus eliminating telltale bubbles from the water, cloaking his presence as he waited. He listened to the din from the street above, the cacophony of violence, which he registered with anticipation and dread, the tumult of a chaotic extraction whose odds of success were diminishing with each passing moment.

Jacobsson's earbud connected him to the SDV that idled directly beneath him, eighteen feet below the surface.

The rat-a-tat-tat of sporadic gunfire started less than a minute after Jacobsson surfaced. It echoed down across the flat water, bouncing between the stone walls of the canal, each round causing Jacobsson's heart to race a little quicker.

"It sounds like fucking Beirut up there," Jacobsson whispered into his commo as he tread water.

Jacobsson's teammate, Davey Wray, was seated in the tight cockpit of the SDV, waiting for him to return.

"Roger that," came Wray. "I can hear it."

In Jacobsson's right hand was an odd-looking weapon: HK P11, a pistol designed for underwater use, capable of firing steel darts.

The flashing lights of a police cruiser abruptly appeared, directly across from him, slamming to a screeching halt on the sidewalk just behind the balustrade.

The shouts grew closer, then were overhead.

Suddenly, an object came flying from above. It was a body, limp, like a corpse. He watched as the object came crashing from above; it was a woman, her long hair unmistakable. She splashed violently into the canal.

Jacobsson lunged beneath the water, kicking furiously, sticking the P11 back in his belt with his right hand as, with his left, he pulled a small red canister from the same belt. The canister—a ditch pipe—was the size of a pack of Life Savers. Jacobsson swam underwater to the place where he guessed she entered the water. He searched frantically for the woman, then found her, at least five feet beneath the surface, unconscious. Jacobsson pulled her even farther beneath the water, aiming for the SDV. He stuck the ditch pipe into her mouth, then pressed a black button on the end. Oxygen poured into her mouth as Jacobsson swam deeper, kicking hard, moving down into the depths of the canal.

Dewey hit the water hard, slamming legs-first only inches from where Katya's limp body had plunged into the canal. He dived below the surface just as bullets struck the water near his head. He dived as deeply and as quickly as possible, fighting to get to a safe depth, reaching down frantically into the water with his hands, kicking as hard as he could, despite the pain and what he now understood was a potentially serious injury to his right knee.

As he kicked lower, Dewey wrestled his way out of the leather Belstaff jacket, pulling his arms from the sleeves, then let the jacket fall away.

Dewey opened his eyes beneath the water, seeing nothing but infinite black. Instinctively, he searched for signs of Jacobsson, of Katya's white pants.

Then Calibrisi's last words came back to him: *We need you in Russia.*

He'd arrived in Russia totally unprepared for deep field work, but he understood that the situation was far graver than anyone back in America had predicted.

Whoever this person or this group was, it was clear they were an enemy far more sophisticated than anyone imagined.

In the cold water of the canal, the trauma from the leap through the hotel room window came into sharp relief. Each movement of his right arm and right leg brought acute pain.

Fight through it. You're not done yet. Not even close.

Dewey had always known how to take pain and compartmentalize it, then put that compartment out of the way, so that even though he was feeling it, it did not affect his work. He would need that strength now. His leg, in particular, felt as if it was dangling, still attached to the knee, but by a thread.

He scanned the water again for Jacobsson and Katya. He would stay in Russia, yet the SDV offered the chance to pick up a medical kit so he could bandage up his leg later.

In the murky water, his eyes suddenly caught a flash of white beneath him. He dived down toward it. It was the white of Katya's jeans. Jacobsson was pulling her down to the SDV.

He swam after them. As he went lower, the darkness became like the blackest of tunnels. Katya's white pants remained the only thing that wasn't black, but they were fading.

Then she disappeared.

Dewey found himself deep in the water, unable to discern which direction was up. He was out of breath.

Let it go.

Dewey stopped swimming. For several seconds, he didn't move. Slowly, he felt his buoyancy pulling him up. Blackness turned into a light-speckled greenish blur.

He knew the Russians would be waiting, their weapons trained at the surface of the water. But there was nothing he could do now. He breached the surface, gasping for air, then ducked back below the surface, diving down. He waited for the dull staccato of gunfire but heard none. He remained below water for nearly a minute, then surfaced again.

When he looked around, what he saw shocked him. The canal had opened up. The channel's current had taken him several hundred feet away from the scene. He was thirty feet from shore, along a marina whose wharves were lined with boats.

Dewey struggled to catch his breath. He side-paddled to the far end of a dock that jutted out into the water. On both sides of the wooden jetty, small sailboats were moored, empty and quiet.

Dewey placed his hand on the top of the dock, holding on to it, remaining there for several minutes as he caught his breath and stared at the brightly lit scene up the canal, where a helicopter now hovered, its spotlights scouring the surface of the water. Both sides of the canal were alight with spotlights and the flashing strobes of police cruisers. From the other side of the canal, Dewey saw police speedboats, sirens roaring as they approached the disordered scene. He turned at a sudden noise. Behind him sped another police boat, its spotlights scanning the surface of the water, moving rapidly across the marina. Soon it would be at him. As the light hit the sailboat to Dewey's right, lighting it up, he dived again, using the bottom of the jetty to hold himself just below the surface. After a half minute, he resurfaced. The police boat was creeping along the canal, toward the Four Seasons, its spotlight panning the canal wall, hunting.

Dewey's eyes shot to the Four Seasons. Along the terraces, at least a dozen gunmen swept the water with guns, searching. He watched the chaotic scene as several scuba divers entered the water, looking for Katya. Looking for him.

Jacobsson swam into a small compartment at the aft of the SDV, pulling Katya in with him. He pressed a button inside the compartment. The door shut tight, then locked.

"Go!" barked Jacobsson, still on commo, speaking into his mask to Wray, who was in a separate compartment just a few feet from him, dry.

The SDV moved out, its nearly silent propulsion system sending it forward into the darkness, away from the Griboyedov Canal and toward the open water.

The compartment still filled with water. Jacobsson pressed another button, and a small but powerful pump came to life, pumping out water. Soon the water level in the SDV started dropping. In less than ten seconds, it was empty.

Jacobsson laid Katya on her back. He felt her carotid artery at the side of her neck for a pulse. There was nothing.

He pulled off his mask, arched Katya's neck gently, and plugged her nose. He started breathing hard into her mouth, in timed puffs, trying to push air back into her water-choked lungs. After more than a minute, she made a soft moaning noise, then started vomiting water.

Slowly, Katya opened her eyes. She looked frightened and confused. She looked slowly around the tiny compartment. Then she started bawling uncontrollably.

The SDV moved quietly through the water, aiming deeper, speeding at fifteen knots toward the USS *Hartford*.

Jacobsson knocked on the glass, getting Wray's attention.

"Heat," he said, asking Wray to crank up the heat inside the compartment.

Jacobsson placed his hand on Katya's forearm, attempting to calm her down. After several minutes of sobbing, she put her first words together.

"Where am I?" she asked.

Jacobsson said nothing.

Twenty minutes later, the SDV locked in place against the submarine. Jacobsson opened the hatch, picked up the barrel of his gun, and rapped the steel grip against the sub. A moment later, a round hatch lowered, opening.

Halogen lights, beamed up from the sub, made the light blue and eerie. Jacobsson crawled down first, followed by a pair of bare feet beneath soaked white denim jeans. Katya climbed down the ladder, sopping wet and dripping. She was placed on a stretcher and carried to the quarterdeck, her eyes scanning the inside of the submarine, then the half dozen men standing in front of her.

"Bring her to the officers' quarters," said Montgomery Thomas, the *Hartford*'s captain. "Get her some dry clothes. Something to drink if she wants it. Do not let her out of your sight."

After Katya was led out of the compartment, Thomas looked at Jacobsson.

"What happened to Andreas?"

"I don't know," said Jacobsson.

46

Calibrisi looked at one of the NCS case officers.

"Get me Montgomery Thomas on the USS *Hartford*. Use a clean uplink."

"Yes, sir."

A few seconds later, Calibrisi's cell buzzed.

"Monty?"

"Hector," said Thomas, "I was wondering how long it would take you to call."

"How's she doing?"

"Fine. She's a bit terrified, but we've got her in some warm clothing. You need to know something. Andreas didn't make it out."

"I know," said Calibrisi. "We need him in-country. We have a problem."

"You want to talk to the lady?"

"Yeah," answered Calibrisi. "I need live stream as she's speaking, along with your EKG."

"Hold on."

Calibrisi put his hand over the phone, then looked at an analyst.

"I want this run through FACS along with the VRA module," said Calibrisi.

Calibrisi, in shorthand, was instructing the NCS analyst to quickly set up two forms of remote lie detection technology for use on Katya. FACS stood for Facial Action Coding System, in which Katya's facial movements would be quickly cataloged, creating a digital bookmark of what Katya looked like when she was telling the truth and when she was lying.

The VRA was voice risk analysis, a CIA-developed remote lie detection technology. At the same time Langley's computers were aggregating Katya's facial movements, a separate software module would attempt to read the inflections in her voice against her heart rate, breathing pattern, and blood pressure.

Together, they would provide a down-and-dirty lie detector, less effective than a classic interrogation setting, but with Katya on a submarine thousands of miles away, it was Calibrisi's only option.

"Park it on line four, sir," said the young woman.

"Starting with a baseline," said Calibrisi. "When you have it, let me know."

"Roger."

A few moments later, a soft female voice came over the speaker system.

"Hello?"

The plasma at the front of Targa abruptly cut to Katya's face. She was seated in front of a steel table. Her hair was slightly messed up, though her beauty was obvious. EKG wires on her arm and neck were visible.

"Miss Basaeyev, my name is Hector Calibrisi. I work for the U.S. government. You were taken out of Russia on my authority. I want you to know that you'll be treated as fairly and respectfully as you treat us. Which means answering our questions truthfully. We mean you no harm. You know who we're after."

"You kidnapped me, and now you torture me and hold me against my will. I don't know anything. I think you have the wrong individual. Pyotr is not terrorist."

"You work as a ballerina, is that correct?" asked Calibrisi.

Katya paused for a brief moment, then looked up. She didn't respond.

"When was the last time you danced in front of a live audience?"

Katya shut her eyes as Calibrisi asked her another question.

"What was the ballet?"

The analyst turned to Calibrisi and shook her head. Without Katya answering the simplest questions, they would be unable to establish a baseline of how the ballerina acted when telling the truth.

"What was your mother's maiden name?"

Katya opened her eyes, then started crying.

Calibrisi muted the line and looked at Polk.

"This isn't working," said Calibrisi. "And we don't have time to be patient."

Calibrisi unmuted the line to the *Hartford*.

"Monty, take me down, please."

A moment later, Thomas came back on the line.

"Where do you want her?"

"Is there a carrier somewhere in the North Atlantic?"

"Negative. *Nimitz* is the closest and that's in Naples."

"Give me live sat," whispered Calibrisi.

A digital map appeared. His finger found the *Hartford*. From there, his finger made a beeline southwest, finding the United Kingdom.

Polk put his hand out, muting the line to the *Hartford*.

"What about MI6?" asked Polk, referring to Langley's closest ally in the trade, Britain's intelligence service.

Calibrisi nodded. "Good idea."

"You want me to call?"

"No, I'll call," said Calibrisi. "You need to focus on getting those men to Moscow."

Calibrisi unmuted the uplink to the submarine.

"Monty," said Calibrisi, "get her to Inverness Airport in Scotland. We'll take it from there."

On the USS *Hartford*, Thomas hung up his cell phone. He climbed a ladder down to the quarterdeck. He went to the digital map, tracing a path with his finger toward the north coast of Scotland. He looked at one of his junior officers.

"Give me the range on an Osprey V-22."

"A thousand miles, sir."

"What if we load it with fuel?"

"With internal fuel tanks, double it, sir."

He picked up one of the submarine phones.

"This is Montgomery Thomas on the USS *Hartford*. We have an Emergency Priority. I need a V-22 as soon as you can get it here, loaded with enough gas to fly to Scotland."

Under a black, starless sky, the *Hartford* rose to the surface of the water, gray-black steel against gray-black sky and gray-black water.

Thomas climbed onto the platform as, in the distance, the low growl of a plane cut above the noise of the ocean.

Behind him, two men lifted Katya by her flex-cuffed arms to the top of the ladder. She was dressed in navy blue pants, black rubber boots, a navy blue shirt, and a fleece jacket. All of it was too big for her. A nylon life vest was strapped around her, tight around her chest, torso, and legs. A pair of large steel O-rings—for transport—dangled from the vest at the waist.

The lights of the plane appeared through the cloudy sky, as the Osprey's turboprops grew louder. Suddenly, a triangle of bright halogen lights illuminated the plane's white fuselage. The lights pivoted and scanned the black ocean until they found the hulking steel of the submarine.

The Osprey descended quickly. For a brief moment, it appeared as if it might fly straight into the ocean. Then it stopped immediately overhead. The props abruptly flipped from vertical to horizontal, like helicopter rotors, enabling the plane to hover overhead.

A steel door opened in the bottom of the plane. A flashing light appeared.

The flashing light, attached to a cable, descended. With a grappling hook, Montgomery grabbed it and clipped the cable to the O-rings on Katya's vest. He checked it to make sure it was secure. Then he held his left thumb up in the air.

The cable went taut, and Katya was yanked up from the deck of the *Hartford*. She disappeared into the fuselage of the plane. The steel door shut, then the plane's engines screamed out of sight, ripping southwest, into the night.

47

ELEKTROSTAL

Cloud listened to Katya's phone ringing for the third time. When it went to voice mail, he shut his eyes and listened.

"*Hello. I'm very sorry but I can't talk right now. Please leave me a message.*"

Cloud hung up the phone, then hit Redial. As he waited for something he knew would not happen, something that would never happen again, namely, for Katya to answer, he shot Sascha a look.

"Have you been able to reach any of the men?" asked Cloud, referring to Katya's bodyguards.

Sascha shook his head.

"I have tried Roman twice, Vladimir three times, and the other. There is no answer."

Katya's phone started ringing, then, after two rings, a voice came on: "Who is this?" the man asked. Russian.

"Where is she?" asked Cloud.

"This is Colonel Polyan from FSB. Who am I speaking to?"

"I am . . . Katya's father," said Cloud. "I have been trying to reach her."

"I'm sorry, sir," said the officer. "She is not here."

"Where is she? There are news reports—"

The phone went dead.

Cloud stood up, a psychotic look on his face. He hurled the cell phone at the wall, where it smashed into pieces. He kicked his chair away and walked to the stairs.

"*Cloud*," said Sascha.

Cloud ignored him.

He descended the stairs three steps at a time. When he reached the basement garage, he climbed onto his motorcycle. He turned it on, revving it hard, then screeched forward, pulling up the ramp to street level. As he was about to accelerate onto the dark street, a figure appeared and lurched in the path of the Ducati. Cloud slammed on the brakes.

It was Sascha.

"Come back inside," he said, panting heavily from his run down the stairs, holding up both arms as if he could direct Cloud to do what he wanted. "Something has happened."

"I have to go to Saint Peters—"

"She's *gone*, Pyotr," snapped Sascha.

Cloud stared into his friend's eyes for several seconds. He didn't say anything. Sascha stood as still as a statue, holding his arms up. Then he put them down and stepped to Cloud, walking to his side, moving to within a few inches of him. Gently, he placed his hand on Cloud's shoulder.

"We knew this was a possibility," said Sascha. "Going to Saint Petersburg will get you nothing, except caught. Now come back upstairs."

Five minutes later, Cloud followed Sascha to his computer.

"The CIA is sending more men into the country," said Sascha.

Cloud went behind Sascha and read the screen. It was a transcription of a CIA conversation.

709	get brainard and fairweather to moscow
710	tell christy she needs to take the bullet out herself

711   then get word to dewey
712   he needs to stay in theater

Their eyes met. They both knew what it meant. They were coming for him.

"They're coming to meet Andreas," said Sascha.

"They're going to try," said Cloud. "Find out where the safe house is. There are agents already there."

Cloud went to his computer. He joined Sascha inside the CIA network, then placed a piece of tracking code, similar to a cookie, on the records of the agents Langley had dispatched to Russia to assist Dewey. Any activity involving either Brainard or Fairweather would trigger an alert, which Cloud could then examine.

When he finished, he looked at Sascha.

"Put Andreas's photograph out on the wire," said Cloud. "Law enforcement, news agencies."

"What about his identity?" asked Sascha.

Cloud was silent as he considered the question.

"Not yet."

48

NEVA RIVER
SAINT PETERSBURG

Dewey treaded water and watched as lights in a marina building went on. A few seconds later, police cars poured in through a fenced-off entrance. Dewey dived beneath the surface and swam into the darkness, away from shore, resurfacing after more than a minute. Searchlights scanned the surface of the water near the shore. He turned onto his back and let the current take him away from the city.

The hum of the chopper's rotors softened, blending into the slapping of the water. He floated for an hour as the lights of Saint Petersburg became a dome of dull yellow, blurry and silent, far in the distance. He came onshore along a rocky stretch of coast, bordered by a dense thicket of trees and brush.

He was exhausted. His knee was badly cut. He was cold and wet. He wanted to sit down and rest. But he couldn't. Now was the time he needed to move. Not later, *now.*

They're coming.

He took a step, then another, his eyes weaving between the starry sky and the tree line, moving east, navigating by the stars. He walked for at least an hour, through a rough country of trees and fields. Eventually, he came to the first sign of civilization: train tracks.

The rail bed had a few weeds, but he smelled fresh oil. The track was still being used.

Dewey moved left, along the tracks. He walked for another hour, then saw the outskirts of a rail yard. It sat quiet but was large. The tracks split into a dozen lines. Boxcars and locomotives filled the sidings.

Dewey's clothing was still damp. He was hungry. Mostly, the gash at his knee hurt. But whatever discomfort he felt, he ignored. There would be time to think about it later. Right now, he needed to focus on a few core issues, survival being at the very top of the list.

He reached to his left calf. Sheathed to his leg was his Gerber combat blade, seven inches of black steel, double-serrated, its hilt wrapped in black hockey tape. He pulled it out, then moved along the outskirts of the big rail yard, at the edge of a tree line, to a simple two-story brick building at the side of the yard.

Dewey studied the building from the shadow of the trees. Seeing no activity, he charged across the exposed side of the building, reaching the far end, then crouching against the brick. He stalked, back pressed to brick, until he came to the corner of the building. Dewey peeked around. He saw a doorway and, beyond it a parking lot, empty except for a pair of pickup trucks.

Dewey walked to the door, jiggling the doorknob. It was locked. He glanced around, making sure he was alone, then heaved his shoulder against the door. It was a steel door. The lock was double-bolt. It wasn't going to be opened by force.

"Fuck," he muttered.

Dewey got down on his knees and felt along the foundation, looking for a hidden key. He went right, crawling all the way to the corner of the building. He found nothing.

A loud, creaking noise, then the slam of steel as, in the rail yard, on the other side of the building, there was activity; a boxcar was being moved.

Dewey repeated his search for a key on the far side of the door, crawling, banging the foundation. A few feet from the door, a piece of concrete seemed loose. Dewey tugged at it. It popped out. Behind it was a set of keys.

Back at the door, he inserted keys until one fit. He went inside, relocking the building behind him.

He felt the wall for light switches, then flipped them on. Clutching the knife in his right hand, Dewey moved inside the building.

He passed two offices, then came to a locker room, with work boots strewn against a far wall, benches, and lockers. He opened and closed lockers until he found one with clothing in it: a pair of jeans hanging from a hook and a dirty T-shirt. He held the jeans up, but they were far too small. He heard the door down the hallway open. Then voices, two men, speaking in Russian.

Dewey stepped quietly along the line of lockers. He wedged himself between the last locker and the wall.

One of the voices was coming closer. He couldn't understand what the man was saying, but his tone was unmistakable. Anger. He heard doors opening down the hallway, then footsteps moving up the stairs to a second floor. The two men were calling back and forth to each other.

From the corner, Dewey watched the room through a small gap between the top of the locker and the ceiling. He saw the man's shadow at first, then the man. He was big, dressed in a dark green uniform. Local police or railroad security.

Dewey stood as still as a statue. His eyes followed the man's as he scanned the room, taking a drag on his cigarette, a small hint of grin appearing.

Dewey's eyes shot to the bench. There, sitting on top of the bench, was the set of keys.

"Fuck," he whispered. *Don't look at the keys.*

The officer left the locker room and shut the door.

Dewey breathed a sigh of relief. He waited for the voices again. But there was nothing.

He should've searched the lockers.

Dewey understood in that moment that he'd seen the keys. He was getting the other officer.

Dewey scanned the locker room. There were two windows. Both were tiny.

The door was the room's only entrance or exit.

Then the lights went off.

Dewey stepped out of the small hiding area. He had precious little time. He crawled to the pile of boots. There were several dozen pairs, piled against the wall. He dug out a crawl space beneath the pile. He covered every inch of his body and head in boots, still clutching the Gerber in his right hand.

Dewey waited for more than a minute. He heard the faintest scratching of metal, as the doorknob was slowly twisted open. He watched as the door opened. He saw the vaguest outline of a gun, moving in, then training right, at the space just inside the door along the wall, then the unmuted explosion of gunfire filled the room as the officer fired at the space next to the door in the same instant another man lurched inside, gun aimed in the other direction, and then, a second later, fired three blasts through the door; whatever was behind the door was now pelted with holes.

One of the men turned the lights on. Dewey watched through a tiny gap in the mass of boots that lay atop him. The two officers looked surprised at the empty corner, at the lack of a dead man just inside the door.

The second man was short and fat. He said something to the taller man.

Dewey guessed, from the shaking of the man's head, that it was something along the lines of: *Are you sure someone is in here?*

The bigger guard stepped to the bench and picked up the keys, as if showing him proof.

Dewey's ears suddenly picked up the faintest hint of a siren in the far-off distance.

The short man barked something in Russian. The other guard

began to open the door to the first locker, near the door, at the opposite end of the room from Dewey. He looked inside the locker, found it empty, then slammed the door shut. He moved methodically down the line of lockers, opening and closing each one.

The siren grew louder, then was joined by more sirens.

They were coming. They were moving quickly, and they were organized. The Russian authorities were angry.

But how could they possibly know he was still in-country?

It didn't matter. There was only one way he'd be able to get out of the rail yard, and it would necessarily leave evidence, likely in blood. In a few short moments, things would get hairy.

A splash of lights cut in through one of the windows.

The larger guard registered the arrival of additional policemen. He muttered something to the other guard, now standing in front of where Dewey lay, covered in a pile of boots.

Dewey watched as the two Russians argued, voices rising as they barked back and forth at each other. The shorter Russian was still clutching a pistol, which was aimed at the ground. His legs were less than a foot from Dewey. Through the man's legs, Dewey could see the larger guard, who held a submachine gun, targeted unknowingly at Dewey's head.

Dewey's left arm pushed out through the boots—quietly, quickly—creeping through the air unnoticed. Dewey snatched the muzzle of the guard's pistol with his left hand as, with his right, he reached for the guard's hand. The guard felt the tugging, yelled, and looked down, eyes bulging, as Dewey clutched the gun, and now his hand. The guard yanked at the gun, trying to pull it away, as he screamed. The larger guard looked back at his partner, an expression of confusion on his face, until he saw Dewey's hand on the muzzle. He waited an extra moment, then swung his submachine gun in their direction, while in the same instant Dewey inserted his right index finger into the trigger opening, over the guard's finger, and lurched up, boots tumbling off him, overpowering the guard. Dewey swung the guard's arm, and the pistol, across the room, firing, just as the other guard triggered the submachine, blasting rounds into the wall to Dewey's right. The pistol's unmuted gunshot was like an explosion. The slug tore into the big guard's forehead, splattering blood behind him. He fell to the floor, on his back, as Dewey forced the small guard's arm to the left. The guard screamed, gripping the butt of the Skyph with both hands. But Dewey overpowered him. He forced the pistol skyward, so that the muzzle was aimed at the guard's chest, then pumped the trigger. The bullet tore into the center of the guard's chest, dropping him.

Dewey climbed onto the bench, glancing at the parking lot through one of the windows. Three police cruisers, lights still on, were surrounded by a cloud of dust. Several policemen moved across the parking lot toward the building, weapons out.

He charged down the hallway and dead-bolted the main door. He moved back down the corridor to the locker room. Dewey took off his damp jeans, removed the big guard's green uniform jacket and put it on, just as the first fist, knocking against the door, made a dull pounding noise down the hall.

Frantically, Dewey took off the man's weapons belt, boots, and pants and pulled them on. The pounding of fists grew louder, followed by shouting in Russian. Dewey pulled his jeans onto the big guard, then buttoned them, as a sudden, very loud explosion boomed from the doorway. Dewey's eyes shot up, watching the door as it rocketed inward, slamming into the wall across from the doorway.

Dewey took the pistol from the first guard and stuck it in the big man's hand. He grabbed the submachine gun with his left hand, and, with his right, dipped his fingers in blood from the dead guard, wiping it across his own cheek and forehead.

Calmly, as the first drumbeat of boots echoed from down the hallway, Dewey lay down, his head arched slightly up. He trained the muzzle of the submachine gun on the dead guard, waiting.

To an observer, the scene was mayhem, the conclusion simple: a battle had taken place, and the guard, Dewey, now holding the gun, had prevailed by a whisker, killing the intruder, after the intruder somehow killed the other guard.

Dewey looked up, pretending to be dazed, registering the arrival of a small horde of officers. His eyes met one of them, who said something, but Dewey didn't respond. Instead, he shut his eyes, lowering the submachine gun to the ground, and let his head fall back.

They carried Dewey to one of the police cruisers and lay him across the backseat. The door shut, then the car started to move.

The driver said something into the police radio, which was followed by a sharp squawking noise, then a female voice, probably a dispatcher, telling the driver where to go with the injured officer.

Dewey felt the weapons belt, removing a handgun. He opened his eyes just a crack, glancing to the front seat. There was only one officer, the driver.

Dewey sat up and swung the muzzle of the Skyph to the back of the driver's head. The driver glanced in the rearview mirror, jerking back reflexively at the weapon held against his skull.

"Do you speak English?" asked Dewey.

The driver nodded.

"Yes," he said in a coarse accent. "Little."

"Keep driving," said Dewey. "Do *not* pick up the radio. Do *not* adjust the lights. Keep your hands on the wheel. You understand?"

The police car was moving quickly. The daylight was rapidly turning the sky a light shade of blue.

"Tell me you understand."

"Yes, I understand."

"Who were you looking for?" Dewey asked. He already knew the answer, but some small part of him hoped perhaps he was wrong. He also wanted to find out how much they knew.

The driver glanced in the mirror, a look of confusion on his face.

"You," said the policeman.

He nodded to his right. On the seat was a fake leather folder. Dewey leaned over the seat, keeping the gun against the driver's

267

head, and opened the folder. There on the inside was a sheet of paper. It was an all points bulletin. The top half was covered in Cyrillic writing. Dewey stared at the paper, then reached his arm down and lifted it up. Beneath it were two photos. One showed him. It had been taken at the Four Seasons, by security cameras, as he checked in. The other showed Katya Basaeyev.

Dewey pressed the gun hard against the driver's neck, then held the sheet up.

"What does it say?" Dewey asked.

The driver glanced at the sheet, then looked at Dewey in the mirror.

"Multiple homicides," he said. "As well the abduction of the ballerina."

"Who put it out?" asked Dewey. "Saint Petersburg Metro?"

The driver glanced at the sheet.

"FSB," he answered, referring to Russia's notorious internal federal security force.

"Is it public yet?"

At this question, the officer turned, before Dewey placed the muzzle against his cheek and forced his head back around.

"You kidnapped someone famous. Your photo is everywhere."

The officer reached to the radio and turned it on. A man was speaking Russian.

"I don't speak Russian."

"Well, it's good for you that you don't. He's talking about you."

"What's he saying?"

"You're wanted: dead or alive."

49

Gant drove to an out-of-the way Best Buy store and purchased a new cell phone, paying for it with a Visa gift card bought under a fake name.

Back in the car, he rolled up his shirt sleeve. A phone number was written on his arm in ballpoint ink. He dialed the number.

"*Hola,*" came a soft female voice.

"Is he there?"

"No."

"He needs to call me. It's urgent."

"Yes," said the woman.

Gant read her the number for the new phone.

"Tell him it's extremely important."

Gant hung up. He glanced around the parking lot, then took out a pack of wipes from the glove compartment. He wiped the number from his arm, buttoned his shirt, then sped quickly out of the parking lot.

50

Dawn was at least an hour away as Poldark trudged along the dank, musty corridor belowdecks. At the cargo hold where the bomb was, he slowly pulled on the hazmat suit.

Each time, the suit took longer and longer to get on, most likely because, despite the self-contained breathing apparatus, radiation from the bomb was getting through. But those small doses were about to become a thing of the past. Today, exposure for him and anyone else on the boat would escalate dramatically. Today marked the beginning of the end for him and the crew.

He opened the steel door, stepped inside, then shut the door tightly behind him.

All extraneous pieces of the original bomb had been removed. What remained was on the stainless steel table. It looked like a giant soup can, four feet long, two feet in diameter. Thick, dark, reddish-green steel. A seam at one end of the cylinder. The other end smooth and rounded and slightly bulbous.

Poldark went to a large red duffel bag against the wall. He opened it and removed a black case. Inside was a set of instruments. After measuring the circumference of the end piece, Poldark attached a series of specialized clamps, then attached a wire to the clamps. This enabled Poldark to pinpoint the precise apex of the seam between the end of the cylinder and the barrel. Once that was done, he removed what looked like a pencil from the case. Placing it at the seam, he hit a small switch, producing a soft hum as a tiny, nearly invisible diamond-tungsten cutting device moved rapidly up and down, etching a minuscule cut into the steel.

It took Poldark six hours to penetrate the seam at the end of the barrel. It took him eight more hours to complete the cut in a manner that would not unintentionally set off the trigger.

Other than bathroom breaks, he didn't leave the room.

Sometime after eight at night, Poldark left the bomb and went back upstairs. He went directly to his bedroom and climbed into bed. He was so tired that he forgot to remove his suit as well as the breathing unit covering his head.

51

John Schmidt, the president's communications director, stepped into the Oval Office. Already gathered were President Dellenbaugh, National Security Advisor Josh Brubaker, and Vice President Daniel Donato.

"Sorry I'm late."

The mood was tense. Schmidt had called the meeting to discuss a subject that made all of them uncomfortable.

"We have to get the fact that a nuclear bomb is on its way to the United States out there," said Schmidt, standing just inside the doorway. "It's going to get out there, so we might as well be in front of it."

"I disagree," said Brubaker. "The level of panic that would be created would not only be hard to manage, it would hinder our effort to find the bomb."

"Josh," said Schmidt, shaking his head in impatience, "how many times have we had this debate on any number of topics? *It's going to leak*. There are too many people at too many agencies, not to mention the terrorist himself."

The door behind Schmidt abruptly opened. Schmidt's deputy, Gary Foster, poked his head in.

"They're breaking the story about Katya Basaeyev," he said. "I thought you'd want to know."

"Who's got it?"

"BBC."

Schmidt opened up what looked like a bookcase. Behind it were six flat-screen plasmas. He took the remote and switched on the BBC.

A female correspondent was on a bridge in Moscow, the lights of the city behind her.

"This is Sarah Rainsford, reporting to you live from Moscow, where a series of incidents tonight have the country rattled and Russian authorities on high alert . . . "

The television cut to an aerial video taken from a news helicopter showing flames coming from a building.

"What you are looking at is live video from Rublevka, an exclusive Moscow suburb, where, according to several eyewitnesses, a loud explosion occurred just a few hours ago. As you can see, the inferno is still burning as firefighters try to stop the flames from spreading to nearby dachas . . ."

The TV cut to live video from Saint Petersburg, where a swarm of police lights flashed on a locked-down street near the Four Seasons Lion Palace.

"In addition, in the city of Saint Petersburg, just a few hours from here, an intense manhunt is under way after the apparent abduction of one of Russia's most famous citizens, the ballerina Katya Basaeyev, taken,

according to one source, from her hotel room following a performance at the Kirov Ballet. This photograph, taken by a hotel security camera, shows an unidentified man whom the FSB called its main suspect in the abduction . . ."

A black-and-white photo of Dewey flashed to the television screen.

Schmidt muted it.

"The story is going to get closer and closer," he said emphatically.

"We can't let any aspect of the bomb get out," said Brubaker, almost yelling. "The American public would panic—"

"You don't get it, do you?" interrupted Schmidt, shaking his head and taking a step toward Brubaker, then pointing. "It's not the White House versus America, Josh. It's America versus the terrorists. We need the public's help. We need their support. If you lie about stuff like this, you'll lose them. They'll blame us for not being up front, and by 'us' I mean the president."

Schmidt turned to leave.

"Mr. President," said Brubaker, looking at Dellenbaugh. "You need to make the call."

Dellenbaugh nodded at Schmidt.

"I understand your argument, John," said Dellenbaugh, "but Josh is right. If America finds out a nuclear device is on its way to our country, there will be widespread chaos. We can't stop the terrorist and deal with that at the same time. For now, this stays close to the vest."

52

Cloud looked out the window at the low-flung buildings of Elektrostal. Until now, the city meant nothing to him. It was a place to work. A place to remain anonymous, off the radar screens of law enforcement and intelligence agencies. Off the radar of men like Alexei Malnikov. But tonight, Cloud felt hatred for the small, shabby city.

Two forces had guided him to this place and to this moment. The nuclear bomb represented the past. It was the achievement of a life's work, and the bomb's detonation on American soil would be the culmination of it all. Then it would end, that life he desperately wanted to step away from, and his new life would start. That new life was Katya. Respectability. Belonging. Above all else, family. *A child.* Yes, a child. He hadn't admitted that part to anyone, not even her, but it was what he wanted more than anything else. A little girl. Now it was gone. The dream was gone.

It was the first time he felt outdueled by anyone. In the span of a few hours, the plan he'd carefully constructed was cracking. Andreas had succeeded in taking away the future. All that was left was the past.

So be it, he thought.

"Has Langley discovered the trapdoors?" Cloud asked.

"No," said Sascha. "They know something is going on. They're running standard procedures to attempt to block us, but we should be fine."

"Very well," he whispered, too softly for no anyone else to hear.

A memory flashed. It was his father. He could hear him speaking. Sitting alone with him, in front of the hearth, playing chess.

"*There are some moves in chess that are not understood, even by grand masters,*" his papa said. "*Moves that are made by some part of the brain that is the part that knows how to win.*"

"But you did know," he whispered. "You knew they would come after her. You exposed Katya. You exposed her the moment you sacrificed Al-Medi. It was inevitable."

Cloud had hired the best three men money could purchase to guard Katya. Perhaps he could've somehow gotten her to cancel her performance, but he knew it ran the risk of alerting the Americans. The entire night had been based on subterfuge, on the Americans believing one reality while in fact another one lurked beneath.

Now, when he should have been on his way to Saint Petersburg to surprise his fiancée, he stood staring into the pitch-black oblivion of his own eyes reflected in the glass.

Had he misread his opponent? Had America been deceiving *him* all along?

"Impossible," he remarked to himself.

Cloud knew the United States would never sacrifice men as part of a deception. They would not allow three soldiers to die at a dacha. This was not in their DNA. Russia, China, for that matter almost any country but the United States, would sacrifice men. But not America.

"Oh, no," he said to himself as a tingling sensation arose from his spine.

He arrived at the conclusion he was after: he was playing chess against an opponent who played by a different set of rules. Tonight, he'd fallen victim to the lowest of rule violations in the game of chess, a move done by children: the United States had placed an extra piece on the board. And not just a pawn or a rook. The abduction had been the work of a knight—bold, reckless, and violent.

"Interesting," said Sascha.

Sascha's words brought him back.

"What is it?"

"Saint Petersburg Metro," said Sascha. "All points bulletin."

Cloud read the document:

** FLASH: URGENT **
Possible mult homicide at rail yard
Kolpinsky Rayon km 554.7
Two dead
** SUSPECT AT LARGE **

"Where is Kolpinsky Rayon?" asked Cloud.

Sascha brought up a map of Saint Petersburg. The town was several miles downstream from Saint Petersburg, then inland, in the direction of Moscow.

"Now is the time to release Andreas's identity," said Cloud.

53

TOSNO, RUSSIA

They drove for several miles away from the rail yard. Dewey remained in the backseat, keeping the gun pressed to the officer's neck. When they came to a small town, Dewey ordered the Russian to pull into the parking lot of a decrepit-looking strip mall, empty at this late hour.

"Behind the building," Dewey ordered.

The policeman pulled in back of the building and parked next to a large black Dumpster.

"Get out," said Dewey.

The officer got out as Dewey climbed from the back of the car, keeping the gun aimed at him.

"Give me the belt," said Dewey. "Hurry up."

The Russian unhooked his weapons belt and tossed it to Dewey, who threw it in the cruiser.

"Empty your pockets."

The policeman had a wad of cash as well as a cell phone. Dewey pocketed the cash, then put the phone on the front seat of the cruiser.

Dewey stepped toward him.

"You saved your own life tonight by not doing something stupid. Don't start now. I'm going to knock you out. When you wake up, you'll be inside that Dumpster. Your head will hurt, but you'll live."

"May I ask you something?"

"What?"

"Did you abduct her?"

Dewey ignored his question, then slammed the Russian's head with the butt of the pistol, a trained, precisely targeted strike that caused him to crumble to the ground, unconscious.

Dewey flex-cuffed the policeman's wrists and ankles. He ripped part of his shirt off and tied it around his head and through his mouth, gagging him. Dewey lifted him over his shoulder, fireman style. He stepped to the Dumpster and dropped him in. The body made a clanging noise as it tumbled to the bottom.

By now, they knew the two dead men at the rail yard were policemen. A search for the officer's car would be under way.

Dewey climbed back in the police car and tore away from the mall, driving without headlights. A few miles down the road, he saw a minuscule black object in the sky, directly in front of him, flying low. A moment later, he heard the dull rhythm of chopper blades slashing the air. He jacked the wheel left and barreled into a parking lot next to an apartment building. The chopper grew louder as Dewey gunned the sedan hard, streaking across the crowded parking lot. He aimed for an empty space, then slammed his brakes, sliding the last few feet as he came to a hard stop.

Clutching the gun in his right hand, the door handle in his left, Dewey listened from the car as the helicopter roared overhead, then was gone.

He stepped from the police cruiser to a white station wagon. With the butt of the gun, he smashed the rear window, then unlocked the car. He tossed the weapons belt onto the front seat.

He popped the trunk on the police cruiser. Inside sat a canvas duffel bag. He ransacked the bag and found a set of civilian clothes. He pulled out a pair of pants and a plaid short-sleeved button-down, changed, and left the police uniform in the trunk. The clothing was slightly baggy, but it didn't rub against the gash near his knee.

At the bottom of the duffel, he found another cell phone, which he guessed was the officer's personal phone.

He hotwired the station wagon in less than half a minute. He gunned the car toward the main road.

Dewey needed time, the time to settle things down and get away from the immediate vicinity of Saint Petersburg and the rail yard. He was in a rapidly escalating mess. He needed to make contact with Langley. The problem was, he was being hunted by FSB, one of the most notoriously hard-hitting law enforcement agencies in the world.

It had to be.

Get away. That's your top priority.

He turned on the phone and went to the map application. He was near a town called Lyuban. Moscow was east. He studied the route, then exited the map application and dialed Langley.

After several rings, a high-pitched monotone could be heard. Dewey punched in a code and a woman came on the line.

"Signal."

"TS 2294 dash 6."

"Hold, please."

A few seconds later, Dewey heard a click, then a voice.

"Where are you?"

It was Calibrisi.

"Running. Do we know where he is?"

"Not yet."

"What am I supposed to do?"

"You need to get to the safe house in Moscow. There's food, weapons, and you can take a shower. There's another operator waiting at the safe house as well as a case officer. Bill is sending in more men."

"Who's the operator?"

"His name is Maybank. He's injured."

Dewey glanced down at his pants. He could see red from the wound, which was continuing to bleed.

"How close are we on the intel?" asked Dewey.

"We're working on it," said Calibrisi. "NSA, Pentagon, Langley—everything is focused on this right now. But—"

"What?"

"It's a needle in a haystack. This guy is an unknown. A ghost."

"FSB is going to be tracking me," said Dewey. "If I'm the only able-bodied operator over here, that's a problem."

"I'm working on other options," said Calibrisi, quieter. "Non-Agency resources."

"Israel?"

"No," said Calibrisi. "Someone outside official channels. I'll tell you more when you get to the safe house."

54

Calibrisi hung up with Dewey, then dropped the cell phone to the floor and stepped on it, smashing it to pieces. He removed another disposable cell phone from his desk and dialed a number in London.

"Gansevoort PLC," came the soft, clipped British accent of a woman. "How may I direct your call?"

"I've been in a car accident on Ratcliffe Highway," said Calibrisi.

"Hold, please."

A moment later, another woman came on the line.

"Director's office. How may I help you?"

"Natalie, it's Hector Calibrisi."

"Hello, Hector. Let me get him for you."

As Calibrisi waited, a tall man with glasses appeared outside the glass door to his office. It was Ted Wendell, the Agency's chief technology officer. Wendell was spearheading the effort to determine how Cloud had hacked into Langley's network infrastructure—and to sanitize it.

Calibrisi held up his hand, telling Wendell to wait.

"Hector," came the aristocratic English accent of MI6's Cambridge-educated director, Derek Chalmers. "How are you?"

"Not so good."

"Did you have a little too much vodka, Hector?" asked Chalmers.

Calibrisi was momentarily quiet.

"What do you know?"

"Very little. But Dewey's photo is on the wire, so I knew something was up. They haven't identified him yet, but there is a manhunt. He's going to get rolled up, Hector. Do you want us to assist in the reconnaissance?"

"I'm not worried about Dewey."

"Did he abduct the woman?"

"Yes."

"Tell me, why is the United States so interested in Russian ballerinas all of a sudden?"

"Her fiancé is a terrorist. He put a thirty-kiloton nuclear bomb in a boat and it's on the way to the United States."

A soft whistle came from Chalmers.

"What do you need from us?" he asked. "It goes without saying, we're at your service."

"Katya Basaeyev is being flown to Inverness," said Calibrisi. "I need your best interrogator. At this point, she's our only connection to him."

"And he's the only one who knows where it's going?"

"Correct."

"How far out is the vessel?"

"Two days."

"July Fourth," noted Chalmers. "Independence Day. You're lucky we Brits don't hold grudges."

Calibrisi cleared his throat.

"Very lucky, Derek. Thank you, as always, for your help."

"I'll fly up right now," said Chalmers.

"You don't need to go. Just send up your top interrogator."

283

"That happens to be me. If she knows something, I'll find it out."

"Dewey thinks she's innocent. He said that she seemed genuinely surprised at the fact that her fiancé is a bad guy."

"As you know, and despite his irascible countenance, I'm one of Dewey's biggest fans," said Chalmers. "But he's an operator. I nearly lost my life due to a Russian honey trap. Never trust a Russian woman. What's the fiancé's name, by the way?"

"Pyotr Vargarin. He's called Cloud."

"*Cloud?*" said Chalmers. "What a pompous ass. Already I don't like the fellow. Send some biographical information, will you?"

"Will do."

Calibrisi hung up his phone, then nodded to Wendell, who pushed in the door and entered Calibrisi's large glass-walled office.

"Where are we on this, Ted?" asked Calibrisi.

"It's bad," said Wendell. "It's some sort of virus. It's going to take awhile. Cloud has been inside for more than a year. He built a bunch of trapdoors. Looks like he can come and go as he pleases."

"Can't we remove them?"

"The problem is, we don't know how many, or where they are. As long as the virus is still active, we could theoretically get rid of all the trapdoors but still not have gotten to the heart of the problem."

"How long to clean it?"

Wendell shrugged his shoulders.

"A couple weeks, maybe a month."

"Can we get some contractors on it? Cyber security specialists?"

"That's like hiring the police to stop a bank robbery after it's happened, Hector."

"What's your point?"

"*He's inside,*" said Wendell. "He cracked the vault and now he's inside. We don't need a cop. We need a bank robber."

Calibrisi nodded, deep in thought.

"Thanks, Ted," he said, nodding to the door. "That'll be all."

Calibrisi waited until Wendell left, then put both hands on top of his desk, bracing himself against the wave of anxiety that flooded over him. It wasn't just the lack of manpower on the ground in Russia. They were exposed here, in the United States, as well. Time was running out. The enemy was attacking on all fronts. Like cancer, he'd laid down his contagion silently, at a level that was invisible to the human eye. By the time Rublevka went south, the cancer had already taken hold. Now they were witnessing the rapid metastasis of the illness. It was spreading. Worst of all, there was no longer a vague premonition as to the day the cancer would take down its victim. Chalmers was right: the attack they nicknamed 9/12 would take place on Independence Day, the Fourth of July, a nation's birthday that in two days' time would be forever marked by genocide.

Calibrisi picked up an object from his desk. It was an old pistol, a Walther PPK, its black patina worn from use. It was a gun that, many years ago, in a Berlin apartment building, had been used by a Stasi agent to try to kill him. The slug had missed. Not by much, but it had missed, and Calibrisi had taken the gun after putting a bullet through his would-be killer's head. He kept it because it reminded him of the thin line that separated victory from defeat, good luck from bad luck, life from death. An inch here, a moment there.

A sudden, violent lurch when your enemy doesn't expect it.

Calibrisi understood then what he needed to do.

He crossed his office and opened the small closet at the opposite side of the room, quickly stuffing a few items in a beat-up leather weekend bag. He went back to his desk, opened a drawer, and pulled out a bundle of disposable cell phones and put them in the bag.

A few minutes later, bag in hand, Calibrisi stepped off the elevator eight floors below and walked down the hallway. He put his hand on a scanner next to the door. A half second later, the door unlocked and he stepped inside Targa.

Polk was standing before one of the plasma screens, watching a live POV video of one of the agents now attempting to infiltrate Russia. The view showed a line of passengers at an airport.

Calibrisi got Polk's attention. Polk crossed the room.

"What's the status on the team?"

"It's set up," said Polk. "Brainard and Fairweather should be wheels-up within the hour."

For the first time, Polk saw Calibrisi's leather bag.

"Where you going?"

Calibrisi paused, then spoke: "I'm going off grid. I'll call you."

55

W hen Poldark awoke the next morning, he leaned immediately to his left and started vomiting.

You're running out of time.

The radiation sickness was already upon him. It would settle in quickly, ravage for a day or two, then kill them all. By the time they arrived at their destination, all of the men aboard the boat would wish they were dead. Poldark, mainly due to his age, would likely *be* dead.

Poldark, Faqir, and the other six men aboard the trawler had all agreed to what was to come. They all signed up to die on behalf of a cause.

For Faqir and the Chechens, that cause was jihad. For Poldark, the reason had nothing to do with jihad. It had to do with a man named Vargarin, though not Pyotr.

Anuslav Vargarin had been Poldark's professor and mentor. He studied under Vargarin and it was Vargarin who convinced Poldark, at age twenty-one, to pursue a life devoted to scientific discovery and academic research. Professor Vargarin had been his undergraduate advisor, his doctoral thesis advisor, and, for twenty-two years, his colleague.

Poldark was part of the team that helped Anuslav Vargarin turn an idea into a theory and then, ultimately, into a formula, a formula that eventually got Vargarin killed. In a few days, it would kill Poldark as well, though in a very different way. It would kill Poldark because he would utilize the formula to divide the nuclear device into two nuclear devices, and, during that process, would be exposed to lethal amounts of gamma radiation. He would die either when the bomb was detonated in New York City or from radiation sickness before they got there.

What Vargarin created, with Poldark's assistance, was a way to achieve supercritical mass with less uranium than a standard nuclear device. Though other scientists had also succeeded in achieving the same goal, all had done so with chemical accelerants that, while not as difficult to procure as uranium, still required the use of apparatus and/or chemicals that only a major enterprise possessed, such as a cyclotron or polonium. Vargarin's theory achieved supercritical mass with a slight twist, using a chemical compound that could be made more easily than had ever been achieved before, without a cyclotron and without the need for a rare element such as polonium.

In essence, it meant two bombs could be created from one. At a time when the Soviet Union and the United States were at war, a Cold War, racing to amass nuclear weapons, Vargarin's idea was revolutionary. A country could double its existing stockpile of nukes without the need for more radioactive material. It was an idea big enough for America to kill for.

When the Americans killed Anuslav Vargarin and stole the formula, they also killed Poldark's hope of a scientific career as celebrated as Vargarin's. He would have been part of the team that designed it. In the Soviet Union, such accomplishments were handsomely rewarded, its scientists treated like rock stars. America had robbed him of his future.

Nearly thirty years later, Vargarin's Theorem was no longer innovative or, for that matter, used.

But all that was secondary to Poldark. All that mattered to him was that it worked.

After carefully removing the bomb's component parts, Poldark took two of the eight uranium rings and placed them in a steel case beneath the table. He reassembled the original physics package. He drilled a small hole through its cap and then welded the cap back on.

Next he went to the duffel and removed a shiny steel cylinder that was longer and wider than the original. Over the next several hours, he replicated the design of the original bomb. Once the gun assembly was done, he welded a similar end cap to it, though this one had a slight modification. At the center was a small threaded hole.

Poldark went to the duffel and removed what was the most important part of the process. It was a large thermos, filled with a liquid, radiogenic isotope of bismuth. It looked like water. Using a plastic funnel, he poured the contents of the thermos into the second device.

From the black tool case, he removed two specially designed copper bolts. At the head of each bolt, three small screws stuck out like small antennae. He screwed a bolt into each of the caps, threading them tightly into the holes at the end of each bomb.

Poldark removed two small, similar-looking devices from the duffel bag. They resembled cell phones except that both had wires dangling out. These were the triggers. He attached the wires from each trigger to the copper bolts atop the two bombs, wrapping them around the screws, then fastening them tight. He wrapped several strips of duct tape over the end of each bomb.

Finally, he removed two detonators from the tool case. These were thin, square boxes the size of television remotes, made of white plastic. On one side of each detonator was a square blue cap that stuck out. Poldark placed each detonator on the table, then lifted up the caps. Beneath were switches, like light switches. They glowed dull red. He closed the covers and wrapped duct tape around them, ensuring no one accidentally flipped either of them before they were in place and ready to be detonated. He marked each detonator with a number so that the right detonator went with the bomb it had been programmed to.

Poldark stepped back from the table. He placed his hands behind his back, leaned against the wall, and slowly slid down and sat on the floor. He pulled the SCBA, self contained breathing apparatus, from over his head. Beneath, he was wet with perspiration, his skin a pale, ashen gray. Poldark crossed his legs. He sat and stared at the two bombs for more than ten minutes.

He looked up at a clock on the wall. He'd been working for twelve hours. His eyes returned to the bombs.

Would Anuslav be proud of him now? he wondered. Would he be proud of him for implementing his vision? For helping his son exact vengeance on those who'd killed his mother and father as he watched, an innocent five-year-old, sentenced to life as an orphan, crippled by a memory that could not be erased? Would Anuslav share the sense of justice when the bombs tore through life and limb of countrymen who'd taken his very life? Who'd stolen his life's work, sacrificing one of the Soviet Union's greatest scientific minds, all for a few sheets of paper filled with letters and numbers? Would the great professor be proud of him now?

Poldark knew the answer.

56

GRAMERCY PARK HOTEL
NEW YORK CITY

Igor heard his phone beeping through a fog of Patrón and extremely expensive marijuana, grown in a laboratory in Oregon and designed for a mild prep school high intermingled with a Viagra-like sexual potency. The beeping was accompanied by a nudge from the foot that was approximately half an inch from his face, a foot that was tan and smooth, with red toenail polish and a heel that looked as if it had never done a hard day's work in its life, despite the fact that it belonged to a runway model, at least, that's what Igor thought she'd said. His left eye opened. He was now staring at the foot. It was a beautiful foot, he thought.

What the hell is her name? Alice? Allison?

The phone beeped for a fifth time.

At the other end of the bed, he felt a girl kissing his ankle, then his knee, then his thigh, and then a little higher.

Whoever's calling, well, they're just going to have to wait.

Suddenly, he felt a hand wrap around his chest. His eyes darted down. It was a small hand, brown, with white fingernail polish. Then he remembered the black girl. *She* was Alice. Now it was coming back to him. La Piscine. Hotel Americano. A shared joint. A limo ride back to the Gramercy. The shower.

Igor was worth more than $100 million. It wasn't as much as Sergey Brin, one of his classmates at Stanford, but it was better than a sharp stick in the eye.

He was the best programmer in his class. If others had made more money, it didn't seem to bother him.

Igor had made his fortune working for an American energy company, KKB. With little help or fanfare, he had designed, built, and then managed a technology colossus that controlled, in real time, all aspects of exploration, production, storage, and distribution for the largest energy company in North America and the second largest in the world.

Igor not only built it all alone, he managed it with a staff of only twelve people. The company's executives and traders knew precisely what was occurring in all parts of the company's massive supply chain, at all times.

Most impressive was the complex algorithm Igor had written that enabled KKB to optimize how it priced its products—electricity, oil, coal—in real time, against location. It was a mathematical piece of software genius. It helped deliver the highest profit margins of any other energy company, large or small, in the world.

KKB, in turn, had rewarded Igor handsomely. The year before, he'd made $25 million. And on New Year's Day, Igor had walked out of KKB for the last time, retiring with enough money to live a life of pleasure and, occasionally, debauchery. Of course, all that was irrelevant at this particular moment. Money, KKB, computers, the world—none of that crossed his mind, as Alice said something in French that he didn't understand.

The beeping started again, and this time it didn't stop. Reluctantly, Igor pushed Alice off and reached for his cell phone.

"Who is it?" Igor asked.

"It's Hector Calibrisi."

Igor sat up. He rubbed the bridge of his nose, trying to expel the hangover and dizziness from his head.

"What time is it?"

"Two o'clock," said Calibrisi.

"Day or night?"

Calibrisi ignored the question.

"We need your help, Igor."

"Call Geek Squad," said Igor.

"I'm not fucking around."

"I'm not either. I retired, Hector."

"This concerns your adopted homeland, the United States of America. I'm assuming you still like it here?"

"Oh, man. What do you need my help with?"

"Catching a hacker."

Igor swung his legs over the edge of the bed and stood up. He walked toward the bathroom as the two girls curled up together and started kissing.

"What do you mean, 'a hacker'?"

"He's Russian. His name is Vargarin, but he goes by the name—"

"Cloud," said Igor, stepping into the bathroom and turning the shower on—cold.

"That's right."

"Okay, first thing, tell your IT people not to shut anything down," said Igor. "No sanitization, no removal of code. *Nothing.* Leave it alone."

"Why?"

"He's inside Langley, correct?"

"Yeah."

"Cloud came in through a path. We need to find the beginning of the path. If we can do that, we can find him."

57

PARK TENISOWY OLIMPIA
POZNAŃ, POLAND

The bleachers were filled with fans, there to watch a second-round doubles match in Poland's sole professional men's tennis tournament, the Poznań Open. Beneath a warm summer evening, the point was already under way.

The French team was leading, having taken the first set over the pair of Americans. Tom Fairweather suddenly found himself in no-man's-land, trying to get to a lob that was headed for the baseline.

Fairweather had gotten lured to the net by a drop shot, and now he had no choice. He leapt, striking the ball with the very edge of the racket. The ball sailed in a wobbly line back down the middle of the court, between the two Frenchmen.

"Watch your alley!" barked Fairweather.

The French player reached the ball and pivoted, ripping a forehand crosscourt, toward Fairweather's alley. At full sprint, he lurched forward, racket extended, diving. The ball hit the racket in the half second before Fairweather landed chest-first on the clay, thumping hard and sliding painfully forward as gasps came from the crowd. From the ground, he watched the ball hit the top of the net, perch for a pregnant moment, then dribble over and die on the clay on the other side of the court.

Slowly, Fairweather climbed to his feet. The front of his white shirt and shorts, as well as his arms and legs, were covered in red clay.

"Nice shot," said one of the French players, nodding at him.

"Thanks."

Above the French player's shoulder, he saw a woman in a white linen pantsuit standing in the entranceway, arms crossed, staring at him.

Fairweather walked across the court to his partner.

"I gotta go."

"Can't you hold it until the break?"

"No, I have to leave. Sorry."

His partner took a deep breath.

"We're in the middle of a—"

Fairweather didn't wait to hear the end of his partner's sentence. He ran to the court exit. In the underground passageway beneath the bleachers, he dropped his racket on the ground and fell into a full-on sprint, charging out through the central clubhouse to the street. A silver Volvo station wagon was idling.

He climbed in the back, joining the woman from the court, and the car sped away.

Panting hard, he looked at her.

"What is it?"

"Moscow," the woman said, nodding to a white duffel bag on the seat. He unzipped it, finding a change of clothes. Beneath the clothing was money, a passport, and a plane ticket.

As the Volvo headed for the airport, Fairweather undressed.

"What do you know?" he asked as he pulled on a pair of dry boxers. He glanced up, catching her appraising his body.

"Tina, what do you know?" he repeated.

"It's Emergency Priority," she said, looking out the window.

Fairweather's demeanor shifted. He stared straight ahead,

watching the other cars on the road, lost in thought, a cold, blank expression on his face.

A few minutes later, the Volvo pulled into Poznań–Ławica Airport. Fairweather looked at her one more time.

"Tell me what you know. I know you know something."

"We lost five men earlier tonight."

"In Russia?"

"Yes."

"How good is the paper?"

She looked back from the window.

"It's one of Mr. Coughlin's old aliases," she whispered. "The ones he kept in the safe. Bill insisted."

58

Alina described to Brainard, for the second time that evening, the car accident. It had happened that afternoon, in front of her office near Victory Square. An elderly woman had been struck by a taxicab, then thrown in the air. Alina had been the first person to find her, lying facedown on the sidewalk, dead.

"*Miortvych*," she said in Belarusian, as again tears appeared on her cheeks. "*Ja byŭ biezdapamožny, Todd.*"

Dead. I was helpless, Todd.

You get used to it, Brainard thought to himself.

"*Jość, jość*," he said.

There, there.

Brainard put his hand on hers, then noticed a man seated at the bar, staring at him.

"*Ja chutka viarnusi*," he said, standing.

I'll be right back.

At the bar, Carter, Minsk chief of station, was having a glass of wine and reading the newspaper. Beads of sweat covered his brow. Brainard stood next to him.

"Moscow," Carter whispered. "Vernacular House. Emergency Priority."

"What's going on?"

"I don't know. Bill called and told me to get you the fuck over there."

"FSB tagged me last week," said Brainard. "I won't make it through Customs."

Carter pushed a section of the paper toward him. The edge of a white envelope was visible.

"The passport's fresh," said Carter, "and it's off grid."

"How fresh?"

"Ten minutes old. Get moving."

59

VERNACULAR HOUSE
MOSCOW

Christy Braga knocked on the door to the bedroom. There was no answer.

"Johnny?"

She was holding a field trauma medical kit, housed in a large stainless steel case. She opened the door.

Maybank was lying on the bed. He stared up at her. His face was bright red. He was drenched in sweat, even though the air-conditioning was cranked up.

"We need to remove the bullet," she said.

Maybank stared at her with bloodshot eyes.

"I'll be fine," he said.

She went to the side of the bed and pulled the blanket away. The mattress beneath Maybank's leg was covered in red.

Braga opened the trauma kit. She removed an electronic thermometer and waved it across his forehead.

His fever had spiked to 104 degrees.

"You will not be fine unless we remove it."

"Fuck off," he panted, weakly pushing her away. "I need a doctor."

Braga searched through the case, finding a syringe, and filled it with oxycodone. She held it in her left hand, thumb on the end of the plunger. She removed a scalpel, forceps, suture material, and a needle, placing them on the top of the case.

"Lie back," she said soothingly.

"You're not touching me," he wheezed.

She lifted the scalpel and moved toward him. He lurched at her, she ducked, then she slammed the needle into his neck. His eyes drifted back into his head and his eyelids shut.

She placed her hand on Maybank's torso, rubbing it gently. He was breathing very rapidly, unconscious but alive.

Braga cut away Maybank's pants at the top of the thigh, above the wound. She took the scalpel and cut four small incisions in the skin near the bullet hole. She put the forceps into the bullet hole, digging down, searching for the slug. After more than a minute, she felt the hard edge of a steel object. Carefully, she gripped it with the forceps, rocked it slowly back and forth, and pulled the slug from Maybank's leg.

Braga cleaned the wound, sewed the skin back together, then wrapped the thigh in a thick bandage. Finally, she filled a syringe with antibiotics and injected it into Maybank's leg.

Braga sat on the bed next to Maybank and placed her hand on his forehead. He was still hot. His eyelids cracked open.

"Get some rest," she said. "They'll be here soon. We need you."

60

DURHAM DRIVE
POTOMAC, MARYLAND

At just before three, under a blazing sun, Calibrisi's black Lincoln Town Car pulled down a quiet road lined on both sides with white horse fence and palatial homes. The car came to a set of iron gates, which parted as his driver took him closer, then moved down a long pebble-stone driveway. The driveway led in a winding arc to a massive white house that looked like a palace.

"Jesus Christ," said Calibrisi, reaching for the car door. "What a fucking eyesore."

Calibrisi walked slowly up the driveway, then climbed marble steps to a pair of ten-foot-high doors. He rang the doorbell. When the doors opened, a young blond woman in a bright yellow tennis outfit was standing there.

"Mr. Calibrisi?" she asked, smiling.

"Yes."

"Follow me. John's in back. Would you like something to drink?"

"No, thank you."

Calibrisi trailed the woman through an entrance hall and out to a stone terrace. Below was a tennis court, a swimming pool, and a rolling lawn that spread out to a white fence several hundred yards away.

John Barrows was seated in a teak chaise. He was wearing white tennis shorts and a striped polo shirt. Barrows's hair was tousled. He had a blank expression on his face. He clutched a glass of lemonade.

"Hi, John," said Calibrisi, taking a seat next to Barrows. "Sorry to interrupt your tennis match."

Barrows was one of Washington, D.C.'s most powerful attorneys. Unlike most high-profile lawyers in town, he wasn't well known, except to the select few who needed to know him.

When *The Washington Post* attempted to write a piece on him a few years before, Barrows succeeded in doing something even U.S. presidents had failed to do, namely, get the story killed. Barrows didn't just have influence. He had power. His clients were the substructure that underlined most criminal activity in the United States. On the one hand, the U.S. government fought him, but at the highest levels, at times like this, they worked with him. They had to.

"What is it, Hector?" said Barrows.

"Before we start, I want you to send Alexei Malnikov a text."

"Why?"

"Tell him to do a sweep of all cell phones, computers, and any other appliances that are connected to outside networks. He needs to sanitize. He'll need a good IT person."

Barrows reached for his cell phone.

"Was Langley penetrated?" Barrows asked as he typed.

"Yes," said Calibrisi as Barrows typed a text. When Barrows was done, he looked up.

"The floor is yours, Mr. Director."

"The conversation we're about to have never happened," said Calibrisi, staring at Barrows. "Dead man talk."

Barrows nodded.

"Okay."

"I want to cut a deal," said Calibrisi.

"I'm listening."

"Alexei pressured a Ukrainian general into selling him a nuclear bomb," said Calibrisi.

"So you allege," said Barrows.

"He admitted to it."

Barrows nodded.

"I figured it was something more provocative than usual."

"The bomb is on its way to the United States."

For the first time, Barrows looked momentarily flummoxed.

"How?"

"Boat. A fishing trawler. It left Sevastopol three days ago."

"So sink it," said Barrows.

"Good idea," said Calibrisi. "Why didn't we think of that?"

Barrows grinned.

"There are four million registered commercial fishing vessels in the world," added Calibrisi. "At least double that if you include unregistered boats."

"How many fishing trawlers?"

"The size of the one the bomb left on? Approximately a million."

"Alexei Malnikov is not a terrorist, Hector."

"The man he gave it to is, however," said Calibrisi.

"Who is he?"

"His name is Vargarin. He goes by the name Cloud. He's a computer hacker."

Barrows took a sip of lemonade. He stood up and walked to the balustrade that overlooked the tennis court and swimming pool.

"What do you need?"

"Alexei's help."

"You think my client knows where this guy is?" asked Barrows.

"Not necessarily," said Calibrisi. "But he might be able to find him."

"How do you figure that?"

"Let's put it this way," said Calibrisi. "If you asked me to go into the woods and find a truffle, I probably wouldn't find it."

Barrows laughed.

"I won't tell Alexei you compared him to a pig," said Barrows.

"There are air wars and there are ground wars," said Calibrisi. "Right now, we need someone who knows the dark alleys of Russia."

"Don't you guys have manpower in Big Red?"

"Of course we do," said Calibrisi. "But we need local access."

"How big is the bomb?"

"Thirty kilotons."

Barrows's mouth fell open in astonishment. He looked ashen.

"If this bomb detonates, it will be a very dark day for this country," Calibrisi continued. "We're talking about the potential for more than a million deaths. We need Alexei's help. We're willing to pay a great deal of money for it."

"You think money would move the dial with this guy?" scoffed Barrows. "If they included Alexei Malnikov on the Forbes 400, he'd be number six. He doesn't care about another fifty million, hundred million, or whatever amount the U.S. government offers."

"I can't leave it to chance."

Barrows leaned back in his chair.

"There's only one thing Alexei cares about, and that's his father," said Barrows. "You want pay for performance, you need to deal with his dad."

Barrows's message was clear: Alexei Malnikov might help find Cloud in exchange for freeing his father from prison.

"A full presidential pardon," added Barrows. "Nothing less."

Calibrisi nodded slowly, deep in thought. This was the precise deal he knew he needed to cut with Barrows. But now that it was on the table, he felt sick to his stomach.

The low electric hum of a helicopter came from the distant sky.

"Fine," said Calibrisi. "We'll do it."

"It'll need to be in writing," said Barrows. "From the attorney general."

Calibrisi stood up as the sound of the chopper grew louder. Suddenly, a navy blue Sikorsky S-76C cut across the tree line, then hooked left and down toward Barrows's backyard, descending with almost military intent.

"It cuts both ways, John," said Calibrisi, his voice rising above the growing din.

"What does that mean?" Barrows shot back.

"We'll do the deal. He helps us find Cloud, we stop the bomb, his dad goes free. But if we don't stop it—"

"All the kid can do is try," said Barrows, protesting. "It wouldn't be fair for you to hold him responsible if this nutjob detonates a nuclear bomb on American soil."

"He sourced it," said Calibrisi, his anger rising for the first and only time during the conversation. "If that nuke goes off on U.S. soil, anyone with any connection to it better make damn sure his affairs are in order."

"That sounds like a threat."

Calibrisi watched as the chopper settled onto the lawn, just behind the tennis court. He paused, then stared angrily at Barrows.

"It *is* a threat. Alexei Malnikov helped create this problem."

Calibrisi took a few steps toward the stairs that led to the backyard, then turned back to Barrows.

"You tell me, John, if this nuclear bomb goes off, and a million people die, do you think Alexei Malnikov deserves to live?"

61

Malnikov's crimson red Gulfstream 200 touched down at Moscow International Airport and taxied to the private aviation terminal, coming to a stop next to a waiting bright green Lamborghini Aventador 720-4. As Malnikov hustled down the stairs of the jet, the car's right scissor door arose like a knife blade into the air. Malnikov climbed in the passenger seat, nodding with barely concealed anger at the driver. Before the door was even halfway down, the Lamborghini's tires screeched high and the sports car ripped across the tarmac toward the airport exit.

Eight minutes later, the Lamborghini braked in front of a low brick building that housed Malnikov's base of operations along with his nightclub. Malnikov stepped out of the car and walked to the door, which opened as he approached. Inside, a gunman stood.

"Hello, Alexei," he said.

Malnikov ignored him.

The club was empty. It smelled of spilled alcohol, cigarette smoke, and body odor. He crossed the litter-strewn dance floor, walking toward the stairs at the back, where another gunman stood.

"Get me coffee," snapped Malnikov as he stepped by the gunman and descended the stairs.

Inside his office, four men were gathered: Prozkya, Radovitch, Leonid, and Obramovitch.

Malnikov crossed to his desk and reached below, opening a small refrigerator. He took out a Red Bull, popped it open, then took a big sip, staring at his men.

"I want you to drop whatever you're doing," said Malnikov. "Right now, we have one job: we're going to kill this motherfucker Cloud. Find him and kill him. I want to put a steak knife in the side of his head. Do you understand?"

"I told you not to buy the fucking bomb," said Radovitch.

"Thank you for pointing that out," said Malnikov. "Do you want a medal? Take your fucking attitude and stick it up your ass."

"This is about the fact that he set up your father, and we all know it. You've put the entire organization at risk."

Malnikov's hand moved imperceptibly to his hip, then swung into the air and threw a knife in Radovitch's direction. The blade somersaulted in a tight arc and landed in the leather of the coach, only an inch from Radovitch's head.

Malnikov stared at Radovitch as a long, pregnant silence took over the room.

"Shut the fuck up," said Malnikov. "Just be quiet. It's not about my father. It's not about the bomb. It's not the money. This is about honor. *My* honor. *Your* honor. We're going to find Cloud. We're going to find him and we're going to stab a steak knife into his fucking skull and cut apart that big brain of his. Do I make myself clear?"

"Yes," said Radovitch, who reached to his right and pulled the knife from the leather couch.

"What is the last information we have?" asked Prozkya.

Malnikov felt a small vibration in his pocket. He pulled out a cell phone and glanced at the caller ID on the screen:

:: CALIBRISI H.C. ::

He stared at the screen for a moment, then answered.

307

"What is it?"

"Alexei, it's Hector Calibrisi."

Malnikov covered the phone with his hand. He looked at his men and nodded toward the door, telling them in no uncertain terms to get the hell out of the room.

"What do you want?"

"We need your help."

"Haven't I already helped you enough?" asked Malnikov.

"This is a zero-sum game," said Calibrisi. "I'll tell you when you've helped me enough."

Silence took over the phone.

"Did you speak with your lawyer?" asked Calibrisi.

"Yes."

Malnikov reached to the drawer of his desk and took out a pack of cigarettes, then lit one.

"The paperwork is in process. We have presidential sign-off."

"How do I know the United States will keep its word?"

"That's why you pay John Barrows so much money."

"I don't know where Cloud is."

"You better start looking, then," said Calibrisi.

Malnikov's nostrils flared slightly. He took a sip of Red Bull.

"Look, I didn't call to argue with you," continued Calibrisi. "You already helped us. I want you to know I'm grateful."

"Then why the threats?"

"Because that bomb you gave Cloud is on its way to the United States. I need you to understand that your life depends on us stopping it. You want to live? You want to see your father go free? Find Cloud."

"I'll find him for you," said Malnikov. "And when I do, I will kill him myself."

"You won't touch him. We need him alive. He has information that is of vital interest to the United States of America. There's an agent on his way to Moscow. He will direct the in-theater aspects of Cloud's takedown."

Malnikov shook his head, then took another drag on his cigarette.

"Do I make myself clear?" asked Calibrisi.

"What's his name?"

"Dewey Andreas."

"You want me to find Cloud and bring him to this agent, Dewey?" said Malnikov, a hint of contempt in his voice. "Treat him like a little baby?"

Calibrisi was silent for a few moments.

"I realize you think this is some sort of deal that's gone bad for you, Alexei," he said calmly, "but it's much more than that, and you need to drop the attitude and accept the situation you're in. If that nuclear bomb goes off inside the United States, we will scour the earth until we find you, and then you'll die. Got it?"

"Yeah, I got it."

62

IN THE AIR

Katie Foxx stared out the window of Delta flight 35, the 9:10 P.M. Chicago-to-Atlanta direct. She was seated in first class. Next to her was Rob Tacoma, leaning against her shoulder. He'd been asleep since taking off from O'Hare.

Katie imagined that everyone surrounding them thought they were married, or a couple, but Tacoma was like a little brother. In fact, his snoring was annoying the shit out of her. She flared her elbow up, cracking him solidly in the neck. He opened his eyes, looked at her with a dazed, confused look, then shut his eyes again and leaned even farther into her seat.

Tacoma and Katie had worked together for more than a decade, first at the CIA, where she ran Special Operations Group under Bill Polk. Tacoma was her most reliable paramilitary agent, a tough-minded, fearless in-theater operator with stunning athletic skills. He was the best face-to-face combatant she'd ever seen. He wasn't the sharpest knife in the drawer by any stretch, but with Katie around, he didn't need to be.

When Katie left Langley to start a consulting firm, Tacoma was the only one she took with her. The firm, which didn't have a name, provided a wide complex of services to individuals and corporations alike, all under the general rubric of security. These services usually involved doing things, in foreign countries, that were against the law.

Katie and Tacoma operated with the express approval and permission of the CIA. In fact, Langley was their biggest client. The firm enabled Langley to occasionally move faster and with more savageness than usual.

The serenity of the first-class cabin was interrupted by an announcement over the intercom.

"Ladies and gentleman, this is Captain Fletcher. I'm afraid we have a slight change of plans. We are having a medical issue involving two of our passengers, nothing to worry about, but we're going to land in Columbus and make sure everything's all right. I apologize for the inconvenience."

Tacoma opened his eyes. He looked at Katie. She returned his look.

"This should be interesting," Tacoma said.

Ten minutes later, the Boeing 737 touched down at Columbus International Airport, then taxied to a stop in the middle of the tarmac. A set of mobile air stairs was driven from the terminal building to meet the jet. Behind it sped a black Chevy Suburban.

A stewardess opened the cabin door as the air stairs were moved into place. Tacoma and Katie stood up, grabbed their bags from the overhead bin, walked to the door, and climbed down the stairs. They sprinted across the tarmac to the Suburban. The Suburban crossed two runways, then came to a stop next to a shiny light blue Gulfstream G100, its engines humming. A minute later, the jet was ripping through the sky, toward New York City.

63

Just before midnight, under a dark sky, Calibrisi's Sikorsky S-76C helicopter dropped from the sky upon a bucolic Connecticut estate, landing on a large, circular pebble-stone driveway before a rambling mansion, now dark, except for a lone light in a first-floor window. Calibrisi, Foxx, and Tacoma jumped from the cabin of the chopper as the rotors continued to slash the night air.

Calibrisi had already briefed Foxx and Tacoma on the situation in Russia.

In the driveway was a pair of vehicles. One was a black Range Rover, the other a convertible Porsche 918 Spyder, yellow with black racing stripes along its sides.

They moved quickly toward the large door that marked the mansion's entrance, a copper lantern dangling from above. Two men stood watch, both dressed in jeans, running shoes, and T-shirts. Both men clutched submachine guns.

Calibrisi, Foxx, and Tacoma nodded at the gunmen as they slipped quickly into the mansion.

The house was fully furnished and appeared lived in. Another gunmen stood inside the entrance hall. He nodded to a door at the side.

They stepped into a library. The walls were lined with bookshelves. Old taxidermy hung from the walls. The room contained only one desk. A man with long blond hair was typing frantically. In front of him, three computer screens were lit up. The center one showed a map of the world, lit up digitally. The other two screens displayed what looked like thousands and thousands of slow-moving rows of numbers and letters, in orange and green, scrolling over a black screen.

Calibrisi shut the door.

"Igor, this is Katie Foxx and Rob Tacoma."

Igor turned, nodded, then turned back to the keyboard and kept typing.

Foxx and Tacoma glanced at each other, then at Calibrisi.

"This is the guy who's going to find someone who just pried his way into the CIA?" asked Foxx.

Igor kept typing, ignoring her.

"Don't take this the wrong way, but Cloud sounds like he might be slightly more capable than some guy in an Aerosmith T-shirt that's two sizes too small."

"Oh, he's much more capable," said Igor as he continued to type without turning around. "He is on a level that is several generations more sophisticated than the U.S. government."

"I doubt that," said Katie.

Igor stopped typing and turned.

"Then you're a fool," he snapped, turning back around. "If you want to catch a hacker, you have to put aside self-delusion about the greatness of the brilliant men and woman at the CIA and the National Security Agency. No doubt they are all patriots, but catching a hacker has nothing to do with patriotism. It is a function of numbers and letters, and their arrangement in a three-dimensional grid, over time."

Igor struck the keyboard.

"Tell me a city where Langley has a sphere of operations, Ms. Foxx."

"It's Katie."

Igor scanned her up and down.

"You are beautiful, by the way," he said, smiling.

"Tokyo," said Katie.

Igor typed for a half minute.

Suddenly, the digital map of the world zoomed down onto Japan, then kept moving in, focusing, until *Tokyo* appeared. Igor typed, and different areas of the city flared up in pockets of red. Igor typed again. The screen to the left flashed a checkerboard of black-and-white photographs; they appeared to be some sort of surveillance photos.

"This is just a small example," said Igor. "In fact, I was able to do this within one hour of arriving at my desk."

Katie stepped forward. She studied the sheet and pointed to one of the photos. It showed a man climbing out of a car.

"That's Kilmer," said Katie, taken aback. "This was an operation. Last year. That's off of my computer."

"Yes, it is," said Igor, "sorry about that. For what it's worth, I didn't look at any of your naked pictures."

"I don't—" said Katie, shocked. "My God. He hacked—"

"That is nothing. Watch this."

Igor typed furiously. The right screen shot white, then came into focus. A note was written and he enlarged it.

```
DEL TT—H9—Unger re:4
979AS.83
                                          NS: 4A
                                          NS: 4B
                     CMD > reroute ATLGA::COLOH
   //                            J/Etd
   > CMD 2
```

"What is it?" Katie asked.

"That is computer code. Do you like it? A few little lines, like a haiku. Those lines were how I got them to drop you off in Columbus, Katie. Is that short for Katherine, by the way? Are you busy after we find this guy?"

"My God," she said again.

"Yes, that is the proper reaction. Self-delusion doesn't work in Cloud's world. What does work is numbers and letters, arranged in a three-dimensional architecture—"

"Over time," added Katie, "yadda yadda yadda."

"Think of a cube," said Igor, ignoring her. "That cube has a wrapper on it, a wrapper that is composed of numbers and letters, and they are constantly changing. But if we can unwrap it, inside we will find our hacker. Where we are going, Katie, there is no room for human emotion. Where you and I are going, however, after we find him, there is plenty of room for human emotion."

"So do they know we're here?" asked Katie.

"No," said Igor.

"Why not?"

"Because I told them you're not," said Igor, smiling at her.

"Can you guarantee with one hundred percent certainty you're going to find him?" asked Tacoma.

"Eventually, yes, I will find him," said Igor. "By the time the nuclear bomb gets here? No, I can't guarantee that. At best, I give it a twenty percent chance."

"Then I want to understand what you're trying to do," demanded Katie.

Igor paused, looked at Calibrisi, then back to Katie.

"I understand," said Igor patiently. "I will explain how we're going to capture Cloud. Then you need to leave me alone."

"Deal."

Igor typed.

"Hacking in point of fact is the process of exposing human frailty, then taking advantage of it," he said, gesticulating with one hand

315

while he typed with the other. "The computer networks that run the CIA, KKB, a bank, a person's e-mail account—they're all a collection of computer code, written by human beings. They're all protected by different forms of encryption, which is also built by human beings. Most of these encryption keys are terribly built. Some are better. Some are, in fact, nearly perfect. But none is perfect. Because a human being built it. Hackers attack by finding those human flaws. Once they find a flaw, they can gain entry into the computer network. The best hackers are not only able to penetrate the most secure networks, they're able to do it without being noticed."

He pointed to one of the screens in front of Katie. The screen showed a dizzying sheet of numbers and letters, which scrolled down very rapidly. She leaned forward to look.

"Is that Chanel Number Five?" he whispered.

Katie glanced at him.

"Can you please focus?" she snapped, but in a whisper.

"Oh, I'm focused," he whispered back.

"What I meant was, could you explain what that is?" she asked, pointing. "You're not my type, anyway."

"What is your type?"

"Not you. Now will you explain what those numbers and letters are."

"That screen shows processing activity at a server farm. A warehouse full of computers are all right now focused on finding errors in the encryption algorithms that safeguard the Central Intelligence Agency."

"Where are they?"

Igor typed. The scrolling letters were replaced by the inside of a brightly lit warehouse, the size of a football field, filled with rows upon rows of high-powered servers.

"Iceland."

"Are they yours?" she asked.

"Not exactly."

"So what you're saying is, we're going to hack into Langley?" asked Katie.

"Oh, we've already hacked in," said Igor. "I've found six separate vulnerabilities thus far. But I haven't found Cloud yet."

Katie nodded, making no effort to hide her doubt. She glanced at Calibrisi, who stared back with a blank expression.

"Cloud is a great programmer," said Igor. "One of the best hackers in the world. In fact, some might say *the* best. But those people would be wrong. There's one hacker who's better than Cloud."

"Who?" asked Katie.

"Another Russian. *He* is the best hacker in the world. At least he was. He hasn't hacked in many years. He disappeared. Some people speculate that he may have died. The truth is, he's not dead. He simply chose to stop breaking the law. Not that he ever would've been caught, but he didn't want to do it anymore."

"Can he help us?" asked Katie.

"He's trying to," said Igor, smiling. "But he's having a hard time getting any work done because you're asking him too many fucking questions."

Katie nodded, then grinned.

"Lawbreaker, huh?" she said.

Igor smiled.

"Is that closer to your type?"

"A little."

Igor pointed at the live video stream coming from Iceland.

"That warehouse generates so much heat that it had to be situated near cold water or else the air-conditioning would've been cost prohibitive. Right now, every computer in that room is scouring Langley's technological infrastructure. Once we find the precise vulnerability point that Cloud is accessing, that is, his trapdoor, that, Katie, you beautiful American girl, is when you will have Cloud."

"How long will that take?"

"If I had to guess, a week."

"A week?" asked Katie.

"Then again, if a certain American woman with the most gorgeous blue eyes I've ever seen were to want to go to dinner with me, it might inspire me to do it quicker."

"Well, I do want to find him," said Katie, smiling mischievously at Igor, "but not *that* badly."

"What happens if you can't find him?" asked Tacoma.

Igor's smile disappeared as his eyes roamed to Tacoma.

"Then we're fucked."

64

ELEKTROSTAL

Cloud saw the red icon in the shape of a star suddenly pop to the front of his screen. He double-clicked it, then scanned the flag:

22:00:15

Reinholt T.C.

Minsk NA MSQ UMMS 223

Withdrawal

NBRB

Exch. 75000 BEL ruble * RUS ruble

Cloud read and reread the alert. Reinholt was not one of the men, so why had the flag popped?

He went into the database and brought up the last two days' worth of electronic signatures for both Brainard and Reinholt. Brainard's last event was the purchase of drinks at a Minsk restaurant. The cash withdrawal at the airport ATM was Reinholt's first. He did a quick directory search on Reinholt, using his passport identification to architect his financial activities—credit cards, bank accounts, and anything else the database had. Reinholt had three credit cards and two bank accounts. All of them had been created that day. In fact, the ATM withdrawals were the first electronic signature—the first transaction—Reinholt had ever made.

"Perhaps he's a mountain man?" said Cloud to himself, facetiously. "Lived in a tree house for his whole life. Just happens to have a few credit cards along with a bunch of money in the bank. Now he wants to go to Moscow. Makes perfect sense."

It was Langley's asset, Brainard. He was at Minsk National Airport, where he'd just exchanged Belarus rubles for Russian ones.

Cloud looked at a publicly available schedule of flights between Minsk and Moscow. There was only one more flight that evening, a 10:07 P.M. Belavia flight.

He glanced at his watch: 10:00 P.M.

Within a minute, Cloud discovered a vulnerability in one of Aeroflot's servers, enabling him to penetrate the airline's computer network. By 10:04, he was looking at the passenger manifest of Belavia flight 9984 Minsk to Moscow. He thought for a minute. Then he copied the list of names and ran it against the Belavia customer database. Only one name was new. Either Langley had an alias they were employing for Brainard's trip to Moscow unaffiliated with his identity, or they'd provisioned new identity in the last hour. If it was the former, there was little Cloud could do at this point.

At 10:06, Cloud dialed Minsk Customs emergency hotline.

"Customs hotline."

"My name is Rudyev and I work for Federal Security Service," said Cloud. "You have a suspected terrorist on flight nine-nine-eight-four. A Mr. Reinholt. He's seated in 9B. Do not let that plane leave the ground."

Two minutes later, from his seat aboard the plane, Brainard watched through a large terminal window as at least a dozen uniformed Customs agents charged through the terminal.

He picked up his cell and dialed Carter.

"I'm blown. Let Bill know."

65

Dewey got on the main highway between Saint Petersburg and Moscow, the M10. With every passing minute, he knew FSB would put more men on finding him. But those same minutes bought Dewey distance and—the farther away he got from Saint Petersburg—anonymity. They would be looking for him near the city. Then he remembered what Calibrisi told him. His photo was on the wire. His likeness attached to the APB posed a significant challenge.

There was something to take his mind off the feeling of being hunted, however . . .

He'd felt it for the past hour now, down his leg: cold, wet, raw.

So far, he'd been able to ignore the pain, as he'd been trained to do, but it was deep and it was getting worse. Dewey's sheer size, and the layers of muscle on his arms, torso, and legs, prevented several bones from breaking when he'd hit the ground outside the Four Seasons, but that was little consolation right now. The bleeding wasn't stopping.

Dewey looked at his leg. From the knee down, the trousers were solid red.

He unzipped his pants. Slowly, as he drove, he pulled them down below his knees, groaning in pain as the rough fabric chafed against the wound. In the dim light, he could see a deep gash glistening in fresh, dark blood.

He'd ignored it thus far, but the blood loss would debilitate him if he didn't deal with it.

At the first exit, Dewey turned off the highway. He pulled into a modern orange-and-white Eka gas station.

He climbed out of the car and stuck the pump nozzle into the fuel tank, then limped toward the gas station, glancing down at the thin, wet trail of blood dripping from his right pant leg.

The wind had picked up. He looked at the black sky and could see clouds undulating with stripes of white and, below, far in the distance, lightning. A storm was coming.

He remembered words from training:

You will learn to operate in the worst types of weather, so when it comes, you're ready. A storm is an opportunity. It's the time when strength and power can be freely used. In this way, the weather is a weapon. The best offensive operations occur at night, during storms.

The store was crowded. Dewey walked the aisles, looking for something to stop the bleeding. He picked up a package of baby wipes, scissors, duct tape, garbage bags, a bag of salt, cornstarch, bandages, and paper towels. He grabbed two large bottles of vodka, then looked up and made eye contact with a teenage girl, who abruptly turned and walked away. Dewey glanced at a mirror in the corner, seeing his face. He was drenched in sweat, and his skin was bright red. His clothes didn't fit. He looked from the mirror to the floor. A small pool of blood had collected at his shoe. He saw an advertisement in the far corner of the convenience store. It was a photo of a fish, hooked to a fishing pole, as the fisherman pulled it flying out of a stream. Near the advertisement, he found a large stainless steel fishhook, a spool of fishing line, and a pair of pliers.

He stepped into line. The chaos of the crowd helped conceal the trail of blood at Dewey's feet. People were too busy to look down, as they fumbled for their wallets and cash. As Dewey got to the front of the line, his eyes shot left, to the door. But it wasn't something outside that caused him to turn. Instead, it was a bulletin attached to the door. It was a large poster, freshly hung. A Wanted poster. Dewey's photo was spread across the center.

Luckily, the photo showed a man with long brown hair. Chopping off his hair had been a good call.

Dewey turned calmly back to the cashier. She was young and plump, with neon-blue-tinted hair, dressed in an Eka uniform.

Dewey pointed behind her to a pack of cigarettes. He added a lighter to the pile as well.

The cashier scanned the items, barely looking up.

Dewey glanced back to the Wanted poster as, to his right, he heard a commotion. He knew it somehow concerned him. He tried not to turn. Then he felt a tap on the shoulder. Looking, he saw a middle-aged man, a father, pointing at the ground and the growing patch of blood on the linoleum floor. Next to him was his daughter, who was crying at the sight of it, her mother's hand over her mouth.

The man said something in Russian. Dewey ignored him, turning back to the cashier as she bagged up his items.

Dewey pulled a wad of bills from his pocket and looked back to the Wanted poster. Two men were reading it and examining the photo of Dewey. As one read the poster, the other's eyes settled on Dewey, staring at him as he waited for his change. From the corner of his eye, Dewey registered the man hitting his friend in the arm, trying to get his attention. The other man turned and joined his friend, staring relentlessly at Dewey.

Dewey picked up the bags and walked toward the door, directly at the men, who remained at the door, watching Dewey approach, suspicion in their eyes. As Dewey came closer, they didn't move. They were blocking the door. One pointed to the ground, at the trail of fresh blood that followed Dewey, then said something in Russian. Dewey paused as he was about to walk into them. When neither moved, Dewey put his right arm between the two men and barreled through the door, knocking both men to the side.

He knew he needed to cut off the distraction immediately.

Dewey looked to the station wagon. It was to the left, at the pumps. He went right. Glancing back, he saw the two men following him.

The first drop of rain struck his head, then another, and then it was a downpour.

At the corner of the building, Dewey went right again. One of the men yelled. Dewey dropped the shopping bags and moved along the wall of the building toward the garage.

He heard the fast rhythm of boots behind him. Both men were now chasing after him.

Both bays of the garage were closed and the lights were out. Dewey moved to the door, slamming his left shoulder against it. The doorframe cracked, sending wood from the doorjamb to the ground. Dewey pushed in the door and was inside a dirty office that stank of petroleum.

The men were now on his heels.

He cursed himself for not bringing the Skyph with him.

Dewey cut left, into the darkness. He sprinted along the near wall, hands out, feeling his way. At a large tool chest, he stopped and crouched out of sight.

The pain in his right knee was getting worse. He shut his eyes and focused on not groaning, lest he alert them where he was hiding.

One of the men charged into the garage. He groped for a light switch, found it, and flipped on the lights. The near bay was empty. In the second bay, a car was raised up in the air.

From his crouching position, Dewey turned his head and searched the wall. Above him, he saw a large black hydraulic lever used to raise and lower the cars.

The first Russian was soon joined by the other.

They both clutched guns. One man flanked left, the other right.

Dewey reached to his calf and removed his combat blade. He held it in his right hand. He watched as one of the men crossed the garage, gun out, searching for him. He kicked over garbage cans, peered behind oil drums, and rummaged along the wall at the far side of the garage.

The second Russian called out something as Dewey squatted against the tool chest, his knee firing sharp bolts of pain up his leg as he tried to keep still and quiet.

Dewey couldn't see the second man, but he heard his footsteps scuffing the ground as he moved toward him. When he felt a small bump on the other side of the tool chest, he held his breath. Then the front of a running shoe came into view just inches away.

Dewey took one last glance across the garage. The other man was inching toward the mechanic's well beneath the raised car, looking to see if Dewey had climbed down inside.

Squatting on the concrete floor, Dewey stared up at where he knew the other Russian would emerge. He clutched the knife in his right hand. The gunman took one more step. His face was visible above the tool chest. A second later, the muzzle of his gun appeared just inches away from Dewey's head.

The other Russian was inching cautiously to the mechanic's well beneath the raised auto.

"Come on," muttered Dewey as his eyes returned to the closer man.

His eyes found Dewey. But by the time he could scream, Dewey had sprung up at him, slashing the knife through the air and spearing it into the man's gut, then pulling it back out and stabbing it into his chest.

Unmuted gunfire shattered the air as the Russian opened fire on Dewey, but Dewey was moving, shielded by the chest. Then he reached over his head and grabbed the hydraulic lever, yanking it just as a slug struck the wall in front of him. The car atop the hoist dropped down on top of the gunman, crushing him.

Dewey pulled his combat blade from the dead Russian's chest. He searched his pockets and removed a cell phone. Then he moved to the door.

Outside the garage, the skies had opened up. Rain was cascading down in sideways sheets of warm water. Dewey welcomed the water against his skin, cooling him, washing away the blood.

At the front of the Eka store, he retrieved the shopping bags. He walked quickly to the station wagon, hung the nozzle back on the pump, climbed inside, then sped out of the gas station. Soon, he was back on the highway. He fell into a line of slow-moving vehicles almost paralyzed by the violent storm.

Dewey moved to the middle of the front seat, steering with his left hand and using his left foot for the gas and brake.

He reached beneath the seat, found the gun, and set it in the driver's seat.

He pulled out a bottle of vodka. He unscrewed the cap and took a big gulp, then another, trying to quell the pain now emanating from his knee.

Dewey put the tip of the Gerber against his right knee. He counted to three, then pushed until the blade punctured the trousers. He pushed the blade down the length of his calf, cutting away the pants. He put the knife between his teeth then grabbed the pants and tore them aside, exposing his knee.

The traffic abruptly came to a halt; Dewey hit the brakes just inches from striking the bumper of the car in front of him. He took another swig from the bottle.

In the dim light, Dewey could barely see his knee, only a sheen of wet blood. When he turned on the overhead light, the sight was gruesome. The knee looked pulverized. The skin all around the wound was black and purple, while the wound itself was open and raw.

Dewey poured vodka over the wound, biting hard on the knife handle and letting out a mumbled groan as the pain seared him.

He opened the glove compartment and set the knife on the shelf.

Dewey splashed more vodka on the gash, then pressed a handful of baby wipes against the wound. He reached into the shopping bag and found the fishhook and put it between his teeth. Without looking, he threaded the fishing line through the eyelet, then tied a hangman's knot.

His eyes were startled by something up ahead. A set of police lights, red and blue, flashed in the distance, coming in the opposite direction, moving recklessly fast. Another cruiser was behind it, then a third. The roar of the sirens couldn't be heard at first, dulled by the rain, then it grew loud as the vehicles swept by.

Dewey removed the bloody baby wipes and tossed them to the floor. He poured more vodka into the wound.

He reached inside the bag for the box of cornstarch. He ripped off the top and placed it on the shelf. Then he found the bag of salt. He set it between his legs, stabbing the top with the knife and ripping it open.

Dewey looked up at the road. The blurry line of lights went straight for as far as he could see. He slowed down a bit, then looked back at his knee. He took a sip, then poured the rest of the vodka into the wound. He poured cornstarch into the gash, then slammed his fist against it, pounding the cornstarch into every possible part of the wound to absorb the blood.

He glanced up at the road, making sure he was still in the line of traffic.

Dewey took a big handful of salt and sprinkled it down into the wound, screaming as the salt cauterized the blood. The pain was like fire. It branched out like electricity, shooting through every part of him. Tears rolled involuntarily down his cheeks. He pounded the salt in, then repeated it, pouring more in, pounding, until the bleeding stopped.

With baby wipes, he cleaned away the excess salt and cornstarch.

He paused for several minutes, allowing himself to get past the pain of the salt. When it had settled into a dull ache, he took the fishhook, glanced at the car in front of him, then looked down and stuck the tip through the healthy skin above the edge of the wound. He stuck his index finger into the wound and worked it up, under the skin, toward the hook. When he found it, he gripped the end and pulled it through, along with the line. He put the hook through the skin on the other side of the wound, pulling it through. He pulled the line semitight, being careful not to rip the skin.

Dewey methodically moved the hook between the edges of the gash, sewing the skin back together.

When he was done, he cut the line and tied the ends together. He wrapped the bandage around the wound, then wrapped duct tape around the bandage.

He moved back into the driver's seat. He lit a cigarette, opening the window slightly, despite the rain.

A large green traffic sign was illuminated above the road ahead:

Moskva 300 km

66

A light blue Bombardier Global 6000 cut down out of the gray clouds, then dropped in a tight line to the ground, coming to a thunderous stop on the tarmac at Inverness Airport. Legally speaking, the runway was too short for the jet. Its occupant, however, insisted on making the landing anyway, and when Derek Chalmers insisted on something, it usually ended up happening.

The MI6-owned jet taxied to a stop near the small one-story terminal.

Chalmers sat in a tan captain's chair looking at an iPad. He was reading the files detailing everything Langley knew about Cloud, including photos and up-to-the-minute transcripts from the USS *Hartford*. There was also extensive biographical research on Katya Basaeyev.

Something troubled him, though he didn't know what it was. Obviously, Cloud was a despicable figure, but it was the dancer who made him uneasy. How could she not have known?

"Director Chalmers?"

Chalmers looked up at the pilot.

"Yes, Brantley."

"They're on approach, sir."

Chalmers nodded.

"Thank you."

Chalmers turned off the device, then looked to a plain-looking middle-aged woman seated directly in front of him, Victoria Smythson, MI6's head of clandestine operations. Though Chalmers was there to interrogate Katya, he thought whatever came out of the interrogation might spill into the need for mission work.

"Is Banchor Cottage ready?" asked Chalmers.

"Yes," said Smythson. "The pharma squad is in place."

"Who is it?"

"Dr. Robbins."

"I thought he retired?"

"To Aberdeen," said Smythson. "He agreed to help out."

"I'd like not to have to use pharmaceuticals on her," said Chalmers. "You read the files. What do you think?"

"You have a nuclear bomb en route to the United States," said Smythson. "Less than three days until it arrives. If it were up to me, I'd have an IV in her arm the moment she walks through the door at Banchor."

Chalmers stared at Smythson but didn't react. He looked out the window as a dark green Range Rover sped across the runway and stopped next to the jet. A moment later came the low-pitched, high-decibel whirr of the Osprey V-22 on approach.

Chalmers stood and pulled on a dark blue Burberry trench coat. He climbed down out of the Bombardier, trailed by Smythson, as the Osprey roared out of the clouds and then seemed to stop overhead as its rotors suddenly tilted upward. The plane descended like a helicopter to the tarmac a few feet away.

Chalmers and Smythson walked beneath the tail of the plane, out of the rain. A moment later, the loading ramp at the back of the Osprey lowered. Standing at the top of the ramp, soldiers on both sides of her, was Katya.

Chalmers nodded to one of the soldiers, who said something to

Katya. Slowly, she stepped down the ramp. She had on a pair of black Gore-Tex technical pants along with a gray sweatshirt. Her wrists and ankles were both cuffed. She was tiny, her skin as dark as leather, her eyes strikingly blue.

When she got to the bottom of the ramp, she glanced around the desolate airport as rain poured down. Seeing little of interest, she stepped before Chalmers and looked up at him, then at Smythson.

"Where am I?" she asked.

"Scotland."

"I didn't know," she said.

"Know what?"

"That he was going to kill the Americans. He's not a terrorist. You have to believe me."

Chalmers reached into his pocket. He pulled out his cell phone and showed her a photo of a room littered with corpses enclosed by walls splattered in blood. It was a photo from the Vietnamese scow. She gasped. She shook her head and closed her eyes, as if she could will away the memory.

Chalmers looked at Smythson.

"Let's go," he said.

67

ELEKTROSTAL

The icon flashed again on Cloud's computer screen and he double-clicked it.

Cloud had stopped one of the CIA agents—Brainard—in Minsk. Fairweather, the other CIA man on his way to Moscow, was all that remained.

The agent had made a phone call from the Poznań–Ławica Airport in Poland. Cloud examined the time stamp on the call. It had been made more than an hour ago.

Cloud searched for flights between Poland and Moscow. There were none left. When he searched for earlier flights the CIA agent might've been able to take, there was one, an Aeroflot flight at 10:58 P.M.

It was now midnight.

Cloud scanned the Aeroflot flight manifest but was unable to find any record of Fairweather getting on a plane. When he ran the passenger manifest against the Aeroflot customer database, there was nothing suspicious. All the passengers on the flight were either Russian or Polish. Every passenger had flown Aeroflot on numerous previous occasions.

Cloud went to a Web site that tracked flights and entered the

Aeroflot flight number. The plane was slightly ahead of schedule. It would land in fifteen minutes.

"How did I miss it?" he asked.

Cloud shut his eyes, remembering the day more than a decade before when he helped Al-Medi hack into U.S. air defenses on 9/11. The day he helped scramble radar at Griffiss Air Force Base and convince the men and women at Northeast Air Defense Sector that American Airlines flight 11 was twenty miles away, even as it bore down on the north tower of the World Trade Center.

It was the day Cloud understood how easy it was to use his computer to bring evil on an unsuspecting world.

When he opened his eyes, Sascha was staring at him.

"Is everything okay?" Sascha asked.

Cloud said nothing.

In 2001, Cloud was shocked to find that data signals between airplanes and control towers in the United States were for the most part unencrypted. Once he succeeded in hacking into the Griffiss tower through their ERP, he altered altitude, latitude, and longitude settings emitted by the plane, fooling everyone until it was too late.

Cloud had hacked into Aeroflot many years before, but altering the plane's signals to the Moscow tower was the opposite of what he needed to do. Right now, he needed to fool the Aeroflot pilot, not the control tower.

"State ATM," said Cloud, referring to the agency that controlled Russia's airspace, similar to the FAA. "Have you ever attempted to penetrate it?"

"No," said Sascha. "But I know someone who did."

"Is it someone you trust?"

Sascha considered the question, then shrugged.

"Yes."

"I need a trapdoor into ATM. I need it immediately."

68

MISSION THEATER TARGA
LANGLEY

Polk hung up his phone after getting the update from Carter, his Minsk chief of station. He looked around the operations room.

"Brainard got blown. They stopped him at the airport."

Polk was seated at a workstation inside the dimly lit command center. The room was half empty. In front of him was a carton of chicken fried rice, which he hadn't touched. All he could do was stare at the screen on the front wall of the room. It showed a digital map tracking Tom Fairweather's flight from Poland to Moscow.

"Ten minutes out," said a case officer. "They're on the final approach."

"Check activity at the airport," said Polk. "FSB and Customs. See if there've been any threat elevations."

"No Customs flags in the past two hours, other than the one on Dewey. Ditto with FSB."

Polk nodded, then picked up a bottle of Gatorade and took a sip.

"Come on, Tommy," he whispered.

Brainard getting stopped by Belarus Customs angered Polk. Having a hacker inside the Agency was like running a race with a thousand-pound weight tied around your neck. Though no evidence existed, it was clear that Cloud had been behind Brainard's removal from the Belavia flight. Polk had already spoken twice to the U.S. ambassador to Belarus about getting Brainard out of jail. Fairweather was different, and Polk felt more confident. The passport Fairweather used was purchased from a corrupt GRU administrator, its numbers clean and designed to withstand a so-called database back-pull at the Russian border.

Polk stood up, clutching the bottle of Gatorade. He stepped to the front of the room, just a few feet from the screen, watching as the flashing red dot—Aeroflot Flight 43—drew closer and closer to Moscow.

"Thirty seconds, sir."

Polk adjusted his glasses. He knew the radar could sometimes show inaccuracies, and yet what he was seeing made a cold shiver run through his body.

He turned back to the case officer.

"They're coming in low," he said. "Are they too far left?"

The case officer highlighted the flight path. Suddenly, the plasma screen view zoomed close up. Lights on the plane's wings became visible against the dark ground below. Digital numbers—representing speed and altitude—scrolled above the plane in bright red.

"They're not going to make it, sir."

Fairweather was asleep when the plane's alarm went off. It was a piercing, high-pitched siren that shrieked so loudly it caused him to lurch involuntarily forward.

Then came the recorded words of a woman, first in Russian, then Polish, repeated over and over: "Emergency. Assume crash position."

Screams engulfed the jet. Several passengers stood up, desperate to run somewhere, to escape, even though there was no place to go. Panic and terror consumed the plane. A man ran by Fairweather for the front of the plane. Several people opened overhead bins, grabbing their belongings.

Fairweather tried to remain calm. He looked out the window. They were flying just barely above a residential neighborhood. The lights of one home were so close he could see the colored movement of a TV show in an upstairs bedroom.

His eyes scanned. In the distance, at least half a mile away, he saw the airport's strobe lights pulsing halogen into the night.

As the siren continued to wail, as the recorded voice repeated its warnings, as screams seemed to reach a crescendo, he felt a hand on his arm gently touching him. He turned. A young woman was clutching her child, her face stricken with fear.

"Is it going to be all right?" she whispered, in Polish.

Slowly, Fairweather nodded.

"Yes," he said, willing himself to smile as he heard the sound of treetops brushing against the fuselage. "Everything is going to be fine."

69

LANGLEY

Gant stepped through one of several back doors at CIA headquarters, swiping his badge. Rather than return to his office on the fourth floor, he went straight ahead and entered the Agency's daycare center.

A woman was seated in a cubicle across from the glass-walled nursery, which was filled with children.

On seeing Gant, she stood up.

"Hello, Mr. Gant."

Gant looked at her badge.

"Anne, is there an empty office where I can make a phone call? I don't have time to run upstairs."

"Of course," she said.

She led Gant to an empty office down the hallway.

"Perfect," he said.

He shut the door, then dialed.

"Senator Furr's office."

"It's Josh Gant."

"Yes, Mr. Gant. Please hold."

Gant reached up and pushed his glasses higher on his nose.

"What is it?" asked Senator Furr.

"You need to cool down on the thing we've been working on."

"Andreas?"

"Yes."

"I just had my fucking counsel prepare a laundry list of re-quests—"

"There's blowback, Senator. It will come back to bite us. Trust me."

Furr was silent for several seconds.

"I can't just—"

"Kill it," said Gant.

70

Katie knocked on the door to the library.

"Can I come in?"

"Yes, yes. Of course."

Katie stepped into the library. She had on green running shorts with yellow piping, a white tank top, and high-heeled leather sandals, all of which showed off her long, tan, muscled legs and arms. As she entered the room, Igor was staring at the computer screen.

She had two Starbucks cups. She stepped to Igor's side and placed one of them on the desk.

Slowly, without taking his eyes off the screen, Igor reached for it. As he did, he accidentally touched Katie's hand, which she had yet to remove from the cup. Igor looked at her fingers, then his eyes traced her tan, sinewy arm all the way up to her shoulder. Then their eyes met.

"Any luck?" she asked.

"Yes," he said. "I found something."

Igor pointed at the screen. On it was a block of computer code.

"This is the attack code that enabled Cloud to penetrate a Langley switch outside of Madrid," explained Igor. "The penetration occurred fourteen months ago. He broke the encryption algorithm. It's called a cold boot attack. He, or someone working for him, actually went to Madrid, found the switch, shut the power to it, then sucked the memory onto a USB. Once he did that, all he had to do was break the key, which he quickly did. He was inside within a week of the Madrid attack. Here's the amazing thing. He didn't alter the CIA encryption algorithm. Instead, he embedded a virus in the actual physical unit of the text. The virus was like a little spy, hiding in the physical representation of the text. It's poetic, if you think about it. Spying on the spies. What appeared to be a relatively innocuous switch failure was quickly closed out and sanitized by Langley's defense systems, its malware and other such useless things. In closing it out, it was, in fact, initiated."

"That's how they got inside the CIA?" asked Katie.

"Getting in was the easy part," said Igor. "That code is how they remained, and how they did so without being noticed."

Katie nodded.

"I'm impressed," she said.

Igor looked up.

"Thank you."

"So what's next?"

"The virus that Cloud placed inside Langley is, in point of fact, just code. Like all computer code, it makes commands. For example, it tells certain internal Langley communications devices, phones on a specific channel, to transcribe their activities, then send those transcriptions, as they're occurring, to him. What I need is to somehow hitch a ride on where they're being sent. If I can do that, I will be able to get a peek at his defenses. His encryption protocols. That is when the real work begins."

"Without being noticed."

"Exactly."

Igor looked up at Katie. She smiled.

"You have a nice smile," Igor said.

Katie's smile disappeared.

"I wasn't smiling."

"Yes, you were. You have a very hard time taking a compliment, don't you? You should consider seeing a shrink. I see one."

"You see one?" Katie asked, a bit surprised.

"Yes. I'm not afraid to admit it."

"You shouldn't be," she said empathetically. "It's brave to admit it. If you don't mind my asking, why do you see one?"

"Sex addiction."

Katie shook her head in disgust and turned to leave.

"By the way, there's something else," said Igor.

"What, I have a nice ass?" she asked sarcastically.

"You do have a sweet ass, yes, but no, I meant I found something else inside Langley."

Katie stepped back to the table.

"Why are you being so mysterious?"

"I might have gone someplace I wasn't supposed to."

Katie crossed her arms.

"Inside the Agency?"

"Yes."

Just then, the door to the library opened. Calibrisi and Tacoma stepped in. Both men looked visibly upset.

"Tommy's dead," said Tacoma, referring to Fairweather, an agent both he and Katie had worked with. Katie had recruited Fairweather.

"His plane crashed on approach to Moscow," said Calibrisi. "A hundred and fifty-five passengers died, all to prevent Tommy from entering Russia."

Silence took over the room.

"I need to get back to Washington," said Calibrisi.

"Igor found something," said Katie. "Inside Langley."

Calibrisi shot Igor a look.

"You read Agency files?"

"Yes."

"Let's hear it," said Calibrisi.

"I scanned Agency logs, archives, directories, stuff that was deleted, you name it. I found a blocked archive. Even with top secret access I wasn't able to open it. Anyway, I figured out a way around it, of course. It's a bunch of projects that were apparently the sort of projects you didn't want anyone to know about."

"What does it have to do with Cloud?"

"Something happened in 1986. Something involving a Russian nuclear scientist named Anuslav Vargarin. It was a project. They called it 'Double Play.' The Agency was recruiting Vargarin. He was supposed to defect and work out of Los Alamos."

"What happened?"

"I don't know. They destroyed everything else."

Calibrisi took a sip from his coffee cup, thinking.

"There are plenty of Vargarins. How do you know he's related?"

"He had a son named Pyotr."

Calibrisi—momentarily taken aback—dropped the cup. It hit the floor and tumbled.

"Are you kidding?" he asked.

"I'm dead serious."

"Show me the scan."

Igor pointed at his screen, which Calibrisi quickly read. The file—what remained of it—was only a few words.

PROJECT 818: DOUBLE PLAY
01/82—07/86
Recruitment of Vargarin, Anuslav, wife Sylvie, son
Pyotr

"We need to know what happened," Calibrisi said. "You need to find that case and decrypt it."

"The data's gone, Hector. Poof. Doesn't exist. What you're look-

ing at is some sort of catalog key. They got rid of it, perhaps because it's so old."

"They didn't get rid of it," said Calibrisi. "I know where it is."

Calibrisi looked at Katie and Tacoma.

"You two, you're coming with me," he said.

71

As dawn broke over the horizon, Faqir was already in the galley, making breakfast for the crew. It wasn't fancy. He brewed a pot of coffee, then cooked oatmeal, which he ladled into six bowls and sprinkled with brown sugar.

At seven, he woke the men.

He left Poldark in his bed. The old professor was now too weak to get up. The night before, when he heard two of the Chechens debating how long it would take for Poldark to die, Faqir had slapped each man viciously across the face, telling them to keep their mouths shut.

Now, even he was beginning to feel the radiation sickness. Though he'd yet to vomit, the nausea had arrived in the middle of the night and hadn't left. Faqir planned to make breakfast just once on the trip, on this day, a critical day, and now he realized it would probably be a waste. If the others felt anything like he did, they would have no appetite.

When they gathered around the galley table, only one man wanted oatmeal. The others weren't hungry.

Faqir spoke in Chechen.

"I want every man ready," he said. "That means weapons in hand, loaded. You wait belowdecks. When the boat arrives, you know what to do. Watch your field of fire."

"How long until it happens?" asked one of the men.

"Who knows?" answered Faqir. "Could be soon. Could be all day."

One of the Chechens leaned forward, then placed his head on the table. He groaned.

"*What the fuck?*" shouted another man.

Suddenly, the man began to throw up, coughing white, thick liquid out in an acrid, chunky splash across the table.

One of the others stood to run.

"Don't move," snapped Faqir, "until I tell you you can move. Do you understand?"

"But he just—"

"*Don't talk back either!*" yelled Faqir, voice rising in anger. "Shut the fuck up and do your job."

Faqir stepped to the sick man, grabbed his hair, and jerked him up.

"You too," Faqir said, his teeth visible as a look of anger crossed his face. "We all feel sick. Either toughen up, or get off the fucking boat."

"What about the old fuck downstairs?" complained one of the others. "Why isn't he here?"

Faqir's eyes moved slowly, deliberately, and hatefully to the young Chechen who'd just asked the question.

"That old man is the only reason any of us are here," said Faqir.

He paused, then looked at all of the men.

"We're about to make history on behalf of Allah," said Faqir. "We will kill as many people as one hundred nine/elevens. You will all be famous. Each one of your names will be known around the world. Your actions today will be studied, hated, and reviled by the West. But they will know you. And where it matters most, you will be loved and honored, forever, by those who matter. Allah will greet you at the fourth gate."

Faqir paused and stepped toward the man who'd mouthed off. He leaned toward him, an intense look, a savage expression on his face as he stared into the young man's black eyes.

"Without the work of that old man, you would be nothing. You would do nothing. If any of you say even one word more of disrespect for him, the next thing you'll know is the feeling of a bullet striking you in the head. Is that understood?"

"Yes," said the young Chechen, bowing his head. "I'm very sorry."

Faqir nodded, acknowledging—just barely—the apology.

"Now we begin," he said calmly. He nodded toward the door. "Belowdecks. And remember, watch your field of fire."

Back in the wheelhouse, Faqir moved the radio frequency to channel 16, reserved for marine distress calls. He picked up the mike.

"*Mayday*," said Faqir. "*Mayday*. Is there anyone who can hear me?"

Over the next two hours, every minute or so, Faqir repeated the call for help. Finally, a faint, scratchy voice came over the radio.

"Roger on that mayday. Over. This is the *Dogfish*. I hear you. What's the situation?"

"This is the *Lonely Fisherman*," said Faqir. "We have a priority problem. We are in need of urgent assistance. Over."

"What's the problem, Captain?"

"We have fuel, but the pump is not transferring. We need a pump."

"Where are you?"

"East of Newfoundland," said Faqir. "Near the Flemish Cap."

He gave the captain of the *Dogfish* his coordinates.

"Let me see what I can do," said the captain. "We're at the beginning of our trip and we'll be heading a little south of you. Let me see if we can we spare a pump. Switch to forty-one."

Fifteen minutes later, the captain of the *Dogfish* came on channel 41.

"*Fisherman*, you there? This is the *Dogfish*. Over."

"We're here, Captain."

"We have a pump we can spare. I expect to be compensated for it."

72

ELEKTROSTAL

Cloud watched the news reports on his computer, volume turned down. The plane had crashed near the airport, in a town called Tolstopaltsevo. The scene was pandemonium.

A low beeping noise sounded from Sascha's computer. Cloud looked up. Sascha was waving him over.

"There's something happening," he said.

"Move over."

Cloud took over the keyboard, sitting down in the seat, quickly scanning the screen. It showed signals intelligence activity over the past day originating at the CIA. The activity had virtually ceased the evening before, then started back up.

The analysis was displayed as a long list. These were precise nodes of activity, fed back to them via the virus infecting Langley. Next to each entry, electronic activity was represented by percentages, over time.

It was clear that Langley had shut down everything following the failed attempt to extract him. That was expected. What he hadn't expected was the resumption of activity. It could mean only one thing: they were hunting for him. Langley would attempt to find him in the same way he'd found them, via the Internet.

Cloud's entire network was protected by several levels of state-of-the-art encryption. The only way to find him was for someone to find the encryption key, then break it. Breaking the key itself would require months. More important, someone would first have to find an instance of the algorithm itself just to have a chance to break it. As of now, Langley was clueless.

Yet, theoretically, it was possible for them to use the trapdoor to find the encryption layer. It didn't mean they could get through it, but even giving Langley that glimpse of his line of defense made Cloud nervous.

He sat back, crossed his arms, and shut his eyes. After a few moments, he opened them. He leaned forward and started typing.

"Go to access four," Cloud said without looking up.

"And do what?" asked Sascha.

"Destroy it."

"If I do that, the trapdoor will be gone," protested Sascha.

"If they find access four, they will be able to find us. Shut it down immediately."

73

BANCHOR COTTAGE
SCOTLAND

Chalmers stepped through the back door of Banchor Cottage, then down a flight of stairs that led to a locked door. He inserted a key and pushed into the windowless basement.

Few who'd been to Banchor had seen this part of the rustic fishing camp.

Behind the door, an intimate, low-ceilinged room looked like an old-fashioned hospital room. On one side, communications equipment was stacked on shelves, all of it tied to MI6 headquarters in London. At the back of the room was medical equipment, including heart and life monitors. A beat-up leather sofa was pushed against the wall to the left. Two hospital beds occupied the right side of the room.

A closet next to the sofa, out of view, held a mysterious-looking device that could be used by an interrogator to elicit information through the moderated application of electricity. For all of the publicity surrounding waterboarding, it was electricity that worked best at getting terrorists to talk, and Banchor, despite England's stated dislike of torture, had heard its share of screams over the years.

Smythson was seated on the leather sofa, reading a magazine.

Robbins, the MI6 physician, was standing against the back wall, back turned, inspecting the contents of a drawer filled with pharmaceuticals.

Robbins turned when he heard Chalmers enter.

"Hello, Derek," he said.

Chalmers nodded but said nothing. His eye went to one of the beds. Katya was strapped to it, a variety of sensors attached to her neck, arms, head, chest, and legs. If necessary, her heart, blood, and breathing patterns could be run through MI6 computers in order to assess her level of honesty.

"Give us a few minutes, will you?" Chalmers said.

"Yes, of course. I'll be upstairs."

Chalmers looked at Smythson, who was still seated. She met his look.

"Me too?" she asked.

Chalmers nodded.

Katya had not moved since being strapped to the bed. She lay beneath a flannel blanket, her clothing having been removed except for panties and a bra. Her head was facing the wall, eyes shut.

What played through Chalmers's mind, as he prepared to interrogate Katya, were the choices before him.

In Chalmers's storied intelligence career, he'd been subjected to a multitude of enhanced interrogation techniques. As a KGB prisoner in 1979, Chalmers wasn't allowed to sleep for extended periods of time. In 1982, the IRA locked him in a Belfast warehouse for almost a month. There, he was waterboarded and electrocuted, though the memory he hated most was of the time they made him kneel in front of a concrete wall for five days with a lightbulb dangling down in front of him. He remembered crying when they finally turned the lightbulb off, as if it had become his only friend, or a god. To this day, Chalmers never changed a lightbulb, an idiosyncratic remnant of his time in that basement.

Chalmers thus had a view of enhanced interrogation techniques that was less theoretical than that of most others in the intelligence community. He'd been there. He knew what worked and what didn't. The challenge was that there was no way to know until the sessions began. Chalmers believed all torture could be effective if there was something there in the first place. If there weren't secrets to be found, however, a prisoner could lead an entire operation down a rat hole simply to stop the pain.

Chalmers could understand Katya having a relationship with someone who had a secret. The question was, did she have real knowledge? It seemed a practical impossibility. How could someone who had to travel all the time, to practice every day for hours on end, be shielding someone with such dark intentions?

The problem for Chalmers was, if he spent the next day trying to get her to confess, he might end up in the exact same place he was now. If she knew nothing, he would get lies in order to stop the interrogation, lies that might misdirect the CIA at a time it needed to be sharpening its focus. He would also destroy any chance he had of eliciting passive but still vital information. If he broke trust with Katya by inflicting pain, she would shut down. He'd been there, and that is exactly what happened. The KGB wanted information he simply did not have. By beating him, his tormentors lost the opportunity to drag other key information out of him.

Chalmers went to a cabinet above the sofa and took out two glasses and poured each half full with scotch. He walked to the bed and lifted the blanket. Gently, he removed the sensors from her body, then unstrapped the bands from around her arms and legs. She remained with her eyes closed, her head facing the wall, motionless.

"Katya," Chalmers said.

He waited for her to turn her head and look up. After more than a minute, she turned and opened her eyes. The aniline blue of her eyes, against the backdrop of dark skin and jet-black hair, was slightly jarring. She stared up at him.

"Would you like to try some single malt?" Chalmers asked. "It's made just down the road. It's quite good. It will calm you."

Chalmers extended the glass. Slowly, Katya sat up. She took the glass, held it beneath her nose, sniffed it, then chugged it down in two large gulps. She held the glass back out to him.

"More," she whispered very softly.

Chalmers smiled. He returned to the cabinet, poured her another glass, and brought it back.

"There," he said as he handed it to her.

"Yes," she said. "Thank you."

Chalmers walked to the sofa and sat down. He took a sip.

"I saw you perform," he said. "Paris."

"Paris. When was this?"

"Five or six years ago, if memory serves. *Coppélia*."

Katya nodded.

"Franz," she said.

"Franz?"

"My lover."

"Ah, yes, in the ballet."

She sipped from her glass.

"Cloud is not a terrorist," she said. "I know him. He's a child. He has the heart of a child. A computer geek."

"And yet he caused the deaths of a boat full of fishermen. He killed American soldiers."

"No, I don't believe it. You showed me pictures, but they could be from anywhere."

"So I'm lying to you? Those men who took you, they did it why?"

"I don't know. Ask them."

"I did. You're engaged to a terrorist."

"No," she said, shaking her head back and forth. "No, I don't believe it."

"You seem quite sure," said Chalmers. "Which makes me wonder is there anything that would convince you?"

"No."

"So if he himself told you he intended to detonate a nuclear device on the U.S., even that wouldn't convince you?"

Katya stared at Chalmers across the room.

"You see what I'm getting at, don't you, Katya? People have secrets. They end up doing things that are quite at odds with what we expect. Secrets. Swanilda has secrets. Franz has secrets. Everyone has secrets. Isn't that right?"

Katya continued to stare at Chalmers.

"I want to ask you a question. Do you like the United States? I assume you've performed there, yes?"

Katya nodded.

"I love the United States. I've performed there many times. I would say perhaps fifty or sixty times."

"New York?"

"Yes, of course, but also other places. Do you know what my favorite place is?"

"No, I don't. Please tell me."

"Kansas City. It was my first tour, when I was only fifteen years old."

"So let me ask you a question. How many people do you think would die if a nuclear bomb went off in Kansas City?"

Katya took a sip.

"I don't know."

"I do. If the bomb Pyotr acquired were to detonate in Kansas City, at least a hundred thousand people would die. Of course, in New York or Boston, cities that are more likely to be the target, that number would be dramatically higher. You, just to be clear, will be forever known as the girlfriend, the fiancée, actually, of the man who did this. If you truly were unaware, and you're lucky, you'll likely spend time in jail, perhaps a decade or so. You'll never dance again. And, to be quite honest, if you are stubborn during this particular time period, when every second matters, when every minute is a precious commodity, when the plot could have been thwarted, even if you don't know anything . . . if you're stubborn now, my guess is you will not live to reach the age of thirty. The American government, if a bomb goes off, will erase anyone involved."

"What do you mean?"

"You know exactly what I mean. It will happen in the jail itself, most likely. They'll hang you, then report it as suicide. Or it will happen afterward. You'll be walking down a street somewhere and a car will pull up, and you'll be dead. It might even happen in the weeks immediately after the bomb goes off. After all, don't forget that you're a ghost now. Nobody even knows you're alive.

"The time for patience, for discussion over a nice glass or two of scotch, that will be gone. You don't need to know what he's doing. You don't need to have been knowledgeable of his activities. But you must help. If you don't, and that bomb goes off, you'll die, and far too young. Moscow, Saint Petersburg, London, Kansas City—you'll never see them again. All for not being willing to simply listen."

"You're threatening me."

"I'm telling you the truth. It's not a threat. It's fact. And you would deserve it. I could torture you, Katya, but I don't want to. I want you to trust me."

"How can I trust anyone? If what you say is true, the only person I have ever loved is a monster."

"You're thinking too much," said Chalmers. "Right now, your singular objective should be survival. What I'm telling you is that if you want to live, cooperate. Do whatever you can to help."

"I want to see your evidence."

"There's a folder on the shelf behind you. Read it."

Chalmers leaned back on the sofa. Katya reached for the folder. For the next twenty minutes, as Chalmers sipped his scotch, she read through it.

When she finished, she stood and walked to the cabinet, poured herself another glass. Then, instead of walking back to the bed, Katya sat down next to Chalmers.

"I will help," she said. "What do you want to know?"

74

ELEKTROSTAL

There's something we're missing," said Cloud. "I want the Langley transcripts again."

"From when?"

"Everything from the explosion on."

"They'll be on your screen in a few seconds," said Sascha.

A green icon appeared, indicating the file from Sascha had arrived. Cloud double-clicked it, then read through the transcripts of conversations from the CIA operations room. His eyes ripped left right with astonishing speed.

"There it is," he said to himself, seething. "I knew it."

706	remember johnnys wounded
707	he has a bullet in his leg
708	how bad is it
709	he has a fever and hasnt left the bedroom

"How could I have been so sloppy?" he shouted. "There are other agents. They must be the ones who took Al-Medi. Did we track him?"

"Yes," said Sascha. "We know where they took him. It's near Pobedy Park."

Cloud stood up. He grabbed his raincoat from the floor.

"I need the address."

"What if they moved him?"

"One of them is injured. Perhaps they're still there."

Cloud zipped up his raincoat, then looked at Sascha.

"What are you doing?"

"*Don't you understand what's happening?*" Cloud screamed. "There are two more agents. We need to remove them."

Cloud turned and moved to the door.

"Stop!" yelled Sascha. "Don't be a fool. You can't go."

Cloud turned around.

"And why not?"

"You're the only one who knows where the bomb is going. If they catch you, they'll dig it out of your head like a peach pit."

"They won't catch me."

"But if they do—"

Cloud shook his head, finally releasing his grip on the doorknob.

"Then you have to go."

Sascha nodded.

"It's raining," said Cloud. "Take the Mercedes. Park a few blocks away. There's Semtex in the trunk."

"Semtex?" Sascha asked, anxiety in his voice. "It will—"

"Level the building," interrupted Cloud. "That's the idea. You don't even need to do anything except stick it near the house. The detonator is already wired. Set it, get at least two hundred meters away, detonate it."

75

MOSCOW

Dewey parked the station wagon on a quiet side street near Moscow University, on the opposite side of the city from the safe house. If FSB was tracking the car, they would find it. When they did, he wanted to be far away.

He grabbed the pistol and cell phone, then climbed out into the pouring rain.

Scanning the street, he put his right hand in the coat and clutched the pistol, finger on the trigger. He took out the cell phone and turned it on, then dialed.

"Hi, Dewey," said Calibrisi.

"I'm in Moscow."

"We're getting closer on Cloud's location."

"What about the team you were sending in?"

"They didn't make it. You have two agents at the safe house. One of them is a case officer, and she's smart. The other is an operator, but he's badly injured."

He walked several blocks, limping slightly, then ducked into a subway station.

"You mentioned someone else," said Dewey as he moved through the brightly lit station, calm, eyes low to the ground, looking for signs of trouble, hand on the gun, ready, if necessary, to kill again.

"Alexei Malnikov."

"Have him meet me at the safe house."

Dewey hung up.

It was late and the station was empty but for a gray-haired woman behind bulletproof glass, waiting to sell tickets. He needed a ticket but didn't want to risk the chance of being identified. He passed the ticket booth and walked to the turnstile and climbed over it. Looking back, he saw nothing to indicate she'd seen him break the law— or at least nothing to indicate she gave a damn.

On a bench near the tracks, he found a newspaper someone had left behind. It was in Russian, but there, above the fold, was his photo, next to a photo of Katya Basaeyev.

The train to Pobedy Park arrived a few minutes later. The car was empty. At the Pobedy Park station, he got out, then climbed the station stairs back into the driving rain.

The neighborhood was quiet and tree lined. Large stucco and brick homes were set back from the sidewalk, behind small gardens. Halfway down the block, across the street, he saw a white stucco town house with black shutters, four stories tall.

He scanned the quiet street. Except for a lamppost at the corner, it was completely dark. The rain had let up slightly. He waited beneath a large tree for several minutes, studying the house. Just as he was about to cross the street, a taxicab turned onto the road. Dewey flinched and stepped back behind the tree. He placed his hand inside the coat pocket, gripping the gun, finger on the trigger. He watched as the cab approached, then sped by.

In the quiet aftermath, he felt his heart beating fast.

Cool off.

Dewey's eyes returned to the safe house. That was when he noticed a man. He was across the street, walking by the safe house.

How long had he been there? Was it Malnikov?

The man had a backpack and long hair. He walked quickly, with a slouch, down the block, away from the safe house.

At the corner, the stranger looked back at Vernacular House. He stared at it for several moments, then turned and kept walking.

Instead of crossing the street, Dewey followed him. When Dewey reached the corner, he crossed the street, just as the man jerked around and looked back. Seeing Dewey, he started to run.

Limping, Dewey charged after the man.

A block in the distance, he watched as car lights went on.

Dewey pulled the gun from his pocket, just as, from somewhere behind him, he heard a horrible explosion. A moment later, he sensed the ground tremor beneath his feet, then felt a violent wall of air kick him from behind. He was thrown instantly forward by the savage blast of air, the red taillights of the escaping car his last sight as he shut his eyes and braced himself for the fall.

76

PRESNENSKY DISTRICT
MOSCOW

Malnikov was seated on a leather sofa in his office. It was hot inside the windowless room. He was in a tank top and jeans, and was barefoot. He could've turned on the air-conditioning, but he didn't. Not for any reason. The truth is, he wasn't thinking about how uncomfortable it was. He was thinking about the conversation with Hector Calibrisi.

In his hand, he held a glass of 1986 Henri Jayer Richebourg, a Burgundy from the Côte de Nuits region of France that cost Malnikov €24,000.

Malnikov didn't like being threatened. It was humiliating. What had started with the meeting with Cloud had only gotten worse. He knew Calibrisi was cutting him a wide berth, and yet there was no mistaking who controlled things. Langley did. He'd done something very wrong, but Calibrisi had laid down a sharp gauntlet.

Find Cloud or die.

"Fuck him," he said, not for the first time, as he replayed his conversation with the CIA director.

Malnikov could take his chances. It would require a heightened level of security. If Cloud did succeed in detonating a nuclear bomb on U.S. soil, Malnikov would have a target on his head. Yet Calibrisi and everyone else in American government would be distracted for years to come.

His head ached. The internal struggle between love and loyalty to his father and absolute hatred at the feeling of being threatened tortured him.

He winced at the memory of Cloud's words: *I knew your father would never be stupid enough to acquire a nuclear bomb, and you would.*

It was true. His father wouldn't have done it. But if he had, Malnikov's father wouldn't shy away from responsibility for his actions.

"You made your bed," Malnikov said aloud. "Lie in it. Be a man."

He felt a vibration in his pocket. Pulling out the cell, he read the caller ID:

:: CALIBRISI H.C. ::

"Hello, Hector."

"I need you to go to our safe house and meet our guy."

Calibrisi gave Malnikov the address of the safe house.

"Is this the guy all over the news?"

"Yes."

Malnikov downed the rest of the wine, then stood up and walked to his desk. From on top of the desk, he took the gun, a Desert Eagle .50 AE, and tucked it into a concealed holster at the front of his pants. He pulled a leather coat from the back of the chair and pulled it on.

"What's his name?"

"Dewey Andreas."

77

GEORGES BANK
ATLANTIC OCEAN
80 MILES EAST OF PRINCE EDWARD ISLAND, CANADA

Four hours later, a boat appeared on the southwestern horizon.

Faqir raised the mike to his mouth: "Is that you, *Dogfish*?" he asked. "Over."

"Yeah. We see you. We'll be there in about twenty minutes."

"Roger that," said Faqir. "Thank you."

"By the way, you guys see anything?"

A small burst of anxiety hit Faqir in the spine. What did he mean? Was there a warning out for them?

He hit the mike.

"Come again."

"Any bluefin? We're headed north."

"No," said Faqir.

"Where you guys sailing out of?"

Faqir took a map of the eastern seaboard. He'd already studied it, but now he realized he could inadvertently get himself in trouble. If the *Dogfish* was from whatever port town he said, he could be fucked.

Faqir felt his stomach tightening.

"Portsmouth, New Hampshire," he said, naming a bigger city where, theoretically, one ship captain might not be aware of another.

"Nice place. We're out of Halifax. See you in a few."

Faqir hung up the mike, then leaned over and threw up in a trash can beneath the console.

He walked down the stairs that led belowdecks. He went to Poldark's cabin. Poldark was unconscious, though still breathing. Faqir tried to wake him, reaching his hand out and gently shaking his shoulder, but there was no response. Faqir covered Poldark with a blanket, then moved down the hall. He opened a door to the bunk-room.

"Let's go."

The approaching boat was smaller, less than half the size of the *Lonely Fisherman*, a purse seiner with a forward wheelhouse. It was dark blue, with long stripes of white along the hull. It was a neat-looking boat, with fresh paint and well maintained.

Faqir stood in the wheelhouse, looking out the window at the approaching boat. His eyes moved to his own deck, and he saw two of the Chechens. They were seated in between piles of ropes, slumped over, hidden by the side of the hull. Each man clutched a submachine gun. They sat in silence, still, watching for Faqir's signal.

The *Dogfish* chugged slowly aft of the ship, then puttered abreast, coming up along the *Lonely Fisherman*'s port side. As it moved across the final few feet of water separating the two vessels, Faqir made eye contact with MacDonald, captain of the *Dogfish*, who stood at the helm. He was balding, with gray hair along the fringes of his scalp and a tan face. Two other men stood behind the wheelhouse on the deck of the boat, both dressed in yellow all-weather fishing gear, creased in stains and wear. One of the men from the *Dogfish* tossed a rope line onto the deck of the *Lonely Fisherman*, just as Faqir nod-ded to the two gunmen.

Faqir stepped through the door of the wheelhouse onto the deck of the ship, waving at the men on the smaller boat.

"Hello," he yelled.

Faqir stepped to the rope line and picked it up.

Suddenly, both of the Chechens stood up, turned to the *Dogfish*, and opened fire.

The unmuted rat-a-tat-tat of submachine gun fire erupted above the sound of ocean and boat engines.

Slugs ripped through both men at the same time; a streak of bullets cut red across one man's chest, spraying blood down his chest and torso as he was kicked backward. The other man was struck in the head; the slugs tore the top of his skull off as he dropped to the deck.

The *Dogfish* made an abrupt lurch as MacDonald jammed the throttle forward, then ducked.

Both Chechens opened fire. But the captain was shielded.

Faqir sprinted toward the bow of the *Lonely Fisherman*. He leapt to the rail, then jumped out into the air. He landed on the back transom of the *Dogfish*, clutching the transom as his feet touched water, now churning in the wake of the boat's engines.

Faqir pulled himself aboard. He sprinted across the deck toward MacDonald. MacDonald turned, saw him, and reached for a knife. As Faqir entered the open-back wheelhouse, MacDonald thrust the blade at him. Faqir ducked, then kicked out MacDonald's legs. MacDonald fell to the ground, screaming. Faqir stepped on the back of his neck and grabbed his forehead with both hands and yanked back, snapping his neck.

He stepped to the bridge and turned the boat around, bringing it back to the *Lonely Fisherman*. He steered the *Dogfish* alongside it, then stopped and moved to the deck.

"Tie us off," he barked to the gunmen. "Give me a gun."

Faqir searched the *Dogfish* for other men but found none. He went back to the bridge of the *Dogfish* and ripped the VHF radio from the wall. He returned to the bigger ship and climbed aboard.

"Are they packed up?"

"Yes, Faqir."

"Get rid of the dead men, then come below."

Over the next hour, the six Chechens, along with Faqir, carried both bombs slowly up the stairs and placed them aboard the *Dogfish*.

Faqir tore the VHF radio from the *Lonely Fisherman* and handed it to one of the Chechens.

"Put it aboard the boat."

Faqir went belowdecks to Poldark's room. He lifted the blanket to carry the old man up the stairs, but Poldark was dead. Faqir sat down for a moment and closed his eyes.

"A prayer for you, Professor," Faqir whispered. "May you find your peace and may the heavens thank you for your bravery."

In the engine room, he grabbed a gas container. He took it up to the deck, then poured it on the deck.

In the wheelhouse, he picked up the mike from the *Dogfish* VHF radio. He moved the dial to channel 17, the international channel for distress calls.

"*Mayday, Mayday,*" he shouted. "This is the *Dogfish. Mayday.* We have a fire in our engine room. We are taking on water and need immediate assistance. I repeat, *Mayday.*"

"*Dogfish,*" came a faint voice.

Faqir stepped from the bridge and threw the *Dogfish*'s radio into the sea. He lit a lighter and touched the flame to the deck. Fire shot out along the wood, quickly spreading out. By the time he climbed aboard the *Dogfish*, the entire deck of the *Lonely Fisherman* was aflame, with clouds of black smoke rising into the sky above.

"Cast off!" he barked.

He stepped to the bridge and pushed the throttle forward, aiming for the East Coast.

"Find the paint," he yelled. "Get rid of anything with the name on it. Hurry up."

78

The helicopter swooped low through the nation's capital, coursing along the National Mall and then banking left and hovering for a moment before descending toward the roof of the National Archives building.

Calibrisi looked at Katie and Tacoma. He handed Katie a thick green card the size of a business card.

"His name is Stoddard Reynolds," said Calibrisi. "Give him this. You'll need it to get in the room."

"What is it?"

"That card gets you entrance into certain places during times of national crisis," said Calibrisi.

"Is that the one for getting on the doomsday plane?" asked Tacoma.

"Don't lose it. I'll be at the White House. Call me if you find anything."

Katie opened the chopper door and climbed out, followed by Tacoma. The blue Sikorsky shot up into the sky as Katie and Tacoma walked toward a man standing at roof's edge.

"You must be Reynolds," said Katie loudly, above the sound of the helicopter.

"Follow me."

They rode an elevator to the basement of the building, then followed Reynolds down a long corridor. A stairway went two stories lower. After another long corridor, they came to a large steel door.

"Swipe the card," said Reynolds.

Katie held the card over a digital scanner. A second later, they heard the steel locks clicking. A green light appeared above the door.

Reynolds reached for the latch and pushed it open, then pointed.

"Go ahead," he said.

"Are you coming?"

"No, I don't have access. I'll be waiting right here when you're done. You need to lock it from the inside."

As they entered the vault, fluorescent lights went on. Tacoma shut the door, then locked it.

The room was massive, at least a hundred feet long and equally wide. For the most part, it was empty, like a library that has been shut down and cleaned out. Only in the center of the room was there anything to see. There, steel filing cabinets ran in a straight line. There were thirty in all.

Katie and Tacoma approached the cabinets. Each five-foot-tall cabinet held four drawers. The cabinets weren't labeled.

Tacoma came to the first cabinet and pulled out a drawer, then reached inside and removed a thick black manila folder. On the cover of the folder, words were typed:

OPERATION TRIANGLE 14

Tacoma opened the folder and started reading.

"Motherfucker," he whispered.

"What is it?"

Tacoma kept reading, but didn't answer. After a minute, he shut the folder, then put it back in the cabinet and slammed it shut.

"What was it?" she asked.

"Nothing," he said quietly.

"Rob—"

"It was Cairo," said Tacoma. "A year ago. Remember Bill Jarvis?"

"Yeah, sure. He was station chief for a while, before he got killed in a car accident."

"It wasn't an accident," said Tacoma. "We did it. These are the termination files."

"Meaning what?"

"When we have to take down an agent. These are the end-of-action reports."

Katie nodded, then started walking down the line of cabinets. She found a cabinet that interested her and pulled out the top drawer.

"These are completely unorganized," said Katie. "We could be here awhile."

She looked back at Tacoma, who was still standing at the first cabinet.

"Don't be so naïve," she said.

"Don't you want to know what happened? Like to Rodney? Haven't you ever wondered?"

"No, I haven't," said Katie. "Shit happens. Look at where we are. What did you think these were? Now start looking."

79

The Situation Room was crowded with the president's top military, homeland defense, and national security team, including Vice President Donato, the seven members of the Joint Chiefs of Staff: the chairman and vice chairman of the Joint Chiefs, the Army chief of staff, the commandant of the Marine Corps, the chief of naval operations, the Air Force chief of staff, and the chief of the National Guard Bureau. Also present were key cabinet members and Agency heads: Calibrisi; Defense Secretary Harry Black; National Security Advisor Josh Brubaker; Tim Lindsay, the secretary of state; George Kratovil, director of the FBI; Arden Mason, secretary of homeland security; Piper Redgrave, director of the National Security Agency; Martha Blakely, the secretary of energy, and John Wrigley, the secretary of commerce.

A variety of key White House and Pentagon aides were also present, including Chief of Staff Adrian King, Bill Polk and Josh Gant from Langley, and Mark Raditz, the deputy secretary of defense.

The walls were covered in a dazzling array of plasma screens. On one wall, several screens displayed photos of the ocean as Defense Intelligence Agency satellites swept for the remote possibility of spotting the boat as it crossed the high seas. Another wall showed a large three-dimensional digital map of the U.S. East Coast, with small lights representing, in real time, all U.S. naval, military, and law enforcement assets and their current positions. A screen at the far end of the room showed live feeds of news media: Fox, CNN, ABC, CBS, NBC, Al Jazeera, BBC, and Russia SkyView, monitoring for any mention of the bomb or terror plot.

On the wall just inside the door was a clock. In red digital letters, it displayed a countdown of time remaining until 12:01 A.M. on July 4.

Outside the room, down the hallway, just past a pair of soldiers with submachine guns, President J. P. Dellenbaugh was standing. He was alone, waiting outside the door. His hand was on the wall and his eyes were shut as he steadied himself and tried to find strength.

Dellenbaugh had just finished the last of the phone calls to the parents and, in two cases, spouses of the six dead CIA men. Telling them they died doing something they believed in. That they died protecting the United States of America.

It was Dellenbaugh's first crisis as president. He'd been a U.S. senator when 9/11 occurred. His memory was permanently scarred by the sight of flight 77 crashing into the Pentagon.

This threat, he knew, was worse. If the nuclear bomb were detonated on U.S. soil, the casualty count would be in the hundreds of thousands, perhaps more. The psychological scars on individuals, on children and families, on schools and communities, on government, on America itself would be impossible to heal.

Dellenbaugh kept his eyes shut for more than a minute, praying silently. Then he stepped into the room. Conversation ceased. Every man and woman in the Situation Room stood up and saluted him. At this moment, he was the commander in chief.

"Harry, where are we on finding the boat?" asked Dellenbaugh, taking his seat at the head of the table.

Black hit the remote. A screen cut to a map of the Atlantic Ocean.

"The boat passed through the Strait of Gibraltar three days ago," he said.

A bright red rectangle appeared on the plasma above a section of ocean. At the top of the screen, Greenland and Iceland were visible to the north.

"Based on our estimates of the boat speed, tides, that sort of thing, we believe the terrorists are somewhere within this band of ocean."

"What's the bottom line?" asked Dellenbaugh.

"They're less than two days out, sir."

Dellenbaugh turned to Brigadier General Phil Tralies, chairman of the Joint Chiefs.

"General?"

"We're throwing everything we have at it, Mr. President," said Tralies, pushing his glasses up on his nose. "We have every long-range UAV we can spare searching for the boat, based on the description of the vessel, estimates of when it passed Spain, and assessments of shipping channels, tide, weather, and of course the speed of the vessel. We have an active interagency protocol that is now live-wired across the U.S. defense and intelligence infrastructure. We're also coordinating with NATO, Interpol, and all major shipping lines that do business with the United States."

Black hit the remote. Another screen cut to a photo of a fishing trawler.

"This is what the boat looks like," said Black. "Approximately two hundred feet long, aft wheelhouse, made to fish in deep water. Unfortunately, there are about half a million of these floating around the Atlantic Ocean right now. And therein lies the challenge of finding it."

"Not to mention the truly scary thing," added Tralies, "which is they might've switched boats by now, in which case we have a bigger problem."

Black tossed the remote across the table to Raditz.

"DIA satellites are scouring that rectangle of ocean," said

Raditz. We're snapping photos at a rate of one thousand per second, sweeping in a controlled arc that we hope will locate the boat."

Raditz pointed to the screens behind him, showing a rapidly changing series of close-up photos of the sea.

"That's the digital feed. We have a lot of people looking at it and, perhaps more important, it's being run against some pretty sophisticated analytical software programs at NSA."

"Have we seen anything?" asked Dellenbaugh.

"We've identified twenty-four boats matching the description," said Raditz. "They were all legit."

"How do we know they're legit?" asked Dellenbaugh.

"We ask for papers, then run them against various registration and commercial filings," answered Raditz. "We also run an interrogation protocol designed to quickly identify possible suspicious behavior and separate those folks from the rest of the pack. We're coordinating those interviews, as they occur, with interrogators from Langley. We also run the audio through lie detectors. If anyone looks suspicious, we will board."

Dellenbaugh stared at the screen—photo after photo of black ocean, interrupted occasionally by whitecaps.

"And if we don't find it while it's out at sea?"

Raditz handed the remote to the man on his left, Rear Admiral Henry Turner, chief of naval operations.

"We're building a cordon off the East Coast," said Turner. "That's a military and law enforcement resource line up and down the coast. Subs, ships, boats, planes, and on-the-ground personnel. Obviously, we're placing particular emphasis on cities and populated areas. We're working with Homeland to coordinate communications with state and local law enforcement so we're not panicking at the eleventh hour."

"What about a blockade?" asked Dellenbaugh. "Why can't we just shut the damn coast down?"

"Theoretically we could attempt it, sir," said Turner. "We've war-gamed it. But there are a couple of very significant challenges. First, we're talking about thousands of miles of coastline. Based on the volume of boats out there versus our enforcement capability set—hardware, manpower—a smart ship captain is going to get through. If we focus on two or three cities, odds are they won't get through; they'll simply go to city number four, five, six. Or they'll wait us out. We believe the best strategy is what we're doing—a flexible line of defense with transparent vertical coordination down through the military and law enforcement complex."

Dellenbaugh was silent for a dozen seconds. Then he turned back to Tralies.

"General, what are the odds we find this thing?"

Tralies nodded, considering his words.

"Normally I'd give it a twenty-five percent chance," he said. "But . . ."

"But what?"

"The vessel has moved very quickly across a challenging navigational course. This suggests an experienced ship captain. He knows what he's doing. That, for me at least, lowers the odds."

"How low?"

"One in ten, sir."

Dellenbaugh paused. He reached forward and poured a cup of coffee, then turned to a woman with long blond hair, seated at the far end of the table: Martha Blakely, the secretary of energy, whose agency was responsible for building America's nuclear weapons arsenal.

"They needed explosives from the Vietnamese boat," said Dellenbaugh. "What does that tell you, Martha?"

"Sir, this sort of nuclear bomb needs conventional explosives in order to trigger the nuclear reaction," said Blakely. "Presumably, their nuclear expert opened up the bomb and found that the explosives were somehow compromised or degraded."

"How hard is it to replace them?"

"Not very hard, Mr. President. There's a chance they'll fail, but it's small."

Dellenbaugh looked at Calibrisi.

"What about intelligence, Hector?"

"We know who's behind the plot, which is a significant first step," said Calibrisi. "Now we're just trying to find him."

Calibrisi nodded to the plasma. The map of the U.S. eastern seaboard was replaced by a tile of photographs, six in all. They were all photos of Cloud.

The key elements of Cloud's biography appeared:

NAME:	VARGARIN, PYOTR ALIAS(ES): "CLOUD"
DOB:	1980 (est.) BIRTHPLACE: Sevastopol, Ukraine
1980–85	Undocumented
1986–93	St. Anselm by the Sea, orphanage (Sevastopol, UKR)
1992	First documented instance of "Cloud"
1994	Enters MSUIEC
1998	First documented attacks involving "Cloud" on computer infrastructure in U.S.
2001	Participates in activities related to 9/11 including manipulating U.S. air traffic control systems in hours leading up to attack
2002	Graduates #1 in university class/various academic honors

2002	Enters graduate school—MIPT—Russia's top science and technology institute
2007	Earns master of science degree with highest honors #1 in class of 1,312 students: GPA 4.33
2008	Indictment in absentia by Switzerland DOJ
2008	Indictment in absentia: U.S. DOJ Russia MOJ China MOJAF
2009	Achieves grand master status following victory at Russia National Chess Championships
2010	Ph.D. with highest honors Pushkin Prize for Highest Academic Achievement

"You've already seen this, everyone," said Calibrisi, "so we don't need to waste time rehashing Cloud's bio. Let me cut to the chase. We believe he's in Moscow. We're doing everything we can to find him. It's a game of hide-and-seek."

"What do you have on the ground in Moscow?" asked Dellenbaugh.

"Right now, we have two operators and a case officer."

"Is that enough manpower?"

"No, and we're doing everything we can to build a bigger team."

"Did we have anything to do with the events that are on the news?" asked Lindsay, the secretary of state.

"That depends."

"On what?"

"On what events you're talking about, Tim."

"You know damn well what I'm talking about. The abduction of the ballerina."

"Yes."

"I've been on the phone four times with the Russian foreign minister."

"How's he doing?" asked Calibrisi.

Lindsay shook his head, slightly exasperated.

"He's pissed," barked Lindsay. "We could've run this through the Russian foreign ministry. We could have—should have—flown over there and sat her down and talked to her, official channels."

"I doubt that."

"Why do you doubt it? Do you think he's lying? We need to work *with* the Russians, Hector. And I'm not talking about the Russian mafia. My God, what has Langley gotten us into?"

Calibrisi nodded, then glanced at Rickards, the attorney general, who had obviously shared the Malnikov deal with Lindsay and others.

He took a deep breath.

"It was your State Department that led the negotiations regarding the disposition of nuclear materials after the Soviet Union imploded," said Calibrisi. "It was Russia's foreign minister who claimed, as recently as last month, that all Soviet-era nuclear materials and weapons were accounted for and safeguarded. This bomb was one of those weapons. If you'd like to play Monday-morning quarterback, I'd start by looking in the mirror."

"I was a United States senator when those deals went down—"

"So it's not your fault?" asked Calibrisi. "Is that what you want us all to know?"

"How dare you—"

"We're in the real world now, Senator," said Calibrisi, interrupting. "In that world, a nuclear bomb is on its way to the United States. In that world, a terrorist succeeded in penetrating Langley's computer networks and killing six American soldiers. I will do everything in my power to stop that bomb from detonating on American soil, including working with people like Alexei Malnikov. You had to take some angry phone calls? All I can say to that is, stop your whining and either start pitching in or get out of the way."

Lindsay, face beet red, lurched forward in his chair. But Dellenbaugh held up his hand, telling him to keep quiet.

"Enough," said the president.

"But Mr.—"

"I said enough. If you two want to take it outside, that's fine with me."

The president was silent for several moments as he took control of the room. He looked at Lindsay.

"I authorized the Malnikov deal," he said, before turning to Calibrisi. "And I was in the Senate when the Soviet Union broke up and we paid lip service to the warnings by Mossad about their nukes. So I guess if you two want to blame someone, you can blame me.

"When I was on the Red Wings, I could always tell when we weren't going to win the Stanley Cup. It was during those seasons when guys would start pointing fingers at each other in the locker room after we lost a game.

"I would trade my life to stop that bomb, and I expect each of you feel the same way, regardless of your title, your rank, or your beliefs. If you don't, I want your resignation right here, right now. If that bomb goes off, our country will be forever, permanently scarred. Hundreds of thousands of people, maybe millions, will die. We have to stop that bomb. There is no other option."

80

*T*y v poryadke?"

The words intermingled with at least a dozen screeching car alarms and sirens in the distance.

How long he'd been unconscious, Dewey didn't know. He was on the ground. There were several people kneeling over him. Everything was cloudy and blurry.

"*Ty v poryadke?*" repeated the man leaning over him, asking Dewey if he was all right. He placed his hand on Dewey's forehead.

Dewey pushed the man's arm aside, then climbed to his feet. He looked to where the car had been. Then he turned. Flames and smoke billowed from up the block. Vernacular House was gone. The buildings on either side were rubble. The cars in front of the house were on fire.

Weaving, Dewey started to move back toward the explosion. He pushed through a line of bystanders, knowing the agents inside were dead yet needing to get back there. As he reached the corner, the first police car arrived, followed by several fire trucks.

Dewey moved up the sidewalk toward the safe house, delirious with shock, his head concussed. He pulled out his cell phone. The glass was shattered. When he tried to turn it on, nothing happened.

He felt for his gun. It was gone.

Dewey turned back toward where he'd landed on the ground.

A woman was pointing at him. She was speaking to a police officer who, Dewey could see, was holding the gun. The officer yelled something in Russian. Dewey turned again. He continued toward the safe house, now blocked by a pair of police cars, their blue and red lights flashing through the rain. He registered two policemen climbing from the first cruiser, looking in his direction.

Dewey turned again. The first officer—the one with Dewey's pistol—was sprinting toward him.

He turned yet again. The two officers from in front of the safe house were also running toward him, weapons out and raised.

He was hemmed in.

Dewey cut abruptly left, away from the two converging lines of policemen.

They were yelling at him, barking at him in Russian, telling him to stop. But he kept moving.

Dewey ran, limping, still weaving, toward a side street, as the officers closed in on him.

He reached the corner of the side street. A block away, he saw lights from a passing car. Suddenly, the car stopped, paused, then jacked right, directly toward him, bursting up the street at high speed.

Dewey heard a gunshot from behind him as the low red sports car ripped up the cross street directly for him. Dewey kept running as the car flew down the thin lane. At the last second, the driver of the car swerved left and slammed the brakes, just feet away. Dewey heard yelling from inside the car. He went to the open passenger window and looked in.

The muzzle of a gun was aimed at him.

"Duck," the man said.

Dewey moved down just as the driver fired. The bullet struck the closest policeman in the head, kicking him to the ground two car lengths away.

"Get in," came the thick Russian accent inside the sports car.

Dewey climbed in as gunfire erupted from behind him.

"Hold on."

The driver put the car in reverse and slammed the gas, tearing backward as, with his left hand, he fired his gun at the line of policemen now charging on foot. The car sped backwards up the street. When the mag was spent, he dropped the gun. In one fluid motion, he jacked the wheel and with his other hand pulled the emergency brake. The car flipped one-eighty. He released the brake, then slammed the gas. Soon he had the car speeding away from the scene, moving rapidly away from the chaotic scene.

"You must be Dewey," he said as he steered without looking up. "I'm Alexei Malnikov. Welcome to Moscow."

81

There's a guy out on the dock."

Saxby looked up.

"Should we call the cops?" he asked.

If Scranton understood the sarcasm in Saxby's voice, he didn't let on.

"Or should we perhaps ask him if we can help him?" continued Saxby. "You are aware that we sell boats, aren't you, Jack?"

"This guy ain't buying a boat. He looks suspicious. That's all I'm saying."

Saxby shook his head. He went out the side door of the marina building and walked to the long pier in back, on the harbor. It was crowded with a variety of boats moored along the teak pier.

When he got to the middle of the pier, he saw the individual. He was on one of the boats, a dark green forty-four-foot Hinckley Talaria. As much as he doubted Scranton, he had to admit the man did look suspect. His hair was long and dark, stubble covered his face. He was Arab. He looked ill, like he was going to get sick right there on the boat.

"Can I help you?" asked Saxby.

"Good morning. I would like to buy this boat."

"You are aware of the cost?" asked Saxby. "That's a four-hundred-and-fifty-thousand-dollar boat right there. Now we do offer financing, but the approval process can take a while."

"I'll pay cash," he said.

"Cash like a check? I can call Mr. Gardiner and ask—"

"Cash like cash," the stranger interrupted. "And I would like it right now."

82

The cell made an incessant high-pitched beeping noise, startling Gant as he ate.

He was alone. Le Diplomate was his favorite restaurant. It brought back memories of different postings in his career. Paris was the most obvious, but for some reason the cozy, eclectic European ambience reminded him of Prague, where he met his first wife.

Gant was feeling sentimental, even sad. He'd been sidelined from the Agency's most important operation in years. When he'd attempted to access status files earlier, he had not been allowed in. He was shut off.

But if he thought Le Diplomate would help, he was wrong. If anything, it only made him realize what he was about to lose.

Or maybe it was guilt finally catching up to him.

His phone started to ring. He looked down at the phone number. It was him, the man who started it all, the one who killed a kindly Soviet scientist as his only child watched.

He picked up the phone.

"Hi, Sage."

"That's not my name anymore."

"Maybe not on that fantasy island where you live, but you'll always be Sage Roberts to me."

"What do you want?"

"Something's happening."

"What's that, Josh? Did you finally worm your way to the director's job?"

"I called to warn you."

"You've never done a fucking thing your whole entire life for anyone other than Josh Gant, so let's cut the bullshit. What is it?"

"Vargarin."

The word shut Roberts up. He was quiet for several moments. Then he let out a loud sigh.

"Oh, boy."

"Boy is right," said Gant. "The son you had me stick in the orphanage."

"Pyotr. Smart kid."

"He's a terrorist now."

"I knew I should've put a bullet in his head," said Roberts. "Why are you calling? To 'warn me'? Because you're such a nice fucking guy?"

"Why did you do it?" asked Gant.

"Do what?"

"Why couldn't you just let the family stay? They wanted to stay in their country, you sick fuck."

"The answer to that question was wired into your bank account fifteen years ago, Josh. Grow up. That's the way the world works."

"All I can say is, you better hope he fails at what he's trying to do. Because if this thing unwinds, they'll be sending the Killer Kanes after you."

83

I gor knew something was happening. In a tight geographic area east of Moscow, the level of defensive activity was spiking. It meant that his target's automated countermeasures were fighting back.

Igor's server farm was pounding against Cloud's 128-bit encryption key, hitting it with attempt after attempt as they enumerated every possible combination of characters. Cloud had embedded logic bombs within the encryption algorithm, so that as someone trying to break the key came closer, countermeasures were instigated. Like a wounded animal, Cloud's defenses were doing what they could to kill, delay, and misdirect the onslaught that was coming from Iceland. A normal attempt at breaking Cloud's key would have long since been stopped. But a warehouse full of single-purpose attackers was not normal in any sense. They smelled blood. They could not be stopped.

Igor had two of his three screens focused on the hunt. One screen showed packet activity in real time—the granular communications between his servers and the servers running Cloud's defenses. At the beginning of the process, those servers running Cloud's protections were distributed all over the world, striking back at the earliest attempts at finding the root line in. But as Igor's overwhelming wall of computing power discovered shortcuts and ways around those first defenses, Cloud's power retreated and focused in a concentric circle. Igor watched the punch-counterpunch in real time, like watching a tennis match in digital form.

The second screen mirrored the locations of the individual battles and displayed them in red dots on a digital map.

As if sensing the end, he leaned forward over the keyboard. A minute passed, then two. Then it hit. The first screen locked on to a 128-bit line of characters. Igor started typing furiously now, re-provisioning the key into his own, then instructing the remaining servers to metastasize. Like a fast-moving cancer, they pounced and started eating into Cloud's network, spidering themselves across every packet, byte, and line of code in Cloud's possession, locking down and freezing a lifetime's worth of cybercrime.

The map zoomed in to a single address:

17 Vostochnyy

Elektrostal

Igor reached for his cell and speed-dialed Calibrisi.

84

Calibrisi remained quiet as Dellenbaugh spoke. He knew he shouldn't have ripped Lindsay in front of the group, but he didn't regret doing it. Calibrisi had a deep distrust of politicians, and that included former ones like the secretary of state. They weren't all that way. He thought Dellenbaugh was growing into being a great president, and he practically worshipped Dellenbaugh's predecessor, the man who appointed him to his post at Langley, Rob Allaire. But they were exceptions. Most politicians cared only about whether people liked them. Most ran for office out of some deep-seated need to prove—to themselves, to their parents, who knows—that people liked them. If they happened to do good things once they were elected, that was a bonus.

Calibrisi was tired. Except for a nap on the chopper ride down to D.C., he'd barely slept in days. Had he been rested, he would've ignored Lindsay during the meeting. Silence was always the best *fuck you*.

As he rubbed his eyes, he felt his cell vibrating. He read the caller ID:

:: JAGGER MICK ::

He put the cell to his ear.

"Hi, Igor," he whispered. "What do you have?"

"I found him."

"You sure?"

"Sure as shit."

Calibrisi looked at the president.

"What is it?" asked Dellenbaugh.

"I need to take a call, sir," said Calibrisi, standing up.

"Anything you care to update us with?" asked Lindsay.

Calibrisi ignored the question.

"Come with me," said Brubaker.

Calibrisi put the phone to his ear.

"Okay, I'm hanging up and calling you back from a tactical line. Stay by the phone."

Calibrisi nodded across the table to Polk, telling him to come with him, then picked up his briefcase and followed Brubaker to the door.

85

BOSTON HARBOR
BOSTON, MASSACHUSETTS

Boston harbor was crowded with boats on a calm, sunny July afternoon, the day before Independence Day.

In addition to hundreds of sailboats, power boats, and fishing boats, there were dozens of police boats and Coast Guard patrol boats crisscrossing the water.

Faqir putted into harbor in the middle of the afternoon.

He noticed the many law enforcement vessels. They were looking, he knew, for the trawler, unless they had somehow discovered the theft of the second boat, though he doubted it.

Besides, at this point, Faqir didn't care. He wanted to execute the plan, and then die.

As it was, he was vomiting every half hour or so. It had turned into dry heaves. He didn't want them to catch him, but if they did, whatever pain or disappointment he might've felt at the beginning of the journey wasn't there anymore. He was physically and emotionally numb with radiation poisoning.

Faqir steered the Talaria the way he imagined a wealthy American might during the summer, at the beginning of a holiday weekend. He cut straight across the water, pushing the boat in a measured way across the crowded harbor.

With the GPS on his phone, he navigated toward Revere. Past a marina filled with sailboats, he came upon an old chain-link fence that ran along the rocky, garbage-strewn waterfront. Behind the fence was an aggregates business. Piles of road salt and gravel dotted a dusty lot. Farther on, lashed to the pier, were several long, flat barges, used for hauling road salt to customers.

Faqir scanned the water for anyone who might see them, but there was no one within a quarter mile. He navigated alongside one of the barges, put the boat in neutral, and then moved to the stern and lifted a storage bin near the transom.

Inside were two nuclear devices, wrapped in a green tarp.

Faqir and the other man lifted one out of the boat, walked to the port gunnel, and lowered it to the deck of the barge.

A minute later, the Talaria was slicing smoothly through the calm water heading south.

86

THE WHITE NIGHT
AVENUE SVERCHKOV
MOSCOW

Malnikov exited the highway, then took side streets through a shabby-looking neighborhood. He parked in front of a bar.

"What are we doing?" asked Dewey.

Malnikov looked at him.

"Finding Cloud. Stay here."

"No," said Dewey. "Fuck that. What are we doing?"

"Seeing an old friend."

"Why?"

"Something I realized this morning."

"And what's that?"

"That people are fuckheads."

Malnikov reached for the door and climbed out.

"Let me do the talking," he said as they approached the front door.

The White Night was nearly empty. Behind the bar was a mirror that stretched the entire length of the room, crowded with hundreds of bottles of liquor, beer, and wine. On the walls were framed photos of famous Soviet athletes: hockey players, soccer players, great sprinters, skiers, and swimmers from past Olympics, including a large black-and-white photo of the gymnast Olga Korbut, heroine of the 1972 Munich Olympics.

There was a lone person there. He was a short bald man with a beard and mustache. He stood at the bar, leaning down, counting out stacks of bundled one-hundred-ruble banknotes. Almost the entire surface of the bar was covered in bricks of the money, like a child's table covered in blocks.

As Malnikov and Dewey entered, the man's head jerked around, along with his right arm, which held a gun, reflexively training it on them. Seeing who it was, he quickly moved the muzzle away.

"Don't shoot, Leo," said Malnikov.

"Alexei," said Tolstoy, putting the pistol back on the bar. "I'm sorry. Instincts. Who's this?"

"Nobody," said Malnikov.

He walked through the empty bar and stopped to Tolstoy's left. Dewey followed behind him and took a seat at the bar.

"Have a seat," said Tolstoy. "Would you like a drink?"

"No, thank you," said Malnikov. "We won't be long."

"You're up early."

Malnikov nodded.

"What is it?" asked Tolstoy, who went back to counting out money.

"I realized something this morning," said Malnikov.

"Yes, Alexei?" said Tolstoy.

"After my father was arrested, you said something to me."

Tolstoy turned. He reached his hand out and placed it on Malnikov's shoulder.

"I said I am sorry he was arrested," said Tolstoy. "You know I love your father."

"You said I could be next. You said I need 'leverage.' Remember?"

Tolstoy nodded, smiling nervously. He removed his hand and reached for a cup of coffee. As he did so, his eyes shot to the gun on the bar.

"I still believe that," said Tolstoy. "If something were to happen to you, we would all be affected. You know this."

Malnikov stared at Tolstoy for several moments, studying him.

"Actually, I will take that drink," said Malnikov. "Vodka."

"Yes, of course," said Tolstoy. "How about you?"

Dewey nodded.

"Whiskey."

Tolstoy stood from the barstool. With his back turned to Malnikov, he picked up the gun from the bar. He took a step, then swiveled, gun out, toward Malnikov. But Malnikov was already standing, anticipating, and his left hand grabbed Tolstoy's gun arm before it could complete its sweep.

Tolstoy yanked his arm back, trying to get free of Malnikov's clutch.

With his other hand, Malnikov reached down and grabbed his gun from the concealed holster.

Tolstoy, unable to get his gun arm free of Malnikov, thrust his leg forward, kicking Malnikov squarely in the crotch, and in the same instant Malnikov fired the Desert Eagle. The slug ripped into Tolstoy's knee, dropping him to the ground. Tolstoy howled in agony.

"*Motherfucker!*"

Malnikov stepped forward and drop-kicked Tolstoy beneath the chin, sending him tumbling against a barstool. He kicked him again, this time in the gut. Then he stepped calmly above him, keeping the long-barreled Desert Eagle trained on Tolstoy's head.

"Who told you to say it?" asked Malnikov.

"Why should I tell you?" groaned Tolstoy, clutching his blood-soaked knee.

Malnikov fired another round. The bullet struck Tolstoy's stomach. As Tolstoy groaned, both of his hands reached for his stomach, trying to stop the bleeding.

"I'll call an ambulance if you tell me right now," said Malnikov, the gun trained on Tolstoy's head.

"Sascha," whispered Tolstoy. "The man's name is Sascha."

Malnikov's face grew red with anger.

"Is he the one who gave you Bokolov's number?"

Tolstoy nodded.

Malnikov paused, looking down at Tolstoy, disappointment, betrayal, and hatred crossing his face.

"Where is he from?"

"Elektrostal."

Malnikov kept the gun aimed at Tolstoy. He pulled a phone from his pocket and hit a speed-dial number, calling a man named Goran, who ran operations in Elektrostal for Malnikov. As it rang, he hit the Speaker button.

"Alexei," came a groggy voice. "What time is it?"

"There's a man named Sascha," said Malnikov, staring at Tolstoy, the gun still trained on his skull. "According to Leo, he's in your city."

"There are many Saschas," said Goran, half asleep.

"He's a computer hacker."

"Yes," said Goran. "I believe I know this man. What does he look like?"

Malnikov looked at Tolstoy.

"Black hair," coughed Tolstoy. "Long. He has a ponytail."

"Yes, that's him," said Goran on speakerphone. "He likes fat girls. What do you want me to do with him?"

"Get me his address."

Malnikov hung up the cell. He kept the muzzle on Tolstoy.

"Please, Alexei," begged Tolstoy. "The ambulance."

"*I to, chto ty, predatel'?*" seethed Malnikov. *And what did you get, traitor?* "Some of the money? Some of *my* money!?"

Blood topped Tolstoy's lips and started dripping down his chin as he looked up at Malnikov from the floor.

"He knew everything." Tolstoy coughed through his clotted throat. "He said I would end up in the same prison as your father. I had no choice."

Malnikov fired. The slug ripped a jagged hole between Tolstoy's eyes, kicking his head back, raining blood, skull, and brains on the floor, killing him instantly.

"You always have a choice, Leo."

87

Cloud had two screens on Moscow network news. One screen showed continuing coverage of the plane crash. The other had live coverage of the explosion near Pobedy Park.

He heard the door open behind him, and turned. It was Sascha. He trudged inside, his clothing and hair soaking wet. His face was red and sweaty.

"It's all over the news," said Cloud.

"He was there."

"Who?"

"Andreas."

Cloud stood, mouth agape.

"He was across the street, like he was watching the building. He chased me."

"What did you do?"

"I detonated the bomb. He was thrown in the air. I think I might have killed him."

Sascha stepped behind Cloud to look at the news. The screen was frozen.

Cloud hit the keyboard.

"We're iced," he said.

Cloud pounded the keyboard several times.

"It must be in our directories," said Cloud.

He walked to the next workstation and ran a series of diagnostic scans of their own servers, then rebooted the system.

The scan of the servers pinpointed a buffer overflow—a massive amount of traffic that clogged the system. In looking at the sequence of its arrival, he was quickly able to find the perpetrator. It was coming from someplace in North America. The perpetrator had no purpose other than to disrupt the streaming of the television station.

Cloud cleaned it out, then rebooted the servers. Within twenty seconds, the screen quickly froze again.

Cloud went back to the log and found the malicious code behind the buffer overflow. He cut out the piece of malicious code, saved it, then ran it through a program that contextualized the code against existing hacker code, looking for similarities, so that he could understand where the code had come from and if it represented a danger. He pasted the code, then watched as it was smashed against hundreds of millions of cataloged malicious code from hackers all over the world, including his own.

After less than a minute, a red flashing block of code appeared:

hwpsraid:/7sxl:0.01

He stared at the screen for several seconds, in shock.

"My God," he whispered.

"What?"

Cloud shut his eyes, deep in thought.

"Cloud, what is it?"

"They found us."

Down the hall from the Situation Room, Brubaker led Calibrisi and Polk to a small, windowless office. The room had photos on the walls

397

of past presidents presiding over meetings in the Situation Room. A desk was against one wall. On top of it sat two large unusual-looking rectangular black phones.

Brubaker stepped to one of the phones and hit the speaker.

A female voice came on: "White House Signal."

"This is Josh Brubaker. I need a dedicated preaction uplink via NSA channel two two."

"Hold, please."

The phone made two distinct beeps, then a male voice came on the line.

"NSC code link, you're live. Agent O'Brien here, go, sir."

"O'Brien, you have a live Emergency Priority action," said Brubaker. "I'm handing it over to Hector."

"Yes, sir. It's an honor, Mr. Calibrisi."

Brubaker patted Calibrisi on the shoulder, then left, shutting the door behind him.

"What kind of encryption is on the link?" asked Polk.

"KEY-5 TLS encryption," said O'Brien. "What's the first number?"

"212-772-1001," said Calibrisi.

"One minute, sir."

Malnikov pushed the red Ferrari F12 Berlinetta recklessly fast—tearing east along the M7 at 150 mph despite the heavy rain.

Dewey, strapped tight in the passenger seat, stared ahead with a hint of unease.

"Alexei?"

"Yeah?"

"You realize if we die on the way there it sort of makes it hard to capture him."

Malnikov glanced at Dewey. He slowed ever so slightly, shaking his head.

"I thought you were tough."

"I never said that," said Dewey. "Besides, I don't care how tough you are, hitting a hunk of concrete at two hundred miles an hour hurts."

"Victory requires speed," said Malnikov. "Americans want to go too slow. Speed limits and whatnot. You're too cautious. Perhaps this is why you lose all these wars? Vietnam. Afghanistan. Iraq . . ."

Dewey's eyes bulged as they came up behind a semitruck, then swerved right, barely missing it.

"The Cold War," added Dewey.

Malnikov braked sharply, then exited the highway. A few minutes later, they came to the edge of Elektrostal. He took a left on Mayakovskogo. The road was rutted with potholes. Trees and shrubs had taken over the sidewalks. Old warehouses stained with rust sat between decrepit structures that had once been office buildings but now appeared abandoned.

"I didn't realize Russia was so nice," said Dewey.

Malnikov laughed.

"We have better-looking women," he responded.

"That's a matter of opinion," said Dewey.

"No, it's a fact."

"Katya's pretty, I'll give you that. But I'll take an Iowa farm girl any day."

" 'Farm girl'?" asked Malnikov, shaking his head in disgust as he steered past potholes. "Who the hell wants to fuck a farm girl? You come out with me sometime. I'll show you what a beautiful woman looks like."

Malnikov slashed right, then slowed and came to a stop.

"There it is," said Malnikov, shutting off the Ferrari's lights.

Two blocks away, an ugly office building sat midblock. Four stories tall, it looked like the countless other structures on the street, concrete, shaped like a rectangular block, with small windows. Lights were visible in the building's top floor.

Malnikov's cell suddenly started ringing. He looked at the caller ID, muted it.

He turned to Dewey.

"In the glove compartment. Get a weapon."

As Igor waited for Calibrisi to call him back, he set the phone down on the desk and began typing, pulling the noose even tighter around Cloud's neck.

First, he built redundant pathways into Cloud's network, in case Cloud somehow shut off the system or was able to contain him. Next, he looked for Cloud's alternative egress points, quickly cataloging the various digital pathways out from the network to the Internet. In all, he found sixteen different arteries out of the single building at 17 Vostochnyy. He infiltrated them all, inserting trapdoors.

Suddenly, his third computer screen lit up. Words appeared:

```
X:\Users\CX7-44 >        who is this
```

Igor thought for a split second, then started typing:

```
C:\Users\002 >        where is it
```

As he waited for Cloud's response, the screen came alive again:

```
X:\Users\CX7-44 >        where is what
```

Igor paused. He knew that right now, every second mattered. He needed to try to delay Cloud long enough for Calibrisi to get people there.

Igor's phone started to ring.

"Igor?" asked Calibrisi.

"Yes, I'm here."

"What do you have?" asked Calibrisi.

"He's in a city called Elektrostal," said Igor.

Polk opened his laptop, quickly bringing up a digital map of Russia. He narrowed in on Elektrostal.

Igor spoke: "Hector, you need to know something. He initiated conversation with me."

"How?"

"Text."

"What did he say?"

" 'Who is this?' "

"How'd you respond?"

"I asked, 'Where is it?' He just responded, 'Where is what?' "

Calibrisi looked at Polk, who was deep in thought.

"We need time," said Polk. "We need to get Dewey there. Let's ask him where the money is. He might think Malnikov has found him."

"Got it," said Igor.

"Control," said Calibrisi. "I need you to add another number."

On one screen, Cloud studied the hack, trying to assess where it had come from.

A second screen showed his opponent's words in white text on black:

```
C:\Users\002 >          the money
```

Cloud found the point of intrusion. First, his opponent had discovered an error in one of the networks Cloud had used to send one of his attacks.

Once his opponent discovered the error, he went directly after the jugular, seeking to break the encryption algorithm that safeguarded all of Cloud's network. The attacker had employed a so-called brute-force attack. Armed with a vast amount of computing power, the person or institution had eventually broken his encryption key by systematically enumerating all possible variants of the encryption key until finding the right one.

Now that he was in, there was no way to get him out. His attacker had already commandeered the network and architected a new layer of encryption, which he, not Cloud, controlled.

"How did he get in?" asked Sascha.

"A fucking fencepost error," said Cloud, shaking his head in disgust.

"I'll do a registry scan," said Sascha, beginning to type. "Send me the bad code."

"It's no use. He broke the key."

Cloud watched a separate screen, which displayed security flags. One by one, so fast he barely had time to read the individual lines of code, his DNS addresses were taken over. Whoever was out there was now commandeering every computer and every program Cloud possessed.

"Mother of God," said Sascha. "It's like a tidal wave."

Whoever it was wanted him to believe they worked for Alexei Malnikov. Perhaps they did work for Malnikov. But Cloud doubted the Russian mobster cared about the money, certainly not enough to invest in the sort of sophisticated attack that just broke through his defenses and brought down his network. Even the response, "the money," gave him pause; he knew Alexei Malnikov would rather kill him than get his money back.

It had to be the United States. Langley.

Cloud turned on his cell, making sure he could use it to continue the dialogue with the attacker. He typed into the phone:

I want to cut a deal

He looked at his computer to see if the phone was still working. On the screen, his words were displayed exactly as they had been written:

Cloud stood up.

"Leave everything," he said to Sascha. "Leave it all, exactly as it is."

Dewey opened the Ferrari's glove compartment. There were four handguns inside. All were the same: Desert Eagle .50 AE. He grabbed one of the guns, then popped the mag, making sure it was full. He grabbed an extra mag and stuffed it in his pocket.

"We need to loop in Hector," said Dewey.

"The time is now, Dewey," said Malnikov. "We call Hector and all of a sudden it's five minutes from now."

Dewey stared at the windshield as rain pelted the glass. He knew they needed to tie in Hector, yet he knew Malnikov was right. It would take time they didn't have. There wasn't anything Hector could tell them that would alter the plan right now, anyway.

"One of us stays here," said Dewey.

"We both go in."

"No," said Dewey. "One of us needs to watch the exits. That's you. Remember, we need him alive."

Though angry, Malnikov nodded. He reached for the door pocket and pulled out another cell.

"Here," he said. "Speed dial one is me."

Dewey opened the door and charged toward the building.

Cloud picked up his gun. He walked to the window. On the street, a block away, he saw the bright cherry red of a Ferrari. They were here already.

"But Cloud," said Sascha, "if we don't at least wipe it—"

"Leave it," snapped Cloud. "Don't even sign off. They're inside.

403

They know precisely where we are. We couldn't wipe it if we wanted to."

Sascha picked up his backpack and started running to the door. Cloud followed. Sascha held the door open for Cloud. As Cloud approached, he raised his arm and aimed the gun at Sascha.

"I'm sorry, my friend," said Cloud. "You will only slow me down."

He fired. The slug struck Sascha in the chest, dropping him. Blood rapidly spread out in a dark pancake through his shirt. Sascha appeared neither surprised nor angry.

From the ground, he looked up at Cloud, staring for a final moment, then shut his eyes.

Cloud heard his phone chime.

C:\Users\002 >   I don't negotiate

Cloud stepped into the stairwell, clutching the gun, staring at the screen. He descended to the next landing, then stopped and typed:

I'll tell you where the bomb is going but I want something in return

C:\Users\002 >   what do you want?

Cloud didn't answer. He pocketed the phone, then ran down the stairs toward the basement.

Dewey sprinted toward the building's entrance. He pulled open the door and was standing in a dim stairwell, lit by a single lightbulb that dangled from the ceiling of the top floor, four flights up.

Dewey scanned the landing, gun out, water dripping from his hair and face. The entrance was quiet and deserted, and yet he'd heard something. Or had he?

The only lights in the building had come from the top-floor windows. Yet Dewey stared down the stairs toward the basement.

* * *

Cloud entered the basement seconds before he heard the door to the building open. He was panting. His heart was beating fast. He lurched behind the wall, raising the gun, then peeked out. It was Andreas.

The American had an angry look on his face as he entered the building. His gun was raised, trained out in front of him, the muzzle moving in time with his eyes, which scanned the entrance area.

Cloud studied him as he looked around the first-floor landing. Cloud's hands were trembling. He heard Andreas's footsteps just above his head as he opened the door to the first floor, searching for him.

Should I kill him?

Cloud remained still, in the basement, hiding against the concrete wall, waiting for Andreas to come back. Then, from above, he heard more footsteps, then the sound of the door shutting. He peered out. He saw one of Andreas's legs, then the rest of his body came into view. Suddenly, his eyes shot down toward him, as if he'd sensed him there. Cloud remained still, holding his breath.

No. He would win that battle. Before you have time to aim and fire, a bullet will rip through you. He won't kill you, not yet anyway. Not until he tortures the information out of you.

Cloud remembered the cell phone in his pocket. He'd forgotten to turn off the ringer. The conversation with the hacker. If he received a message now, the chime would be loud enough for Andreas to hear. Yet if he moved his arm to shut it off, even the faintest scratch of friction might be caught by the American . . .

Cloud held the gun tight, wanting nothing more than to not drop it or make a noise.

Gently, he slipped his left hand into his pocket and turned off the phone's ringer, keeping his eyes on the landing one flight above.

Andreas's eyes stared into the dark stairwell for another two or three seconds. It felt like an eternity. Then he turned and moved out of view.

Dewey opened the door to the first floor.

The room was empty and dark. He glanced down toward the basement, seeing nothing but darkness. He climbed the stairs, moving floor by floor. At the second floor, he opened the door. It too was empty. When he opened the door to the third floor, heat escaped from the darkness. As his eyes adjusted, he saw hundreds of computer servers, stacked together in rows, with large coils of black cable interspersed between them. Their pulsing lights casting a red and green hue.

Dewey climbed the stairs to the top floor. Quietly, he twisted the door handle and opened the steel door.

He entered quickly, gun raised, sweeping the muzzle of the Desert Eagle .50 AE across the air as his eyes scanned for movement. The room was large, mostly empty, except for tables, a few chairs, and computers.

Then he registered the corpse on the ground. It was the man he'd seen in front of the safe house. His eyes stared up at the ceiling, seeing nothing, his chest was drenched in red.

Dewey moved into the room. He held the gun out in front, searching corner to corner, but the room was empty. Cloud was gone.

Cloud waited several minutes, listening for the sound of doors opening and closing as Andreas ascended. When he heard the door to the third floor open, then close, then heard the faint pounding of footsteps climbing to the fourth floor, he ran across the garage to the wall nearest the exit. A steel box was bolted to the wall. He opened it, then took out his cell phone and trained its light on the inside of the box. There were four red switches. Their purpose was simple: they controlled the fire doors to each floor.

In one fluid motion, Cloud flipped all four switches. Even from the basement, he heard the faint slamming of steel from the floors above as the dead bolts locked the fire doors on each floor.

He went to his motorcycle, pulled on the helmet, and raised the kickstand. He turned the ignition key. The Ducati roared to life. He juiced it once. The sound of raw power exploded across the windowless basement. Cloud flipped on the lights, then scorched out of the building into the rainy night.

The silence was interrupted by the sound of metal slamming into metal, like a hammer striking an anvil.

The unmistakable sound of dead bolts slamming shut.

Dewey walked to the door. It was sealed tight. He pulled his cell from his pocket as he moved back toward the exit. He pressed 1 and held the button down, speed-dialing Malnikov.

"Do you have him?" asked Malnikov.

"He's not here," said Dewey. "And I'm locked in."

"I'll be right up—"

Malnikov's words were interrupted by a high-pitched squealing noise: the unmistakable screech of rubber ripping too fast against tar.

Dewey ran to the window and looked to the street below. Through the rain, he saw the orange of a motorcycle breaking from the building's basement.

"He went out a side entrance," said Dewey. "You need to move. Go up a block, then left. *Follow him.*"

"I'm on it."

Dewey watched as Cloud sped up a side street into the rain-crossed darkness. A few seconds later, the red Ferrari burst around the corner after him.

"Are you sure he got it?" asked Calibrisi, referring to Igor's last message.

"Yes, I'm sure. He also read it."

Calibrisi glanced at Polk.

"Any ideas?" asked Calibrisi.

"It's time to sacrifice our queen," said Polk.

Calibrisi nodded.

"Tell Igor to offer up Katya," said Calibrisi, picking up the phone. "Control, get Derek Chalmers on the line."

Chalmers was seated in front of the fireplace when his cell rang. Despite the fact that it was July, the temperature in Scotland, aided by the rainstorm, remained in the fifties, and so he'd built a fire. Katya was downstairs. After two six-hour sessions, Chalmers was allowing her to sleep for a few hours, though the truth was, he didn't think there was much more to find.

"Chalmers."

"It's Hector."

"Hello, Hector."

"We found him. He wants to do a deal."

Chalmers stood up.

"Hector, I don't need to tell you the criticality of not being played," said Chalmers.

"No, you don't. But I'm going to offer him something in exchange for the bomb."

The door to the basement suddenly opened. Katya slowly popped her head out. She smiled at Chalmers.

"I'll have her ready," said Chalmers. "One question though: What happens after he tells you where the bomb is?"

Calibrisi was silent. Both men knew the answer. The moment the bomb was stopped, Cloud would die, and it would likely be a strike from a drone high in the sky. The collateral damage would destroy anyone within fifty feet of Cloud.

"Don't you get played either," said Calibrisi. "It's unavoidable. I'll let you know what he says, but in the meantime, I'd get airborne."

"And go where?"

"Set a course for Moscow. I'll have the secretary of state arrange the permissions."

"Does Russia know about the bomb?"

"No. As far as they're concerned, we're simply returning their ballerina."

"At this point, why not tell them?" asked Chalmers.

"Because I'm not a hundred percent sure they'd want to stop the bomb."

Dewey searched for another way out of the room. In the far corner was another door, but it too was bolted shut. He tried to kick open each of the doors, but it was futile. He was trapped.

He went to the window and looked out, trying to think of a way out.

Glancing around, he saw cables linking the different computers and screens together. There weren't many, but perhaps there were enough to lower himself at least another floor, maybe two, and then jump.

He raised the gun, aimed at the window, and fired. The slug tore into the window and made a dull thump, and that was all. He fired again, same spot, same thud. Then again. This time the slug hit the embedded slug and ricocheted. He fired again and again, until the mag was spent.

"Fuck!" he yelled, hurling the gun against the glass.

He called Malnikov.

"Talk fast," said Malnikov.

"I can't get out," said Dewey. "The windows are bulletproof. The doors are bolted shut."

"Can you get to the roof?"

Dewey looked up.

"Maybe."

88

IN THE AIR
OVER THE NORTH SEA

One of the pilots looked back from the cockpit.

"There's an alarm going off in the loo, Derek," said the pilot.

Chalmers unlatched himself from his seat. He stood up and walked to the rear of the jet. He knocked on the door to the restroom.

"Katya?" he asked. "Is everything all right?"

Katya didn't respond. This time, Chalmers banged harder.

"*Katya!*"

Both pilots emerged from the cockpit.

"Where's the key?" barked Chalmers.

One pilot charged to the door and inserted a key. Chalmers tried to push in the door, but it was blocked by Katya's body. Chalmers slammed his shoulder at the door and was able to stick his head in.

Katya lay unconscious on the floor. Her wrists were exposed and bleeding.

"Get the first-aid kit," said Chalmers. "We need to land and get her to a hospital."

Chalmers reached his arm down and moved her body, then pushed the door in. He pulled Katya out, lifted her up, and carried her to one of the leather sofas midcabin and laid her down. She was covered from her chest down in blood. He felt her neck.

"She's still alive," he said.

Chalmers shook her shoulders, trying to bring her out of unconsciousness. When that didn't work, he slapped her hard across the face. Her eyes opened.

"I didn't know," she said. "I swear."

"Know what?"

"Where the bomb is going. But I remember. I heard him speaking. It was through the wall."

"Where?" asked Chalmers, pulling his cell out and dialing Calibrisi.

"I'm sorry. I didn't know. Then I remembered."

"Where is it going, Katya?"

"Boston."

89

THE WHITE HOUSE

Calibrisi and Polk were in the small office down the hall from the Situation Room when Calibrisi's cell vibrated. It was Chalmers.

"Hi, Derek," said Calibrisi. "Are you in the air?"

"Yes. She gave me a target."

Calibrisi snapped his fingers, getting Polk's attention. He put it on speaker.

"Do you believe her?"

"Yes. She tried to commit suicide. I think she's starting to realize that if she doesn't help us, she's complicit, if not legally, then morally."

"Where's it going?"

"Boston."

"Does she have anything more specific?"

"No."

Polk nodded at Calibrisi, then sprinted out of the office to the Situation Room.

"We're going to land," said Chalmers. "She needs medical attention."

"You're going to have to patch her up on the plane," said Calibrisi. "We need to get her to Moscow."

"She's going to bleed to death."

"At this point, we have the name of a city and that's it. And who knows if it's even the right city. Until we find that bomb, Katya is the only card we have to play. Please, Derek, get her to Moscow."

90

Inside the Situation Room, there wasn't a spare chair or place to stand. The mood was surprisingly calm.

In addition to President Dellenbaugh, most key White House, Pentagon, and intelligence officials were gathered. Anyone not there in person was patched in, their faces adorning plasma screens along the walls.

President Dellenbaugh was seated at the head of the large mahogany conference table. The plasma to Dellenbaugh's right showed live video from Boston, taken from a satellite in the sky. The Boston waterfront was fully visible. All Coast Guard, FBI, police, and military assets were highlighted in red, including a pair of Navy Aegis destroyers, three Coast Guard cutters, and more than one hundred FBI, Boston Police, and other law enforcement vessels.

Superimposed atop the live satellite image was a bright green grid, which was tied into the Defense Intelligence Agency. They were running the feed against a Milstar satellite and its IONDS platform, which was sweeping over the harbor, searching for signs of tritium, uranium, or plutonium emissions.

All eyes were glued to one of the screens. Bob Schieffer of CBS

News was speaking, the volume turned up. Six other screens displayed different TV channels, all of which had the volume down as they continued to show normal programming.

As Schieffer spoke, one by one the other screens cut away from normal programming and went live to special reports, cascading like dominoes down the wall.

Dellenbaugh flashed a look to an aide who controlled the TVs, and the volume from the screen behind him abruptly lowered.

"How are we going to find it?" asked Dellenbaugh.

"We have eight hundred people with Geigers spreading out across the waterfront," said Kratovil, the director of the FBI. "General Electric is bringing in Geigers from their Pittsfield facility. Siemens emptied their warehouse to fill in the gap. We're going boat by boat. If the bomb's there, Mr. President, we'll find it."

91

As his Ferrari ripped west on the freeway, Malnikov hit speed dial.

Stihl, Malnikov's helicopter pilot, answered.

"Alexei, it's three thirty in the morning."

"I don't have time to talk," said Malnikov. "You need to pick someone up. He's outside the city."

"Where?" asked Stihl.

"Elektrostal. A building at the corner of Vostochnyy and Michurinskiy."

"When?"

"Right now."

"The S-92?" asked Stihl, referring to Malnikov's most luxurious helicopter, a Sikorsky S-92 VVIP.

"No," said Malnikov. "Take the Dauphin."

"There's no seating, Alexei. I had it retrofitted for tactical assaults."

"That's the idea. Now get going. His name is Dewey."

* * *

Every time Malnikov thought he was getting closer, Cloud seemed to sense it, finding an extra burst of speed at precisely the right moment. He was running the bike recklessly, stabbing left and right, dodging the occasional car or truck, trying to get away.

Malnikov owned six motorcycles. He'd climbed aboard his first when he was only twelve. But the thought of going as fast as Cloud was now going—and in the rain—was unfathomable.

He glanced down at the speedometer: 144 mph.

He couldn't go any faster, and yet, when he saw the straightaway, he throttled the Ferrari even harder. He watched as the distance between the Ferrari and the Ducati slowly decreased. A quarter mile became a few hundred yards, then only a hundred.

Above the blurry lights of the motorcycle, Moscow's skyscrapers came into sharp relief, spires of glass and steel illuminated against the dark sky.

As Malnikov came within a dozen feet of the Ducati, Cloud suddenly slowed, then burst right down an exit ramp. Malnikov didn't see it coming. He hit the brakes, put the car in reverse, then slammed the gas, ripping backward until he was even with the ramp. He jammed the car into forward then shot off the highway.

Again Cloud opened up distance, but Malnikov tasted blood. He trailed Cloud along the river, soon closing the gap. Near the center of Moscow's business district, Cloud abruptly slashed right, charting a course that led into the crowded warren of steel and glass that constituted Moscow's skyscrapers.

Malnikov pushed the Ferrari as fast as it would go without skidding out of control. Looking down, he saw the number: 160 mph.

As he brought the Ferrari alongside Cloud, time seemed to freeze. Despite the low primitive growl of the Ferrari, despite the high-pitched roar of the Ducati, despite the rain and the chaos, Malnikov felt nothing but stillness and calm.

* * *

Cloud felt the lights on him. He heard the low rumble of the Ferrari; even as wind torched his ears and bended with the Ducati's roar, he still heard it. He glanced quickly left. It was Malnikov after all.

Cloud saw into the open window. He'd been wrong about the Americans. It hadn't been their hackers who found him. It had been Malnikov. He overestimated the United States and underestimated the brute who, at that moment, was half a car length back, raising a gun toward him. He heard the loud boom from the gun in the same moment he heard the frame of the Ducati being struck. The next shot would come any second, and so . . .

In one startling motion, Cloud flexed his right knee out, dived forward and to the right, as if he were trying to dive off the bike, and pushed the left handlebar with every ounce of strength in his body. The bike slashed hard right, the back tire slid but held. He was now alone on a deserted street. In front of him stood Moscow's newest skyscraper, Evolution Tower, half constructed.

He throttled the Ducati. Now was the time. He had to lose Malnikov *now*. When he heard the sound of gunfire, he ducked lower and rolled the throttle to its max.

With his left hand, Malnikov lowered the passenger window. He put his hand back on the wheel as, with his right hand, he reached for his gun from the center console.

He came alongside Cloud, raised the gun, then aimed it at Cloud's head. For several seconds, he held the target in the muzzle. Instinctively, Cloud turned, the black glass of the helmet all Malnikov could see.

Malnikov felt the steel of the trigger. He wanted nothing more than to put a bullet in the head of the man who put his father in prison, who stole a hundred million dollars from him, who caused him nothing but embarrassment and anger. But he didn't fire. Instead, he swept the muzzle lower, aiming for the Ducati's back tire.

Then he pulled the trigger. The slug hit metal, just above the tire, and Cloud banked abruptly right.

Malnikov slammed the brakes. He opened the door and jumped from the car, his gun out in front of him. Cloud was getting away. Malnikov fired, once, twice, and then the third bullet ripped into the motorcycle's back tire. The bike popped right as Cloud tried to keep it vertical. He weaved sharply left, fighting to slow the Ducati before it tumbled. Then the bike's front tire jackknifed and the motorcycle collapsed backward, with Cloud still on it, and slid down the Moscow street. Sparks and flames arose from the friction of metal and tar. Cloud's horrific scream pierced through the noise.

Malnikov sprinted toward the crash. Smoke and flames shot up from the engine, doused only partially by the rain. He ran until he was just a few feet from the smoking wreckage, then slowed, pistol extended in front of him.

On the other side of the badly damaged Ducati, he came to where he knew Cloud now was lying, unconscious, maybe even dead. He stepped past the smoking pile of steel, gun out, muzzle trained, finger on trigger, cocked to fire.

Cloud was gone.

Dewey scoured the ceiling, looking for a way to get to the roof. In the center of the room, at least fifteen feet in the air, was a small hatchway.

He pushed the tables together in a line that ended beneath the hatchway. He went to the far end and sprinted down the line of tables, leaping from the end, into the air, legs and arms kicking, then grabbing the frame of the hatchway. As he dangled from the ceiling, he held himself up with his left hand as he punched at the steel hatchway with his right. It was lodged shut. After several minutes of trying, he dropped to the floor. An involuntary yelp of pain came out as he landed, the drop exacerbating the wound in his leg.

A few minutes later, after catching his breath, he walked to the window, picked up the gun, and put it in his coat pocket. He climbed back onto the table and repeated his run, charging as fast as he could go, then leaping and catching the edge of the hatchway. He pulled the gun from his pocket and smashed it viciously into the steel. This time, after less than a minute, the seam between the hatchway and roof, sealed tight from decades' worth of rust, cracked. He pushed the square hatchway up and pulled himself onto the roof.

Rain was pouring down in sideways sheets. Dewey sat atop the roof for several minutes, catching his breath. He closed his eyes and allowed the rain to wash over him. He pushed away the thought of Cloud and of Russia. He pushed it away and thought of nothing, knowing that any other thought would bring him back to the harsh reality facing him. He knew that if he sought mental refuge in thoughts of family, it would only remind him of the bomb—the nuclear bomb that was now somewhere close to America's shores.

Cloud limped toward the base of the skyscraper. Looking back, he saw Malnikov running toward him.

He needed to get to a hospital. But that wasn't going to happen until he killed Malnikov.

He looked up at Evolution Tower. Its curvilinear half arcs swerved like steel ribbons, as if they'd been interwoven and then hung a thousand feet in the sky. Even half constructed, it was stunning. He'd admired it before, from afar. Now it represented his only hope of escape.

The building was ablaze with lights from cranes and scaffolding and, from within, bright halogen lights for the crews of workers who, at this hour, were not there.

Cloud pushed open the steel chain-link fence. He dragged his right leg, using his right hand to help pull it. He limped through the base of the tower, between stacks of steel girders, past massive construction trucks, huge piles of cement to be mixed into concrete, cranes, and other materials.

He looked up. Wind made the top of the structure move. The skyscraper appeared as if it might simply fall over on him.

He heard a clang from the chain-link fence. He didn't bother glancing back.

Cloud's eyes moved to the ground. For the first time, he realized he had on only one shoe. His right foot was exposed and covered in blood. He couldn't see some of his toes. He registered a raw sensation on his right side. Most of his pant leg had been scraped away in the crash. The sight of his injuries sent a wave of fear through him. Because he didn't feel them. Because, left untreated, they would kill him.

If you want to live, you must kill him.

Beyond a pile of lumber, Cloud saw the construction elevator. He limped to it, climbed inside, and slammed the gate shut. He hit a red switch, and the elevator bounced, then started climbing into the tower.

Malnikov came running into the light, saw the elevator rising, then raised his gun and fired. The slugs struck the steel cage just to Cloud's right. He ducked into the corner, shielding himself from the fusillade.

Even on a calm night, the all-black, heavily customized Eurocopter EC155 B1 Dauphin was difficult to spot. Its lights could be extinguished completely at the pilot's discretion and flown via advanced thermal night-vision optics, either in-helmet or imposed on the inside of the chopper's cockpit glass. Tonight, in the hell of a storm, what was usually difficult to see was nearly impossible.

For Stihl, the elements were nothing. Twelve years in Russian special forces, including more battles in Chechnya than he could count, battles that nobody in the outside world knew about, had forged skills no standard training could match.

When Malnikov told him to create the most lethal helicopter he could, Stihl had spent a week in Marseille, testing what Eurocopter had to offer. He spared no expense outfitting the machine with every technological feature available—and some that weren't, including flight envelope protection, as well as navigation and weapons systems that could be managed by Stihl through helmet-based optics and exoskeletal motion sensors.

He let the nav system take him to the coordinates Malnikov had provided. A thermal module in the helmet illuminated the building from a mile out. As he swooped in close, a red apparition of heat appeared atop the roof. His passenger.

He hit a button on the controls, bringing up commo. A few moments later, Malnikov's cell started ringing. As Stihl descended out of the sky toward the roof of the building, he listened to the phone ring half a dozen times. Malnikov didn't answer.

Stihl brought up more controls, visible inside his helmet shield. He ordered the chopper's nav to locate the cell by GPS. A second later, he saw the words flicker in green digital letters:

: MOSCOW RUS :
: EVOLUTION TOWER :

A faint electric whine, then the shifting of wind and rain, startled Dewey from his thoughts. He stood up, searching the sky, seeing nothing.

Dewey listened, sensed a change in the wind, then spun around, just as the thunder of the Eurocopter's rotors exploded behind him, ripping the air. As sudden as a lightning flash, the chopper surged down at Dewey, dropping from the cloaking wall of clouds and water, nearly landing directly on top of him before punching back up a few feet and then settling next to him atop the concrete roof.

Dewey opened the back door and climbed inside the chopper,

nodding to the pilot, then slid the door shut. The chopper shot up from the roof, cut left, and then tore away from Elektrostal.

Dewey looked quickly around the cabin. It was bare-bones, stripped down, without any sort of creature comforts. Everything inside the cabin was single function, designed for assault. There was no seating, just open space. The doors on the opposite side looked custom—they could be slid open for maximum assault flexibility.

From the ceiling, steel hooks with polymer cables dangled like coat hangers, there to be attached to body harnesses. The doors on both sides of the cabin could be opened wide. The combination of the harness locks and the doors enabled gunmen in the chopper to engage enemy from the air, at all angles, without fear of falling from the sky, especially useful if the pilot was forced to take sudden, hard-angled evasive measures.

The floor was like sandpaper, good for grip, but could also, with the press of a button, drop out like a trapdoor for low-hover jumps. The back wall was chain-link fence in front of a rack of advanced firearms and other weaponry, lined up on vertical shelves. Dewey scanned and saw all manner of firearms, including RPGs and MANPADs.

He pulled out a drawer underneath. Inside was enough ammunition to start a small war.

The chopper bounced violently in the undulating rain and wind.

Dewey stepped to the cockpit. The pilot's face was invisible behind a black-visored helmet. There were no lights on the controls.

The pilot's head turned. He handed Dewey a set of wireless earphones.

"I'm Stihl," he said in a hard Russian accent. "Hold on, it's going to be choppy."

"Where are we going?"

"Alexei is in a building downtown," said Stihl. "We'll be there in three minutes."

"Can you raise Alexei on commo?"

"I'll try," said Stihl as the chopper abruptly lurched left, buffeted by a crosswind.

Dewey heard the phone ring, then Malnikov's voice.

"Where are you?" asked Malnikov.

"We're in the air," said Dewey. "What's the situation?"

"He's wounded. He escaped into Evolution Tower. I'm in the elevator on my way to find him."

"Should I land on the roof?"

"There is no roof," said Malnikov. "It's half built."

"You need to wait at the base," said Stihl. "I'll be able to pick up his thermal from the air once we get there, then you can move in."

"It's too late for that," said Malnikov. "I'm already there."

92

Erika Highland, a third-year associate at Goulston & Storrs, was biting into an apple as she read the purchase agreement. One of Goulston's clients, a real estate developer, was buying a building in downtown Los Angeles.

Her eyes were drawn to the harbor. As usual on a summer Friday evening, it was crowded with boats. It was especially true tonight, July 3, the beginning of a long holiday weekend. But something was going on. She counted six separate flashing police lights.

Highland reached for her binoculars. A large Coast Guard cutter was speeding across the harbor and boats were swiftly moving toward the deeper ocean, away from the harbor, as if being asked to leave.

Her binoculars shot to the open ocean, out beyond Revere. She saw a large gray military boat—an Aegis destroyer—moving in.

"Donna," she yelled.

Highland's assistant came running into the office, her eyes moving to where Highland was looking. She stared at the scene.

"What the fuck?" she asked.

"Who's that guy you know over at WBZ?"

"Hagen?"

"Yeah. You should call him."

Eight minutes later—one minute before CNN, two before NBC, and five before Fox News and ABC—CBS cut into its regularly scheduled programming. The words CBS NEWS SPECIAL REPORT blazed across millions of American TV screens:

"Ladies and gentlemen, this is a special report from CBS Evening News. I'm Bob Schieffer, coming to you live from CBS News headquarters in New York City with breaking news. The footage you're seeing is live aerial coverage from Boston, Massachusetts, where Boston harbor is swarming with federal and state law enforcement, including two United States Navy Aegis destroyers. According to CBS sources, a suspected terror plot is, and I quote, being investigated.

"We now go live to Hagen Ward at our local CBS affiliate in Boston . . ."

93

H & M AGGREGATES
REVERE, MASSACHUSETTS

McLaughlin moved along the last pier at Revere Marina, a hand-held portable Geiger counter in his left hand. He was one of forty FBI agents now moving along the Revere waterfront, searching boat by boat for signs of nuclear material.

Standing on a pier, he keyed his mike, which was clipped to the collar of his dark blue windbreaker.

"Marina's clear," said McLaughlin, reporting back to the central Boston command post being run from a U.S. Navy Aegis destroyer.

"Move to the industrial docks."

McLaughlin looked past the marina and down the rocky spit of land between the marina and the industrial docks. The first dock at the facility was at least a hundred yards away.

It would be easier to go back to the marina and drive, but it also would take more time.

He hiked quickly along the rocky coast, just above the water, which slapped calmly at his feet. In a few minutes, he arrived at a rusty chain-link fence. He scaled it, then dropped onto an ancient wood-and-steel pier. Moored alongside the pier was a barge. It was piled high with road salt. He swept the Geiger along the barge. Suddenly, the low static of the Geiger picked up. McLaughlin moved toward the front of the long boat. With each step, the static grew more frenzied.

Then he saw a tarp. He slowed, holding the Geiger counter in front of him. The small device went from frenzied to sharp monotone. He pulled the top of the tarp aside, revealing a long steel cylinder. At its end was a square device with a flashing blue light.

He keyed his mike.

"This is McLaughlin," he said. "I found the bomb."

94

CHERRY HILL ROAD
GLOUCESTER, MASSACHUSETTS

H ey, Scooter. How do you like your hot dog?"

Saxby Ruggierio, in a blue-and-white apron, was standing on the back terrace, over the barbecue. The backyard of Ruggierio's home was crowded with friends, family, and most of his employees from the marina.

"Medium rare," said Ruggierio's neighbor.

Ruggierio laughed, took a swig of beer, then walked back inside to the kitchen. His son, Billy, was seated at the table with a girl from down the street, both eating cheeseburgers and watching the Red Sox game.

"Who's winning?" asked Ruggierio.

"I don't know," said Billy. "They cut into the game."

Ruggierio glanced at the TV. On the screen was a special report from Boston harbor.

"Turn it up," he said as he stepped closer to the TV. An aerial view of the harbor showed a swarm of law enforcement boats, their red and blue lights bright.

"*. . . while it's difficult to see, the area they seem to be focusing in on is Revere, just across the water from the city of Boston. Again, a terror plot* *is apparently being investigated on this, the evening before the July Fourth weekend . . ."*

"Holy shit," he muttered.

Ruggierio reached for the phone and dialed 911.

95

The elevator came suddenly into the open air, more than thirty floors in the sky. The wind ripped across the steel heights, stinging Malnikov with driving horizontal rain. The cage groaned loudly as it climbed.

Malnikov looked down through the yellow grate. Moscow was a different city, a darker city, dense with whole pockets of black, and lights diffused by rain.

Malnikov registered a puddle of crimson at the edge of the cage. Blood from Cloud, now washing away as rain hit it from above.

The sound of gunshot cut through the air, joined by the loud clang of the slug striking steel near his head. Malnikov ducked just as another bullet was fired, then felt his shoulder being kicked hard and back. He let himself fall to the floor as more bullets hit the rising cage.

A floor above, the elevator came to a loud stop.

Malnikov looked at his shoulder. Blood oozed through a hole in his jacket.

He crawled to the edge of the cage, trying to peer down to the floor below. But just as his head came to the edge, another shot rang out. It hit the steel of the elevator floor. A small dent appeared just beneath his chin.

"Did that hurt, Alexei?" yelled Cloud.

Malnikov lay on his back, staring up at the black and gray clouds. His breathing was becoming difficult, as if he'd just run sprints. He unzipped his coat and pulled it away from his shoulder. Blood was everywhere. His first impression—that the bullet was in his shoulder—was wrong. A black hole sat just a few inches above his nipple. With every labored breath, a fresh wave of blood gushed out.

"I need the elevator," said Cloud. "Do you mind bleeding to death somewhere else?"

Still on his back, Malnikov reached up and lowered the latch to the cage door. He kicked the door open. Slowly, with a painful moan, he turned over onto his side and climbed to his knees against the back wall of the cage. He got into a crouching position, then stuck the muzzle of the gun to the edge of the cage and aimed down at where the shots had come from. Malnikov fired as fast as his finger could flex, then charged through the open door of the cage.

Dewey moved back to the cabin, cutting to the weapons rack. He took out a pair of night optics and pulled them down over his eyes, then flipped them on. He put on a weapons vest, then grabbed a body harness and quickly put it on. He scanned the row of firearms, choosing a Desert Eagle .50AE and sticking it in the vest holster atop his left chest. Then he grabbed a KSVK 12.7 anti-materiél sniper rifle.

Another gust of wind slammed the chopper, kicking it left and down.

Stihl turned from the cockpit.

"We're coming in hot," he said. "Strap in."

Dewey hooked himself to the harness rail in the middle of the cabin.

He stepped to the cockpit, the cord automatically releasing line

432

as he moved. He looked out the front window. In the distance, Evolution Tower looked like a pair of steel ribbons spiking into the sky. The unfinished floors made the top appear as if it were disintegrating.

"Give me a perimeter," said Dewey. "Let's see what we can see before we get in there. It'd be nice if we could surprise that little bastard."

Calmly, Stihl reached to the right side of his helmet, feeling blindly for a small button, then pressing it as, directly in front of him, through the rain-splattered helicopter windshield, the unfinished, wildly curving steel spires of Evolution Tower arose through the mist in sporadic halogen yellow.

After the button was pressed, a black, specially designed glass visor slid down from the top of his helmet and covered his eyes. The visual became like a video game; the building snapped into a three-dimensional digital grid. Isobars of green, red, and yellow against black, in geometric patterns, filled the screen.

Stihl reached to his left, grabbing what looked like a glove. He pulled it on, then repeated the gesture with his other hand. The gloves suddenly went from being black to white, completely lit up, as if his hands were covered in some sort of glow-in-the-dark material. Stihl then began what looked like he was gesturing to himself, as the controls of the chopper became part of an advanced exoskeletal driving and weapons computer controlled by his hand movements, and the chopper responded, cutting abruptly left into the chasm between the unfinished skyscraper and a neighboring seventy-three-story office tower.

Stihl saw glimmers of heat on a high floor. He made an almost imperceptible movement with his left pinkie. The digital camera zoomed close, enlarging the green holographs. Another image flashed in the upper right part of Stihl's visor. Two floors were visible, the separating concrete slashing horizontal. On the higher floor, a man was crouched inside the elevator cage. On the lower floor, another man was limping toward a set of stairs near the side of the building. He was clutching a weapon, trained at the floor above as he climbed the stairs.

Stihl then saw red flashes of gunfire coming from the elevator, aimed at the floor below.

He flicked his finger again, engaging the cabin speaker system.

"We have a firefight," he said. "Better get up here."

Stihl flicked his thumb, and the windshield of the chopper abruptly transformed into the same digital screen he was seeing inside his helmet, like a large television screen. The rain was gone. The two figures looked like ghosts against a black backdrop.

Dewey moved to Stihl's right, studying the scene.

"Can you get a closer shot?" asked Dewey.

They watched as the gunman in the elevator kicked open the side of the cabin, then charged into the blackness, just as, at the other side of the same floor, another man climbed slowly up the stairs.

"Who's who?" asked Dewey.

"I don't know."

The screen showed the man running across the empty floor, sprinting, his path leading directly toward the man now climbing the stairs.

"That's Alexei," said Stihl.

"Which one?"

"The one running," said Stihl. "He's running right into him. He's going to get killed."

"Take me in."

"I'm going to level the guy on the stairs," said Stihl, suddenly engaging the weapons command.

"No, you're not," said Dewey. "Take me in."

Dewey stepped back into the cabin.

"He's going to die if I don't—"

Stihl's words were abruptly cut off as, inside his visor—and across the front screen—a blinding white light hit the left side of the view. He knew, in his bones, what it was.

"Hold on!" he screamed.

A ferocious torrent of wind shear, funneled like a tornado up into the valley between the skyscrapers, slammed like a wall of steel into the helicopter. They were kicked back and to the right, so hard that Stihl's helmet went flying from his head, struck the ceiling, and tumbled to the floor.

The chopper was jacked instantly sideways, its rotors vertical, as Stihl fought—using the exoskeletal gloves—to right them before they smashed into the building.

96

LONG ISLAND SOUND
OFF THE COAST OF STAMFORD, CONNECTICUT

Faqir steered a mile offshore, keeping the lights of the coastline in view, tiny yellow and white lights, from homes along the shore, a typical American evening.

It was pitch-black out on the water. He wore night optics. On the radio was news about a suspected terrorist plot in Boston. The American president had just announced that it had been stopped.

He knew that if the White House was announcing it, it meant they had no clue as to the existence of the other device, the bomb lying on the deck next to him.

Most of the crew were inside the cabin. Every hour or so, Faqir walked among them, feeling if they were still alive. Occasionally, a man would open his eyes. For the most part, they were all dead to the world. Vomit covered the ground.

Faqir stopped vomiting sometime during the night. Aswan, another crewman, had made a similar transition before dying an hour after they departed Boston. He'd tied a concrete block to Aswan's ankle, then dumped him overboard.

Though he didn't say anything, Faqir grew increasingly worried, wondering whether he would last long enough to get the boat to New York harbor.

One of the Chechens, a light-skinned teenager named Naji, was the only crew member still in relatively decent shape. He had enough energy to puke over the side of the boat. When there was work to be done, it was Naji whom Faqir turned to.

Faqir had taught Naji how to run the boat, as well as navigate, just in case he died unexpectedly.

The Talaria was now near the shore, as Long Island Sound narrowed the closer they came to New York. As he looked to the shore, he saw a busy marina. People were sitting out front, eating at a waterside restaurant. Hundreds of watercraft, from beat-up skiffs to gaudy million-dollar cigarette boats, were moored along piers that stretched hundred feet into the water, then ran along the busy coast, beneath office and apartment buildings, for a quarter mile.

A memory flashed in Faqir's mind.

Many months ago, Faqir imagined that the night before the bomb was detonated—his last night on earth—he would celebrate, like Mohammed Atta had done the evening before 9/11. He imagined docking the boat and taking the others out for dinner, perhaps ordering wine.

A small grin came to his emaciated face as he thought about how much fun it would have been. Then he looked around the cabin. His grin disappeared as he realized that, except for Naji, all the crewmen were dead.

97

The wall of wind shear pummeled the Eurocopter sideways. The chopper's rotors tilted into a vertical position, then the chopper dropped more than two hundred feet in just seconds, before starting a somersault. The three-and-a-half-ton helicopter was out of control, in the rain and dark, sixty stories above the street.

Dewey felt the onset of the first gust, and all he could do was stick his hand out to shield his head before he was thrown into the back wall. He slammed into it, then dropped to the floor.

Desperately, he grabbed along the wall, searching for something to hold on to. He found a utility bar and clutched it with every ounce of strength he had, holding on as the chopper whipped violently upside down.

Stihl was strapped tightly to the pilot's chair, focused on the digital screen inside his visor. He'd already flipped the Eurocopter's avionics to his control, and now the chopper's fate was fully vested in the pair of highly advanced exoskeletal gloves on Stihl's hands. He had to right the helicopter before it crashed.

The wind shear should've hit in a straight wall, like a wave. But the tall buildings altered the wind, each steel-and-concrete spire cutting into it, making the gust choppy and uneven.

Stihl, who'd flown in blizzards in the hills outside Grozny, who'd tangled with hurricanes in the Hindu Kush, now had a serious situation on his hands, certainly the worst he'd ever faced.

Stihl reached his hands out, trying find some level of stability within the maelstrom. He tried to focus on the graphical of the wind. Its white blur was now dead center, shaped like an upside-down U. It was moving. The air was clear on the other side.

Stihl's eyes shot to the top of the screen. In bold green, a square box of geometric isobar lines was approaching the center of the screen. This was a skyscraper. Three hundred feet and closing. They would slam into it in seconds.

He waited one extra moment, unsure if what he was about to do would work, then realized it didn't matter. It was all instinct now. A quarter century's worth of gut, all funneled into one move.

"*Hold on!*" he screamed.

Stihl dumped fuel from all but one tank, then slammed on both front and rear rotor brakes. A half second later, he released the rear rotor.

The chopper tilted down, its nose suddenly going from aiming at the sky to the ground, as, in the same instant, the craft dropped. Gasoline poured down around the chopper, mixing with the rain, displacing weight.

Then Stihl jacked both engines to the max. Front and rear rotors churned ferociously. The chopper kicked forward and down. Stihl was slammed back in the seat. Whatever fuel hadn't been emptied juiced the Eurocopter's turbos, which crushed the gas into a barely controlled, sudden explosion of power. Every ounce of thrust the Eurocopter was capable of providing was being used as, on the digital screen, the skyscraper and chopper appeared as if they were in the process of merging.

Dewey, still clutching the utility bar, was pulled sideways, toward the front of the cabin. The chopper's momentum was too powerful. He couldn't hold any longer. He careened through the air and slammed into the front wall.

Stihl took the chopper below the wind shear, down into the chasm between the two buildings, thrusting lower and lower toward the ground. The street grew larger as the helicopter charged to earth. Buildings, which were wider at their bases, grew up on both sides of the chopper; Stihl would soon run out of room to steer or turn.

On Stihl's digital visor screen, the bold geometric lines of buildings on both sides arose in sharp green relief as the chopper looked as if it would slam into the ground. For the first time in half a minute, Stihl felt that he had the chopper under control. He was below the shear. The only problems now were the walls of steel and concrete on either side and that wall of dirt below called earth.

Stihl straightened the chopper, then bottomed out and turned. The chopper climbed back up the face of a building.

Stihl took one extra breath, then swerved around the spire of a building, aiming the chopper back toward the top of the tower. He brought the thermal interface back up as, in the distance, the unfinished pair of steel ribbons appeared directly ahead.

He triggered the loudspeakers in the cabin.

"You still alive back there?" he asked.

"Yeah," said Dewey.

Malnikov sprinted away from the elevator, across the empty concrete, which was wet with windblown spray from the storm.

His chest and shoulder throbbed as he ran. He felt tightness and a recurring stabbing pain down his leg, like an electric shock. But he ignored it. He could live with anything now, any pain or punishment.

He glanced back at the shaft. It was still, motionless.

Had one of his bullets hit Cloud?

He stopped near a concrete piling. He heard metal scratching metal, a round being chambered. It was close, just behind him.

Malnikov turned.

Cloud was barefoot, and that foot was covered in blood. His leg was badly damaged. The pants were torn away from the knee down. The skin was raw, pink and black, most of the skin scraped away.

He held a gun.

"So you want your money back?" asked Cloud.

Dewey stood up and stepped to the front of the cabin.

He stuck his head inside the cockpit. On the screen was a three-dimensional digital pictograph of the tower.

Stihl had the Eurocopter blazing straight for it.

As they moved closer, two men were visible on the high floor. Dewey studied the screen. The men were now standing next to each other. Malnikov was larger. He stood before Cloud, who had a gun aimed at Malnikov's head.

"We won't be able to land," said Stihl.

"He's about to die. What options do we have?"

"Machine guns," said Stihl. "But I must tell you, there will be no survivors."

Dewey stared into the large digital screen that still occupied the view where the windshield was.

"Can you take that off?" asked Dewey, pointing to the digital screen.

The screen abruptly turned off. It was replaced by the actual view through the windshield. Raindrops coated the glass. Evolution Tower looked apocalyptic, sporadically alight in neon yellow, its shape otherworldly. The unfinished floors appeared to be disintegrating, their edges rough and unhewn.

"Take me in closer."

"Hold on."

As Stihl maneuvered in toward the upper floors of Evolution Tower, Dewey turned back to the cabin.

Working quickly, he unclipped himself from the hoist bar, removed his harness and dropped it on the ground. He found the KSVK rifle. Dewey tightened his helmet and returned to the cockpit. They were now hovering fewer than a hundred feet from the high, empty floor. Dewey pulled his night optics down over his eyes and flipped them on. The screen lit up in dark blue, then sharpened. He looked toward Malnikov and Cloud. Malnikov was now on the ground, writhing in pain. Cloud stood over him. Dewey watched as Cloud stepped closer, then aimed the gun down at Malnikov.

"Take me in," barked Dewey.

"I can't do it."

"You have to do it."

"I can get you ten feet away. But even if I could get you closer, even at five feet, the wind is too strong. You'll be blown sideways."

"Open the door and swing it around," ordered Dewey sharply. "Get me as close as you can."

Stihl shook his head, disagreeing, then motioned. The chopper abruptly shot forward, then right and down.

"I'll come at it from below," said Stihl.

"You need to tell me when to jump," said Dewey.

"Fine. Stand back and hold on. It's about to get wet and windy in here."

Stihl shut the cockpit door.

Dewey grabbed a canvas strap with his right hand as, in his left, he clutched the rifle.

The chopper doors slid open. A fierce torrent of wind and cold rain blasted into the cabin, drenching Dewey and pushing him back against the wall.

He studied the digital screen inside his helmet as the chopper flew directly at the skyscraper.

He felt it then. Warmth, his heart beating, then the adrenaline.

Risk it all, Dewey. Now is the time, the moment.

The chopper tore through the wind-crossed melee toward the tower, getting closer and closer.

Stihl's thick Russian boomed over the in-helmet commo.

"Three! Two! One!"

Dewey charged toward the open door of the helicopter. He took one big step and then heard the last word from Stihl: "*Go!*"

Dewey's right foot hit the outer edge of the cabin floor just as the chopper was within feet of the building. Then Stihl slashed the chopper hard right. Dewey leapt into the breach, fifty-five stories up.

Dewey kicked his arms and legs furiously in the free air. He struck the floor's outer edge, throwing the rifle out from his right hand, then hit the building, the thick concrete catching him at the waist. He grabbed the floor, his hands scratching wet concrete, just as a squall of wind from the chopper pulled at him, yanking him out as he tried to hold on. But it was too strong. He slipped back, then his hands were pulled to the very edge of the precipice.

Dewey felt himself dropping. His hands grasped at the last edge of the concrete, then slipped off and he started to drop. His hands grabbed at air, then his right hand felt something sharp. He clutched it and held on. For an awful moment, he swung in the air by one hand, his fingers wrapped around the jagged end of a steel rod.

He glanced down. He was dangling more than fifty stories in the air. He took a moment to catch his breath, then pulled up. Heaving, he hoisted his body up and then swung his left leg over the end of the floor. He slowly pulled his body onto the concrete.

Dewey grabbed the rifle, scanning for the thermal outlines of Cloud and Malnikov. Malnikov was on the ground. Cloud stood above him, behind a concrete piling. Dewey targeted the piling, then triggered the rifle. A low thunderclap boomed as, in the same instant, a hole tore through the piling. Behind it, Cloud screamed as he was kicked backward and down to the floor, landing next to Malnikov.

98

Katie Foxx was seated on the floor, against a filing cabinet. Tacoma was several feet away from her, also on the floor. Both were reading through the files.

Each file in the room detailed CIA agents, case officers, paramilitary, and nonofficial covers who, in the Agency's mind, merited termination. There was no single cause, but there were recurring themes. Treason was the main one. A close second was nonsanctioned murder.

Files were stacked up in piles.

"I have something," Katie said.

In her hand was a small stack of paper, yellowed and fraying at the edges.

LOS ALAMOS NATIONAL LABORATORY

MEMORANDUM

FROM: H. Agnew

TO: N. Bradbury

SUBJECT: IMPLICATIONS OF A. VARGARIN THEORY

DATE: September 10, 1982

Norb—I was able to meet with Anuslav Vargarin in Vienna, where we were both attending the conference. As you said, he is a most charming man. We spent most of our time talking about wine!

However, he mentioned something that, if true, would be significant. Dr. Vargarin stated that he and some colleagues have been experimenting with various divalents as adjunct to nuclear moderation and reflection. He would not say which ones, though, as you and I both agree, Z seems to show the most promise. While most of this was chitchat, as we were of course being watched, Dr. Vargarin stated something I should pass on. He said, "We have now succeeded in three successive tests."

The implications of this are clear: if the Soviets are able to predictably moderate fast neutrons in a lab setting using Z (or other), it would mean the Soviets could double the scalability of their HEU and thus double the size of their nuclear stockpiles in a matter of months.

Let me know what, if anything, you want me to do.

Harry

"What is it?"

"Cloud's father was a scientist who developed a formula," said Katie. "It's all about his dad's formula."

She stood up and dialed her cell.

"I must be missing something," said Tacoma. "So fucking what?"

Katie listened to Calibrisi's phone ringing.

"It's a formula for how to convert one nuclear device into two."

99

J. P. Dellenbaugh poked his head inside the small, cluttered office of John Schmidt, his communications director, the person charged with managing the unruly group of reporters that constituted the White House press corps.

Schmidt, at 11:38 P.M., had just taken a large bite of a steak and cheese sub as he watched, eyes scanning left to right, six television screens on the wall of his office, all showing the same images: live video, taken from news choppers, of the chaotic scene in Boston. The harbor was awash in the blue and red lights of police boats, Coast Guard cutters, and a pair of Navy destroyers.

The voice of Dan Harris from ABC News was turned up.

"You're watching live feed from Boston," said Harris, "which ABC News can now confirm was the site of attempted terror strike. Less than two hours ago, law enforcement—acting on a tip—discovered something near the Boston waterfront. We have been unable to determine who was behind the attempt, or what was found, but we do know that several vessels have departed the harbor in the last hour."

"Hey, John," whispered Dellenbaugh. "You need a shovel for that?"

Schmidt nearly coughed up the bite of steak and cheese.

"If you have a coronary before reelection, I'm going to kill you," added Dellenbaugh.

Schmidt finished chewing. He took a quick swig of Diet Coke and then turned, slightly embarrassed, to Dellenbaugh.

"John, I apologize," added Dellenbaugh, before Schmidt could get in a word, "I didn't realize you were having a *Diet* Coke. That should cancel out any unhealthy effects from the steak and cheese."

Schmidt burst into laughter, then was joined by the president.

"I didn't eat dinner," said Schmidt.

Dellenbaugh's attention was grabbed by one of the plasma screens, which showed a lit-up stretch of coast. It was surrounded by military vehicles, ambulances, police cars, and hundreds of people, most armed and wearing uniforms or tactical gear.

"You are looking at an aerial view of Revere, Massachusetts," said Harris. "This is as close as we are allowed to get. As you can see, various law enforcement agencies as well as military are now clearly in control of what was apparently to have been a strike, by terrorists, on Boston. There are still many questions."

Dellenbaugh and Schmidt stared at the screen in silence.

"Thank God, sir," said Schmidt, looking at Dellenbaugh.

Dellenbaugh put his hand on Schmidt's shoulder.

"I was just thinking the same thing."

"Do you want me to write up some quick remarks for the press conference, Mr. President?"

"No," said Dellenbaugh. "I know what I'm going to say."

Schmidt pressed his phone. The speaker came on.

"Get them seated and quiet, Joanne," said Schmidt to Joanne Hildebrand, his deputy.

In the background, the live news report continued.

"We're waiting for a statement by the president of the United

States," said Harris, "who we're told was very much personally involved in the government's response to the terror plot. And, I'm told,
we're going there right now. Ladies and gentlemen, we take you to
the White House, where President J. P. Dellenbaugh is going to address the nation."

100

Dewey stood—dropping the rifle—and charged, yanking the handgun from his chest holster. He sprinted toward the concrete piling, gun out, then came around it, acquiring Cloud in the muzzle's fire zone.

His eyes shot to Malnikov, lying on the ground. The left side of his chest was drenched in blood.

Cloud was facedown.

Dewey scanned for his gun. It was on the ground next to his head. With his sidearm trained on the back of Cloud's head, Dewey stepped forward and kicked it out of reach.

He put his foot beneath Cloud and flipped him over. His eyes were open. His right leg looked badly damaged. His hip was worse. A small chunk was missing, the slug from the anti-materiél rifle having blown it off.

Dewey looked back at Malnikov.

"You gonna make it?" he asked.

"Yeah," said Malnikov, as he struggled to climb to his feet.

Dewey's eyes moved back to Cloud. Without shifting his gaze, he dialed his cell. A moment later, a female voice came on the line.

"Name?"

"Andreas, Dewey."

"Flag?"

"NOC 2294-6."

"Go."

"I need Calibrisi. Crisis Priority."

"Protocol?"

"Dayton."

"Hold."

Dewey heard a series of clicks, then Calibrisi came on the line.

"Where the hell are you?"

"We have him, Hector. What do you need to know?"

"We found the bomb," said Calibrisi. "We stopped it. It's been disarmed."

Dewey was silent for several seconds.

"You should know, it was Katya who provided the intel."

"Where was it?"

"Boston."

Dewey's eyes moved from Cloud's eyes to his hip. He'd seen injuries on the battlefield and had long ago been hardened by those horrible sights. But even with that knowledge, the sight of it was gruesome. The dull white of bone was visible within the blood. Tendrils of skin and parts dangled down to the concrete, now awash in blood.

Cloud stared up at Dewey. He said nothing.

He was the opposite of the sort of person Dewey expected. He didn't look angry or mean. He looked frail, intelligent, curious, above all innocent. Perhaps, at one time in his life, he had been. But something destroyed it.

He heard Malnikov's footsteps to his left.

Both stared down. To Dewey, he was the one who wanted to kill a million Americans. To Malnikov, the one who took his father away.

Dewey still held the cell to his ear.

"So what you're saying is, Cloud is expendable?" Dewey asked.

452

Calibrisi was silent for several seconds.

Then he spoke: "Affirmative."

Dewey hung up and stuck the cell in his vest. He clutched the Desert Eagle, its steel muzzle aimed at Cloud's head.

"Boston," Dewey remarked to Cloud. "Original."

Suddenly, the elevator cage rattled and started descending.

"We need to get out of here," said Malnikov.

"Here," said Dewey, extending the gun to him.

"You take it," said Malnikov. "You saved my life."

"Do you want to do it, Alexei?" asked Dewey. "It's all the same to me as long as he ends up dead."

Malnikov shrugged.

"Well, I will tell you, I have had this desire ever since he fucked me to put a bullet in that big brain of his."

Dewey handed Malnikov the gun.

"All yours."

101

Adrian King was seated in his office, along with Calibrisi, Josh Brubaker, and George Kratovil, head of the FBI.

Two plasma screens showed live coverage from Boston. A third screen streamed live video feed from the scene, taken by the FBI. Three individuals in bright yellow hazmat suits were preparing the nuclear device for transport out of the area. A fourth screen displayed the White House Briefing Room. The dais was empty, though the room was crowded.

A knock came at the door, then Arden Mason entered. He had a concerned look on his face.

"What is it?" asked King.

Mason handed out manila folders.

"I think you should all see this. It was sent in a few minutes ago."

The folders contained copies of a police report, filed by the Gloucester, Massachusetts, police department, detailing the purchase of a boat that day by someone whom the owner of the marina found to be "suspicious-looking."

According to the marina owner, the customer was young and

looked Middle Eastern. Perhaps most important, he bought a used Hinckley Talaria, which cost $450,000.

"He paid cash," said Mason.

"So this is the boat?" asked King, looking at Mason, then Kratovil. "Let's put out an APB for a green Hinckley Talaria. That would be a pretty good start to the weekend, first we stop the bomb, then we catch the terrorists."

"President Dellenbaugh is about to go live," said Brubaker. "I think we should hand him a note before he goes on. If he can mention the precise boat we're looking for, my guess is we'll find it pretty quickly."

Calibrisi's cell phone vibrated.

"Calibrisi."

"It's Katie."

"I need to call you back."

"No. I need to talk to you. It's about Vargarin. We found something."

"We found the bomb, Katie. Why don't you grab whatever you got and we'll meet over at the Willard. I could use a drink."

"Wait, you said you found the bomb?" asked Katie.

"Yes. It was in Boston."

"How many were there?"

"How many what were there?"

"Bombs."

"One."

"And was it the original device?"

"What do you mean?"

"Was it repurposed? Was it altered in any way? Smaller than the one they took from Kiev?"

Calibrisi looked at the screen showing the FBI feed. The bomb was being lifted by two men. It looked brand-new, like a long stainless steel canister, very different from what the original bomb looked like.

"It's different," said Calibrisi. "Looks like a big soup can."

Brubaker was trying to get Calibrisi's attention.

"Hold on, Katie," he said, covering the phone.

"Do you want to read this before Schmidt takes it out to the president?" whispered Brubaker. "We need to get this on the news right now."

"Katie," said Calibrisi, "I have to call you—"

"*There are two bombs, Hector!*" yelled Katie. "That was his father's big idea. How to take one bomb and convert it into two. We killed him for the formula."

Calibrisi stared at Brubaker. He hung up the phone, then hit another number.

"Control."

"I need an immediate patch to that last overseas caller."

"Hold."

Everyone in the room stared at Calibrisi as he sat, eyes closed, waiting for the phone to ring.

"What's going on?" demanded King.

"There's another bomb," said Calibrisi.

Silence took over the room.

"The president of the United States is about to take a victory lap," said King. "I'm canceling this press conference."

"Don't," said Calibrisi, still holding the cell to his ear. "The American people need to know what's going on. The best thing right now is if the terrorists think we're done. Let J. P. Dellenbaugh lull them into a sense of complacency. It'll buy us time. And do *not* let him mention the boat."

Finally, he heard a pair of beeps, then Dewey's voice.

"How can I miss you if you won't go away?" he asked.

"Whatever you do, don't kill him."

102

BRIEFING ROOM
THE WHITE HOUSE

Dellenbaugh entered the White House Briefing Room. He stepped to the dais, the front of which showed the seal of the president of the United States.

Dellenbaugh paused. Except for the rat-a-tat-tat of cameras clicking, there was absolute silence. His look was confident, calm, with just the slightest hint of anger on his ruddy face.

"Late this evening," said Dellenbaugh, "an attempt by terrorists to attack the United States was stopped. The location of the failed attack was Boston, a place that holds an extremely important place in the history of our country, especially this time of year. We will have much more to tell you in the coming hours, days, and weeks. For now, it's important that we complete our investigation before getting into too many details. But I can tell you that we do not believe this is part of a broader plot. This was a small group of individuals, acting alone."

Dellenbaugh's eyes swept across the crowd of reporters.

"I'm outraged that anyone would attempt to use the July Fourth holiday—a time families and friends gather together to celebrate the day our country was born—to hurt innocent people. Some people,

I know, are scared. You're asking yourself, what if there's another threat out there? The worst thing we could do would be to quit, to cancel the parade, to not put the red, white, and blue icing on that cake Mom made. Because then they will have won.

"Tomorrow, with my family by my side, I'm going to barbecue. Then I'll go to the parade in town. If you're there, I hope you'll come up and introduce yourself. I won't march, I'll watch, because on July Fourth, I like to think I'm just a plain old United States citizen. Oh, yeah, I'm going to get revenge on my brother-in-law for his victory over me in Ping-Pong last year, a match that, in case he's listening, we both know was rigged."

Dellenbaugh smiled as laughter burst out from the gathered White House press corps.

"This Independence Day weekend is already shaping up to be the best in my lifetime. Because today I saw what brave Americans are capable of. The fact that it happened in Boston, well, I have to tell you, there's something mighty poetic about that. The place our country was born was tonight the place where freedom was preserved.

"May God bless you, and God bless the United States of America. Have a happy Fourth of July."

"Mr. President, can you tell us anything more?" yelled a reporter.

But Dellenbaugh was already off the stage and stepping quickly down the hallway. As he rounded the corner, he came face-to-face with King and Brubaker, both standing outside the Oval Office, arms crossed.

Dellenbaugh had a big smile on his face. He ripped off his tie as he walked past them.

"There's nothing you can say that would upset me," said Dellenbaugh, entering the Oval Office, tossing his tie on a chair, then opening a closet and grabbing his fly rod.

"There's a second bomb, Mr. President."

103

Dewey looked at Malnikov, making a gesture across his neck and shaking his head, telling him not to shoot.

"*Why?*" asked Malnikov, anger in his voice. "Fuck that."

"There's another bomb," said Dewey, making eye contact with Cloud.

Dewey spoke to Calibrisi: "He's going to die soon, Hector," he whispered.

"What do you mean?"

"He's bleeding out."

"What happened?"

"He got in the way of a bullet."

"How long do we have?"

"Maybe an hour. Two if I can stop the bleeding for a little while."

Just then, voices echoed up from the elevator shaft. Both turned their heads.

"You need to get that chopper back here," said Dewey.

Malnikov pulled out his cell and dialed Stihl.

Dewey returned to Calibrisi: "What do you want me to do?" he asked.

"Can you get him to the airport?" asked Calibrisi.

"He's not going to survive a flight out of Russia, if that's what you're thinking."

"No, that's not what I'm thinking. Just get him to Ostafyevo Airport."

Calibrisi, escorted by Secret Service agents, stepped through the Oval Office and out onto a stone terrace, then walked through the Rose Garden.

On the South Lawn of the White House, the rotors of the Sikorsky S-76C were already slashing the air in anticipation.

He dialed Chalmers as he climbed into the cabin and the chopper flew into the dark sky above Washington.

"Hector," said Chalmers.

"Is she still alive?" asked Calibrisi.

"Yes," said Chalmers. "We bandaged her wrists. She's stable."

"Where are you?"

"We land in Moscow in fifteen minutes. You should know we're being met by Russian authorities. They're meeting us on the tarmac."

"Which airport?"

"Domodedovo," said Chalmers, referring to Moscow's largest airport.

"Tell your pilot to take the plane into Ostafyevo," said Calibrisi. "We need a few minutes before the cops take Katya away."

"Why? I read the Interpol tear sheet. You stopped the bomb."

"We stopped *one* of the bombs. There's another one. We're down to our last out here."

"She's in bad shape," said Chalmers. "She cut both wrists. She lost a lot of blood."

"You said she feels guilty?" asked Calibrisi as he glanced out the window at the Washington Monument, already lit up in red, white, and blue for the Fourth of July. "Tell her she's already saved at least a hundred thousand lives. Thank her on behalf of the American people.

Then tell her she's going to get the chance to save ten times that number."

"Will do."

A minute later, the chopper swooped down to the roof of the National Archives building. Katie and Tacoma were waiting, Tacoma holding a cardboard box filled with files. The door to the helicopter opened. They climbed aboard, then the door shut and the chopper quickly took off.

"You find anything else?" asked Calibrisi.

Katie nodded.

"Guess who one of the case officers was who witnessed Vargarin's murder?" she asked.

"Josh Gant."

"How did you know?"

Calibrisi stared at Katie but said nothing.

"Let's table that discussion for later," he said. "Right now, we have a nuclear bomb in a Hinckley Talaria that we have to stop. I want you to call Igor. Give him the make and the model on the boat and see if there's anything he can do."

Katie pulled out her cell.

"What do mean, 'anything he can do'?"

"Some sort of variation on facial recognition technology. I want whatever ad hoc software he develops to be live on every possible video feed and security camera from Providence to Washington, with an obvious focus on New York."

"Is that where we're going?"

"Yeah," said Calibrisi. "I might be wrong, but I have to believe that's where the final target is."

Dewey stepped over to Cloud. His eyes were shut. He was unconscious. Dewey felt his neck for a pulse. It was weak, but it was there. He was still alive. Dewey lifted him up onto his shoulder, fireman style.

The voices from the elevator shaft were becoming louder now.

"We have to move," said Malnikov.

He followed Malnikov to a set of stairs. They climbed up three flights, emerging at the top floor of the skyscraper. Wind ripped across the unfinished concrete, drenching them in rain.

The sky was starting to turn a silvery gray as dawn approached. The Moscow skyline was dimly illuminated in sporadic cuts of light from other buildings. Twin ribbons of steel jutted up from the concrete, arched in curvilinear black against the sky.

Blood from Cloud's wound covered the right side of Dewey's coat and pants. Dewey could feel the wetness, warmer and stickier than the rain.

Malnikov clutched his shoulder as he searched the sky for Stihl.

"Pull it aside," said Dewey to Malnikov, nodding at his blood-soaked shirt.

"No," said Malnikov. "It hurts too much."

"Pull it aside."

Malnikov paused.

"You'll have to do it," said Malnikov.

Dewey reached his hand out and gently ripped Malnikov's shirt away from the left side of his chest. The bullet hole was visible—a small black opening that continued to ooze dark blood. Dewey pulled the shirt down, then looked at Malnikov's back. It was covered in blood. But there was no exit wound.

"It's still inside you," said Dewey. "It didn't hit your heart, but it needs to be removed."

Malnikov nodded.

"You're not going to like what I have to say," said Dewey.

"What is that? That I'm going to die?"

"No," said Dewey. "Go back downstairs. Let the cops or whoever they are get you to a hospital."

"No fucking way," said Malnikov.

Just then, the black Eurocopter plunged from the clouds, knocked by the crosswinds, then cut toward the top of the building.

"Promise me something," said Malnikov.

"What?"

"If I die, you will make Calibrisi live up to his end of the bargain."

"You're not going to die, Alexei," said Dewey.

The chopper dropped down quickly as Stihl used the speed of his descent to counter the violent winds. The front of the Eurocopter was tilted forward. As it came closer and closer, it appeared it might slam nose-first into the slab. At the last second, Stihl pulled the chopper back, rear wheels hitting first, then the front.

Dewey and Malnikov moved through the rotor chop toward the door.

"Then the promise won't cost you anything, will it?" yelled Malnikov.

"Fine," said Dewey. "I promise."

Dewey stepped inside the cabin and lay Cloud down on the steel floor. Malnikov followed him on, then the door slid shut behind them. Seconds later, Stihl lifted off.

Dewey went to the back and started pulling out drawers and opening compartments, searching for the trauma kit. He carried the steel case to where Cloud was lying. He pressed several large gauze pads against the wound. Cloud jerked from the pain, though his eyes remained shut. Dewey wrapped a large bandage around Cloud's hip, as tight as he could, keeping the pads pressed to the wound.

He took another gauze bandage and moved to Malnikov. He pulled Malnikov's shirt aside and pressed the bandage against the bullet hole, then wrapped a bandage across Malnikov's chest to keep it in place.

"How do I know you'll keep your promise?" asked Malnikov.

Dewey looked at Malnikov.

"I never break a promise," said Dewey.

* * *

Chalmers's Bombardier touched down at Ostafyevo Airport and came to a stop at the end of the runway.

Chalmers unbuckled and stepped to the cockpit.

"Take it over toward the terminal building but stay at least a hundred feet away."

"Sure, Derek."

Chalmers walked back into the cabin. He sat down across from Katya.

"Katya," he said. "I need to talk to you."

Katya was lying on the leather built-in sofa, eyes shut. She didn't respond.

"The United States found the nuclear bomb," he continued. "It was in Boston. They stopped it. They believe, had it been detonated, at least one hundred thousand people would have perished. Your information prevented that from happening. You saved a lot of lives."

Katya remained still.

"But we need something more from you. There is another bomb. There were two bombs. There's only one individual who knows where it's going."

Katya's eyes opened, then tears came to her eyes and started to roll down her cheeks.

"I don't know where it's going," she whispered, looking at Chalmers. "That was just a conversation I overheard. You must believe me. *I don't know!*"

"But Pyotr does know," said Chalmers.

"I don't know where he is," she protested. "What do you want me to do? He's a monster. He wouldn't listen to me."

The faint din of a helicopter hit the cabin, causing Chalmers to turn to the window. Katya's eyes followed Chalmers.

"No," she cried. "*No!*"

"He will listen to you," said Chalmers. "I need you to be strong. One more time, then it will be over. You can do it. I see how brave you are. I know you can do it. Lives are depending on you."

Dewey tapped Stihl's shoulder as the chopper cut across the Moscow dawn.

"How long until we get there?"

"Five minutes."

Dewey stepped back into the cabin. Malnikov was seated quietly. He looked weak. Dewey knelt next to Cloud and checked the wound. The bandages were soaked through and a small pool of blood was on the ground beneath his hip. Dewey felt his pulse. It was weaker than before. Dewey shook his shoulder, trying to revive him. It didn't work.

He pulled out his cell and dialed Calibrisi.

"We're about to land," Dewey said. "Is she there?"

"Yes," said Calibrisi. "Is he still alive?"

"Barely. He's unconscious. I'm going to try and revive him. I'm not sure it's going to work."

"You need to know something," said Calibrisi. "It's about his father."

"His father?"

"He was a nuclear scientist. Before the breakup of the Soviet Union, we recruited him. He was going to defect. He had second thoughts."

The chopper arced forward and right, descending. Dewey glanced out the window. He could see the small airport in the distance.

"Can this wait?" asked Dewey.

"An agent named Roberts shot his father and mother in front of him. He was five years old."

Dewey stared at Cloud.

"What'd we do with the agent?"

"The Agency put a sanction on him, but he escaped. I don't know if he's still alive."

"Understood."

Dewey hung up. He went to the trauma kit. In a compartment on the side of the case were several small bottles of drugs, including painkillers and antibiotics. He found a bottle labeled EPINEPHRINE. Adrenaline. Dewey took a syringe from the kit, removed it from its sterile packaging, and filled it. He left the loaded syringe in the case and stood up.

He glanced out the window. The tarmac was visible in the distance. A light blue jet was parked. Running and cabin lights were visible.

"Put it next to that plane," said Dewey.

Stihl banked left and descended. A half minute later, the chopper stopped and hovered just a few feet above the ground. Its wheels lowered, then the Eurocopter settled smoothly onto the tarmac.

Dewey opened the side door and crossed a thin stretch of tarmac to the jet, whose cabin door was now lowering. He climbed the stairs and stepped into the cabin.

Looking right, he saw Chalmers, seated, legs crossed.

"Hi, Dewey," said Chalmers.

Dewey's eyes moved to Katya, who was seated across from Chalmers.

"Let's go," said Dewey.

Katya glanced at Chalmers, who stood up and extended his hand.

"It's time," Chalmers said.

Dewey led Katya and Chalmers down the stairs and across the tarmac. Halfway to the helicopter door, Chalmers took Dewey's arm at the elbow.

Dewey shot Chalmers a look.

"She tried to kill herself," said Chalmers, out of Katya's earshot. "Make this quick. She needs to get to a hospital."

"I'll do my best, Derek. But right now, I only care about one thing."

Dewey opened the door of the helicopter and climbed inside, followed by Katya. Chalmers paused at the door, then followed, sliding it shut behind him.

Katya searched in the dimly lit cabin, her eyes finding Cloud. She dropped to her knees beside him. A horrified look crossed her face as she registered his right leg, cleaved of its skin below the knee. Then she saw Cloud's hip, the dark red bandage, the blood on the floor.

She looked at Dewey. As much as Cloud's actions horrified her, Katya's expression showed an even stronger reaction. Her eyes betrayed revulsion at what Dewey had done to him.

She looked back to Cloud.

"Pyotr," she said. "Pyotr, it's me."

Cloud's head remained limp.

Behind Katya, Dewey removed the syringe. He knelt next to her.

"This is adrenaline," said Dewey. "I'm going to try and bring him back. Let me speak first."

Katya nodded.

Dewey pulled the collar of Cloud's shirt down, exposing his chest. With his left hand, he felt Cloud's chest, locating the breastplate. He kept two fingers pressed to a specific spot almost directly in the center of the chest, then placed the end of the needle between his fingers and pushed the needle in. Blood spurted from the puncture. He moved the needle in several inches, then pressed the plunger and pumped adrenaline directly into Cloud's heart.

Cloud's eyes opened up, then shut. A moment later, he screamed. He said something in Russian, repeating it over and over.

"What's he saying?" asked Dewey.

"Kill me," said Malnikov.

"Pyotr, listen to me," said Dewey.

Cloud continued to scream. His eyes again opened. He turned and looked up at Dewey.

"I know what they did. What we did," Dewey told him.

"You couldn't know," whispered Cloud.

"We killed your father. Your mother. I know about it. But the man who did that was a killer. One man. He was slated for termination because of what he did."

"You lie!"

467

"Roberts," said Dewey. "That was his name. He did it. The people you're planning on killing, the people in Boston you tried to kill—they didn't kill your parents. One man did. An evil man."

"Lies," Cloud groaned.

Dewey stood up and moved toward the front of the cabin.

For the first time, Cloud saw Katya.

"Oh, God," he said in a pained whisper. "I'm . . ."

"Pyotr," she said as she began to cry, "you have to tell them."

Cloud looked away from her, shutting his eyes.

"You have to tell the Americans where the bomb is going. It's not fair. It's not right."

"There's no such thing as fair, Katya," he said. "Don't you see that?"

"You're going to kill a million innocent people. What they did was wrong, but God will judge the man who did that."

"I was innocent too. My mother was innocent. My father, he was innocent."

He stared into Katya's eyes. He was blinking rapidly, trying to hold back his emotions.

"Tell them," Katya pleaded. "Please, for me."

Cloud stared at Katya.

"Do you love me?" she asked.

"Of course I love you."

"And if I was there? If I was in the place where you are sending the bomb? Would you tell them? Or would you let me die?"

"I would tell them," he whispered. His eyes moved to Dewey, then back to Katya. "But you're not there."

She leaned over him, her head just inches from him, her lips nearly touching his.

"Pyotr," she whispered. "Please show them the person I know. Show me the person I love."

Dewey took a step back. He leaned into the cockpit. Stihl turned and looked at Dewey.

"Take us up," Dewey said.

468

104

BENEATH THE 145TH STREET BRIDGE
HARLEM RIVER
NEW YORK CITY

Faqir steered the boat up the Harlem River, away from New York harbor. The running lights were off. Over his head was a pair of night optics. He had the Talaria moving slowly, its engine barely above a whisper, as he cut north.

The logical approach to the Statue of Liberty would be from the sea. The authorities would not be looking in the Harlem River or the Hudson. And if they were looking—if they did find him—Faqir possessed the ultimate backup plan: detonate the bomb. As soon as he entered the Harlem River, he had the ability to level untold acres, to bring down building upon building, to kill hundreds of thousands.

He stared up at the green steel of the bridge as he purred north. That was the moment he realized that he'd already won. There was nothing the Americans could do now. All he had to do was press the red button on top of the device.

Faqir pulled out a drawer next to the steering wheel. He picked up the detonator. Ever so lightly, he rubbed his index finger across the button. Then he placed it on the teak table that adorned the center of the deck.

Suddenly, the door to the cabin opened. Naji stepped onto the deck. His hands and clothing were spotted in white paint.

"I painted above the waterline, as you asked," said Naji.

Faqir held a finger to his lips as an angry scowl came to his face. He motioned for Naji to come closer. He pushed the optics to his forehead so he could look into Naji's eyes.

"First," Faqir whispered, "shut the fuck up. Look around you. We're in the belly of the beast. They could very well be looking for us."

"You heard the radio," Naji whispered. "Their own president thinks they stopped us."

"Unless they're playing a game," said Faqir. "The Americans are not very smart, but even a blind squirrel finds an acorn every once in a while. So do us both a favor, shut the hell up."

Naji nodded.

"Yes," he said. "I'm sorry. I finished painting the hull. That's all."

"Good. How does it look?"

"Like Rembrandt."

"We'll drop anchor here for a few hours and let it dry."

Faqir steered close to the west side of the river, so that the boat was now hidden by a combination of the bridge and the riverbank, a concrete wall that arose thirty feet into the air above the water. He pressed a button that controlled the anchor, dropping it from a built-in compartment at the bow. When he felt the anchor hit the riverbed, he let go of the button and looked at Naji.

"It's important you understand what I'm about to tell you," said Faqir, barely even whispering, eyes casting about. He nodded at the detonator.

"We're now free and clear. It is July Fourth. We did it. So if they catch us, press the button."

"I thought the Statue of Liberty is our target," said Naji.

"It is. But if somehow they find us before we get there—"

Naji nodded.

"I understand."

Faqir removed the optics and handed them to Naji.

"You keep watch for a little while. I'm going to try and sleep."

105

The rotors of the chopper picked up discernibly, then the wheels bounced and they rose into the sky.

"Where to?" asked Stihl.

"Doesn't matter. Just get us up."

Dewey turned back to the cockpit. His eyes met Chalmers's, who stared back with a blank expression. He looked down at Cloud, then out the window. Within moments of takeoff, they were several hundred feet in the air.

Dewey reached to the wall and hit a button. Suddenly, the side doors slid open. The roar of the rotors burst into the cabin. Wind and rain came in, dousing the cabin and everyone inside.

Dewey reached down and grabbed the front of Katya's jacket.

"*Dewey!*" yelled Chalmers as, in the same moment, Katya screamed.

With one hand, he lifted her up and carried her toward the open door as she screamed, punched, and kicked at Dewey, but he held her—like a doll.

With his left hand, Dewey grabbed a strap above the door so he wouldn't fall out with her as, with his right hand, he clutched her jacket and thrust her out the open door. Dewey stood, holding the strap, dangling Katya out the side of the chopper. She grasped at his forearm, trying to hold on, then looked below at the buildings rushing by. Then her mouth opened again in panic and she tried to scream, but no noise came out. She was hysterical. Her hair whipped in a chaotic swirl, the slapping at Dewey's arm as she tried to hold on the only sound, and it blended darkly with the rain and wind and roar of the rotors, and the voice of Chalmers.

"*Don't do it, Dewey!*" he called. "*She's innocent.*"

Dewey held Katya there for a dozen seconds, then turned and looked into Cloud's eyes.

"You have exactly five seconds to tell me where the bomb is going," Dewey said, a calm look on his face. "Then I drop her."

Cloud shut his eyes. He rocked his head back and forth.

"Five," said Dewey, beginning the countdown, "four . . . three . . ."

Katya tried to say something to Cloud, but she was so panic-stricken that no sound came out as her mouth moved in silent terror.

"*Two . . .*"

Cloud stopped moving his head. His eyes blinked rapidly, as if he was calculating something. He struggled to move his lips, ushering the last remaining strength he had left. He looked at Katya, his eyes finding hers across the mist.

"New York City," he said in his dying breath, blood seeping from his mouth and nose. Then, his last words: "The Statue of Liberty."

106

At 5:30 A.M., the CIA Sikorsky helicopter touched down at Haverstraw Airport just north of Manhattan.

Calibrisi had a pair of Catch-22s on his hands.

The first: a nuclear device was in a boat headed for the Statue of Liberty. Assuming the terrorists hadn't switched boats, the U.S. government knew the precise make and model of the vessel the nuclear bomb was now on. But if the terrorists suspected anything, they would simply detonate the bomb. Cloud had coveted the idea of hitting one of America's most sacred and important historical structures. But a nuclear bomb detonated anywhere along America's coastline would do damage no less dramatic and permanent.

The second conundrum was his own government. They needed to pinpoint the boat, then move without being noticed. It would require patience, subterfuge, and utter secrecy. Any inkling that they were being watched would cause the terrorists to act preemptively.

Calibrisi had little faith in the ability of law enforcement to pull off a delicate covert mission. He had more confidence in the Navy.

Greer Ambern was the in-theater commander of the Navy team. The week before, in anticipation of what might come, Ambern had moved the Navy's newest combat vessel, the USS *Fort Worth*, into the mid-Atlantic.

But even knowing and trusting Ambern as he did, Calibrisi still felt uneasy.

Calibrisi, Katie, and Tacoma were met at the Haverstraw helipad by a black Suburban, which took them to a private entrance at the Carlyle Hotel. They boarded an elevator to the tenth floor, where there were two private apartments. Standing outside one of them was Igor.

Igor's hair looked as if he'd just stuck his finger in a plug. He was barefoot and was wearing jeans. His white tank top had AK-47 embossed in gold across his chest, and sewn beneath the lettering was a figure of the rifle in pink thread.

"Nice shirt," said Tacoma as they stepped through the door.

"This shirt cost me eight hundred dollars," said Igor.

"I'll sell you mine for a hundred," said Tacoma.

They stepped inside and followed Igor to an office. On the desk was a panel of six plasma screens, three on top, three on the bottom, all attached. The two side screens on the bottom showed aerial maps of New York harbor. Every few moments, a small red circle appeared, then shot down to a vessel, highlighting a boat. The middle screen was computer code, black text on a white screen. The three screens on top all showed people. The left was the operations room aboard the USS *Fort Worth*. The second screen was a conference room at the FBI's New York field office. The last was the White House Situation Room. The audio was turned off.

Overnight, the president had ordered a multiple-layer approach to the management of the government's military and law enforcement assets. The first level of coverage and preferred method of stopping the terrorists would be with snipers, managed by the FBI. The second layer would be provided by the Navy, using SEALs in

SDVs beneath the water around the statue. The *Fort Worth* would also be prepared, if necessary, to fire RIM-116 missiles, or simply let loose with its 57mm cannons.

NYPD's marine units would patrol as usual. It was important to maintain normal appearances.

"Do you want to start the call?" asked Igor.

"Not yet," said Calibrisi, pointing at the video feeds from the harbor. "Tell us what you have. First, any police or Coast Guard reports of missing or stolen boats?"

"Nothing from Maine to Florida."

"Tell us about the software."

"I did as you suggested," said Igor, nodding to the screens. "The two shots of the harbor are live. The cameras are scanning the water. What you're seeing is, for lack of a better expression, the world's first boat recognition software."

"How often does it run the scan?"

"Ten times a second. When the software finds a vessel close to the dimensions of the Talaria, it locks, rescans, then runs the photo against the database."

"Whose video are you using?" asked Katie.

"It's actually a feed from a Google satellite. I was able to call in a favor, although the person I called it in from isn't aware of it yet."

"Does it work?"

"Yes, maybe a little too well. It will find the Hinckley Talaria if it comes into the harbor. The problem is, it also captures boats of the same length and width of the Talaria, and there are quite a few. It's six A.M. now. The program has already cataloged thirty-one boats of the same size."

Calibrisi glanced at his watch: 6:10 A.M.

"Fire up the call," he said.

Igor hit a few keystrokes, and suddenly the voice of President Dellenbaugh came on the line.

"I want a status," said Dellenbaugh. "What assets do we have in or around the statue?"

"We have snipers in four places, sir," said someone from the FBI. "Ellis Island, Governors Island, Liberty State Park, and in or around the statue itself. That's fifty-two in all. In addition, we have another two dozen in boats. We're using a combination of commandeered tour boats and civilian vessels. Everyone is in plain clothing."

"Captain Ambern," said Dellenbaugh. "What were you able to do overnight?"

"There are five SDVs in the water as we speak, ten frogmen, all in a tight frame around the island," said Ambern from the USS *Fort Worth*. "In addition, we are at battle stations and prepared to take out the Hinckley, on command. If you ask me, Mr. President, once we have a lock on the target, I would use our missiles in addition to any snipers."

"What would be the damage to nearby boats?" asked someone in the Situation Room.

"There would be collateral damage," said Ambern. "But blowing up the bomb is different from detonating it. We're talking a few lives versus several hundred thousand."

"What's the flight time on a missile to the statue?" asked Dellenbaugh.

"From button press to target? About five seconds, maybe less."

"Let's talk about the target itself," said Dellenbaugh. "Hector?"

Calibrisi looked at Igor.

"You ready to live-wire this?" whispered Calibrisi.

Igor nodded.

"Yes, Mr. President," said Calibrisi. "What you're all about to see is real-time visual of the harbor as filtered through a software program based on facial recognition technology. The software is scanning every square foot of water, detecting the make and model of the boat we believe the bomb is on. As a camera locks the target, it pushes the image against a database, removing anything that doesn't match."

"Hector, Greer here, how do we triage? I'm assuming we're going to get some false positives. Worst thing that could happen would be if we identify the wrong guy and the terrorist just goes on his merry way and detonates the bomb."

"You're right," said Calibrisi. "The software can only take us so far. There needs to be a human cipher at the end of the line."

"That's you, Hector," said Dellenbaugh. "Everyone else, get ready. Let's keep all lines open."

Calibrisi looked at Igor.

"Mute it."

He looked at Katie and Tacoma.

"You guys all set?" he asked.

Tacoma nodded.

"Yeah, we're good."

107

WALL STREET
NEW YORK HARBOR

Polk carried two Styrofoam Dunkin' Donuts coffee cups, which he passed to Katie and Tacoma as they climbed into the speedboat.

Polk fired up the engine. He was dressed in a madras button-down and shorts. His legs were the white that comes when skin hasn't seen sun in a few years.

Tacoma took a sip.

"I fuckin' hate Dunkin' Donuts," he said.

"Fuck you," said Polk.

Polk untied the boat from the dock, then stepped to the wheel and put the boat in gear, putting out from the dock.

Tacoma glanced in front. The water was crowded with boats. There were hundreds of them, power boats and sailboats, small cruise ships, ferries, even dozens of kayaks. He looked at his green Rolex. It was 7:10.

Polk glanced back, then nodded to the transom. A small cardboard box was on it. Katie opened it. In the box were two tiny glass cases, inside of which were earpieces. Katie and Tacoma each put one in their ears.

"You guys hear me?" asked Polk.

"Yeah," said Katie.

"I'm good," said Tacoma.

"Get your eyes on," said Polk, pointing to a duffel bag on the floor.

Tacoma pulled out two pairs of sunglasses, handing one to Katie. They were specialized; the right lens was a high-powered monocular.

"Guys, it's me," said Calibrisi over commo. "We have our first hard target. Putting it on your screen right now."

A digital tablet was Velcroed to the transom of the boat. On it was a brightly illuminated map of the harbor, with the boat's location at the center. A flashing red dot hit the screen, indicating the boat Calibrisi and Igor had marked, then a line between the two boats cut in yellow across the screen, along with the precise distance between the boats: 1,071 feet.

"Got it," said Polk, cutting left, then speeding up.

"I want you guys to make the first sweep," said Calibrisi. "That's why you're out there. If and when we mark the bomber, we'll make the call as to whether we use the frogmen or the snipers."

"Or us," added Katie.

"Or you," said Calibrisi. "Robbie, you ready if we need you?"

"Just put me in, Coach," Tacoma whispered as he stepped to Polk's side and scanned for the boat.

"Not too fast, Bill," said Calibrisi.

Polk eased up a little as he steered through the crowded harbor.

Tacoma scanned the water, counting boats, losing count when he got to two hundred.

In the distance, he saw the Statue of Liberty. It was the first moment he realized not only the gravity of the situation, and the hard truth about what could be lost that day, but that if they didn't stop the terrorists, he too would die.

He closed his eyes briefly, then shook his head.

"What is it?" asked Katie.

Tacoma looked her.

"Nothing."

His gaze returned to the horizon, then the boats.

"We're getting close," said Polk.

"I see it," said Tacoma. "Slow down. At one thirty, next to a sail-boat."

Polk steered in a curving arc toward the boat as all three of them studied it from afar.

"We have another match," said Calibrisi. "Are you guys ready?"

"It's blue," said Katie. "I see a bunch of girls on the boat."

Polk changed his course.

"That first one is a negative, Chief."

"Okay, second should be on your screen right now."

"Got it," said Polk.

As Cloud had demanded, they came from the north via the Hudson River.

The assumption that guided them—that the Americans were searching for them—had guided them from the moment they set out from Sevastopol.

The radio was on. A news station continued its coverage of Boston. There was no mention of the bomb, only a plot by terrorists. The news was filled with quotes by various American officials, cautiously gloating about the foiled plot.

Faqir stood next to the Talaria's steering wheel. He leaned against a railing as Naji maneuvered the yacht into New York harbor. Faqir's olive-colored skin had turned grayish, as if someone had spread chalk across his now gaunt, hairless head and face.

He felt weak and slightly dizzy. But something had happened during his sleep. He'd awakened with newfound energy and purpose. Perhaps it was the coming achievement of an objective he'd sought for as long as he could remember. Or maybe it was the determination and toughness that Faqir so prided himself on.

He often felt that, in different times, he would've been a military leader, perhaps even a king. But that wasn't the world he'd been born to. Instead of a country or a battalion, he'd been chosen by a different battle. Jihad.

Naji pointed to a building to the left. It was the gleaming glass-and-steel spire of the Freedom Tower. The sight gave Faqir goose bumps.

You're at war. What you do today will live forever. You'll be revered for the horror you deliver into the heart of the enemy.

After centuries of enslavement and silence, Allah's soldiers were finally taking what was theirs. It would take time. Hundreds of years. But it was happening. They were coming. And today would be the second chapter in the great book that would be written about Islam's victory over America. This day, July Fourth, would be looked upon by Muslims the same way Americans looked at the Boston Tea Party.

Faqir's name would be as famous to Muslims as Paul Revere's was to Americans.

On both sides of the boat, the water was crowded with boats, so many boats—sailboats and motorboats, even kayakers, close to shore, paddling beneath the warm sun.

If any of them were worried about a terror plot today, they certainly didn't act like it. It felt . . . *easy.*

So far, they had seen only three police boats, all near the Brooklyn Navy Yard. A Coast Guard cutter loomed a quarter mile offshore, beyond that was a U.S. Navy destroyer, but its presence seemed ceremonial.

Naji steered in a slow, casual way, remaining in a line behind a smaller boat filled with a family.

"Naji," Faqir whispered.

"Yes?"

"We're here," he whispered.

Faqir pointed into the distance at the Statue of Liberty, raising his arm slowly in the air.

Naji reached to a shelf above the console. He removed a small cardboard box and handed it to Faqir.

Calibrisi was seated next to Igor. His jacket and tie were removed, his sleeves were rolled up.

Igor's fingers flew over the computer keyboard so fast Calibrisi stopped trying to understand how he did it.

By ten o'clock, they had spotted nine suspicious vessels. Polk, Katie, and Tacoma had swept six of them. The other three were checked out by plainclothes FBI agents in sniper boats.

Every passing minute brought with it increasing anxiety. With each possible boat, Calibrisi sensed the anticipation and urgency from the White House, revealed on one of the screens above, revealed in the way Dellenbaugh paced the Situation Room, eager to see if the terrorist had been found.

Igor suddenly elbowed him.

"We got something," he said, hitting the keyboard. "Coming into the harbor from the Hudson."

The camera shot down and focused. The passengers were beneath the bimini roof, out of sight line. The boat was green. The photo was so clear that the small gold Hinckley insignia was visible along the side of the boat.

"Bill," said Calibrisi, "we have something behind you. Putting it on your screen right now."

"I got it," said Polk.

Calibrisi looked at the plasma upper left. Greer Ambern was standing on the bridge of the *Fort Worth*, surrounded by his battle team.

"Greer?"

"I see it, Hector."

"Where's the nearest SDV?"

"A couple hundred yards away," said Ambern. "They'll be there in less than a minute."

* * *

Faqir placed the cardboard box on the table. He leaned against the table for stability. Carefully, he lifted the top of the box. Reaching inside, he took out a small square device made of stainless steel, with a small red button on top. The detonator.

Faqir looked at Naji.

"Naji," he said.

Naji's face was turned away from Faqir as he steered.

"Think quick," said Faqir.

He tossed the detonator through the air. Naji's face took on a look of horror as he removed his hands from the wheel then stabbed them out, catching the detonator before it tumbled to the ground.

He held the detonator gently as he studied Faqir's grinning face.

"What are you doing?" he asked, shocked that Faqir would be so reckless.

"It doesn't matter now. We're here. Go ahead. Do you want to press it?"

The SEAL Delivery Vehicle pushed silently through the water, a dozen feet below the surface. There were three SEALs now clutching the submersible. The pilot and copilot sat near the front of the minisub in tiny compartments open to the water. Burns, the combat swimmer, clutched a handle near the rear.

Above, the waterline was chaos. Each boat engine churned the surface of the water, creating eddies that blurred the view. There were so many hulls they seemed to blend together.

Burns listened to his SDV pilot over commo as they steered toward the target boat.

"Captain," said the pilot, "I need a hard GPS lock on that boat's position. There are too many boat hulls out here."

"Roger, that," said someone on the *Fort Worth*. "I'm going to take your nav over for a sec."

On the pilot's nav screen, illuminated dots, representing the boats directly above the SDV, suddenly started to flash. Then a green circle appeared around one, pulsed three times, and locked on. A bright green target symbol flashed.

"Got it."

The pilot locked the nav onto the target boat. The SDV hovered beneath it at precisely the same depth and speed. The SDV now moved in conjunction with the target boat, tracking it. The pilot let go of the controls. He and the copilot were now ready to join Burns in the attack.

The pilot turned back to Burns.

Over commo, he asked, "You ready, Burnsy?"

Burns put his free hand to the airtight pocket on his chest, feeling the bulge of his gun, a suppressed Beretta 9mm.

"Affirmative, Captain."

"*Fort Worth*," said the SDV pilot, "on your go."

"Hold until we get the surface sweep."

On Polk's screen, the boat's location flashed red.

Then the words appeared: *705 feet.*

Polk steered toward the target boat. He weaved between vessels, all moving slowly, many distracted by Lady Liberty in the distance. Polk glanced at his watch: 10:28. There were, he knew, four fireworks displays scheduled for the day. The first, he knew, started at 10:30.

As he watched the screen, he heard a sudden yell.

"*Watch it!*"

Polk looked up just as the bow of the boat grazed a cigarette boat, its engine growling loudly.

"Sorry," Polk said.

A tall man with a potbelly was behind the wheel. Behind him was a woman, who came running to the side of the boat, looking to see if there was damage.

"If that left a scratch—" the man began.

"*It did!*" the woman exclaimed. "It left a big black mark, Rudy!"

The man ran to the side of the cigarette boat. Polk put his boat in reverse. As he started to back up, the man grabbed one of the boat's cleats, holding the vessel against his boat.

"Let go," said Polk, debating whether to accelerate, fearing that if he did he would bring the man overboard, resulting in his wife screaming.

Before Polk could do anything, the man threw a rope around the cleat.

"I want your insurance," he yelled.

"What's going on down there?" asked Calibrisi over commo. "Get to the Hinckley, now."

Tacoma moved from the back of the boat. He pulled out his combat blade, placed it under the rope, and sliced the line. The cigarette boat owner swung, but Tacoma ducked.

"Go," he barked to Polk.

Fearing the man might fall in, Tacoma punched him in the mouth, sending him backward, tumbling to the deck.

Katie sat on the transom, ignoring the commotion. Through her monocular, she studied the suspicious vessel, just a hundred feet away now. It was a green Talaria. There was a man steering. He had longish dark hair and was shirtless.

"I think that's it," she said over commo. "Hector, I think that's the boat."

"I'll be there in ten seconds," said Polk.

"No, you won't," said Calibrisi. "Greer, get those SEALs up there."

Burns let go of the handle in the same moment the other two SEALs leapt from their seats. Burns reached the bottom of the Talaria just ahead of his teammates. He placed his hand on a brass handle along the back, removed his flippers, unzipped his weapon pocket, and silently hoisted himself up onto the ski platform at the back of the boat.

The other two men soon joined him. Burns climbed onto the deck.

Burns signaled his teammates using his left hand: *my shot.*

A door opened. A teenage girl stepped from the cabin, saw Burns, and screamed.

The man behind the wheel turned, then held up his hands.

"Whatever you want," he whispered, trembling.

A scream abruptly rattled the air. It came from another boat, a sailboat just a few yards away, as a woman saw the three frogmen, all in black, clutching weapons on the Hinckley.

Naji's head turned as the scream echoed through the throng of boats. He stared, his eyes transfixed, at the three divers, all clad in black.

"Faqir," he said, pointing to the green yacht a hundred feet away from them.

Faqir quickly registered the men. SEALs or FBI. Then he saw the dark green of the boat's hull.

They're here.

"Where is it?" he asked, desperation in his voice.

"What?"

"The detonator!"

Naji pointed. The detonator sat on the table, its red button sticking up in the air.

Faqir stepped toward the table, his hand extended.

Polk stood at the wheel, watching from a distance as the three SEALs climbed aboard the boat. He waited to see the man fall. Then the long white-blond hair of a girl emerged onto the deck.

"Oh, my God," he whispered. *"Hector—"*

The scream cut across the water, interrupting Polk. He turned to see Katie. Their eyes met.

"*Shut it down!*" yelled Calibrisi. "Greer, tell your SEALs to stand down and identify themselves and calm those people down. If the terrorists see them, it's all over—"

"Roger," said Ambern.

"On our way," said Polk.

Polk pushed the throttle forward and sped toward the scene.

"Goddammit," he muttered, shaking his head. He glanced at Katie.

"That was my fault," she said.

"No, it wasn't. It was mine. I should've let Tacoma drive. Rob, you take over."

Polk turned around.

"Where's Rob?" he asked, looking at Katie.

Katie swiveled her head, looking for Tacoma, but he was gone.

108

Tacoma saw him just after Polk rammed the cigarette boat. The moment just before Calibrisi ordered in the SEALs.

He was standing on a different boat, a pretty white boat, behind the cigarette boat, far away from the boat that was about to be attacked by the SEALs.

He was bald. But it wasn't normal-looking. It was the unmistakable grayness of death, the sickly color of a person after he's been irradiated. It was the look his mother had just before she died.

In that second of recognition, Tacoma knew that the SEALs were approaching the wrong boat. And that once the bald man saw the frogmen, it would all be over. Everything.

Shielded momentarily by the cigarette boat, Tacoma ripped off his shirt and jeans. Beneath, he had on an Olympic-style tactical warm weather swimsuit, armless at the top, thin material down to midthigh, all black. He slipped into the water as Polk and Katie were turned in the opposite direction, watching the other boat just as the SEALs made their approach from below.

He dived down until he was safely beneath the hulls of boats overhead.

Tacoma navigated as he'd done as a kid—before he knew what

UDT stood for, before Hell Week, before SEALs, before there were masks with digitally imposed maps, before he knew what commo was, when it was just the water at the lake and the moonlight.

He swam as fast as he'd ever done, arms lunging, legs kicking furiously, lungs burning, desperate for another breath of air. When he couldn't hold his breath any longer, he kept going, until he saw it: the dark green hull of the Talaria and, just above the waterline, the fresh white paint the terrorists had slapped on to cover it up.

He felt a rush of warmth as adrenaline flamed inside him. Time seemed to stand still. It was as if he'd been born to be here.

He grabbed the wooden ski platform and climbed up.

He slipped silently onto the transom at the same moment his hand pulled the SIG Sauer P226 from his weapons pocket, then raised the gun, its black suppressor targeted toward the two men.

He climbed onto the deck. He stood without moving, dripping wet, clutching the gun. He trained the muzzle on the driver, then waited in silence. And then a young girl's screams echoed across the water.

Both men turned.

Tacoma fired a slug into the side of the driver's head, spraying blood and brains across the console, dropping the man to the deck in a contorted heap.

In the half second that followed, the bald man raised his withered arm. He stretched it out toward Tacoma, as if pointing.

It was then that Tacoma saw it.

In between where they stood was a table. On the table was the detonator. Its red button stuck up in the air, as if asking to be pressed.

His eyes locked with Tacoma's. Small eyes, clever eyes, black eyes filled with hate. They moved to the gun, carefully studying the hole at the end of the suppressor, still aimed at his head.

A long, pregnant silence took over the deck.

Both of them knew where the detonator was. Both knew that if the terrorist lunged, even if Tacoma shot him at that same moment, the momentum of his lunge would enable him to land on the detonator.

"I know what you're thinking," said Tacoma calmly, still breathing heavily. "You're thinking, should I go for it? Even if he shoots me, I'll probably land on it. Am I right?"

The bald man didn't respond. Instead, he crouched ever so slightly, coiling his legs, waiting for the precise moment to go.

"The thing is, if I shot you in the head, you'd be right," continued Tacoma, still holding the man's skull in the center of the gun. "It would go right through your brain and out the back. In fact, it would probably go pretty damn quick because of how small your brain is."

Tacoma grinned slightly, then swept the muzzle down, stopping when it was aimed dead center at the terrorist's chest.

"But the breastplate is a lot stronger," said Tacoma. "Runs down through your body. That's where you fucked up. You should've gone for it when I had it aimed at your head. You would've won. Now that I got your breastplate, it doesn't matter how hard you jump. Doesn't fuckin' matter anymore. As long as I can hit that breastplate, you're going backward. No way around it. It's physics, dude."

The terrorist jumped toward the table, surprising Tacoma. But the surprise lasted less than a second. Tacoma pumped the trigger. A telltale metallic *thwack* was the only sound as the suppressed gun sent a slug through the air. It struck him dead center in the chest, kicking him off his feet and back into the wall. He dropped.

Tacoma walked across the deck, gun aimed at all times on the man. He stepped above him, then stared down into his eyes.

"You see? I told ya."

He inched the suppressor up a few inches, then pumped another slug between the terrorist's eyes.

"Happy Independence Day, motherfucker."

EPILOGUE

Freemans was crowded. The New York City restaurant, located at the end of a dark alley, was like an old hunting club on the inside, with dark wood and stuffed moose and deer heads hanging from the walls. There was barely enough light to see.

Dewey was a few minutes early and he stepped to the bar, ordering a bourbon and a beer, both of which he deposited down his throat so quickly that the bartender did a double take.

"Another round?"

Dewey nodded.

The bar was packed. Most of the people there were in their twenties. Of the two dozen or so people at the bar, Dewey guessed that three-quarters of them were female, and three-quarters of them were models.

Tacoma, he thought as he drained the second bourbon, then sat down and took a small sip of beer.

Suddenly, a magazine landed on the bar in front of Dewey in the same moment he felt a hand on his shoulder. He turned. It was Calibrisi.

"Hi, hotshot."

"Hi, Hector."

On the bar was the most recent issue of *People* magazine. The cover showed a male movie star Dewey didn't recognize. Below his face, the cover read: "The 50 Sexiest Men Alive."

"Oh, goody," said Dewey, enthusiastically. "I haven't seen this issue yet."

Calibrisi took the stool next to Dewey and ordered a glass of wine.

"Page sixty," said Calibrisi, nodding with a smile at the magazine.

"You finally made it," said Dewey, flipping through the magazine. "It's about time they started considering large protruding hairy guts sexy."

"Fuck you. Read it."

As he flipped through the magazine, he stopped at an earlier article. It featured a large photo of Katya Basaeyev. She was seated in a chair, legs crossed, smiling. Behind her, a window showed the skyline of Moscow on a sunny day.

"She's dancing again," said Calibrisi.

Dewey said nothing.

"Would you really have dropped her?" asked Calibrisi.

Dewey paused at the question, staring at Katya's beautiful face for a few extra moments before continuing to flip through the magazine. He didn't answer the question.

He found page sixty. He looked down at the photo. It was a glossy, full-page portrait of Tacoma. He was standing in a tight all-black Olympic-style swimsuit. His hair was slicked back and he was dripping wet. His arms and shoulders were tan and ripped in muscles. Each hand clutched a gun, and both were aimed at the camera. Kneeling to each side of him were females clad in skimpy string bikinis, one blond, the other brunette, both staring up adoringly at Tacoma.

"I'm going to puke," said Dewey.

Calibrisi laughed.

#4 Rob Tacoma, America's Hero

The only thing hotter than the bullets flying out of ex–Navy SEAL Rob Tacoma's gun are the smoldering green eyes on his luscious Virginia-born face. With his Fourth of July heroics, 29-year-old Tacoma earned his place in America's pantheon of legends. With his movie star good looks and chiseled physique, Tacoma earns #4 on this year's list of the World's Sexiest Men Alive. Tacoma is single and plans to stay that way—unless some girl out there can figure out a way to deliver a kill shot to this studmuffin's flak jacket–covered heart.

Dewey shut the magazine and looked at the bartender.

"I need another bourbon."

Just then, a commotion came from the door. Katie was standing just inside the door, waiting for Tacoma. Tacoma was outside, surrounded by girls. He had a pen out and was signing autographs. Katie's eyes found Dewey. She rolled them and shook her head, then came over to the bar.

Katie was dressed in brown linen pants, high-heeled sandals, and a sleeveless see-through silk chemise. She'd let her hair grow out a bit. She resembled a young Ingrid Bergman.

Dewey looked at her as she approached, scanning her from head to toe, without taking his eyes off her.

"What are you looking at?" she asked.

"You."

Katie blushed slightly.

"You look nice," he said, reaching his arms out and wrapping them around her.

"Nice?" she whispered, holding Dewey tightly. "I like that. By the way, how are you, cutie? I missed the hell out of you."

"I missed you too," said Dewey. "I'm good."

Katie let go of Dewey and wrapped her arms around Calibrisi.

"Hi, big fella."

"Hi, Katie."

Dewey nodded to Tacoma, who was still at the door.

"Is it like this everywhere?" he asked.

"Yes," Katie said, exasperation in her voice. "It's crazy. He had two girls in his room this morning when I went by to meet him. I think they were cheerleaders."

"What makes you think that?" asked Dewey.

"They had cheerleader uniforms on."

Dewey laughed.

"You guys are not going to believe his ego," said Katie. "If you thought it was out of control before—"

"Let him enjoy it," said Calibrisi. "He did something important. He's young and single. Let him bask in his fifteen minutes of fame."

"Easy for you to say," said Katie, shaking her head. "As happy as I am that bomb didn't go off, there are times I find myself wishing it had."

Dewey, Calibrisi, and Katie all started laughing. They turned to see where Tacoma was. He signed the last autograph, then entered Freemans.

His hair was slicked back and combed neatly down the middle. He had on a light tan leather jacket. It was partially unzipped. He didn't have a shirt on. He wore madras shorts and cowboy boots.

"I think I agree with Katie," said Dewey, smiling and waving to Tacoma. "Hector, do you have Bokolov's number?"

Tacoma nodded to Dewey, raising his hand like a gun and firing his index finger at him.

"Did he just wink at me?" asked Dewey.

"He doesn't have a shirt on," said Calibrisi, incredulous.

Tacoma stepped to the bar. He wrapped his arms around Dewey, then Calibrisi. He nodded to the bartender, who brought him a bottle of beer.

"Okay, before you guys say anything, I have three points I wanna make," said Tacoma, looking at Dewey.

"Let me guess," said Dewey. "You met someone who delivered a kill shot to your flak jacket–covered heart."

Tacoma shook his head.

"First, I can't help it if some magazine names me to their sexiest man alive list. Now, if you ask me, I should've been number two, but that's water under the bridge. Second, I didn't know about those two chicks they stuck in the picture."

"*Chicks?*" asked Katie. "Can you possibly be more offensive?"

Tacoma took a big swig from the bottle.

"And what's third?" asked Dewey.

"What?" asked Tacoma.

"You said you had three points," said Dewey. "That was two."

"I think I said two. I had two points."

"Do us all a favor and put a lid on it for a few minutes, will ya, Mr. Sexy?" said Dewey.

Tacoma, slightly chastened, nodded, then grinned.

"Yeah, I'm sorry, man."

Just then, the hostess approached.

"Your table is ready."

They followed the hostess to a table in the dimly lit back room. They ordered several bottles of wine along with dinner. They caught up as they ate, eventually enjoying Tacoma's regaling them with his various exploits since the fateful day he killed the terrorist in New York harbor. At some point, they all realized Tacoma was not, in fact, bragging. He was as surprised, dumbfounded, and amused by it all as they were.

After dessert had been cleared and there followed a lull in conversation, Dewey glanced at Calibrisi. His mind flashed to the beginning of it all. Castine. Calibrisi had flown up not because of the coming attack, not even because he needed Dewey. He came that day to rescue him. Dewey wasn't good at saying thank-you, at least not with words, but he allowed a smile to come to his face. He picked up his wineglass.

"Here's to Hector," said Dewey.

"Here, here," Tacoma chimed in, raising his glass.

"To our fearless leader," added Katie.

497

Calibrisi smiled in silence and raised his glass, moving it to the other three.

"So what are you going to do about Gant and Roberts?" asked Dewey, after downing the remaining wine in his glass.

"Josh is spending some time in one of our more out-of-the-way stations," said Calibrisi. "If there's ever a terrorist threat in Biak, he'll be the first to know."

"Biak?" asked Katie.

"An island near Papua New Guinea," said Calibrisi. "Apparently there're still some cannibals running around, but personally I have my doubts."

"What about Roberts?" asked Dewey.

Calibrisi smiled knowingly, but didn't answer Dewey's question.

Just then, the waitress brought over the check, which Calibrisi grabbed before anyone else could.

"So what are you up to tonight?" he asked Katie.

"Nothing too exciting," she said. "I might stay in the city. I don't know."

"Doesn't Igor live near here?" asked Tacoma, grinning at Katie.

"Yeah, I think he does," said Calibrisi.

Katie smiled mischievously and then turned to Calibrisi.

"How about you?"

"I'm headed back tonight. I haven't seen Vivian in a week."

Calibrisi looked at Dewey.

"What about you?"

"Me?" asked Dewey. He looked at his watch. "Oh, shit. I'm actually going to see something."

"Something?" asked Katie. "Or someone?"

"Someone. It's nothing."

Dewey got to his feet.

"You're not leaving yet," said Tacoma. "Let's hear it."

"No way."

"Come on, Grampa. Who is she?"

Dewey shot Tacoma a look.

"Someone whose identity is above your pay grade, studmuffin."

"So you won't tell us who the lucky lady is?" asked Tacoma, flashing a smile.

"Tell you what, tough guy," said Dewey, "let's arm wrestle. You win, I'll tell you her name. I win, I get that leather jacket."

Dewey sat down. He put his right arm up, resting it on the table. Tacoma placed his arm on the table. Their hands met and clasped tightly together.

A small crowd started to gather in the back room to watch— waiters and waitresses, a few people from the bar—until there wasn't any more room left.

"We go on three," said Dewey. "Katie, you call it."

"Honestly," said Katie, "you two are like little children."

"Katie," said Dewey.

"Fine," she said, smiling. "One . . . two . . . *three.*"

ACKNOWLEDGMENTS

Last year, I brought my then six-year-old daughter to the Flatiron Building in New York City. This is the headquarters of my publisher, St. Martin's Press. When Sally Richardson, the company CEO, heard we were in the building, she insisted on us coming up to her office to say hi. Sally was, as usual, incredibly busy. But she put everything on hold to welcome us. We caught up and shared some laughs. Feeling bad that we were taking up so much of the boss's time, I suggested we should go so that Sally could get back to work.

"Now hold on just a minute, Ben," said Sally. She then turned to Esmé. "Esmé, before you leave, could you do something for me?"

"Sure, Mrs. Richardson."

Sally patted the empty seat next to her.

"Would you please read aloud to me?"

Esmé walked over and sat down next to Sally on the big sofa. For the next ten minutes, she read aloud to Sally and the rest of us. It was a moment that reminded me why I became a writer, and why, with every book, I'm fortunate enough to have St. Martin's Press on my side.

So thank you everyone at SMP, with special gratitude to Sally, Keith Kahla, Jennifer Enderlin, George Witte, Martin Quinn, Jeff Capshew, Lisa Tomasello, Krista Loercher, Paul Hochman, Justin Velella, Kelsey Lawrence, Melissa Hastings, Rafal Gibek, Jason Reigal, Ervin Serrano, and Hannah Braaten. And a special thank-you to the late Matthew Shear, whose laughter and kindness I will never forget.

I would also like to thank the talented group of people who represent me: Nicole James, Aaron Priest, Chris George, Terra Chalberg, and Rachel Sussman.

As with every book, a number of technical experts offered me their guidance and thoughts. Thank you for your help: Gail Riley, Matthew Bunn, Alex Mijailovic, Kevin Ryan, Jonathan KomLosy, and Rorke Denver.

An extra, very sincere thank-you to Nicole James and Keith Kahla, who demand nothing but the best from me, and then help me find it with their brilliance, toughness, patience, and, above all, humor.

Finally, a heartfelt thank-you to my family, Shannon, Charlie, Teddy, Oscar, and Esmé. I'm very proud of you—each of you—for your own unique and wonderful gifts. You make me laugh, keep me humble, and always find a way to show me your love when I need it most. A hundred times a day, I think to myself, look at how lucky you are, the only person alive who can look at the five of you and and say the words, this is my family.